The Only Exception

I hope you enjoy
Lucinda & Alex's story!

Claire Huston.

Claire Huston

Published by Goldcrest Books International Ltd
www.goldcrestbooks.com
publish@goldcrestbooks.com

ISBN: 978-1-913719-57-9
eISBN: 978-1-913719-58-6

For Mum and Dad
xx

Chapter 1

Later, as she sat with the police explaining what had happened in the lift, Lucinda found she could remember little about the start of her day.

She was certain it had been brimming with optimistic promise. A trip to London always put a spring in her step. The April sunshine had warmed her bones as she wove between black cabs and red buses towards the offices of the Richards Group. Striding through the revolving glass door, she had smiled in anticipation of a renewed contract and a third year of lucrative city business. And her smile had widened as she imagined waving the paperwork in Chris's face and dismissing all his doom-laden rumours as rubbish.

Thirty dismal minutes later, she strode to the fifth-floor lift. Holding her head high, she strutted with faux nonchalance, refusing to let her dejection show on her face. Instead she gave vent to her wounded pride, frustration and disbelief by giving the call button a particularly vicious prod.

Undercut! How had she been undercut? And by whom? Were they growing all the food themselves? Did they not have to pay their staff?

And of course Chris had known. She rubbed her forehead, kneading the growing ache above her brows. He'd be unbearably smug. Worse still, his eyes would fill with sorrow and he'd give her the look that said, *'Poor Lucinda. Another contract lost. When will you accept you're not cut-throat enough for this game?'* The look which made her want to both scream and sob.

Consumed by thoughts of Chris's *'told you so'* face, she barely heard the ping as the lift opened or noticed her three fellow passengers as she filled the vacant space just inside the doors and dropped her leather shoulder bag between her feet. The throbbing in her forehead had crept behind her eyes and she lowered her gaze away from the glare of the ceiling lights. Past the ends of her smartest black trousers jutted the tips of her cobalt-blue stilettos. Flipping torture devices. Oh-so chic and professional when she had slipped them on that morning, but now the pain in her heels suggested she would have to treat sizeable raw blisters before she changed back into the comfort of her steel-toed clogs.

'Excuse me? Which floor?'

The owner of the deep voice to her left was a tall man standing next to the panel of floor buttons. She blinked at him, noting the sandy waves of his short hair, his lightly tanned skin, large brown eyes and the suggestion of stubble on his cheeks and strong jawline. The words 'handsome' and 'familiar' were creeping to the front of her mind when he cleared his throat and pointed at the buttons.

6

'Which floor?' He spoke more slowly and a touch louder this time. Normally this sort of patronising behaviour would have riled her but, as she had been gawping at him, it was probably fair.

'Um, sorry. Ground floor.' Flustered, and hoping to show she was more capable than her slack-jawed staring suggested, she extended her arm and took a swift step towards the panel to push the button herself, but her right stiletto caught in her bag strap, which had curled itself next to her foot like a lurking viper. She stumbled and was inches from hitting the floor buttons with her head when her slide was stopped by Mr Handsome who stepped in front of her and grabbed her upper arms.

'Woah!' His brow creased with concern. 'Are you OK?'

A blush tickled the base of her throat: part embarrassment, part irritation. Great. In addition to vacant, she must look like a clumsy damsel who needed rescuing.

'Yes. Thank you.' She pulled away, her hands sliding down his forearms, over his wrists, and as her fingers brushed his she was jolted by a mighty crackle of static which made her hiss and snap her hands away.

His raised eyebrows and parted lips told her he had felt it too. His features settled quickly but there was a curl at one side of his mouth as he turned to press the button for the ground floor and said, 'Shocking,' in a low rumble which sent the heat in Lucinda's neck rocketing up into her cheeks. Fantastic. He was laughing at her.

She flicked her gaze back to the floor and drove her annoyance down after it. Stupid bag. Stupid fancy shoes. That certainly wouldn't have happened if she'd been in her clogs. They were anti-static, anti-slip and had withstood everything from the points of plummeting knives to splashes of scalding water.

Keen to train her gaze anywhere other than the man to her left and his mocking smile, she tilted her head to her right and used the cabin's mirrored walls to peek at the other passengers. By now they too had likely concluded she was a clumsy nitwit.

They were a mismatched pair: a squat young man sporting a mustard-coloured Aran knit sweater and an astoundingly full beard she believed would officially qualify him as a hipster; and a petite lady who Lucinda struggled to place in her sixties or seventies, her delicate bone structure showcased by an elegant black skirt suit and loose chignon which held her grey hair back from her face.

Lucinda had just decided the woman had an air of the older Audrey Hepburn about her when the lift shuddered, the quaking accompanied by an ominous clanging and ticking. With a final squeal the cabin came to an abrupt halt, causing Lucinda to stagger once again into the rescuing embrace of Mr Handsome.

Surprise and concern had widened his eyes. His gaze locked on to hers before dropping to where his hands were supporting her waist.

Lucinda felt no embarrassment this time, but the former irritation lingered. She was a highly capable person! How did she keep ending up in his arms? Her annoyance pricked her, even as her gaze lingered on his dreamy brown eyes which were ringed with long black lashes ...

A wistful sigh flowered in her chest. The view from his arms was actually rather nice. And the sensation of his strong hands on her waist wasn't bad either.

It might have been a strange sort of vertigo caused by the cabin's sudden halt, but the few inches of air separating them seemed to vibrate with possibility. His lips twitched into a lopsided smile and he murmured, 'Not so shocking this time,' in a suggestive, secretive tone which made the fine hairs on Lucinda's arms stand on end.

Her heart began to race and she couldn't be sure if the culprit was the prospect of being trapped in a lift or her closeness to Mr Handsome. Or perhaps it was the idea of being stuck *with* him that was the problem. Surely anyone would find his ridiculously gorgeous face, delicious figure and impressive reflexes unsettling?

He even smelled good, for heaven's sake! As she took a step back from his capable hands, the air stirred and she caught tantalising hints of citrus and … What was that? Pepper, yes! But there was an undertone she was unable to place. Sage? Fennel? Perhaps—

'Er, help?'

Hipster guy had backed himself into a corner. His hands were trembling and angry red patches blotted his pale cheeks. Lucinda presumed he wasn't a great fan of cramped spaces, but when she turned to follow his stare she realised his SOS hadn't been for himself.

The older lady was slumped against the back of the lift, her head hanging forwards and face ashen. Her breathing was laboured and the hand she was pressing to her chest trembled.

Lucinda glanced at Mr Handsome. 'I don't suppose you're a doctor?' she asked, although given her luck so far that day, she assumed he wasn't. Besides, the building was home to a leading talent agency and she had already guessed—given his handsomeness—he was a model or actor.

He didn't respond but stared open mouthed at the Audrey Hepburn lookalike. Had he not heard her? Never mind. His stunned expression didn't suggest someone at home with dealing with medical emergencies.

Lucinda rolled her shoulders back. Her first-aid training would have to suffice. And, after all, she had wanted to appear capable.

'Hello,' she said, gently placing a hand on the lady's elbow. 'Can you tell me your name?'

'Carol.' The reply was a rasp. From the shallowness of her breathing and the pallor of her skin, it was a wonder she was still standing.

'I'm Lucinda. I'm going to help you sit down.' She put her hands under Carol's arms and together they completed a controlled slide to the floor.

'Hey.' She turned her head to Mr Handsome. 'Can you ring the call bell? Tell them we need a doctor.'

But he continued his stunned statue impression, horror reflected in his watery eyes and every line of his drawn expression. Meanwhile, on the other side of the space, Hipster-guy had sunk to the floor, tucked his knees to his chest and was hiding his beard behind them, like a furry hedgehog.

Lucinda silently cursed them both. Bloody useless men!

Carol's breathing hitched and Lucinda pushed her exasperation to one side as she knelt beside her and untied the silk scarf at her neck. 'Do you have any pain, Carol?'

'My chest,' she whispered, her voice ragged with effort.

'Anywhere else?' asked Lucinda, unbuttoning Carol's

jacket and praying what she was looking at was a panic attack rather than something far worse.

'My neck. And jaw.'

Oh crap.

'Hey!' Lucinda raised her voice in the direction of Mr Handsome-but-Useless. Experience from years of delegating in stressful situations kicked in, and she swung a hand to strike his shin. 'Hey! Wake up!'

He blinked and the distance and tears in his dark eyes retreated as he gazed down at her. 'What?'

'Get over there'—she jabbed a finger towards the panel of buttons—'and tell them to call an ambulance and get us out of here.' When her best head chef tone failed to take immediate effect, her last shred of patience slipped from her grasp. 'Move!' she barked, causing him to jump out of his trance and whirl over to the panel.

The cabin lights flickered. Ignoring the whimpering sounds coming from the hedgehog hipster, Lucinda focused on Carol, whose wheezing had quietened and eyes closed.

That wasn't good.

Dimly aware of Mr Handsome talking to a disembodied voice coming from the instrument panel, Lucinda moved Carol so she was lying on her back. 'Carol!' When shouting and patting her face produced no response, Lucinda pinched her earlobe as hard as she could. Still nothing.

Not good at all.

An eerie calm descended on Lucinda. She swept her hair away from her face and lowered her cheek to Carol's open mouth. A heaviness pooled in her stomach as her worst fears were confirmed: not a whisper of warmth and Carol's chest was ominously still.

Right then.

Lucinda glanced left and right at the men. The quivering hedgehog would be of no use; Mr Handsome would have to do.

'Hey!' she said to him as she placed a hand on Carol's forehead and used the fingers of the other hand to tilt her chin. 'Tell them she's not breathing and to call that ambulance. Then get down here. I need your help. Now!'

Shifting to her knees, she placed the heel of her right hand in the centre of Carol's chest, put the left on top and pressed down, counting to herself with every thrust.

Having delivered the news of their emergency, Mr Handsome knelt next to her. 'Are you watching?' Lucinda asked, her words broken into syllables accompanying the chest compressions. 'I'll need you to take over.'

'Um, well—'

'You have to press quite hard.'

'I don't know … I haven't … I wouldn't …'

'Two compressions a second.'

He stuttered again as she moved to give rescue breaths. 'But … but … How fast is—'

'You can use a song for the beat. "Stayin' Alive" is a good one.'

'Certainly fitting.'

Was that a *joke*? *Really*? Lucinda's frown deepened. 'Watch me and imagine it,' she said. 'You do the next set.'

'But the guy I spoke to'—he gestured to the control panel—'said we'd be out of here in five minutes.'

Oh for goodness' sake! He was lucky to be gifted in the looks department given he wasn't overburdened with brains. Or gumption. 'I'm getting tired. You're stronger. We'll take turns.'

'But—'

'Look, it's like this!' Lucinda came up from giving more breaths and interlocked her fingers on Carol's chest. She drove her frustration downwards, wishing she could fire it into Carol's heart and bully it into beating. 'We're not going anywhere soon. Carol needs our help or she'll die.'

His cringe told her she was holding the right gun to his head. Time to take the safety off. 'If *you* don't help me. Carol. Will. Die.'

Bingo! He gave a sharp inhalation and pressed his lips together, apparently steeling himself.

'Ready?' He nodded and, as she ducked to give more breaths, he placed his hands in the centre of Carol's chest in a good imitation of her previous efforts. 'That's it. You can press harder.'

He winced. 'I feel like I'm hurting her.'

'She won't mind if it saves her life. Keep going.'

He was a mercifully fast learner and, as they slid into a regular, collaborative rhythm, Lucinda lost sense of time passing. Her world contracted to the area immediately surrounding Carol and seemingly endless counts of thirty. In the wordless space, disturbed solely by their own movements and breathing, she began to feel strangely disconnected. It was as if she were standing outside herself, observing the scene, and the one thing tethering her to her body was how aware she was of the man next to her, his warm, steady presence a vibrant and shocking contrast to the greyish-blue tinge of their patient's skin.

'When do we stop?'

'What?' The sound of a voice in the stillness had startled Lucinda as much as what he had said.

'When do we give up?'

Was he exhausted? She doubted it. His lips were pressed into a tight line and his jaw was tense, but these were the lone signs of effort. Rather than being tired, perhaps he just didn't see the point in carrying on. Perhaps he didn't care about the life of an elderly lady he didn't know. Or perhaps he was a quitter as well as tending towards the useless and dim.

Whatever the reason for his question, there was only one response Lucinda could give. She had never known when to give up on anything and took pride in her tenacity in the face of all opposition. Although her determined nature hadn't proved to be popular with everyone, and Chris would often shake his head and say she was stubborn to the verge of bloody-minded madness.

She waited until he began a new set of compressions and said, 'We don't. We don't stop.'

His lips twitched and he threw her a glance. 'That's what I thought.' He turned his gaze back to his hands and nodded. 'Good.'

Lucinda's eyebrows flew upwards as she watched him work with renewed energy. Well-versed in all her flaws, Chris also enjoyed pointing out she was too quick to judge and too slow to change her mind. Maybe she needed to reassess Mr Handsome when they weren't trapped together in a life-or-death scenario.

Minutes, hours or perhaps years later, they began to descend and the doors opened. A pair of paramedics bustled her and the two men out of the cabin. Hipster guy whimpered and scurried away, leaving Lucinda standing a few metres from the lift doors, craning to get a view of the paramedics. She stood shoulder to shoulder with Mr Handsome and, when she sneaked a peek in his direction, a flicker of the whites of his eyes made her suspect he had been stealing a glance at her too.

'I'm Alex, by the way.'

'Lucinda.'

As the paramedics and their equipment formed a protective wall in front of Carol, Lucinda's sight—which had been unnaturally acute while in the lift—fogged. She swayed and would have staggered if Alex hadn't placed a hand on her elbow.

Her vision clearing, Lucinda focused on the medical drama before them and willed Carol to pull through. At the same time a fine strand of her consciousness was connected to Alex. It was a link beyond the physical connection of her arm and his hand, one which seemed to shimmer in response to his proximity. The sensation was unnerving and insistent, like … like … she struggled to find a fitting comparison for an entirely new feeling. What was it?

With their fingers to Carol's neck, one of the paramedics called out, 'I've got a pulse!'

Lucinda whisked her arm from Alex's touch to clench her fist in triumph. As Carol was hurried to an ambulance, Lucinda let her hands fall to her sides and a twinge bolted down her back as the tension in her neck slipped free. She allowed herself a small smile. Carol wasn't out of the woods yet, but at least they had given her a fighting chance.

'I can't believe it.' Lucinda turned to Alex and was surprised to find his eyes were once again filled with tears. His voice, whose gravelly edge she had noted earlier, carried an additional rasp. 'You did it.'

Over the course of several bitter run-ins with back-stabbing colleagues, Lucinda had learned the importance of taking the credit for her efforts before someone else did. But, she considered, as she rummaged in her bag for a packet of tissues, she had also come to appreciate the importance of teamwork. Even when your team was made up of people who couldn't tie their shoelaces without you to guide their hands.

'*We* did it,' she said, offering Alex a tissue.

'Thanks.'

As Alex pressed the tissue to the corners of his eyes, Lucinda was again struck by the feeling she knew him. His tears dried, he pushed his hands into his pockets, a gesture which raised his shoulders and created a slightly bashful posture. Her former irritation now swamped by relief, Lucinda watched him shuffle his feet and realised she found his awkwardness bafflingly adorable. She frowned at this latest development. Perhaps being stuck in the lift had starved her brain of oxygen? Or maybe it was low blood sugar?

'Lucinda,' he said, lifting his gaze to meet hers. 'I don't suppose you—'

'Excuse me.' They snapped their heads towards the source of the interruption: a police officer giving them a textbook smile of reassurance. As he stepped forwards, his height, breadth and casual air of authority caused Alex and Lucinda to shuffle back from each other. 'I'm PC Stamp. Would you both be happy to have a quick chat?'

'Of course.'

'No problem.'

'Great. It shouldn't take long.' He turned to Alex. 'Sir, if you could speak to my colleague, PC Khan'—he pointed at another officer who was standing by the reception desk—'and I'll stay here with you, Ms ...?'

'Green. Lucinda Green.'

He led Lucinda to a corner of the lobby where, after they had perched on a pair of black leather armchairs, he impressed her with a brisk line of questioning. His breezy efficiency helped draw Lucinda out of the dreamlike place she had entered during the crisis and complete her return to a mercifully mundane reality.

He closed his notebook with a snap. 'OK. I might need you to put that in writing.'

A grizzled veteran of licences, insurances and permits, Lucinda understood the flicker of sourness at the corner of the officer's mouth. 'Endless paperwork?'

'Indeed.' He sighed and stood. 'I won't keep you. I'll be in touch if we need anything else.'

Lucinda picked up her bag and turned to face the lobby. She scanned every corner, but Alex was nowhere to be seen. While the previous half hour had swept her mind gloriously free of any business-related worries, now they crowded back in, jostling for her attention. Even so, there was a part of her that continued to linger on Alex's cute display of shyness and was curious about what he had been about to ask when PC Stamp had appeared. Perhaps she should ask at reception if they'd seen—

Somewhere in her bag, her phone jangled and buzzed. Cursing under her breath, Lucinda rummaged through her jumble of belongings in a desperate bid to get to the phone before the caller gave up. Her efforts were rewarded by the pleasurable sight of Jay's name on the screen. Thank goodness. She wasn't ready to endure Chris's smug sympathy yet.

'Hi! How's it going?' Jay's usually cheerful, musical voice sounded over bright.

'Oh, you know. OK,' Lucinda lied. 'I'll fill you in later. Are you all right?'

'Um, well. Not exactly.'

Lucinda gritted her teeth and marched towards the revolving doors. 'Tell me.'

'Peter can't help me this afternoon.'

'What?' The roar of traffic assaulted Lucinda as she stepped out onto the pavement. She blinked against the glare of the sun and the pressure of another problem. 'Why not?'

'It's that bug that's going round. He's been throwing up all night.'

Lucinda muttered another curse. Peter had been supposed to help Jay prepare a supper for one of their more demanding customers. 'I'm coming back now. I'll help you.'

'Weren't you supposed to take the rest of the day off?'

'When you're self-employed there are no days off. I'll be back in about an hour.'

'So soon? Have you tied up everything there already?'

Lucinda paused and glanced back to the Richards Building. If she waited a couple of minutes could she catch Alex on his way out? The thought she would never see him again stirred a troubling pang of disappointment.

'Lucinda?'

Jay's voice startled her, and she gave herself a mental shake. The last thing she needed was any sort of entanglement with another hopeless guy who would drain her time and energy. She was better off on her own. Definitely. No question.

'Yes, all wrapped up here,' she said as she strode for the station. 'See you soon.'

Chapter 2

'Alex! Are you going to be much longer?' Nicole's voice rapped off the other side of the bathroom door. The size and volume of it belonged to someone large and looming, rather than a five-foot, petite blonde. 'I need to get in or I'll be late!'

Alex took a deep breath and clenched the edge of the sink, willing the lingering tremor in his fingers to still. Alone in the peace of the shower, he'd made the mistake of letting his mind drift back to the elevator. An initially pleasant trip down memory lane, taking in Lucinda's enchanting green stare, gorgeous hair and full lips, had swiftly strayed into the darker territory of Carol's slumped form and ashen skin.

He shook his head, clearing the last of the wooziness. He had believed he was past all this. The paralysing panic, the nausea, sweating and shaking … He hadn't experienced anything like that since his late teens.

Judging the residual trembling in his hands to be under

control, he unlocked the door and Nicole almost fell across the threshold.

'At last!' She grabbed her mascara and set about painting her eyelashes with swift flicks. 'Are you sure you won't come with us? It'll be a great night. A huge celebration.'

Leaning against the wall, Alex welcomed the distraction of Nicole's frenetic preparations as his pulse settled into a steady rhythm. He forced his mind away from Carol and towards the impossible task of recalling where Nicole was getting ready to go. Should he pretend he remembered the details or give Nicole another chance to mock his ever-worsening short-term memory?

'You've forgotten what we're celebrating, haven't you?' Nicole gave him a sly grin. 'Jackson got that BBC period drama gig.'

'Of course. I remember you said.' He didn't. He wasn't even sure which one of her glitter of friends Jackson was.

'There!' Nicole stabbed the mascara wand into its tube. 'Bathroom's all yours.' She paused in front of him on her way out and reached up to tap the end of his nose. 'Are you OK?'

Alex nodded. How would he even begin to explain to Nicole what was going on? He hadn't spoken to anyone about it for decades. 'I'm fine. Just thinking about tonight.'

'Cheer up! It's only one night of menial labour, right?'

'Right. I'm sure it'll be fine.' He gave her a small smile as he closed the door, conveniently allowing Nicole to attribute his anxiety to his upcoming job. In reality, he was looking forward to spending the evening serving food to strangers, something else Nicole wouldn't understand.

As he stepped up to the mirror and picked up his moisturiser, he conceded his excitement was slightly odd.

But he had always enjoyed learning, and preparing for a role gave him a reason to pick up a new skill.

Alex traced his index finger over the lines on his forehead, coming to a halt at the particularly concerning wrinkle at the bridge of his nose. Perhaps the time had come to give in and get Botox. Ray said he'd started on it years ago. But then Ray was the vainest person he had ever met and one who revelled in recounting his adventures of getting jabbed with ever more exotic poisons.

Blinking away intrusive thoughts of Ray—which were almost as unpalatable as the man himself—Alex glared at the white flecks of toothpaste speckling the mirror from top to bottom and rubbed his annoyance into his wrinkles along with some face cream. He'd reminded Nicole to clean that off only recently, hadn't he?

'Alex! Have you seen my large gold hoops?'

Alex rolled his eyes as he stepped into their cramped bedroom where a pile of jewellery was strewn across the bed. Nicole was spreading it wider in an effort to find her missing earrings.

A cloud of her vanilla perfume made Alex cough as he reached into the wardrobe for his clothes. 'I think I saw them on the coffee table in the front room.'

Nicole jumped off the bed. 'Thank you!' she said and fired a kiss onto his cheek before bouncing out of the room, leaving Alex to finish dressing.

Doing his best to ignore the jumble of accessories littering the duvet, he turned to the wardrobe door and inspected his outfit—black trousers, waistcoat and tie and a white shirt—in the mirror. Running a hand over the front of his tie, he scrutinized his face again and concluded he had as many wrinkles as he should have at forty-three. Besides, while the business certainly placed a premium on youth, surely there was a need for some actors to look the age of the characters they were playing? If all of them were chock full of Botox, wouldn't they all have an eerie, ageless appearance, as if they were wearing plastic masks? And how could he use his face to convey the whole range of human emotions if he couldn't move parts of it?

'Alex?' Nicole rocketed back into the bedroom, flung the wardrobe open and rifled through its contents, causing several items to slip off their hangers. 'I can't find my red jacket.'

'Um ...' Alex fought the urge to tell her it would be easier to find her clothes if she hung them up. 'Maybe try the cupboard by the front door?'

'Yes!' She whirled round, training one of her brightest smiles at him, and for a moment all of Alex's annoyance vanished. 'You really are wonderful!' This time she laid her hands on his cheeks and kissed him with a loud 'Mwah!' of appreciation before darting out of the room.

Mollified, Alex shook his head in affectionate exasperation and followed her into the lounge, a room which lacked the space to encourage lounging of any kind. One corner featured the front door. The opposite corner housed the tiny kitchenette. The area between them was filled by a two-seater sofa, a coffee table and a television unit. They really did live in a shoebox. Although, Alex thought, as he pondered where his black shoes were, apparently one large enough in which to misplace jackets and footwear.

Furthering her display of subtle detective skills, Nicole set about throwing items out of the cupboard in the general direction of the sofa. Alex ducked as his left shoe flew over his head. 'Hey! I need the other one of'—the right shoe landed at his feet—'those. Thanks.'

With her head in the cupboard, and her voice having to compete with muffled sounds of yet another argument between the occupants of the upstairs flat, Alex struggled to hear Nicole as she asked, 'Why are you doing this job out in the sticks anyway? When was the last time you waited tables?'

'Twenty years ago.' He frowned. Had it been that long? Christ, Nicole would have been … what? Ten? Nine? He shook his head to drive the thought away. 'And that's why I need the practice. It's research.'

Nicole paused her ransacking to glance in his direction and raise an eyebrow. 'You and your endless preparation. Some might say over-preparation.' The pink gloss on her lips glistened as she shot him a sardonic smile.

'No such thing.' He returned her smile, then glared at the shoes. They needed a clean. Three strides took him to the cupboard under the kitchen sink, where he hoped he'd find polish and a cloth. 'I can't relax into a role unless I go in prepared. And this is a good part. The movie will do well.'

'Sure, babe. But with all the buzz around you at the moment, you know I think you should be thinking beyond this next part. You should be capitalising on the attention.'

He was grateful to be crouched behind the slim counter unit which separated the excuse for a kitchen from the rest of the lounge so she couldn't see his grimace. He loathed the 'buzz'. You spent your whole career hoping for an audience to get excited by your work only for a gig you took out of sheer mercenary desperation, a gig you would prefer never to appear on your IMDB listing, to be the one the sodding internet noticed.

He directed his grumbling response towards the floor as he stood and began to clean his shoes over the sink. 'Yeah. Attention.'

'I don't understand why you're touchy about it. All actors have done some advertising at some point.'

'Yeah.'

'And it's just a voiceover.'

'Thank God.'

'No!' Nicole paused her decimation of the cupboard's contents to glare at him. 'You're looking at this backwards. You should be thinking, "Wow! If I can cause this sort of fuss with a thirty-second voiceover, what could happen if I get those same people excited about my next performance." A performance that actually features your face. You're a brilliant actor, Alex, and you work damn hard. You deserve an army of adoring fans.'

Alex rubbed at a scuff on the toe of his left shoe. 'Thank you. But you know I'm not comfortable with the attention being on *me*. I'd like people to be interested in my work. But I've never wanted them to be talking about my—'

'Yes! Got it!' Nicole slipped into her cherry-red jacket and pulled her hair over the collar. Taking out her phone, she stood among the scattered jackets, shoes, scarves and handbags and used the front-facing camera to inspect herself.

Alex seized the opportunity to change the subject. 'You look great,' he said with genuine conviction. Nicole was stunning and it sometimes worried him how she never seemed to be satisfied with her appearance, no matter how much she buffed and bronzed her pale skin or styled and sculpted her golden hair.

She gazed at him long enough to smile and say, 'Thanks, babe,' before returning to a thorough appraisal of her selfie readiness.

Alex sighed as he stooped to rehouse the polish and cloth in the cupboard. In the early days of their relationship, he remembered how thrilled he was by the way Nicole's blue gaze would never stray from his face as they spoke to each other, as if she was fascinated by every flicker of his features. But lately, the few times she looked directly at him, he wondered if she was staring into his eyes only for the chance to check her own reflection.

'Hi guys!'

Nicole's sunny tone signalled the start of another video. Straightening, Alex watched as she blew a kiss to her phone, the prologue to the show. Scattered around the globe, her tens of thousands of Instagram followers were being treated to the full Nicole glamour. And though she must have seemed an aspirational model of confidence to her audience, the growing frequency of these live recordings made Alex uneasy.

'Whatever you're up to, have a great night! And I'll see you later.' A final wink and a wave, and Nicole pocketed the phone. She crouched to grab her bag from the scattered items on the floor and turned to face Alex, her lips in a neutral line, the unassailable cheeriness she had given to the camera gone. 'I'll tell everyone you said "hi", yeah?'

'Please do.'

'OK.' She waved, a half-hearted version of the enthusiastic finger wiggle she had given her followers, and made for the front door. A glitch in the latch made opening the door a two-handed task, but the second it was free of the frame Nicole retrieved her phone from her pocket, no doubt already preoccupied with how many likes her video should have received. Without turning back or looking up from the screen, she said, 'Hope work goes well.'

'Thanks. Could you—' The door slammed behind her. Alex addressed the rest of his words to the empty room. 'Pick up all that stuff before you leave, please.'

Stifling another sigh, Alex set his shoes by the sofa, collected up the various items of outerwear from the floor and hung them in the cupboard. Maybe Nicole was right. Perhaps he should try to capitalise on the hoo-ha the advert had created. Do his best to get over the fact that the highly *personal* nature of the attention it had brought him made his skin crawl. After all, he wasn't getting any younger and his chances to break through were becoming slimmer every year. Life was short: a lesson he'd learned at an early age. And if he'd needed a reminder of the importance of seizing the day, what had happened recently in the lift with Carol had been a stark one.

He winced as his excellent imagination dragged him back to the lift once more. Nope. No. Not now. A few more seconds dwelling on Carol lying unconscious and he'd freeze again.

He gripped the last pair of shoes he was putting back in their place until the tips of his fingers turned white and stared at them, focusing on details to force his mind into a more colourful, safer place. Blue sandals with pencil-thin heels. Lucinda's shoes had been blue too, a flash of colour in the greyness of the lift cabin. And her eyes were a bright emerald, with an enchanting feline tilt and black lashes.

She'd trained her green stare on him for so long his initial assumption—that she'd been trying to place him—was replaced by a suspicion she was interested in him. And then there had been that static spark. He was pretty sure the real electricity had been accompanied by something more intangible. After all, she'd blushed at his 'shocking' comment. Which had been a stupid thing to say, although apparently the best his dull brain could come up with when an attractive stranger fell into his arms.

But then Carol had become ill and he hadn't been able to shake himself into action. Lucinda's frosty glare in response had made it clear he'd spoiled any favourable first impression he might have created. Although later she had seemed to thaw somewhat ... Had he done enough to redeem himself?

He placed the shoes on the rack at the back of the cupboard and unhooked his own jacket. What would Lucinda have said if he'd managed to finish his suggestion they go for a well-earned drink?

Ugh! He shook his head. While thoughts of Lucinda were undoubtedly helpful in distracting him from disturbing memories of Carol, why did her opinion of him matter?

He slipped on his jacket and out of the noisy, cramped flat. And, as he made his way to his car, he turned his mind back to the evening ahead which would be hard work, requiring total concentration. For one night only he would be playing the role of the best waiter Compton Hall had ever seen. No distractions.

But as he started his car, his mind drifted back to Lucinda. What was she doing tonight? Like Nicole, was she spending her Saturday evening out with a huge group of friends? Or, like him, was she heading to work?

Argh! He shoved his foot onto the accelerator, channelling some of his frustration towards the road. It was time to declare the rest of the day an imagination-free zone. For the next few hours he would have laser-like focus and keep himself so busy he would be unable to entertain a single solitary thought about the lift incident and certainly not about a strangely captivating, green-eyed woman he was guaranteed never to see again.

Chapter 3

'Working? I thought you were taking the weekend off? Honestly, Lucinda, it's like I'm always telling everyone at the club, you'll have no friends left at the rate you're going!'

Lucinda let her gaze settle on the details of the framed movie poster on the wall opposite her bed while silently counting to five. Had her mum instinctively mastered the subtle art of identifying and prodding her sore spots? Or was there some sort of covert training involved?

She took a deep breath and dived back in. 'Good to know you're talking about me to everyone in town, Mum. Make sure to tell the postman I bought some new underwear last week. Black lace trim in case he needs details.'

'Don't change the subject, young lady. Why are you working on your day off?'

Though there was a relatively safe distance of a thousand miles between them, Lucinda could picture Marion's stance: splayed fingers on a jutting hip, pursed lips and an indignant head tilt sending chandelier earrings swinging. Which reminded her, where were her favourite silver studs?

The tangle of necklaces and earrings in the porcelain dish on the dresser was likely to be harbouring the silver discs inlaid with blue opals. She prodded at the pile as she dragged up an excuse that had a chance of mollifying her mum.

'It's that bug that's been doing the rounds. We're short-staffed'—an exasperated huff from the other end of the line broke Lucinda's flow but she soldiered on—'and I can take a weekend off when everyone's back.'

'Hmn. Well, as long as it's not an excuse to stop speaking to me.' Her mum's tone was playful, but Lucinda winced as she remembered the times she had gone to similar lengths to avoid these kinds of conversations.

'Of course not.' Earrings successfully located, she propped her phone against the wall as she put them on. 'What are you doing tonight?'

'You know it's bridge club on Saturdays.'

Lucinda wished she did know, but it was hard to keep track. Marion's calendar resembled a bus timetable: bridge club, book club, art club, bowls, dances … No wonder she despaired at Lucinda's lack of social life.

'Of course it is. But weren't you thinking of swapping bridge for something more interesting?'

Her mum laughed. 'I was, but Graham has livened it up no end.'

Which one was Graham again? How was she supposed to remember every member of Mum's potpourri of expat chums?

Encouraged by Lucinda's stumped silence, Marion ploughed on. 'He was telling me that Bella, his eldest daughter, has just been promoted to head of her section. She's the accountant, remember?'

'I'm sure he's very proud.' Lucinda stomped into the bathroom and, her nostrils flaring at the residual stink of Chris's musky cologne, set her phone down next to the sink before rifling through her drawer under the sink for a comb and hair clip. How could she bring this conversation to a close? If Mum ran on much longer she'd be asking about Chris next.

'And her fiancé is an architect,' Mum said, her tone rising ominously. She was building up to something. 'Speaking of which, how's Chris?'

Lucinda squeezed the comb in her fist, letting the plastic teeth bite into her palm. 'He's fine. And still not my fiancé.'

'Well we all know that's more your doing than his.'

'Actually, that's not—' The staggering inaccuracy and injustice of her mum's last comment momentarily broke Lucinda's resolve and she was about to set her right when she realised maybe that had been Marion's cunning plan all along: to shock her into talking about Chris. She shook her head. If there were courses behind Mum's skills then she must have a doctorate.

'I must be keeping you back, Mum. Don't want you to be late for bridge. Everyone at La Cala would be lost without you.'

'Too true. But take some time off! You could come here for a visit. Some sunshine would do you good. Make you look less pasty and tired.'

Lucinda glanced at her reflection in the mirror. The dim lighting in the bathroom never did her any favours, but she had to admit she was a little pasty. The light worry lines which had been settling across her forehead in the second half of her thirties were, now she had reached forty, subsiding into full-on wrinkles. But she didn't look exhausted. In fact, since she had started delegating more tasks, she had been treating herself to the occasional evening at home and lie-in.

'It'd be lovely to be able to visit, Mum. But I should really get going—'

'Yes, yes. It's been lovely talking to you, darling, but I can't be jabbering to you all day, I have to get ready. Speak soon!'

'Bye, Mu—' Lucinda managed to get out before the line went dead. Lucinda's small growl of exasperation echoed loudly in the sudden silence as she tugged the comb through her hair. Her company would soon have been running for six years. Most of that time had passed in a blur, but recently operations had settled into well-managed patterns. She had built a competent team, they had a roster of regular clients and enough work to keep them open.

She should follow everyone's advice and take a weekend off. For while she was delighted that over five years of ceaseless effort had paid off at work, her recent periods of downtime had made her realise her life had shrunk. Aside from dropping into some parties with Chris, she couldn't remember the last time she'd spent any quality time with anyone outside work. And she had no hobbies aside from reading, watching TV and cooking. She had somehow drifted into a somnolent loop: not enough sleep, work, worry about work, eat, read, not enough sleep. And repeat.

As she twirled her hair up into a clip, Lucinda pictured her mum darting between all her activities in an endless sparkling whirl, the human disco ball of the Costa del Sol. In contrast, Lucinda's day-to-day had atrophied into an automatic existence, as reflexive and unconscious as breathing. And Lucinda didn't want to merely exist; she wanted to live. Though a cliché, her recent milestone birthday had caused her to reflect on what she had achieved so far. Her first four decades had scudded past in a bewildering haze, leaving her certain it was only now, as she entered middle age, that she was truly getting started. And what had happened with Carol a few weeks previously had reminded her no one has time to waste.

Downstairs the front door slammed, causing the bathroom door to vibrate in sympathy and Lucinda's head to drop forwards in despair. There went her plan to leave before Chris got home! Ugh. Speaking to her mum had drained her diplomatic reserves and she didn't have the energy for an argument.

'Lu? Are you still here?'

There was no point in pretending. The house wasn't big enough to hide in. Lord knows she'd tried. 'I'll be down in a minute!' A knot tightening in her stomach, she turned back to the mirror and smiled, trying to dispel the slightly grumpy, unimpressed expression which her features always seemed to arrange themselves into.

As she glided down the stairs, an unforced smile came to her lips as she ran her hand along the surface of the bannister rail. Hours of sanding layers of old paint from the beautiful light oak and a final polish had left it as smooth as glass. It was one of dozens of little features she loved about the house. Finishing touches which went unnoticed by everyone else, but which brought her joy. The modest library recess to the left of the old chimney breast in the living room was another. Chris's dad had installed the shelves, allowing her to arrange her books on them according to spine colour. And no matter how grey the weather, the sight of her literary rainbow always lifted her mood.

'Tea?' Chris called from the kitchen, raising his voice over the bubbling of the kettle.

'No, thanks. I'd best be off.' She wandered into the room and leant against the countertop as Chris reached for the kettle. As he gripped the handle and tipped water into a mug, his right bicep strained against the tight fabric of his red sweater. Suspicious, Lucinda shifted her gaze to his waist, which was trimmer than she remembered. Had he been exercising more lately? And, more importantly, when had he met the woman behind this latest bout of self-improvement?

Keeping her tone casual, she asked. 'You're not working tonight?'

'No.' He grinned, his eyes filling with a cheeky sparkle. 'The bosses have given me the night off for good behaviour.'

Chris was head chef at The Olive Grove, one of the best and busiest restaurants in the Comptons. Its pleasing Mediterranean menu and fantastic location on the High Street made it a perennial favourite. And, while they'd had their ups and downs in the decade since they'd met, Lucinda would never deny that Chris was a brilliant chef who would no doubt steer the place towards ever-greater success. A fact which delighted his parents, who had founded the restaurant when Chris was five years old.

'Are you staying in?' If he didn't have a date, Lucinda would insist he do some cleaning. She'd gone easy on him the past few weeks. His lack of smugness or pitying looks when she'd admitted to having lost the Richards Group contract had bought him her goodwill. But her tolerance had limits. And the bathroom mirror was covered in his sodding toothpaste splatter *again*.

Chris's grin shifted into a nervous smile and he ran a hand over his short brown hair. 'Er, actually, I'm meeting someone for a drink. Possibly dinner.'

Aha! She knew it! She tried to catch his eye, but Chris was deliberately fixing his attention on stirring his tea. When would his awkwardness when it came to dating other women end? They hadn't been an item for over two years. Why he thought he had to sneak around was beyond her. Especially as Lucinda had never experienced so much as a pang of jealousy even when they were together.

It certainly wasn't jealousy that kept her awake at night. Chris finding a long-term partner was only a nightmare scenario because it would—bar a miraculous windfall—result in her losing the house. And as much as she tried not to think about it, she knew it was a case of when, rather than if. After all, annoying as he could be, Chris was a kind, creative, good-looking guy. And no woman was going to be happy with him continuing to share a house with his ex-fiancée.

The thought of having to leave the cosy nest she had poured so much love into feathering made the knot in her stomach twist. She grabbed her keys from the counter, squeezing the large heart-shaped key-ring charm between her fingers. The crimson enamel key fob, with its dented and scratched metallic border, had served her as a makeshift stress toy for decades. Although now, as she stared at the puzzle piece-shaped hole in the centre of the heart, she doubted her dad could have realised how well his gift would one day reflect the state of his daughter's love life.

Pressing a hand to the heaviness in her belly, she forced some levity into her voice. 'Great! Hopefully you'll get to dinner. Have a good night and I'll see you tomorrow.'

'Right. OK.'

Chris nodded as he stirred his tea, the sparkle in his eyes and his smile replaced by the hangdog look he gave her when he'd forgotten to buy milk. Pouting and biting back a sigh, Lucinda marched to the front door, stamping any residual guilt into the carpet. She was tired of being responsible for Chris's feelings when—no matter what her mum or anyone else thought—he was the one to blame for his single status.

Chapter 4

In the seventeenth-century setting of the Compton Hall Grand Saloon, the annual dinner of the Norton Cricket Association was passing off swimmingly. The aroma of perfectly braised beef welcomed Lucinda to the kitchen seconds before the relaxed smile of her head chef. And, as she listened to a rundown on how the evening was proceeding, Lucinda quickly grasped why Jay couldn't understand her need to visit.

'Honestly, you should have enjoyed your night off. It's going great.'

'The mains are—'

'All the mains are out and Misha says service is going smoothly. The desserts are already plated up.' Jay nodded towards the trolleys whose tiers were carrying over one hundred plates of individual *tarte au citron*: parcels of buttery shortcrust heaven filled with a sharp citrus kiss.

'And the cream is—'

'In the fridge. Of course if they'd gone for the clotted

cream we could already have it out.' Jay let out a sigh of exasperation at their client's lack of adventurousness.

Lucinda smiled in sympathy. Having your creativity thwarted and the most delectable menu options rejected in favour of safer, blander fare was an occupational hazard when catering for the masses.

'The customer gets what they want. And, more importantly, what they're willing to pay for. Did you also prep some—'

'Raspberry coulis, vanilla ice cream and whipped cream on standby, as instructed.'

'Excellent.' Lucinda often suspected Jay regarded her as an overcautious worrywart and was thankful the younger woman suffered her interference with good humour. She gave Jay's shoulder a tap of gratitude. 'Thanks.'

It would have been inappropriate to hug an employee, but Lucinda was often tempted to embrace Jay. She was talented, industrious and, crucially, on Lucinda's side. This final feature made her extraordinary and invaluable. Sometimes Lucinda's entire life seemed like a fight: a battle to carve her own trench across a rocky minefield while surrounded by people seeking to divert her or hold her back. But now, at least at work, she had Jay in the trench with her, watching her back.

She scanned the kitchen. In the absence of staff the hum of the fridges seemed deafening. 'Where is everyone?'

'Ethan and Nina are out on a break. They'll be busy with the dishes soon. I sent Peter and Tyler home when all the mains were out.'

'Good.' Lucinda bit her lip. Jay clearly had everything under control and there was no need for her to have come.

But this was an important night. Compton Hall's list of caterers who were approved to use the facilities was short. Her business had only been on the roll for two years and tonight was the first time they had catered for this customer. So when Misha had made an offhand comment about staff shortages, it had created a worry worm which had burrowed into Lucinda's subconscious and refused to sleep.

Jay ran a cloth over the already-gleaming countertop. 'You should go home. You still haven't had a day off since your brush with death and that was nearly three weeks ago.'

Lucinda shrugged in response to what was likely another attempt by Jay to dig for details about what had happened in London. There was no malicious gossip-hunting in her persistence, simply the natural curiosity of someone whose own life was an open book and who enjoyed reading passages from it aloud.

'I'm fine,' Lucinda said. 'It wasn't me who nearly died.'

'Still, you should put your feet up more, read a— Oh!' Jay bent down and slid open a door to one of the under-counter cupboards. 'I nearly forgot. Something for you!' She handed Lucinda a hefty coffee table book and continued to speak over Lucinda's gasp of delighted surprise. 'My cousin, Sheena—I told you about her, always unlucky in love, bless her. She thought she'd finally found a winner with her latest bloke, who's into a lot of the same geeky stuff as you—'

'Hey!' said Lucinda, clutching the volume to her chest. '*Star Wars* is solidly mainstream.'

'You keep telling yourself that.' Jay grinned. 'Anyway, for this guy's birthday Sheena bought him that'—she waved her cloth towards the book—'which is like a nerd's guide to the making of the first film, 'cos apparently there's more than one of them—'

'Please stop.' Lucinda held up a hand. 'Your lack of classic film knowledge is actually painful.'

Jay huffed a laugh. 'And then he dumped her a couple of days before, and she called me and said she was going to burn it—'

'What?' Lucinda wrapped both arms around the book, wondering if putting it under her top would be a step too far.

'I know, right? But I said I knew someone who would appreciate it. And so, there you go.'

'Thank you.' Lucinda dragged her gaze from the book to Jay's animated features and wondered, again, if she could hug an employee. 'Are you sure? I'll pay her for—'

'Nope. No need. Honestly, she was chuffed to get shot of it. She really has had a terrible time lately. I think I mentioned before, her mum's been ill. Oh … speaking of health issues, have you heard anything about how the lady who had the heart attack in the lift is getting on?'

'She's recovering well, apparently.' Lucinda stooped to return the book to the safety of the under-counter cupboard while hoping a clipped response would halt Jay's questions, thereby preserving something of her own and Carol's privacy. After Jay had given her such a thoughtful gift, she didn't want Snappy Lucinda to appear and turn on her.

'You were right about going on that first-aid refresher course after all,' said Jay as she returned to polishing the counter. 'She was lucky you were there. Did you ever hear any more about the guy who helped you? Aren't you curious about—'

'Did Misha manage to sort out the waiting staff shortage?'

Jay froze and, after a brief pause, whipped the cloth away from the countertop. As she busied her hands with tucking the cloth into her apron ties, Jay's features remained composed and the only sign she had noticed Lucinda's snippiness was in her cheeks, where the usual gold tones of her brown skin had darkened to bronze. Like Lucinda, Jay had worked in too many kitchens run by explosive screamers and swearers to be fazed by a curt boss.

When Jay replied, her voice was subdued. 'Yes, she got a couple of cover staff. And, actually'—her upbeat tone returned, heralding exciting news—'one's interesting! He's an actor who's going to be working on a film here at the Hall.'

'An actor? Does he have silver service experience?'

'Of course! Misha knows what she's doing. Apparently he's been terrific.'

'Then that's all that matters, I guess. Wait ... He's not recognisable, is he? Waiters are supposed to be invisible.'

Jay tilted her head, considering. 'Hmn. Not really. He's that guy from that thing.'

'What?'

'An actor who's been in loads of stuff but in minor roles. So you're watching something and you recognise the guy but you can't remember their name or where you've seen them before. And it drives you mad until you google it. Right?'

'Uh ... I guess. Has he been in anything I might have seen?'

'How about *Napier*?' Jay's eyes widened in response to Lucinda's blank stare. 'I can't believe you don't watch it! It's a cop show. A cult hit. The third episode of series three is tomorrow night.'

'But if you think I should have seen it, won't someone out there recognise him?'

Jay waved a dismissive hand. 'I don't think it's the sort of thing that would appeal to this crowd. He should pass unnoticed. As long as he keeps his mouth shut.'

Already disorientated by the direction of the conversation had taken, Lucinda gave herself over to complete bafflement. 'Huh?'

Jay giggled. 'He's the advert voice guy all the mums have gone nuts about!'

'Sorry, you've lost me.'

'You must have heard about it. The thread on Mumsweb about weird crushes that went viral? It's been all over Twitter!'

'I have zero idea what you're talking about.'

Shaking her head at her boss's lack of social media prowess, Jay steered Lucinda towards the swing doors and the corridor beyond, which connected the kitchen to the Saloon. 'Come on. It'll be easier if I point him out.'

The women huddled behind the glass panel in the door to the dining room. Ignoring the decor—though the mahogany panelling, gilded ceiling mouldings and eighteenth-century portraiture were always distracting— Lucinda focused on the faces of her customers and was relieved to see laughter, enthusiastic chewing and conversation. Although, as her glance skimmed over the far left of the room, her stare snagged on a familiar figure lurking in the shadows between a pair of crimson velvet curtains. Lucinda smiled and made a mental note to seek out the friendly shade for a chat when everyone was busy enjoying dessert.

'I see Becky's here,' Lucinda said as the figure disappeared behind the curtains.

'Who?'

'Rebecca Watson. I'm not sure you've met her yet.' Lucinda knew Becky had worked a few of the same events as Jay but was unlikely to have introduced herself unless strictly necessary.

'Oh. No I haven't but I think you've mentioned her. She's the event planner, right?'

'Hmn. Not really. More of a crisis manager. She's sort of an insurance policy. Event planners actually recommend her to their clients. People hire her to make sure nothing goes wrong—'

'There!' Lucinda startled as Jay hissed and jabbed a finger to the right of the room. 'That's him! The tall guy topping up glasses on table four.'

Lucinda followed her gaze. Her heart stuttered and jaw dropped.

Apparently not having noticed her dumbfounded expression, Jay broke into a hushed commentary not dissimilar to a wildlife documentary voiceover. 'He's better looking in real life, if you ask me. And he must be at the gym all the time to have a bod like that. But that's part of an actor's job, I suppose.' She paused to glance at Lucinda before rattling on. 'Do you reckon that tan's natural? Only I always think—'

Lucinda swallowed the lump forming in her throat and said, in a hoarse whisper, 'It's Alex.'

'I know! That's what I've been trying to tell you. Alex Fraser.'

Lucinda stuttered, unable to tear her eyes away from him. With his left hand tucked behind his back, he was leaning forwards to top up a customer's wine glass using a graceful one-handed motion. The red-faced, portly gentleman with a towering comb-over didn't deign to gift his waiter a glance, but Alex smiled at him as he stepped back and glided to the opposite side of the table.

Lucinda recovered sufficiently to close her mouth, but continued to stare. Most of her brain was busy processing and slowly accepting the evidence of her eyes. Meanwhile the rest—a small but vocal part—was musing on how Alex's surname suited him, how harmoniously the sounds of his first and last names chimed together, and how flipping fantastic his trim muscular figure looked in a close-fitting waiter's uniform.

She stammered a reply. 'No, well, yes. But—' Lucinda took a breath and aimed for coherency. 'He's the guy from the lift. The one who helped me give the older lady CPR.'

'What?' Lucinda glanced at Jay and saw her own shock mirrored on her head chef's face. 'You didn't say anything about him being fit!'

In the three weeks since she had met Alex, in the brief moments Lucinda hadn't been occupied by work, worrying about Chris or avoiding her mother's calls, she had found her thoughts wandering back to Alex's slanting smile, electric touch and the beautiful burnt umber tones of his dark eyes. Now, as she stared at the deft way he handled the bottle with his strong hands, the lump in her throat returned. She coughed and said, 'I didn't really notice what he looked like.'

Jay's pitch rose further as she continued to express her amazement, but to Lucinda her voice was a distant cloud of sound. A flutter of butterflies was performing loops in her tummy and when she raised a hand to her neck her pulse raced under her warm fingertips. That had to be the result of the surprise, didn't it? Such an amazing coincidence would make anyone jittery. Of course it would.

'Lucinda?' Jay nudged her with her elbow. 'Are you OK?'

'What? Um, yeah, fine. Never better. What's up?'

'I said, I'll take my break now. If that's all right?'

'Of course!' Lucinda pressed a trembling hand to her tummy. 'I think I'll go find Becky. See what she's doing here.'

'Great!' Jay grinned as she began to unfasten her jacket, revealing a fitted top in sunny lemon tones. 'And you can catch up with Alex later. Perhaps you could introduce me properly? I said "hi" when Misha gave him the tour earlier, but it'd be great to ask him some questions about *Napier*.'

'Um, sure. Yep.'

'Fantastic! This is so the best event we've ever done.' She beamed and clapped Lucinda on the back, sending her stuttering pulse racing once again. 'Cheer up! You worry too much. We're nearly finished here and it's all going great. I mean, what's the worst that could happen?'

Chapter 5

Despite Jay's cheerful reassurance, Lucinda's heart continued to pound as she strode down the staff-only corridor concealed behind the outer wall of the Saloon. Becky's presence at an event meant its organiser had foreseen trouble. Over the past two years Lucinda had witnessed Becky's work behind the scenes at various venues, watching as she employed an array of tactics to deal with explosive brides, drunken guests and clueless groomsmen. Tactics which were at best reckless and at worst morally questionable. Moves which Lucinda could never imagine using herself and which surely weren't required at a cricket association dinner?

Normally Lucinda was happy to do Becky the odd favour while remaining in blissful ignorance of the specifics of Becky's mission. But Alex's appearance that evening had already been a shock and, never a fan of surprises, Lucinda wasn't sure she could cope with another. For once, the cautious and prudent move would be to track Becky down and ask if there was anything else she should be prepared for.

Finding the library and drawing room empty, Lucinda made her way to the entrance hall. Someone had turned off the dazzling lights of the enormous crystal chandelier, leaving the grand sweep of the mahogany staircase, the first-floor gallery and the columns supporting it illuminated only by a few wall sconces. In the dim light, the room resembled a cloister, albeit one with gilt-framed artwork and decorative cornices. Jay had thrilled in telling Lucinda that the Hall was said to be haunted and, while Lucinda had found it easy to rubbish such rumours at the time, the current gloomy silence would be the ideal setting for a headless apparition or two.

She shuddered. If she didn't find Becky soon she'd go back to the kitchen before she started believing in all kinds of nonsense. Even if that did mean having to deal with Alex. Not that she was avoiding him. Obviously. Why would she need to avoid him? That would be as daft as believing in ghosts!

Shaking her head, she stalked away from the Saloon entrance and crossed the black-and-white checked floor with the determination of a woman who had no time for the supernatural or astounding appearances by weirdly attractive actors. But her progress was soon halted by the sound of a woman's voice coming from the far corner of the room.

'No, thank you. I need to get back to work now.'

Hang on. Was that Jay?

Lucinda inched around the corner pillar and was rewarded with a clear view of Jay at the far side of the room. She was backed against the wall, her exit towards the cloakroom and kitchens blocked by the stout man with the ludicrous comb-over whom Alex had been serving earlier. Perhaps this was his first time as a guest at the Hall and he was asking Jay for directions to the toilets? But— Lucinda reasoned as she peered at the pair, her breathing accelerating as misgivings writhed in her stomach—if he were merely asking Jay an innocent question then why was she crossing her arms protectively across her chest and pressing herself against the wall so urgently it looked as if she were hoping she could melt into it?

Lucinda took two steps forwards as the man chuckled, mumbled a reply and lifted a finger to stroke Jay's arm. Jay's voice rose in response, 'I said no. Now let me pass.'

Lucinda's nostrils flared as the man chuckled again and slouched even closer to Jay as he slurred another response, looming over her like a portly Nosferatu. Her head chef's features twisted in horror as he laid his chubby hands on her waist. And, as Jay squirmed against the wall and shouted, 'Get off me!', Lucinda saw red.

Casting caution aside, she bore down on them, her anger boiling into rage with every step. The guy could be the owner of sodding Compton Hall, she was still going to rip the ratty excuse for hair from his greasy head and ram it down his throat. How dare he lay a finger on Jay, the miserable—

'Jay! How wonderful to see you again.'

Lucinda halted in the shadow of the nearest column as a fair-haired woman glided through the cloakroom door and, speaking to Jay as if the man in front of her didn't exist, continued in a pleasant, untroubled tone, 'It's been ages. How are you?'

Sidelined by the newcomer, the man took a wobbly step

back. Lucinda now had a clear view of his red cheeks and jowls and could imagine his sour, booze-soaked breath.

Jay muttered a response as the woman stepped deftly into the space left by the man, forming an effective barrier between predator and prey. Through her outrage, Lucinda had to hand it to Becky: the woman was a professional diplomat. She could probably defuse a bomb with a few civil words and a smooth smile.

'We should catch up later.' Becky gave Jay a reassuring nod and tilted her head towards the cloakroom door. 'Please don't let me keep you. Lucinda's sure to have missed you.'

Jay nodded and muttered a thank you as she turned and hurried towards the exit. Meanwhile, Becky had spun round to address the man. 'And I'm sure you're keen to get back to the party, sir,' she said through a sharp, frosty smile.

The man harrumphed and shuffled back to the Saloon, his smug, oily expression devoid of any shame. Lucinda exhaled noisily and was considering removing one of her trusty clogs and hurling it at his head when a low voice at the back of her neck said, 'Nice to see you, Lucinda.'

Lucinda yelped and startled as she spun round to face Becky. Where had she learnt to sneak up on people like that? She took a breath to regain her composure and said, 'Perfect timing, as always, Becky. Whatever they're paying you tonight, it's not enough.'

Becky's clear blue eyes narrowed and her brows drew together. 'Not quite perfect. I should have got here a few seconds earlier.'

'You and me both. But you stopped me throttling the rancid slug, so he should be grateful.'

Becky glanced down at Lucinda's quivering hands. 'Why don't you go and check Jay's all right? Ask her for the whole story and then come and meet me out on the veranda? Perhaps between the two of us we can come up with a solution to the problem of the charming Mr Wilson?'

'A permanent solution? I have more than enough knives—'

'Preferably a solution which doesn't involve violence, jail or you getting struck off the Hall's list of approved suppliers.'

Lucinda huffed and planted her hands on her hips. As usual, Becky had a point. 'Fine. I'll meet you out there in fifteen. But'—she raised a finger and an eyebrow—'if Mr Wilson makes the mistake of so much as breathing in the direction of another member of my team in the meantime, all bets are off.'

Chapter 6

Alex couldn't remember the last time he'd enjoyed a Saturday night so much. He'd had a shaky start, but his jitters had died down as his experience and recent practice began to pay off. The guests were content, the staff friendly and Misha kept the team of waiters so busy he had slim chance to ponder the exact date and time his social life had died.

He was also pleased he had arrived early and taken the opportunity to familiarise himself with Compton Hall. Originally built in the 1670s, and surrounded by fragrant formal gardens, neatly mown lawns and acres of parkland, the Hall's three storeys of red brick and rows of white-framed windows enclosed an equally cinematic interior. He had no doubt it would photograph beautifully. All in all, it was a great choice of location.

Preoccupied with thoughts of the upcoming movie shoot, he was one of the last to finish delivering the desserts. As he made his way back to the kitchen, he paused to run a hand over his face and straighten his tie. Perhaps he should make the most of his ten-minute break by stepping outside to cool down and collect himself?

To the left of the swing door to the kitchen, a set of French windows had been left ajar. The veranda and superb view over the rose gardens beyond them were obscured by a pair of thick crimson curtains which had been drawn over the opening.

As he paused by the gap between the curtains, the fresh rose-perfumed air caressed Alex's face and he decided spending a moment outside was one of his better ideas. He raised his fingers to the plush material and was about to lift it to one side when a voice outside said, 'I knew when I saw you that something would be up.'

'I was hired to make sure the whole event went smoothly, but the organiser was especially concerned about Mr Wilson's behaviour. And sadly it turns out she was right.'

Edging closer to the space between the drapes, Alex peered into the relative gloom outside. Illuminated by the light from the dining room windows, a fair-skinned, dark-haired woman was standing on the veranda, leaning against the waist-height stone balustrade. His jaw dropped as he stared at her, his heart racing in recognition and disbelief. During the team's pre-meal break, he'd noticed the Lucinda's Catering logo on the side of one of the vans outside and had done a double take. If Misha hadn't confirmed what he was reading, he might have believed he was imagining the name, a manifestation of his recent preoccupation. If he'd known Lucinda—*the* Lucinda—had been in the building when he was serving, he suspected a few diners would have ended up with a lapful of gravy and potatoes.

Lucinda was facing a woman Alex thought he might have seen in the corner of the dining room earlier in the evening. At the time he'd noticed her clothing—black trousers, white blouse and black cardigan—and assumed she was either a member of the catering staff or an employee of Compton Hall. But the relaxed way the women were standing inches apart and the content of their conversation made him think he'd got that wrong.

'Did Jay tell you exactly what happened?' The other woman tilted her head and the moonlight glinted off the lenses of her glasses and her light brown hair which was drawn back into a simple ponytail at her nape.

Lucinda growled and unfastened her hair. It tumbled over her shoulders, forming a luxurious raven mane which framed her pale face. Alex gawped. As Lucinda lifted her chin and shook her head to sweep it back, Alex's heart stuttered and skin prickled. What he wouldn't give to tangle his fingers in those stunning inky waves! To run his hands over the soft lustrous curls and—

Lucinda set about tugging her tresses back behind her head. Blinking, Alex closed his mouth and swallowed. He was being ludicrous. It was just hair. Sexy mermaid hair, but hair nonetheless. The important thing was what she was saying ...

'She was on her way back to the kitchen from the loos and he cornered her. Made some inappropriate comments, then made a grab for her.' Lucinda growled again, her eyes narrowing as she refixed her hair with an aggressive snap of the clip. 'Not his first offence either. Misha says he'd been harassing and trying to grope Nina during early service, so much so she switched her to another table.'

'I'm so sorry.' The other woman bit her bottom lip. 'I was told he was a flirt and might be a problem around the younger female guests.'

'A flirt!' Lucinda swung her foot at the balustrade. 'A perve with a thing for intimidating women young enough to be his daughter in dark corners, more like.' Lucinda aimed another kick at the stone barrier and a steely note crept into her voice which suggested she was the sort of person who had a shotgun and a shovel in the back of her car and wouldn't hesitate to use them.

'I was watching him with the other guests, but I should have thought of the staff—'

'It's not your fault, Becky.'

'And then I let him get out of my sight because Phoebe called with a question about Dylan—'

'No one should have to police the guests!' Lucinda threw her hands up, her fingers rigid with vexation. 'Although if anyone should have been watching out for Jay, it was me. She's a member of *my* team.' She dragged her hands down over her temples and sighed. 'How did he even get invited if they knew he was likely to do this sort of thing?'

'He's on the board of the Association. And a generous donor.'

'Ugh! I could've guessed.'

Becky smiled ruefully. 'And his niece is the one organising the dinner.' She shrugged and said, 'A little more than kin ...'

'And less than kind.' Alex grimaced and froze. His short-term memory was increasingly unreliable, but for some weird reason every play he'd ever been in stuck firmly in his mind and finishing the line had been a reflex.

Squeezing his eyes shut, he listened to his pulse thundering in his ears and prayed he hadn't spoken aloud. But that faint hope shrivelled and died when a short burst of laughter was followed by Becky saying, 'How now, a rat?' She laughed again and said, in a teasing tone, 'We know you're there. Come on out.'

While scurrying to the kitchens like a frightened rodent was highly tempting, Alex was fairly certain fleeing would impress Lucinda far less than admitting to eavesdropping. So he parted the curtains and ducked onto the veranda, feeling more awkward than if he had been stepping out onto a stage in front of thousands.

Lucinda crossed her arms as she glared at him with her piercing green glower, while Becky blinked at him, the corners of her eyes crinkled with amusement. 'Do you regularly hide behind an arras on the off-chance you'll get to finish quotes from *Hamlet*?' she asked.

'Sorry.' He rubbed a hand over the back of his neck, where the skin was hot. 'Occupational hazard.'

'You're the actor! Misha mentioned you were working here tonight to prepare for a role.' Her lips curled. 'And have you played the Dane?'

'Sadly not. I was Laertes.'

'Don't be sorry. It's an important part.' Becky's smile widened and a shine stole into her cornflower-blue eyes. 'Were you double cast or did you have to hang around backstage for half the play like another ghost?'

'I was the Player King too.' He returned her smile, finding himself relaxing—as he always did—in the company of someone who shared his love of Shakespeare. And, although it had been fifteen years ago, he held fond memories of that production. It was a thrill to work in Stratford and then tour the regional theatres with the company.

'Ah.' She nodded. '"The play's the—"'

'Hey!' Lucinda thrust her hands onto her hips and directed a look charged with an impressive degree of aggression towards them both. But when she spoke, she addressed her comments to Becky alone. 'I'm sure this is fascinating and not at all irrelevant, Becky, but could we please get back to our real and present problem? Please?'

At any other moment, Alex would have been upset by the brusque way Lucinda was sidelining him. Would a *'Hello'* and *'Nice to see you again'* be too much to ask for? But, given the circumstances, he was relieved not to be on the receiving end of her ire, particularly as he'd just been caught listening in on her private conversation and probably deserved it.

How to make amends and get on her good side? Or at least get a toe over the line. He frowned and replayed the part of their conversation he'd overheard. What they'd said would explain why he'd been asked to switch to table four before serving the main course. He'd lay money the guest responsible for harassing Nina and Jay was the same one who had been making lewd comments about the female diners. The charming specimen in question had a gravity-defying comb-over held in place by bombproof denial and presumably an entire can of hairspray. As he pictured him, Alex's nose wrinkled in revulsion. If Lucinda and Becky confirmed his suspicions that the charmer he had in mind was the culprit, he'd happily volunteer to light a match above his head.

Becky's smile faded. 'I know it's annoying, but I'm not sure how much we can do.'

Lucinda spluttered and her cheeks darkened. 'But ... But ... We can't let him get away with it!'

'I agree.' Becky's voice was calm and conciliatory, but her expression was pained. 'But a guy like that isn't going to be frightened off by you or me. And he'll get a kick out of having upset another woman and being able to lord his untouchable position over us.'

'Can't we report him to the police? It's assault and harassment, surely?'

'Yes.' Becky nodded. 'And there are a couple of people at the local station I could call, but it'd be wasting their time.'

Alex, seeing the logic of Becky's position, muttered, 'He'd probably say you'd misinterpreted his actions.'

Lucinda snapped her head in his direction and fired him a look so poisonous he had to fight the instinct to recoil.

Becky either hadn't noticed Lucinda's laser-like stare, was used to her temper or simply a far braver person than he was. She nodded in agreement with him and said, 'Exactly. That he was only being friendly, he didn't mean to cause offence ... The same old story. And I don't think my client would be too pleased at me having her uncle officially cautioned.'

Lucinda pointed to the balustrade and the sunken gardens a storey below. 'Ugh! Honestly, can't I just throw him off the balcony?'

Alex grinned, imagining the comb-over remaining perfectly immobile as its owner fell, flailing and wailing before crunching into a hideously thorny rosebush. He said, 'I'd be more than happy to be your alibi. Or I could carry him, if you prefer.'

'Fine,' Lucinda said. 'But I get to push him over.'

'Deal.'

Lucinda smiled at him, the violence momentarily leaving her eyes. It was only a fleeting, conspiratorial smirk, but it sent a rush of adrenaline through Alex so powerful he felt as if he'd scored the winning goal in the World Cup.

Becky laughed. 'All right you two. Calm down. I don't want to have to get you out of jail tonight.'

The sudden rush which had hit Alex nudged a thought to the front of his brain. One which, given all the previous talk of police, he couldn't believe hadn't occurred to him before. 'Actually, I think I might have an idea.'

The women turned towards him. Both had their eyebrows raised: Becky's in apparent polite surprise, Lucinda's in impatient disbelief.

Undeterred by the pressure of their collective gaze— even though it did rival that of the most intense casting panels he'd experienced—he continued, 'Technically, it might ... be a bit illegal. And if not, then it would definitely be in a morally grey area.'

Becky grinned. 'Sounds like my kind of idea.'

'Wait a minute.' Lucinda held up a palm. 'Does it involve kicking Mr Wilson's arse?'

'Literally? No.' Alex held back a smile at Lucinda's wince of disappointment. 'Figuratively? Yes.'

The women looked at each other and Becky shrugged. In response, Lucinda pouted and turned back to Alex. She splayed the fingers of her right hand over her jutting hip and said, 'OK then, *Player King*. What did you have in mind?'

Chapter 7

He had to be kidding.

As she stared at Alex, her mouth agape and knees weak, Lucinda was relieved she had been leaning against one of the upright freezers in the corner of the kitchen when he had returned from his mysterious trip to the car park.

She was also pleased Ethan was busy at the other end of the kitchen. Wearing luminous blue earbuds, the teenager sprayed and loaded dishes into the dishwasher while humming along to his music. Absorbed in his work, he was one less person to explain Alex's appearance to.

It was like looking at a shifting mirage. There, in front of her and Becky, with the confident stance of a man who belonged, stood the Alex who moments ago had been the image of a quintessential waiter. But now, in a black uniform which included a tactical vest and was topped with a flat-topped visored hat ringed with a black-and-white chequered band, he was Police Constable Fraser.

Running her gaze from the shine of his sturdy patrol

boots to the badge on his hat, taking in—but obviously in no way dwelling on—his toned thighs, trim waist and broad shoulders, she couldn't decide which was responsible for the greater part of her disorientation: the speed and degree of the transformation, or the accompanying change in his appearance from very handsome to 'best tie yourself down and watch out you're probably drooling' handsome.

'What do you think?' One of the corners of Alex's mouth twitched as he completed a slow twirl, the room's cool lighting showing up every crease and curve in his outfit, and his body underneath it.

Lucinda struggled to keep her eyes on his face. Even his neck was distracting. He had a great neck, strong and— Ugh! She had to close her mouth and focus. 'You carry a police uniform in your car all the time?' She came a breath away from asking if he was a part-time strippergram, and though the thought remained unspoken it warmed her cheeks.

Alex chuckled as he removed the cap and placed it on the counter next to him. 'I got it from a friend who moved to America. He was a supporting artist on a few cop shows, so he bought a uniform.'

'Why?' asked Becky.

'You can get paid more if you bring your own costume. And we're roughly the same build, so he gave it to me.'

Lucinda eyed the pile of menus on the worktop next to her. Could she use one as a makeshift fan? Would that be too obvious? 'But why did you have it in your car?'

'I'm passing it on to another friend. He lives the other side of Barnsby so—'

'As it's just down the road from here, you were going to drop it off after work this evening,' said Becky.

'Right.'

Lucinda remained sceptical. 'But what if the real police stop you and find that in your car?'

'There's this police-backed scheme. You register, you get a card to show them and they won't detain you. I've got one.'

'That's good,' said Becky, narrowing her devious blue eyes and tapping her index finger against her lower lip.

Uh-oh. Lucinda's guts twisted. She had seen that look on Becky's face before. It usually prefaced some kind of madcap plot. 'You're not actually going to send him after the creep dressed like that, are you?'

Becky ran her tongue over her bottom lip and, her gaze fixed on Alex, nodded. 'Yes. I think our friendly officer here having a quiet chat with Mr Wilson could be just the thing.'

'But—'

Becky raised a hand. 'I'll speak to his niece. Fill her in on the plan. If any of it backfires, she can claim she hired Alex—although she'll have conveniently forgotten his name—to have a word with her uncle. That leaves us pretty much in the clear.'

'But ... But ...' Lucinda's gaze shuttled between Alex and Becky, hoping for a sign one of them was having second thoughts. She'd been all for luring the guy out onto the veranda, sneaking up behind him and shoving him off a high wall, but she didn't approve of a plan which involved the lowlife getting a good look at Alex's face while he was impersonating a police officer.

Becky misinterpreted her concern. 'We won't say we've had complaints from anyone on your team, don't worry.

Alex can be vague. He can say he's gathering information as part of an investigation into several complaints made over time and Mr Wilson's name came up during the course of his inquiries. He won't accuse him directly of anything, but make it clear Big Brother is suspicious and watching.'

'But …' Lucinda continued to flounder. Ugh! Why was she tongue-tied this evening? Why was Becky so good at covering all the angles?

Lucinda's frustration with her own lack of persuasiveness soared as she scanned the faces in front of her and found only quiet confidence. And, in the way Becky was fiddling with her glasses and Alex was bouncing on the balls of his feet, she suspected they were both barely containing their excitement. The reckless idiots.

Aware of some of the crazy things Becky had done in the past, Lucinda gave her up as a lost cause. But perhaps, she thought as she turned to him, Alex would see sense. 'And you're OK with this?'

Alex raised a hand towards Becky. 'If you can speak to his niece and then tell me what you need me to do and say—'

'Perfectly happy to.'

'Great. Let's go!'

'You're both crazy!' Lucinda called after them as they made their way to the exit with a foolhardy spring in their step. 'Hey! Wait a sec!' She scooped up the police cap from the counter and strode after them. Offering it to Alex, she looked up at him and their eyes met. 'Good luck.'

He gave a small nod and, reaching out with both hands to take the hat, his fingers brushed against hers. A faint echo of their previous spark made her hand tingle.

'Thanks,' he said, his lips curling as he dropped his dark gaze and turned away.

The last one out the door, Becky glanced back to give Lucinda a reassuring smile, but it did nothing to settle Lucinda's jangling nerves and the horrid writhing sensation in her guts.

She attempted to distract herself while they were gone by helping Ethan with the dishes. Scraping the plates with an unnecessary viciousness, she examined the source of her unease. Obviously, their plan was nuts. But, with Becky in charge, she begrudgingly accepted it would probably be a success and was unlikely to cause any real harm. So what else was bugging her?

Her heartbeat hadn't settled into a regular rhythm since she'd seen Alex in the dining room. And when he'd stepped out onto the balcony and their eyes had met, she'd experienced something similar to the static shock when she'd fallen against him in the lift. An unsettling, powerful charge. And then, as if things weren't strange enough, he'd swiftly proceeded to prove himself useful. Again!

In fact, he'd come up with a creative solution to the problem and been quick to volunteer. Perhaps, she conceded, as she hacked and stabbed at a stubborn piece of pastry welded to the plate in her hand, her initial judgement of him had been off. Which would mean she'd have to admit to being wrong …

Cursing silently, she pursed her lips and dropped a plate into the sink, sending water flying and forcing her to make a hasty apology to Ethan. She was passing the poor kid a towel when Becky and Alex bowled back into the kitchen. From their chatter and easy laughter, Lucinda assumed their mission had gone well and some of the tension in her shoulders eased. Although, as Becky grinned at Alex and hit him playfully on his upper arm, Lucinda felt another murky emotion stir.

'It went well then?' Lucinda asked, experiencing a stab of pique. Look at them! Would they be able to tear their eyes away from each other long enough to answer her?

Becky nudged Alex again, who had his hands on his hips and chest thrust forwards in a proud victory pose. 'If the unhealthy shade of puce he turned is anything to go by, I think Mr Wilson has been successfully scared straight. Thanks to Officer Smith here.' She gave Alex's bicep a wholly gratuitous squeeze. 'Alex was brilliant.'

'I can't take all the credit.' Alex patted Becky's hand, which remained on his upper arm for reasons which escaped Lucinda. 'Ms Watson was great. She's a natural.'

'Rubbish!' Becky slid her hand from his arm—finally!—and gazed up at him, eyelashes fluttering. 'And please, call me Becky.'

Squeezing her fingers into a fist, Lucinda whirled away from them, opened the nearest fridge and pretended to study its contents. She contorted her features into an ugly, simpering expression and mouthed, *'Call me Becky,'* actions which both relieved the press of spite threating to overwhelm her while also making her hate herself. Taking deep breaths of the cool white air in front of her, she resolved to push pettiness aside and, closing the fridge door, tuned back in to Alex and Becky's conversation.

'Have you done any other Shakespeare?' Becky asked Alex as she leant against the nearest steel counter.

'I was in a production of *Romeo and Juliet* ages ago.'

'As Romeo?'

'No.' Alex dropped his hat onto the counter between him and Becky and ran a hand over his hair, making his luscious blonde waves stir and settle. 'Mercutio.'

Wait, thought Lucinda, as Alex took a step closer to Becky and ran his hand through his hair again. Was he flirting with her?

'Mercutio's the best part!' Becky said. 'I mean, come on! You get to reel off cracking one-liners while dying. And there can be nothing better than getting to shout, "A plague—"'

'"—o' both your houses!"'

Alex joined her to complete the line in a triumphant chorus which sent them both into a bout of hysterics. And while Lucinda might have been able to attribute some of the laughter to the success high they were riding, why did Becky need to rest her hand on Alex's arm? *Yet again.*

Knowing next to nothing about Shakespeare, having struggled in English lessons at school, Lucinda felt as if she was standing behind a glass wall being forced to watch two close friends on the other side exchanging private jokes. Clever private jokes that were beyond the slow kid at the back of the classroom. The sense of exclusion stoked her irritation, as did Becky's bizarre behaviour. At every event where their paths had crossed in the past, Becky had been in work mode, sliding through the shadows at the edges of rooms like an invisible, chaos-defying ninja. Always professional, she spoke to a select few, and gave permission to use her given name to even fewer. But here she was, on first-name terms with Alex after meeting him minutes ago? And all over him like a rash? It was almost embarrassing to watch. Digging her nails into the palm of her hand, Lucinda fought an urge to reach out and pinch Becky. Really hard.

And Alex certainly seemed to appreciate the attention. Lucinda wouldn't have been surprised if he'd forgotten she existed as he tilted his head and asked Becky, 'Do you have a favourite?'

'Shakespeare play? Uf! That's like trying to choose a favourite child.' Becky gave Alex a sickeningly soppy smile. 'I suppose, I do have a soft spot for *Macbeth*.'

'Can't blame you. I was Macduff in a—'

'Sorry, but have you actually played any main parts? Ever?'

Lucinda hadn't planned to interrupt Alex. The words spewed from her, having originated in her spleen rather than brain. They flew from her lips easily and, unable to stop them, she could only brace and watch as they landed.

A grenade would have had less impact. The words wiped the smiles from Alex's and Becky's faces. Slowly, they turned their heads to stare at her. Becky's eyes widened. She shook her head and raised her shoulders a fraction. The sum of the gestures amounted to a non-verbal '*What the hell?*'

And while Becky's unspoken reproach struck her like a sobering blow, far worse were Alex's parted lips, knitted brows and the sheen of hurt in his eyes. The expression was a flicker, there and gone in a second, replaced by a smooth untroubled mask. And yet, in that moment, it was as if he had reached into Lucinda's chest and crushed her heart.

He shrugged and huffed a short laugh. 'I guess not everyone is leading-man material.'

'A good performance by a supporting actor can steal any show,' said Becky with deliberate cheerfulness. 'And a team is only as strong as every one of its members. That applies to a cast as well as a catering team. Wouldn't you agree, Lucinda?' She gave Lucinda a pointed stare.

'Yes.' Lucinda crossed her arms and looked down at the granite-coloured linoleum. Her mouth had gone dry and, swallowing with difficultly, she grudgingly grasped the opportunity Becky was giving her to undo some of the damage she'd done. 'Yes, I would.'

The drone of the dishwasher and Ethan's humming grew ear-splitting as the awkward silence thickened. Rational Lucinda knew she should say something else. Something kind and reassuring. But Rational Lucinda could only listen and cringe as Mean Lucinda said, 'Is Charlie not expecting you back home soon, Becky?'

This time, as Becky's gaze settled on Lucinda, it was cooler and reflective. It pierced her like X-rays and made Lucinda want to fold in on herself. Becky's tone was equally level as she said, 'He's still in New York. But he'll be back next week.'

'You must miss him. And haven't you been ill recently? Was it the stomach bug some of my guys have had?' Lucinda paused, giving part of herself the chance to scream, 'What are you doing?' at the other.

'Yes, but I've been feeling better lately, Lucinda.' Becky's eyes glimmered with what could have been amusement. 'Thank you for your concern.'

'Maybe best not to be hanging around in the kitchen though. If you've been poorly.'

Becky's lips curled and she gave a swift nod of satisfaction, as if she had just cracked a puzzle. 'Quite right. It's time I pushed off.' She turned to Alex and dialled her smile up a notch. 'It was a pleasure to meet you. I understand you'll be back here in June.'

'Um yes. But playing a butler. Not a waiter or'—he pointed at his costume—'a PC.'

This time Lucinda managed to smother the apparently monstrous part of herself which itched to sneer that she assumed the butler wasn't the star of this latest project either. She bit the inside of her cheek and focused on the pain which, all told, she deserved.

Continuing to be as graceful as Lucinda had been graceless, Becky said, 'I look forward to seeing the result on the big screen.'

'Thank you.' Nervously rotating his cap by pinching it along its brim, Alex glanced at Lucinda, then turned to Becky. 'I should be going too. This uniform won't deliver itself. I'll walk you out.'

'Great! Bye, Lucinda.' Becky's tone was breezy and she no longer seemed upset as she turned and made for the door. That was a partial relief. It had taken months of small favours for Lucinda to gain her trust and she knew Becky's quiet recommendations had resulted in some excellent contracts she wouldn't have won alone. Losing her confidence would be as bad for business as for Lucinda's own morale. Recently Becky was one of the few people she saw regularly enough to think of as a friend.

So, given the importance of her relationship with Becky, why was she more interested in watching Alex? In analysing his striking features and posture as he stared at the floor, tapping the visor of his cap against the fingers of her left hand?

Lucinda opened her mouth to speak. But what could she say that could make things better? Or at least not make things worse?

If she made a start, perhaps inspiration would strike. 'Alex, I—'

'Goodbye, Lucinda.' Alex delivered the words with a curt nod and strode after Becky. Seconds later, a light scent of citrus, pepper and the mysterious aroma Lucinda had yet to place were the only evidence he had ever been in the same room as her.

She watched as the door swung on its hinges and when it came to a complete stop she chided herself for standing idle. Since she was eighteen, Lucinda's go-to response to all sorts of difficulties had been hard work. And those dishes weren't going to scrape themselves.

She paced back over to Ethan, grabbed a knife and snatched up the dirty plate on the top of the pile. The repetitive task was usually oddly comforting, but no matter how hard she scratched and rubbed, she couldn't shake the queasiness in her stomach. An unease which redoubled when she recalled the flash of hurt in Alex's eyes.

She shook her head. It was all ridiculous. Why should she care about the feelings of some bloke after two random brief encounters? She knew next to nothing about him and his actions that evening had shown he was quite prepared to be reckless and a dreadful flirt. Anyway, in the unlikely event they ever met again, she doubted they could even be friends. After all, unlike him and Becky—his new bestie— they'd have nothing in common.

This looping string of reassuring half-truths eventually calmed her mind and saved the dishes from permanent scoring. So why was she left with the urge, as she finished scraping the last of the plates, to smash each and every one of them to the floor?

'You didn't kill him, did you?'

Lost in her thoughts, Lucinda hadn't heard Jay approach and almost dropped a plate.

'Sorry!' The chef smiled. 'Didn't mean to scare you. I've just checked in with the Hall manager. She's delighted with us and didn't mention finding any dead bodies, so I'm guessing you and Becky found a peaceful solution?'

'Yes. With a bit of help from Alex, actually.' Lucinda sighed. 'Do you mind if I tell you the whole story tomorrow? All the drama has left me wiped out. And you should get home too. You've had enough to do, let alone having to deal with that idiot.'

'I'm OK.'

Jay wore her normal relaxed smile, but Lucinda couldn't be certain she wasn't concealing a deeper upset. 'Are you sure?'

'Yes. If it makes you feel any better, when Becky interrupted him I was a second away from following your advice about dealing with guys like that.'

'A swift knee to the groin?'

'Yep. And if all else fails: bite.'

Lucinda grinned. 'I'm not sure I have anything left to teach you, my young Padawan.'

'I have no idea what you just said, but I'm guessing it's another Yoda, feel the force, *Star Wars* thing?'

'I knew it! You're secretly an expert, aren't you?'

'Oh sure, yeah. I just have to watch the movies and then I'll know everything.' Jay returned Lucinda's wide smile and nodded over to where Ethan was finishing with the dishes. 'Ethan's almost done and Misha says she can do final checks. Can you give me a lift home?'

'Absolutely. Sounds good.' Lucinda nodded. 'Just let me finish this and I'll be right with you.'

Jay laid a hand on Lucinda's arm. 'Are *you* all right?'

No, thought Lucinda as she gave her trusted lieutenant a reassuring smile. She patted Jay's hand to show gratitude for her unshakeable positivity and steadying touch, although they had done little to return Lucinda's balance. She had never felt so mixed up, so at war within herself. What was going on with her lately?

Chapter 8

A week after moonlighting as a police officer, Alex spent his Sunday in another unpaid role: home removals assistant. One of his oldest friends was leaving town and had recruited Alex to help lug furniture down five narrow flights of stairs.

Shortly after six, and brushing the last traces of dust from his T-shirt with weary fingers, Alex opened his front door to find two sets of cutlery and a pair of wine glasses sitting neatly on the coffee table. In the kitchenette, Nicole—her sleeves rolled up and hair back in a high ponytail—was glaring at a sizzling wok. Her efforts had filled the flat with a fantastic smell which made Alex's empty stomach rumble.

Nicole glanced up and her frown melted into a relaxed smile. 'Perfect timing!' she said, gesturing to the pan. 'Take a seat, dinner's ready.'

Alex closed the door and approached the table cautiously as he racked his sluggish brains. Had he forgotten a special occasion? Nicole's thirtieth birthday wasn't until September, so at least he could be sure this surprise intimate meal had nothing to do with that.

Nearing the sofa, he did his best to focus on Nicole's swift movements and ignore the shambles she had made of the kitchen. The dirty utensils and pots covering every surface were understandable, but his skin prickled as his gaze snagged on the splashes of various lurid substances on the walls and across the cupboard fronts. And was that a splodge of something on the *ceiling*? How had she managed that? He bet every surface of Lucinda's kitchen sparkled—

No. He gave his head a sharp shake. He refused to go there again. Particularly after a day of intense physical labour which had given him very little opportunity to dwell on memories of a certain incomprehensibly grumpy caterer.

His lovely girlfriend had made him a lovely meal. Which was great. Even if it might mean he'd forgotten an important occasion and was about to be in a lot of trouble.

As Nicole scraped the last of the food from the pan, his lips curled into a nervous smile. 'That smells amazing. What's the occasion?'

'Completing day ten of the Vegan Challenge!' Nicole shot the large spoon she had been brandishing into the sink, sending a wave of grey water slopping to the floor. 'You've been so brilliant doing it with me. I thought I'd make veggie stir-fry for dinner so you aren't tempted to sneak a bacon butty when I'm not around.'

Alex's belly grumbled again at the thought of his much-missed bacon butties. 'That's lovely, thank you. I'm starving.'

'I'm not surprised. I bet Ryan worked you hard.' She picked up the plates and swished to the table. 'I still think he was cheeky to ask you to help.'

'He's a good friend. It was nice to spend time with him.' Nicole took out her phone to photograph their dinner and Alex ducked into the bathroom to wash his hands. He raised his voice to continue defending his friend. 'And Eve's seven-months pregnant. You can't expect her to lift stuff.'

With the clicking of her camera app running underneath her voice, Nicole replied, 'Hmn. Well, I think he's a cheapskate for not hiring movers. But then I suppose penny-pinching is how you afford a house. That and moving out of London.'

'Getting a nine-to-five job helps too,' Alex added, grinding his teeth at the sight of more toothpaste spatter on the bathroom mirror.

Nicole put her phone on the table and sat down as Alex returned to the sofa. 'Ah yes, the endless excitement and creative fulfilment of being an HR manager.'

'He has a pension, paid holidays and—'

'But he doesn't love it.' Nicole poured the wine and handed Alex a glass. 'I'll never find another job I love as much as acting. And neither will you. We're lifers.' She grinned as she clinked her glass off his and Alex nodded, mirroring her smile. 'Now, eat! I hope it's OK. The recipe's got great reviews.'

'It's really good.' Alex was telling the truth but he found it difficult to concentrate on the tangy flavours on his tongue. Though he had turned his back on the kitchen chaos, to his left a tangled pile of Nicole's shoes, which had been lobbed in the vague direction of the hall cupboard, seemed to scream at him. He swallowed hard. No matter how hard he tried to turn a blind eye to it, Nicole's mess continued to gnaw at his nerves. If they were going to continue living together he needed to bite the bullet and confess how much it annoyed him. Even if his previous gentle requests that she do a little tidying had resulted in daunting displays of whining and sulking which he would rather not revisit.

His throat dry and tongue heavy, he laid his fork beside his plate. 'Nicole?'

'Hmn?'

'I wanted to talk to y—' Alex's phone buzzed and he snatched it up. An unknown number flashed on the screen. Staring at this serendipitous means of escape, Alex knew he should ignore the call. After all, they'd leave a message if it was important. He really had to talk to Nicole—

'Aren't you going to get that?' Nicole asked, lifting her gaze from her own phone.

'We're eating. And I don't recognise the number.'

'I don't mind.' Nicole shrugged and twisted more noodles around her fork. 'It might be work. Just see who it is and if it's not important, tell them to call back later. Go on.'

Alex frowned as he accepted the call, a little annoyed but mostly relieved that the mystery caller had saved him from a potentially difficult conversation. 'Hello?'

'Hello? Is that Alex Fraser?'

Alex's frown deepened as he struggled to place the unfamiliar, confident voice, with its round vowel and firm consonants. 'Yes.'

'Hello! I'm Veronica Russell, Carol Russell's grand-daughter. You helped save Grandma's life. In the lift at the Richards Group. I hope you don't mind my calling …'

'No, not at all.' Alex's heart raced as it filled with pleasure and surprise. 'How is Carol?'

'She got back home from the clinic a few days ago,' Veronica said. 'The doctors are thrilled with her progress. And she's certainly well enough to be bossing me around again.' Her bright, breezy voice gave way to a snorting chuckle. 'That's why I'm calling, actually. She'd like to invite you to a small afternoon tea so she can thank you properly. Three weeks from now. The second Saturday in June. That's the thirteenth. We're only over in Berkshire. Are you free?'

Alex didn't usually memorise his agenda, but he started filming at Compton Hall on the fifteenth and had made a point of keeping the weekend before his next job clear. 'Yes, I'm free on the thirteenth and that's very kind of Carol. But I wouldn't want to trouble her if—'

'She says she's fit enough to eat some lemon drizzle with guests. Besides, she told me not to take "no" for an answer. And, believe me, if you knew Grandma you'd know it'll be quicker to say "yes".'

Alex huffed a laugh. 'If she insists, I'd be delighted to accept.'

'Wonderful! Grandma will be so pleased.' As Veronica giggled in delight, Alex grinned in anticipation of a pleasant, tranquil afternoon in the Berkshire countryside savouring a few slices of lemon drizzle cake, one of his all-time favourites. Veronica continued, 'I'm so looking forward to meeting you. And I'm sure you'll be happy to know that Lucinda Green will also be coming.'

Oh. Alex's smile faded and his neck muscles stiffened as Veronica's words splashed icy water over his cosy mental image of enjoying tea and cake with a harmless elderly lady.

'Righty-ho!' Veronica breezed on. 'I'll message you the address but if you have any problems finding us, please give me a call. Bye!'

'Um, bye.' Alex lowered the phone to the table and stared at it until Nicole's voice jolted his gaze back to her.

'What was that about? Where are you off to on the thirteenth?'

Alex picked up his fork and poked at a piece of broccoli, his appetite suddenly absent. 'Carol, the woman who had the heart attack in the lift, she's invited me to hers for afternoon tea.'

'That's nice.' Nicole ran her free hand over her ponytail as she scooped up another forkful of stir-fry. 'But that'll be the last day of the Vegan Challenge so tell her you'll need vegan options. Cakes are always stuffed full of eggs and butter.'

Oh.

Alex raised his left hand to the ache blooming in his temple as Nicole's words stripped another layer of shine from what mere minutes ago had been an entirely appealing invitation.

Chapter 9

The flimsy tripod collapsed for a second time, tumbling to the floor along with another colourful string of expletives from Nicole. Her frustration chimed with Alex's own as he knelt in the scrap of floor space by the hall cupboard and engaged in a grudge match with some slippery wrapping paper and a lethally sharp tape dispenser.

'Are you sure you don't want to take a break and come with me?' he asked, though he knew Nicole would rather be without her phone for a week than suffer through his seven-year-old niece's birthday party.

'No, I have to get this done. And anyway, you know a kid's party isn't exactly my scene.'

Nicole was underplaying her aversion to anything child-related, but the swift wrinkle of her nose gave her away. They were only a couple of months into their relationship when Alex had first noticed how she seemed to consider spending time with family a chore. She had only ever met James and Sarah—his brother and sister-in-law—and their daughters once, having successfully conjured reasons to avoid meals and parties. However, today her excuse was a good one: she was preparing an audition tape for the pilot of a new US drama series.

Nicole swept the tripod off the floor and glared at it. 'Perhaps I can make the next one. Emma's birthday is soon, right?'

'Emily.' Alex frowned and yanked another piece of gummy, rubber-scented tape from the dispenser. 'Emily's sixth birthday was only last month.'

'Right, yeah. Not long until it comes round again.' Nicole sighed and flicked her hair from her shoulders. 'And at this rate I'll still be trying to get this thing to work on Emily's eighteenth.' The tip of her tongue in the corner of her mouth, she tightened the tripod's retractable legs and set it back on the miniscule coffee table. 'You know, I have a really good feeling about this one. This is going to be *it*.' She glanced at Alex, her beaming smile sending a bright shimmer of hope into her eyes. 'I can tell.'

'I'm sure you'd be perfect for the part.' He glanced up and gave Nicole a tight-lipped smile. It was almost painful to watch her buzzing with youthful optimism, putting so much into a few minutes of video which Alex knew would be stacked in a mountain of similar clips and most likely viewed with barely casual interest. His own frustrating experiences of pilot season during his twenties had left him somewhat jaded. But that was no reason to rain on Nicole's parade. 'Would you like me to get some of my books and we can prop your phone up on those?' he asked.

Nicole waved away his offer as she moved to slot her phone into the spring-loaded holder on the tripod. 'I will make this bloody thing work for me. Just you watch. Besides, those presents won't wrap themselves.'

Alex grunted and returned his focus to the glittery purple paper from hell while Nicole fiddled with her camera set-up. The gift wrap crackled over the lull in conversation, competing only with the muffled din of the upstairs neighbour's obnoxious rock music.

Alex had just succeeded in sealing the last corner of paper over Olivia's present with a satisfying zip and crinkle of tape, when Nicole said, 'Speaking about putting things off ... Have you decided if you're going to see the heart attack woman. Carol, wasn't it?'

'Yes,' said Alex, his own heart dropping. 'No, I haven't decided. Not yet.'

Though Alex had been quick to accept Veronica's invitation, he had been having doubts about going ever since. He was mostly worried that seeing Carol would transport him back to the moment of her collapse, making him freeze and filling him with dizziness, trembling and nausea. In the days after Veronica's call his sleep had been fitful. His dreams had turned dark as he sprinted to reach someone or something forever beyond his grasp. Not wanting to explain all that to Nicole, he had shared his secondary reason for wavering over the invitation.

'I think you should go.' Nicole gave her phone a prod and sank back onto the sofa. 'I mean, the woman who's putting you off, the one who you helped with CPR ...'

'Lucinda.'

'Right. She can't be that bad, can she? I know you said she was seriously rude and annoying, but you can put up with her for a couple of hours, can't you? You've been stuck in companies for months with people you didn't gel with. What's one afternoon?'

Nicole made a good point. And Alex would have had greater confidence in his ability to face any insults Lucinda might sling his way if it hadn't been for his recent nightmares. As it was, perhaps it would be best if he politely wriggled out of afternoon tea at Carol's and tried to let everything that had happened in the lift and everyone who had been there fade into dim, distant, manageable memories. That said, following the sour finale to his most recent encounter with Lucinda, forgetting her was proving extremely difficult. The crushing disappointment he'd experienced when she'd dismissed him and his profession in such a callous way continued to sting. For a foolish moment he'd believed there could be a genuine spark between them but then she'd shown herself to be a rude, judgemental, dismissive cow who looked down on acting as some sort of mucking about which failed to meet her superior standards for a 'proper job'.

He shook his head as he drummed his fingers off the nearest gift box. He didn't need Lucinda's sort of negativity in his life. If he wanted to be made to feel small, to be reminded how he was lacking, he'd call his brother.

'And,' continued Nicole, a sly smile at the corner of her mouth, 'if she's still awful, just be rude back. I've always said you're too nice.'

'Hmn. I'm not sure that would help.'

'OK. Why not look at it this way instead?' Nicole raised her eyes to the ceiling and pursed her lips. 'You're all about preparation for your roles and you're about to play a butler who spends his life keeping a straight face while posh people are mean to him. Think of it as a chance to practise being polite, but distant. Formal and civil … What's the word I'm after?'

'Aloof?'

'That's it! Channel your best aloofness. That should get you through it.'

Alex snorted. It wasn't a terrible idea. 'You really think I should go to Carol's?'

'Yes. And if she really wants to thank you, you should ask her to let you take some selfies to put up on Insta.'

Alex's jaw dropped. He gawped at Nicole, blinking and stuttering. Was she really suggesting turning Carol's medical emergency into a photo op?

'Why would I do that?'

'You saved a life, Alex. If she's happy for people to know about it, you shouldn't keep it a secret. It's a great opportunity to boost your visibility. And I know you don't like putting yourself out there—'

Alex grunted, but Nicole was used to his tetchiness around the topic and continued, 'I know you like it to be all about the work—'

'My job is to help tell a story. I don't want to *be* the story! It's embarrassing!'

'It doesn't have to be, Alex. Not in this case. You saved a nice lady's life. People get nominated for awards for doing less.'

'I didn't help save her life to get an—' He took a sharp breath in through his nose and bit his lower lip. The back of his neck had warmed with his rising temper and he would have loved to have given vent to the heat, but there was nothing to be gained from debating the ethics of self-promotion with Nicole. Their views on the subject were as different as their approaches to cleaning.

'There! That's almost perfect!' Staring at the phone screen, Nicole continued her inspection of her smiling face.

Alex hauled himself up to standing, holding in middle-aged grunts of effort. Nicole entering full preening mode always brought conversations to a close, and he should hurry or he'd be late for the party. He'd never been able to stomach tardiness.

'I'd best be off.' He gathered up the presents and peered over the top of them. 'Are you sure there's nothing I can do to help before I go?'

'Hmn?' Nicole glanced at him before returning to tweaking her camera settings. 'No, no, you get on. Have a nice time. Say happy birthday to Emily for me.'

'Actually, it's Olivia's …' Alex trailed off as he watched Nicole rearrange the sofa cushions. Deaf and blind to everything but her own voice and appearance, there was no chance she was about to leap up and hold the front door open for him.

Alex threw a final glance at Nicole as he wrestled with the door catch and bulky gifts, rolled his eyes and muttered, 'Break a leg,' in lieu of goodbye.

Chapter 10

The drive to James and Sarah's house took Alex south of London and back down the road to the Comptons. His destination was Wolston, a forgettable commuter town where his ever-prudent brother had sensibly invested in a detached four-bed family property.

The house was a regulation brick-and-slate construction to the west of the town centre. It had recently been elevated out of total mundanity by the installation of wood cladding on the upper storey. The horizontal beams had been stained dove grey, a muted choice Alex suspected was motivated by a desire not to further disturb the neighbours, none of whom had dared to alter the original aspect of their homes. Although, as a senior planning officer at the county council, James could probably have secured permission to bulldoze the house and erect a turreted fort complete with portcullis, drawbridge and crocodile-infested moat.

That Saturday his brother's grey corner of the sleepy suburbs was filled with an assault of colour and shrieking as a gaggle of children ran riot in the sunny garden. The outdoor space had been decked with bunting, balloons and a banner declaring *Happy 7th Birthday Olivia!* Mauve tablecloths, sparkly plates and paper cups covered a series of folding tables at the back of the house. When Alex stepped out onto the patio, some of the guests were sitting at the tables painting each other's nails, but most of them hadn't yet matured beyond the joy of throwing themselves around the giant bouncy castle at the bottom of the garden, their screams of delight soaring over the drone of the fan blower.

His brother served him a characteristically warm reception. 'You're finally here then.' He lifted his sunglasses to fix Alex with his disapproving stare. 'Better late than never.'

Not wanting to mar a happy occasion with a fraternal spat, Alex swallowed a comment that he had gone to great trouble to arrive on the dot of four, as instructed. Anyway, he found it impossible to take his little brother's temper seriously when he was sporting what appeared to be a Prince Charming costume.

Doing his best not to smirk at James's pale blue tunic, red epaulettes and cuffs, Alex nodded at the enormous gift-wrapped boxes he was carrying and asked, 'Where should I put these?'

'Over there with the others. Then make yourself useful, will you?' James frowned as two children sped past him, sending the plastic sword hanging at his side swinging. 'It's a ruddy circus here is what it is.'

Hovering over the folding tables, Alex's sister-in-law was overseeing the organised chaos with her usual mixture of no-nonsense pragmatism and good humour. Sarah greeted Alex with an enthusiastic hug, unburdened him of the giant presents and assigned him the task of bringing plates of food out from the kitchen.

Unwrapping the cellophane from a plate of sandwich triangles, she said, 'I was delighted to hear you'll be filming at Compton Hall soon.' She paused to readjust her plastic tiara, pushing it into its place among the fibres of the white-blonde wig which was tied into two long plaits falling behind her ears. Its artificial sheen was a perfect match for her icy blue gown, whose thin iridescent layers stirred in the late May breeze. 'It's lovely you'll be working down the road.' She gasped in delight as a thought came to her and, for a moment, her wide smile and shining brown eyes belonged to a Disney princess as much as her outfit did. 'You must stay here!'

The idea had already occurred to Alex. Commuting every day from his place in north London would be exhausting, while Compton Hall was a short drive from Wolston. It would save him a lot of time, energy and, not unimportantly, money.

He emptied a packet of crisps into a bowl and glanced at Sarah. 'I wouldn't want to get in your way.'

'No, really. It makes sense. How long will it be for?'

'They need me for three weeks. It might stretch to four, depending on scheduling.'

'Well then.' Sarah took a step back from the table and nodded. 'That's settled. And it'll motivate me to clear the girls' old stuff out of the spare room.'

Alex didn't doubt the sincerity of Sarah's welcome; the roadblock to the plan would be elsewhere. He frowned and gazed towards the side of the bouncy castle where his brother was standing next to a candyfloss machine. James's arms were crossed and he was scowling at a child who had dared to request he spin them some of the pink confection. 'I don't want to be any trouble. And James might not be thrilled about me hanging around.'

'Nonsense!' Sarah tossed her head and the tiara slid forwards again. 'The girls will love having you here. We hardly see you these days what with you being so busy. Although, obviously, it's great that work's going well for you.'

'Thanks.' Alex touched the top of Sarah's arm and gave her a small smile. He hoped she knew how much he appreciated her support. It had been such a pleasant surprise that the woman his brother had persuaded to join the family had turned out to be far more supportive of Alex's career than any of its original members.

Sarah patted Alex's hand. 'You're welcome. And you're a saint for coming today.'

'I'd have come in costume if you'd asked.'

'You're a darling, but I don't think I have a dress that would fit you.' She grinned. 'Although, if anyone could pull it off, it would be you. And, speaking of people with style, how is Nicole? It's such a shame she couldn't make it.'

'Yes.' Alex lowered his gaze to another packet of crisps. It made lying easier. 'She was sorry she couldn't come.'

'Uncle Alex! Uncle Alex!'

Two glittery cannonballs careered into Alex's legs in a burst of sugary candyfloss perfume. Olivia was dressed to match her mother, although as her auburn hair was in two plaits, she clearly hadn't been able to persuade her parents to let her have a blonde wig. Emily's skirt was as blue as her sister's, but the bodice was black and she was revelling in her dark pink cape, which she tugged and swung about her with gap-toothed glee.

'How are my favourite nieces?'

Olivia huffed and shot Alex a withering gaze which would have made her father proud. 'You don't have any other nieces.'

'That just makes you more special!' he called after her as she skipped off to the end of the table to supervise her guests' nail art. Grinning, he squatted down to have a proper chat with Emily. He rescued a strand of candyfloss from her skirt and handed it to her as he asked, 'Who are you today?'

'Duh!' Emily rolled her eyes, expressing the disgust common to children forced to contend with adult ignorance of the most basic and essential facts. 'I'm Anna, silly. And Olivia is Elsa and so is Mummy. From *Frozen*.'

'Ah. Of course.' Alex had vague notions of the film but knew he was out of his depth. He glanced up at Olivia, who was letting her friends paint her nails, and realised she had probably already aged past the point where he had a chance of understanding her. And, having recently reached the grand age of six, Emily would soon be joining her.

It seemed only minutes ago that the girls had been five and four. That summer he had been given the title 'Uncle Dinosaur' as he happily gave in to demands to carry one of them on his back and channel his best velociraptor impersonation while chasing the other in a giddy, giggling whirl round the garden.

Sarah's voice cut across his reminiscences. 'Emily! Please tell Daddy it'll be time for food in five minutes.'

Emily nodded at her mother, then leant closer to Alex and whispered, 'Did you bring me a present too?'

Alex assumed his serious business face. 'It's inside.'

'Yay!' She beamed and threw her arms around his neck, and Alex had to fight to keep his balance while experiencing a rush of happiness possibly equal to Emily's.

As she scurried off across the lawn to her father, Alex got to his feet—somewhat stiffly, he must start doing yoga again—and Sarah came to stand at his shoulder.

'Emily adores you. So does Olivia, although she's getting too grand to admit it.'

Alex returned his gaze to the busy bouncy castle. The girls were growing up terrifyingly fast. He should try to spend more time with them before they were teenagers and didn't want to hang out with tragic old Uncle Alex.

'Now I have more of an idea what I'll be working on—thanks to *Napier*—perhaps … Perhaps I could come and visit the girls once a month or something?'

'That would be fabulous! You could take them out. They'd love it. You're much cooler than their parents.'

Alex frowned. Chasing the girls around their own garden in shouting distance of their mother, who was handily also a doctor, was one thing. Being in sole charge of two lively kids in open spaces when they could easily give him the slip, was another. 'Um, we might have to work up to that—'

'You'd be fine.'

While flattered by his sister-in-law's confidence in him, as he watched her rub her brow and squint at the howling children doing laps of the apple tree, Alex wondered if Sarah's faith in his babysitting abilities had more to do with her own need for a break.

'Right,' she said, uncovering the final plate of sandwiches and planting her hands on her hips. 'Brace yourself. It's feeding time.' Taking a deep breath, she turned to face the juvenile hordes and hollered, 'Food's ready!'

Alex took down the last of the bunting and wrapped the string of rainbow-coloured flags around his fist as he strolled towards the kitchen. The eerie post-festivity hush in the garden washed over him and he was struck by a bitter epiphany: he had to break up with Nicole. The inevitable end of their year-long relationship had been creeping towards him for a while. The weird blip of his powerful attraction to Lucinda had helped him face the truth, but there had always been too great a distance between what he and Nicole wanted professionally and personally for their relationship to last. And if he couldn't be bothered to argue with her or so much as mention the small things she did to irk him, it was a sure sign he didn't care enough about making their relationship work.

He ambled into the kitchen and dropped the bunting on the counter by the sink where Sarah was transferring the remaining slices of birthday cake from a silver board to a plastic container.

Sarah tipped the candle stubs down a chute into a concealed bin. 'You must be pleased with the reaction to *Napier*, Alex. I think series three is the best to date. Is Sunday week the last episode?'

'I'm afraid so.'

'I can't see how there's time to wrap it all up! Does it end on a cliffhanger? Oh, please say it doesn't!'

'My lips are sealed.' Alex mimed zipping his mouth shut. He'd become expert at giving away nothing about the show's various red herrings and plot twists. Although, as a relatively minor character, he didn't get harassed for spoilers as much as some of his co-stars.

James came in from the garden, bashing the bulging rubbish sack in his grip off the door frame with a crunch and rustle. Alex was disappointed James had swapped the fancy dress for his preferred uniform of jeans and T-shirt. Sarah was still in her dress but the wig had gone and her chestnut hair was drawn back in a ponytail.

James bent forwards to set the bag on the floor next to the island and Alex noticed—with a degree of guilty pleasure—his brother's mousey hair was thinning at his crown. It wouldn't be long until he'd have a bald circle resembling a monk's tonsure. In contrast, Alex's sandy hair continued growing in thick. Further proof of how much better people aged when they were unproblematic.

James straightened up and, gazing at Alex, rubbed his hands together. 'So it looks like you might be getting something out of your stint as a first-aider, eh?'

Alex knew exactly what his brother was referring to but never liked to pander to his mercenary instincts. 'Sorry?'

'The old bag you saved the other week? Sarah tells me she's asked you to visit so she can show her gratitude. Hopefully she'll make you her sole beneficiary. Especially if her health's still shaky.'

'Watch out there, darling,' Sarah muttered to James as she dropped a plastic cup into the rubbish sack at his feet. 'Your grasping bastard is showing.'

'What?' James's eyebrows shot up in protest. 'Come

on!' He gestured to Alex. 'It's not like he doesn't deserve a reward.'

Alex was surprised by this crumb of what might conceivably pass for praise. He was edging towards a tentative smile, when his brother continued, 'And God knows he certainly needs the cash.'

And there it was: the inevitable dig. Not wanting to glare at his brother, Alex picked up the refuse sack and held it open to allow Sarah to drop in another cup. '*Carol* has asked me to afternoon tea at hers on Saturday a couple of weeks from now. Although I'm still not a hundred per cent sure I'll be going.'

'Oh come on! Even without a reward, surely it's a good idea for you to vanish off to the sticks for a bit?' James sniffed. 'Once *Napier* finishes, what will those mums who worship you do for their Alex Fraser fix? They'll be stalking you in packs around the city.'

Alex cringed. How did his brother always know the exact location of his sore spots? And why did he feel compelled to prod them?

Ever quick to extinguish the flames of friction between the brothers, Sarah stepped in. 'It'll be a shame if you can't make it. It's wonderful Carol's mended up enough to be back home and having visitors. And it'll be lovely for you to see her looking well. Recovery from cardiac arrest is no picnic.'

Emily, who had covered almost every inch of the kitchen tabletop with miniscule and evasive beads from the craft set Alex had gifted her, asked, 'Is that what happened to Malachy? Caryak rest?'

James and Sarah exchanged a meaningful glance and

Alex remembered their tenth wedding anniversary was fast approaching. Had they always been able to reach an agreement without speaking? How long did it take a couple to develop their own private telepathy?

'No darling,' Sarah said. 'Malachy got some food stuck as he was swallowing it. But the teachers helped him and he's fine.'

Emily nodded and returned to the task in hand, extending her tongue as she threaded a golden charm onto a plastic thread.

Sarah gestured with a tilt of her head for Alex to follow her and James to the sink. Once there, she said, in a low voice, 'A boy in Olivia's class choked at lunchtime this week. He's fine, the midday assistants stepped in. But seeing him struggle to breathe, well ... it understandably shook Olivia up.' She flicked her gaze to Emily. 'Emily has obviously been listening in on her big sister's version of the story. Poor Olivia said she didn't know what to do and thought Malachy was going to die. She blames herself for not doing more.'

Alex's stomach rolled and a dull queasiness scuttled through his veins, making his throat burn and head light. He had been pleased James's mention of Carol hadn't brought on any symptoms of panic, but apparently they had been waiting for their moment.

He took a deep breath and focused on the sparkle of a single silver thread trailing from Sarah's sleeve. He opened his mouth to speak, but James got there first.

'She's seven. What was she supposed to do?' James trained a steady gaze on Alex, one loaded with significance. 'We told her it wasn't her fault.'

As he stared back at his brother, Alex's mouth went dry and his nausea lifted. The acid in this throat hardened into a stubborn knot which threatened to bring tears to his eyes as his brother slapped him on the back and squeezed his shoulder. They were simple words and small gestures. But to Alex they spoke of the acceptance and forgiveness he had craved for over thirty years.

He should leave before the wooziness returned, he burst into tears or James spoiled the moment with one of his crass quips. Alex glanced towards the door and said, 'I should get going.'

Alex noticed James and Sarah lock gazes and Sarah widen her eyes at her husband. This second instance of silent spousal communication was followed by James saying, 'I'll walk you out.'

They processed in single file through the house and down the drive to Alex's car. Alex composed his features as he turned to face his brother, preparing himself for the inevitable awkward farewell. Most brothers would hug or pat each other on the back. In their case, parting usually involved Alex running away while James fired poison verbal darts after him.

'Sarah said she's invited you to stay while you're filming at Compton Hall. And I said—'

'It's fine. I can find somewhere else.'

'It's a good idea. You can visit this Carol of yours for tea on Saturday afternoon, use that evening and Sunday morning to pack and sort out whatever you need back at yours and then come over here in the afternoon. All ready for starting at the Hall on Monday.'

'Oh … um … right …'

'Doesn't that work?'

'No. I mean, yes. It works perfectly. Thanks. That would be great.' Unbalanced by James's unusual display of graciousness, Alex opened the car door and slid inside before his brother had the chance to retract his invitation.

James knocked on the window and began speaking before Alex had wound it down. 'Seriously though. I think it's great. What you did for Carol.'

Looking at his brother's—for once—sincere expression, tears finally came to Alex's eyes. He had been struck by a sudden memory of what it had been like when they were a little older than Olivia and Emily. Back when their family had been whole and James had gazed up at Alex—his amazing big brother—as if he were a god.

It didn't take James long to ruin the moment.

'But mate,' he said, 'if the old bat wants to leave you anything, take it.'

Shaking his head and blinking to clear his vision, Alex started the engine. He said, 'I'll let you know how it goes,' and pulled away before James could get in another shot.

But he wasn't fast enough. Always keen to have the last word, James called after him, 'Take it! You might finally be able to afford somewhere decent to live!'

Chapter 11

'Of course you should go to Carol's! I can't believe you're thinking of giving it a miss!'

Lucinda grabbed a lipstick and brush from her bathroom drawer and strode to her bedroom as Jay delivered her pep talk. While she had been quick to accept Carol's invitation to afternoon tea, she had spent the following two weeks wavering. Alex would be there. And as never seeing him again was her best excuse for not apologising for her rudeness at their last encounter four weeks previously, meeting him again would force her to swallow her pride. A prospect as appealing as swallowing broken glass.

She threw the lipstick and brush into the gaping maw of the handbag which perched on the bed in expectation of her imminent departure. Shoving the rest of the bag's contents to one side, she fished out her keys and clasped the key fob tightly as she sank onto the foot of the bed. The heart-shaped charm filled her palm and she trailed her thumb over the golden border of the puzzle piece-shaped hole in the centre. It was an activity which often helped her straighten out her thoughts. And right now she needed to cook up a reason to stay home which stood any chance of cracking Jay's solid wall of go-getting positivity.

'The journey will be a bit of a pig,' said Lucinda. 'If any of the vans had been free I could have driven to Berkshire easily, but as it is I'll have to take trains and a taxi.' She glanced at the thick grey clouds filling the square of sky visible through the bedroom window. The first two weeks of June had been marked by heat, humidity and downpours. She'd be lucky to make it to Carol's without getting caught in a shower. 'And it's going to rain.'

As excuses went, it was flimsy but plausible. Unfortunately for Lucinda, Jay was having none of it. 'It isn't that far and you won't melt. Besides, it'll be worth it to see Carol looking well.'

'That's true.'

'You'll get to see Alex again too! Please remember to say "thank you" to him for helping you guys put the fear of God into that creep.'

'OK.'

'You promise?'

'I promise,' said Lucinda, stifling a groan. Fantastic. Now she'd have to apologise *and* thank him.

Jay chuckled. 'I wish I'd got to see him in the uniform.'

'Hmn.' Lucinda lifted the key fob to her lips to prevent herself saying anything more. For while she would have loved to tell Jay she hadn't missed much, there were only so many lies she could tell in one phone call. And she certainly didn't want her head chef to know that the memory of Alex in police uniform made her heart stutter and cheeks flush.

'And you deserve the time off and some fun,' Jay said, ploughing on with her unassailable cheeriness. 'Enjoy being catered for and waited on for a change.'

Lucinda tapped the heart charm against her chin as she strained to remember: when was the last time she'd had fun? Relaxed and enjoyed some pampering? Since starting the business it was like there was a heavy cloud of worry permanently stationed over her head. An axe waiting to fall. She used to laugh a lot more. She used to make jokes! They weren't very good, but she'd made Chris laugh. He used to say her sense of humour was one of the things he liked most about her.

She frowned and traced the tip of her finger around the hole in the middle of the bright heart charm. The puzzle piece wasn't the only thing missing: where had fun, funny Lucinda gone?

'Have you ever considered getting a pet?'

'Huh?' Lucinda frowned, puzzled by Jay's latest non sequitur.

'My friend Samara got a dog last year and she says looking after him helps her relax. He's a great mood booster apparently.'

Lucinda snorted, amused by Jay's not-so-subtle hint that she found her boss as uptight and grumpy as she did herself. She often thought about getting a pet, but her work hours had been so crazy the last few years she wouldn't have been able to take care of one properly. And then there were Chris's allergies. Which was definitely something else Jay didn't need to know about.

'I used to have a dog,' Lucinda said and braced herself for Jay's incredulity.

'You never did! Well, you know what, that's great. So you'd know what you're doing if you got another one. You should think about it.'

'It was a long time ago'—Lucinda paused and swallowed the lump which had suddenly risen in her throat—'but I might consider it.' With a deep sigh, she tossed her keys into her bag. 'And in the meantime, you've convinced me. I'm going to Carol's.'

'Yes!' Lucinda's lips curled at Jay's squeal of victory which was quickly followed by more reassurance. 'You really don't need to worry about the jobs we've got on today and tomorrow. There's nothing huge and I've got it all under control.'

'I'm sure you have,' said Lucinda. 'But, if you need anything—'

'I'll call you. But I won't. Have a fantastic time and I'll see you on Monday.'

As she ended the call, Lucinda checked the on-screen clock. She'd have to leave in the next quarter of an hour or risk arriving late. And as being late was possibly the one thing she hated more than apologising, she should get her skates on.

She had just retrieved her black ballet pumps from the back of the wardrobe when her phone trilled. Jay must have remembered a question about the weekend's jobs once she stopped imagining Alex in police uniform. Without looking at the screen, Lucinda grinned and swiped to accept the call.

'I thought you said you wouldn't need to call me?'

'Lucinda? Darling, what on earth are you talking about?'

Lucinda winced. She didn't have the time for this now. 'Hi Mum. Sorry, I thought you were Jay.' She wriggled her feet into her shoes and took another glance at the clock on her phone before asking, 'What's up?'

'I have the most wonderful news, darling! I'm getting married!'

'Sorry?'

'I'm engaged!'

Shock punched the air from Lucinda's lungs. She staggered and collapsed onto the foot of the bed. Pulsating spots of static crept into the edges of her vision and her mum's voice became muffled and distant.

'Lucinda? Are you still there?'

Lucinda rubbed her forehead and focused on the widest section of the crack in the ceiling. Somewhere outside, further down the street, a car alarm wailed a piercing scream. But even its incessant screeching was less disturbing than her mum's news. She must have misheard. 'Did you say you're getting married?'

Marion laughed, a fluttery, girlish sound which Lucinda had never heard her produce before. 'Silly girl! Of course!'

The snowstorm at the edges of Lucinda's vision gradually cleared, but left behind a jagged ache in her temples. She scrunched her eyes shut. Surely this was a misunderstanding? 'But … when … who …?'

'To Graham! He asked me last night, although I'd seen it coming for a while. And it was beautiful! He took me to the beach and—so thoughtful, so like him—he'd prepared …'

Her mum rattled on, but the details of the moonlight picnic were obscure murmurs to Lucinda. Not caring if she was interrupting the greatest proposal story of all time, she said, 'But, Mum! Why?'

Her earnest question was met with more giggles and an exasperated gasp. Lucinda could imagine Marion rolling her eyes at her daughter's slowness. 'Because we love each other. He's completely wild about me and I feel the same. Why else?'

Why else! Lucinda bit back a scream. Because true love doesn't exist! It's a load of rubbish fed to us by greetings card manufacturers, florists, jewellers, confectioners and makers of comforting fictions. Cupid's arrow, the lightning bolt, soulmates, happily ever after: all dangerous baloney.

Lucinda knew this to be true. Or rather she *had known*, because the person who had drummed these self-evident truths into her was the same person who was now regaling her with a lovey-dovey proposal story.

'You'll have to come out for the wedding. Bella, that's Graham's eldest, is already on the case. I've mentioned her, haven't I? She's the accountant. Just been promoted and she's only thirty-two! Her fiancé's an—'

'Architect. You've said.'

Her mum giggled yet again and Lucinda had to squeeze her phone to stop herself smashing it against the wall. 'It's good to know you've been listening to something I've told you recently,' her mum continued. 'You can't have been paying attention when I've mentioned Graham or this wouldn't be a surprise.'

A surprise? Surprise! Your colleagues organising a furtive whip-round to get you a birthday cake and card was a surprise. Her mum's news was an atomic bomb. Sure, Lucinda hadn't given her complete and undivided attention to every word Marion had said during their regular phone calls. And while Mum had dropped Graham's name into conversation a few times since last Christmas, those oblique references had always been in the context of her wider group of bridge-playing buddies or as a way to remind Lucinda of lucrative career paths she should have pursued.

'But you never said you were an item!'

'An item! Lucinda! What language!' Her mum gave a huff of disdain. 'We became bridge partners and then we started walking out together.'

The car alarm gave a final squeal before giving way to blessed silence. Even so, a persistent throbbing pulsed at Lucinda's temples. She had to pause the conversation to process or her head would explode. 'Mum, it's great news. Congratulations! Send me pictures of the ring, OK?'

'I will. Thank you, darling. Such a beautiful setting and so thoughtful of him to include my birthstone. And I was thinking, you're a little older than strictly acceptable, but I think you could still be a bridesmaid if you were—'

'I'm sorry, Mum. I have to go. I have tea with that lady who I helped in the lift. Remember?'

'Well of course I do! You're off to her charming cottage in the country.'

When Lucinda had spoken to Carol's granddaughter, she had called the afternoon tea venue Carol's 'modest place out of town'. And while Lucinda didn't know exactly what that meant, her imagination had conjured an ivy-covered, thatch-topped bungalow which was likely in line with her mum's ideas.

'That's right. It'll be nice to see her looking well. And—'

'All right, darling. I must dash!'

'Right. OK. I'll tell you how I get—'

'Oh, Graham's here! Speak soon!'

Lucinda dropped her phone onto her bed and plunged after it. Her heart was racing so hard it made her ribs vibrate and, though she was lying down, she needed to cling on to something, as if the world had tilted in an attempt to tip her off.

A tentative knock on her bedroom door made her groan and roll up to sitting. It was followed by a muffled voice. 'Hey, Lu? Are you OK?'

She laid her hand against her chest. Under her fingers her heart was slowing. Even so, she wasn't sure she could deal with Chris right now. But then again, could things get any weirder?

'Come in.'

Lucinda stared dead ahead as Chris entered the room, his footsteps swishing across the carpet. The mattress dipped as he sat next to her and joined her in contemplating her favourite movie poster: that for *Back to the Future*. She'd owned it for nearly twenty years but had only framed and hung it two years ago when she and Chris had moved into separate bedrooms. He had refused to let her decorate the walls with film posters in any 'shared spaces'—which had been the whole house while they were together—so putting up three of them in her own bedroom had made the change in their relationship feel definitive. And she knew the sight of them needled him, which brought her a childish pleasure.

She could sense his disapproval now. His breathing was interspersed with tiny sighs, as if he were offended by the sight of Michael J. Fox standing next to one of the most famous cars in film history.

'I wasn't eavesdropping, but from my room I could hear your voice getting squeaky,' Chris said. 'What did your mum say this time?'

Lucinda's shoulders sagged. 'She's getting married.'

Chris laughed and, for once, Lucinda found his characteristic snorting and wheezing oddly reassuring.

'No,' she said. 'She's really getting married. To Graham.'

'Bridge guy Graham?'

'Yes.'

'Graham with the marvellous accountant daughter—'

'That's the one.'

'Your mum? The woman who has repeatedly and very loudly said to anyone who'll listen that romance is humbug and a … a …'

'Joke.'

'Right. The woman who lectured me on true love being a load of crap is getting married?'

'So it would appear.'

'Is someone holding her at gunpoint?' Chris frowned and Lucinda could hear the cogs grinding round in his head. 'Is he a billionaire?'

'No.' Lucinda shook her head. 'No practical reasons. She's besotted.'

'Well I'll be. Huh.' Chris closed his mouth and used his elbow to nudge Lucinda's arm. 'Are you OK?'

'I'm not sure.'

Chris wrapped his left arm around her shoulders and, apparently not noticing how Lucinda tensed in response to his uninvited touch, squeezed her to him. 'Don't worry—'

'I'm not.'

'I'll call your brother.' Chris removed his arm and squirmed to retrieve his phone from his back pocket.

'No.' Speaking to Michael was the last thing she needed right now. She had to get her own thoughts in order before hearing her brother's. She turned her head to look Chris squarely in the eye. 'It's fine. I'll call him later.'

Chris glanced down at his phone, scrolling to find the number. 'You should speak to him now, Lu. He'll be the best person—'

'I said, no!'

Chris's slack-jawed, puppy-eyed expression managed to stir a glimmer of guilt in Snappy Lucinda as she watched him lock the phone screen and put it on the bed.

'Sorry,' she said. 'I'll speak to him later when I've processed all this. Anyway'—she glanced at the clock on her phone—'I have to go or I'll be late.'

She was halfway to her feet when Chris shot out a hand to grab her wrist. 'Don't go.'

For a moment, Lucinda was tempted. The idea of cocooning herself in her room, easing into fleecy pyjamas and fluffy socks and snuggling under the duvet to watch a marathon of her favourite movies was seductive. But she'd made Jay a promise and she would keep it. No matter how painful or awkward doing so might be.

'I have to,' she said. 'It'd be rude to cancel at such short notice and Carol's probably gone to a lot of trouble.'

Chris kept a firm hold on her wrist as he got to his feet and positioned himself between her and the doorway. 'You can tell her you've got family stuff going on. Stay here. We can finish the last two episodes of season three.'

Over the previous fortnight, Lucinda and Chris had watched series one and two of *Napier*. Chris had already seen them but, as a keen fan of the show, he was happy to sit through them again. Meanwhile, for Lucinda, it had been disarmingly pleasant to lounge next to him on the sofa, sharing the experience of the drama without fearing he was going to start a serious chat about living arrangements.

And the show wasn't bad either. Lucinda had imagined a programme Chris described as '*Luther* meets *Line of Duty* meets *Silent Witness*' would be muddled and incoherent. But, somewhere around the middle of series one, she was hooked.

By the end of series two, she was so heavily involved with the plots and characters, she could almost believe it when she told Chris she'd wanted to watch *Napier* because Jay had insisted she must. And that her whim to catch up with the show had nothing to do with the actor playing former DI Dexter Hartford, husband of no-nonsense investigative genius DCI Alisia Napier.

In fact, she found the plot so engrossing, she barely noticed how Alex seemed to sparkle on screen, drawing the viewer's eye to him with inescapable magnetism. He was also brilliantly convincing and his performance shifted seamlessly from funny to earnest to moving. It was odd he hadn't been given more—

'Lucinda?' Chris gave her wrist a shake, waking her from her pleasant daydream. 'Come on. You should stay here. You know you want to. It's a bugger of a train journey.'

'It's under two hours.'

'It's complicated.'

'It's one change and I think I can cope with Waterloo. I was a Londoner once, remember?'

Lucinda slipped her wrist out of his grip and moved to pass him, but Chris stepped to his right, blocking her exit. He laid a hand on her upper arm and fixed her with a pleading stare. 'Please stay. Let me look after you.'

Ugh! His protectiveness which, long ago, had seemed an attractive quality, now only angered her. Lucinda had hoped that after years of dating and cohabiting, Chris would have learned she was many things—including brash and confrontational when provoked—but never a defenceless damsel.

She bit back an angry snap, hoping one of her meanest stares would serve as sufficient warning. 'That's kind,' she said through gritted teeth, 'but I have to go.'

Lucinda shrugged off Chris's hand and scurried downstairs to the hall, her thoughts flying ahead of her feet. Chris didn't follow her. Huh, she thought as she glanced over her shoulder. Perhaps this once he'd got the message.

She was swinging her handbag over her arm when his voice sailed down to her. 'You'll get hot walking to the station. And it might rain again. I'll drive you!'

Keeping her eyes firmly ahead, Lucinda growled as she yanked open the front door and slammed it behind her. Nothing ever changed. When it came to reading her body language, Chris always had been and always would be illiterate.

Chapter 12

'Could you stop here a moment, please? Please? Stop!'

The taxi pulled to the side of the drive as Lucinda rolled down her window and removed her sunglasses with clumsy, trembling fingers. She hadn't thought it possible to experience two seismic shocks in one day, but here she was, staring awestruck at Carol's small place in the country: an enormous mansion surrounded by freshly cut lawns shimmering on the horizon, like a luxury ocean liner in a calm green sea.

'Um.' She glanced at the taxi driver. 'Are you sure we're in the right place?'

The driver flung his arm around the back of the passenger seat as he turned to her. He grinned, his teeth a crooked grille of amusement nestling under a bristling ginger moustache. 'You wanted Russell House.' He nodded towards the palace in the distance. 'There she is.'

'And does Carol Russell live here?'

'Lady Russell, you mean?'

'Lady ... Lady ...' Lucinda paused to get her stammer under control. 'She's a lady?'

The driver sucked in air through his teeth as he shook his head, a weary sage reluctantly imparting his knowledge to a foolish apprentice. 'She's the daughter of the Duke of Berkshire. He's hanging on, God love him. Must be in his late nineties.'

Lucinda gazed across the lawns at the cream stone of the house and the comparison which came to mind was Buckingham Palace, because the monarch's central London residence was the only other building of a similar size Lucinda had seen in person. The mansion's symmetry was its most striking feature. The three-tier central core of the complex was flanked on either side by a single storey colonnaded construction connecting to a two-floor building large enough to have been a sizeable family house on its own.

'I'll carry on to the house, shall I?'

'Sorry?'

'Should I take you to the door? Save you the walk?'

Lucinda's gaze flicked down to her comfortable flat pumps. The courtyard in front of the house appeared to be lined with a quicksand of shifting gravel. Thank goodness she hadn't worn her slippery blue stilettos. They would forever carry associations of the day of Carol's cardiac arrest and she had made the considerate decision to leave them at the back of her wardrobe.

But while she was happy with her choice of footwear, horror gripped her as she took in her smartest blue jeans, white Breton-striped cotton jumper and black cardigan. It had seemed appropriate attire for visiting a fellow commoner in her humble dwelling, but now she felt underdressed. And what on earth did her hair and face look like?

She pulled her bag onto her lap and rummaged for her hand mirror. 'Yes, please,' she said to the driver. 'But could you drive slowly?'

Further rummaging turned out her brush and seconds later all stray hair had been tucked into the clip at the back of her head. Retrieving her berry-pink lip crayon, she dabbed a few dots onto her inner lips and used her finger to smudge them wider.

The driver didn't seem to mind the snail's pace. Possibly because it gave him time to practise his hobby as an amateur tour guide. 'The house is Georgian, designed in the 1730s but not finished till the 1760s. Over eighty rooms, more if you count the servants' quarters, and there's two hundred and fifty acres of grounds. Gardens, lawns, deer park ... and then the rest of the estate.'

Half listening, Lucinda rubbed the lip colour which clung to her lightly shaking finger into her cheeks. While the journey had proved useful in giving her the time to calm her anxiety about facing Alex, she hadn't bargained on the additional stress of her host turning out to be a mansion-dwelling aristocrat.

The car's wheels crunched to a halt in front of a huge protruding portico with a triangular roof resting on the scrolled heads of four ionic columns. The driver took his fare from Lucinda and, as she opened the door, added, 'We come every year to the open day. If you get to the gardens, the fountains are worth a look.'

'Thanks?' said Lucinda, her nerves making the word sound more like a question than she had intended.

As it rumbled away from her—the driver waving and shouting, 'Good luck!'—Lucinda stared longingly after the taxi and fought the urge to pursue it. A shudder rippled through her as she raised her gaze to the tonnes of ancient stone hanging over her, impervious to her attempts to stare them down. The shade should have been welcome on such a warm, muggy day, but the chill air only added to Lucinda's trembling.

She pressed her lips together, hitched her handbag strap over her shoulder and told herself to get a grip. She'd worked in many grand and intimidating places, this couldn't be that different.

Ah! But that was *work*, her unhelpful inner voice reminded her. At work she trod the same old trenches; this was an unknown slice of no man's land.

The jet-black front door, the proper entrance for the great and good, loomed as solid and foreboding as a tombstone. Perhaps she could sneak around the side of the building and find a tradesperson's entrance? There had to be an alternative—

The door swung open and a beaming blonde woman trilled, 'There you are! Come in!'

Drat. Too late.

Ducking her head as she crossed the threshold, Lucinda endeavoured to process the size of the entrance lobby. A mahogany imperial staircase rose in a majestic sweep to a shallow landing before splitting in two. Its wooden newel posts were topped with intricately carved acorn caps. To the sides of the room, sizeable floral arrangements posed on twin antique side tables. The soft purple delphiniums and sweet-scented blush roses were reflected in tall ornate mirrors.

'I'm Veronica.' The blonde spun towards her, sending her ponytail swinging away from her slender, freckled neck, and extended a slight pale hand. 'We spoke on the phone.'

'I'm Lucinda. Nice to meet you.' She took the proffered hand and was pleased to find Veronica's grip as confident as her voice. Lucinda guessed she was in her early twenties, an age where many people had handshakes like dead fish. 'You're Carol's … or should I say, Lady Russell's granddaughter?'

Veronica laughed, a tinkling sound finishing in a short bray, which chimed perfectly with the woman's shiny teeth and glossy mane. 'Did her title come as a shock? Sorry! We're super informal here.' She waved her hands around her, taking in the mind-boggling grandeur of her surroundings with a casualness which must have come from years of habituation. 'Grandma will insist you call her Carol. And please call me Vee. We should head for the drawing room. Grandma is dying to meet you. Oops!' She covered her mouth with her dainty fingers. 'Probably not the best expression given your last encounter!'

Vee released another peel of high-pitched laughter and Lucinda smiled, finding the younger woman's bubbliness was going some way to settling her nerves. She was further distracted from her jitters when the sound of joyful barking joined Vee's giggles and a beagle shot into the hall through a doorway at the rear of the room.

The small dog jumped around Lucinda, its nails scrabbling on the polished marble floor. Lucinda crouched and dropped her bag by her feet, freeing her hands to stroke the beagle's head and admire the smart line of white fur running between his brown floppy ears and down to his large black nose. Staring into the dog's eyes, which were glowing with delight, Lucinda was struck by how much she missed having her own pet. Losing her canine best friend when she was twelve had done nothing to diminish her fondness for the animals. And this one, whose tail was wagging so fast the white tip was a draft-stirring blur, was a beauty.

Relaxing for the first time since she'd laid eyes on Russell House, Lucinda grinned as she looked into the dog's warm hazel eyes and, stroking his neck, said, 'Well, hello there. Aren't you the handsome chap?'

A deep voice replied, 'Thank you. That's very kind.'

Lucinda's heartbeat accelerated to a gallop. After watching almost all of *Napier* over the previous two weeks, she knew the voice as well as that of any of her friends or family. Though, even without the television marathon, she'd have remembered the bass tones with raspy edges from the first time she'd heard them. If the voice had been edible, it'd have been smooth dark honey with a final crunch of sweet comb.

She glanced up and found Alex sauntering towards them. Lucinda's breathing grew shallower and the room seemed to tilt as Alex's dark stare collided with hers. Was he taller? And—her mouth went dry as the thought came to her—was it possible he was more attractive?

Lucinda gave herself a mental shake and retreated to the safer ground of considering Alex's clothes, rather than the contours of the muscles underneath and the clinging fit of his— *Agh!* She gave herself a harder shake and forced her focus to his faded black jeans and fitted navy sweater, choices which made Lucinda suspect that, like her, Alex had been unaware of the luxurious splendour of Carol's home.

Vee drifted closer to Alex as he pulled up a few feet from where Lucinda was kneeling. 'Yes, my Hubert is handsome. And such a good boy.' While Vee was presumably talking about the dog, her interest was fixed on Alex and a dreamy expression slackened her features as she laid a hand on his bicep.

Lucinda glared at Vee's hand, and had just begun to wish her stare could burn when Hubert came to the rescue—he *was* a good boy!—by emitting a piercing howl which jolted Vee out of her shameless contemplation of Alex's assets and her hand from his arm. She blinked and turned to Lucinda. 'Obviously you and Alex are already acquainted.'

Hoping to calm her pulse, Lucinda sought refuge in Hubert's laughing eyes and took a moment to steel herself. This was it. She was going to apologise and then they could bury the hatchet and move forwards. After all, today they were both fish out of water and should probably stick together.

She gave Hubert a final pat between his fabulous ears, got to her feet and joined Vee in training her newly positive attention on Alex.

As her gaze met his, she noticed an unusual coolness in his eyes. Perhaps her callous comments the last time they'd met had upset him more than she'd dared imagine? A dart of shame spurred her heart back to racing and strengthened her resolve: she had to try to put things right.

Lucinda willed some of the genuine, unconditional

affection she had absorbed from Hubert into her smile and was moving her lips to greet him when he cut across her.

'Hello again, Ms Green.'

Lucinda closed her mouth as her brain scrambled to catch up with Alex's words. Had he called her *Ms Green*?

Wrong-footed, Lucinda blinked at Alex, taking in his clenched jaw and crossed arms as the final remnants of her smile faded.

She had prepared her apology for the amiable, relaxed, smiling Alex she thought she knew. Not for this aloof imposter.

Her throat dry, she swallowed and didn't bother to summon her smile as she replied, in a level, lifeless tone to match his, 'Hello, Mr Fraser.'

As her words landed, she thought she saw the rigidity in his jaw and posture slacken, but her view was partially blocked by Vee who threw herself into the gap between them. 'It's marvellous to see you two together!' She placed a hand on the small of their backs and ushered them towards the back of the hall. 'A life-saving team reunited! This is going to be wonderful!'

Lucinda bit back a snort as she glanced up at Alex and took in his furrowed brown and stern gaze. Vee's optimism seemed bulletproof, but would it be enough to get them through the afternoon if Alex, or this evil twin version of him, was unwilling to put the past behind them?

Chapter 13

God but he was a complete and utter arsing idiot!

Alex cursed himself as he stared at the flames dancing in the drawing room fireplace. The wood in the grate crackled, blackened and disintegrated, and he wished he could follow it.

He supposed his moronic behaviour might be, in part, due to an ongoing lack of sleep. In addition to the recurring nightmares, over the past few days his mind had been occupied by worries about starting the film shoot on Monday. He'd always suffered from stage fright, although with experience he'd learnt to accept it and use the energy in his performance. But that didn't make it any easier to sleep in the run-up to opening night or the first day of filming.

And his restlessness wasn't entirely work-related. In the two weeks since his niece's party he had repeatedly tried, and failed, to speak to Nicole about ending their relationship. He knew he should do it before leaving to stay at his brother's house for a few weeks, but the moment never seemed right. That morning, as he ran through his lines for the hundredth time, even though he'd had them by heart for a while, he'd watched her filming herself for her followers. She was vibrating with happiness at the possibility of being called back after her most recent audition and he didn't have the heart to sour her mood.

So instead, like the perennial conflict-avoider he was, he'd used visiting Carol as another reason to avoid breaking up with her. He'd been so keen to leave the flat and run from his guilt that he'd arrived at Russell House early, giving him time to recover from the shock of the ludicrous splendour of the place before Lucinda's arrival.

He had imagined his fellow guest would be as wrong-footed as he had been when he walked through the front door and was dwarfed by the dimensions of the entrance hall, like some bizarre scenario from *Alice in Wonderland*. He thought he could capitalise on Lucinda's momentary confusion and greet her with aloof cordiality to make it clear he hadn't forgotten her previous cruel comments.

But, when he entered the hall, Lucinda had been on the floor playing with the family pet and grinning as if she owned the place. The image had thrown him and made him come out with a ridiculous line in response to something she'd said to the dog. And then when she'd looked up at him, her expression open and inviting, it had been a golden opportunity for him to be the bigger person, to extend the olive branch and start anew. But, oh no, Alex the sleep-deprived imbecile had turned up masquerading as a pompous git doing some sort of achingly poor Mr Darcy impression.

Her reaction had been instant: her feline eyes had narrowed and her even lips had drawn into a stern pout as she no doubt thought what an arse he was. And now Lucinda was treating him with the sort of frosty civility a state-appointed defence lawyer might use to address a new client who was still covered in their victim's blood.

'Another cucumber sandwich, Alex? Or another slice of the vanilla cake?' asked Carol, gesturing to the blue porcelain cake stands on the oval-shaped coffee table which were loaded with an impressive display of dainty sandwiches, golden scones and layered cakes.

Alex summoned a polite smile, trapping a sigh behind his teeth. While he was grateful to his host for including vegan options, he struggled to summon enthusiasm for the rubbery eggless sponge or triangles of white bread slathered in margarine. 'Um, no thank you,' said Alex, leaning forwards to place his empty plate on the table.

'And you, Lucinda?' said Carol, turning to her right where Lucinda was perching on the edge of a wing-backed armchair which matched her own. Alex envied them. He was sharing a two-seater, rolled-arm sofa with Vee, who insisted on fidgeting her knees towards his legs, and no matter how hard he pressed himself against the side of the seat it was difficult to avoid contact.

'No, thank you,' said Lucinda, who still had half a slice of chocolate cake to finish. 'Do you not want any?'

'I've been told to improve my diet,' Carol explained.

'Staying off the gin would do you more good,' said Vee.

Carol laughed too loudly and brushed aside Vee's blunt comment with a casual wave, although the cutting glare she shot her granddaughter made Alex think Vee's observation was probably close to the mark.

'Well, either way, I can never thank you both enough,' Carol said, glancing at Alex and Lucinda. 'If I hadn't had the good fortune to be in the lift as the same time as the two of you ...' She shuddered.

Alex was delighted to find that, for once, he didn't share Carol's quaking horror at the memory of her brush with death. He had expected his palms to turn clammy and breathing to quicken with every mention of her heart attack, but seeing her alive and well seemed to have done him a lot of good. And her near-death experience certainly had done nothing to diminish her sense of style: Carol's long grey hair was tied back in a loose bun and she was wearing wide-legged trousers and a sweater in a matching shade of cream wool.

'As I was saying earlier,' he said. 'You should thank Lucinda. She was the one who knew what she was doing. I just followed her instructions.'

Lucinda looked up from the cake she was sampling. She blinked at him and inclined her head a fraction. The miniscule gesture detonated a blazing grenade in Alex's core, a hot jolt of triumph at having made the tiniest crack in her armour. Although, the heat might have come partly from the fire, which Carol insisted Vee keep feeding despite the room being warm and stuffy, a close atmosphere not helped by the pungent scent of lilies from the bouquets on the side tables.

Carol repeated her dismissive wave. 'All I know is what the doctors told me. I wouldn't be here if you hadn't—Veronica!' Carol's bark made Alex startle and his foot caught the leg of the coffee table, making the teacups rattle. 'Remove that blasted dog at once! He's a menace!'

Hubert had trailed Lucinda in from the hall and taken up a happy residence at her feet. Alex had noticed her sneaking the dog tiny pieces of ham sandwich, the animal's tail semaphoring his joy. When not being offered snacks, Hubert would complete a lap of the coffee table, forcing the humans to shuffle their legs and feet aside.

'He's just pleased to see new people,' said Vee as she stood. 'Come on, Huey. You need a trip outside anyway.'

As Vee exited the room, Alex sighed and spread into the middle of the sofa. During her short absence, Alex, Lucinda and Carol indulged in the supremely English pastime of enjoying tea while getting a full update on the state of their host's post-operative health and exchanging observations regarding the weather, particularly the recent rain.

'It would be nice for some fine weather so I can go out walking,' said Carol. 'Perhaps finally get back to a state resembling my former self.'

'I think you look great,' Alex said.

Carol smirked and straightened in response to the compliment as her granddaughter trotted back into the room. 'Poor Hubert shot out of the kitchen door,' Vee said as she returned to the sofa, causing Alex to shuffle towards the arm again.

'He's your dog?' asked Lucinda.

'Yes.' Vee gave a sigh of contentment. 'My one true love.'

Carol produced a guttural sound of exasperation. 'I have told Veronica many times if she gave the men who court her half the attention she lavishes on that hare-brained creature, she would already be engaged.'

'Oh Grandma! I'm only twenty-five. And getting married isn't that important nowadays.'

'Poppycock!' Carol placed her cup and saucer back on the table with an aggressive rattle. 'What will become of the world if it is full of nothing but ageing spinsters and bachelors?'

Alex glanced at Lucinda. She was giving Carol a determined stare he recognised and, from her narrowed eyes and parted lips, he feared she was gearing up to deliver a barbed reply.

Perhaps Carol sensed the oncoming rebuttal too because, as Lucinda was drawing breath, she fired a question at her. 'Lucinda! You are forty and yet I understand you've never been married?'

Lucinda snapped her mouth shut and the muscles in her jaw clenched before she replied. 'You understand?'

'Yes. From my investigator. Obviously I asked her to look into you and Alex before I invited you here.'

The skin next to the ribbed collar of Lucinda's pretty jumper began to turn a pale pink. 'Obviously?'

'Of course! You could have both been thieves or murderers for all I knew!'

The pinkness inched up to Lucinda's cheeks and threatened to darken into what Alex assumed was a blush of pure fury. Lucinda struck him as someone who liked to keep her private life private. A desire he could sympathise with having seen friends unsettled by intrusive and unkind press attention.

In contrast to the deepening flush in her face, the fingers Lucinda was using to grip her teacup had turned white. 'You had someone investigate us?' she asked.

'Naturally. And they turned up you are unmarried, yet you were engaged. Although sadly for less than a year. Is that correct?'

There was a pause in which Alex, staring at the carefully blank expression on Lucinda's face, swore he could hear the scrape of the knives she was sharpening in her head. When her reply finally came it was low and curt. 'Yes.'

'You and your former fiancé had been courting for five years before your engagement and'—Carol paused to insert a slight wince of disapproval—'living together for the latter three years of that period?'

'Yes.'

Apparently not regarding Carol's digging around in their lives at all strange or, frankly, completely unacceptable, Vee jumped in, bringing her own enthusiastic style of questioning to the interrogation. 'And you're no longer engaged. To Chris?'

'That's correct.'

Lucinda flinched when Vee used Chris's name, and Alex wasn't surprised when the lawyerly tone she'd used to speak to him earlier now became increasingly pronounced. She'd be using legalese next. If that happened, he'd have to step in before she overturned the tea table.

Vee continued, blithely unaware the woman sitting opposite her was slowly morphing into a ball of barely contained violence. 'But you and Chris still live together? Even though you're no longer an item?'

'That's correct, Veronica.'

Vee shifted forwards in her seat as if following the scent of blood, apparently not having noticed the way Lucinda had uttered her full name through clenched teeth. 'So a reconciliation is still possible? Are you hoping you might still get married?'

'I have had, and continue to have, no plans to that effect at this time.'

Oh Lord help us all, thought Alex. There it was: full barrister mode.

'But surely,' said Carol, continuing the pursuit, 'if you are to have a relationship with anyone else, one of you quitting the property would be the wisest course?'

'You know what, Carol?' Lucinda straightened and fixed the older woman with a narrowed glare as her tone sharpened. 'If I were to have a relationship in future, and if I were to think about selling my home, I think I can safely say it would be absolutely none of your—'

'I was married!' Alex said, blurting the words out in a desperate attempt to prevent bloodshed.

And … hallelujah! His gambit worked! Vee and Carol, who had been training their hunting instincts exclusively on Lucinda, swung their stares towards him. Alex exhaled and, determined to keep their focus until Lucinda's colouring had dialled down from puce to a lighter shade— one which suggested she'd abandoned any plan to burn the mansion to the ground—he decided to treat his latest audience to the best version of the story.

Imagining he was talking to friends he had known for years, he smiled with genuine warmth, shuffled nearer to Vee and leant to close the gap between him and Carol. Follow me, he thought, as he lowered his voice and began.

'I met Kelly on one of my early jobs after drama school. We were both twenty-one and it was love at first sight.'

Vee's swoony sigh competed with a grunt from Lucinda. Having faced tougher crowds, Alex continued.

'We spent every second we could together and started hunting for a flat to share. And then one day I joked about getting married. It was just a joke, but once I'd said it, it began to seem like the only idea that made sense.'

His gaze drifting past Vee's entranced stare, Alex pictured Kelly as she had been back then and remembered the jolt of electricity that had hit him when she'd shook his hand and fixed him with her hazel eyes. There was something unusually intense about their connection and from that first meeting he couldn't stop thinking about her. Each day, with every little thing he learnt about Kelly, she grew more beautiful. He loved her laugh, the wrinkle at the top of her nose when she found something unpleasant and the way she would sometimes push the tip of her tongue to the corner of her mouth when she was concentrating.

'How long was it until you married?' asked Vee.

Alex risked a glance at Lucinda and ... *yes!* The angry blush had calmed and retreated. Rather than annoyed, she seemed pensive, and was watching him with her head tilted to one side as if trying to make up her mind whether to believe a word he said.

'Three months after we met,' Alex said. 'And, knowing our families would try to talk us out of it, we went the whole nine yards and eloped to Gretna Green.'

'Oh how romantic!'

Alex gave Vee a tight-lipped smile. The truth was, twenty years later, most of his memories of the wedding day were fuzzy. He had thought he was ready, though. Bursting with eagerness and keen to embark on their happily ever after.

'So what went wrong?'

Alex glanced at Lucinda, unsurprised she had chosen to play the chorus of doom. 'We were young. Our circumstances changed. She got an opportunity in the States and wanted a clean break.'

Alex was being charitable to Kelly. For her, their love affair had been a romantic fantasy and when they returned to London it wasn't long until it collided with reality. Under the pressures of irregular employment and contingent money worries, the collision came fast and was head on. Disappointed and unwilling to put in the work that could have saved their relationship, she walked out. Alex's heart shattered and, during the two years it needed to mend, the former hopeless romantic became a guarded one.

'And you never remarried?' asked Vee.

'No,' said Alex, turning to look her in the eye, 'but I wouldn't rule it out.'

Vee giggled and gave his knee a playful push. A snort of derision from Lucinda drew his gaze to the other side of the table in time to see her stab a morsel of chocolate cake, ram it between her teeth and chew with considerable malevolence.

Carol gave a polite cough and asked, 'Perhaps Nicole is waiting for you to propose?'

'Sorry?'

'Oh dear. Did I get that wrong?' Carol frowned. 'Your current girlfriend, or partner, or whatever you call it nowadays. The young lady you live with. Her name is Nicole, isn't it?'

'Yes. Yes, it is.'

Carol sighed. 'All these young people who seem unable to settle down. I do wonder if it's something to do with being raised by only one parent. I mean, after what happened to your father, I'm sure your mother did her best, but it couldn't have been ...'

Carol's voice grew distant as Alex's heart thundered. All his muscles tensed and the back of his neck prickled with sweat.

Oh no. He'd been doing so well. Why did she have to mention Dad?

His vision began to blur as his mind's eye filled with old memories he wished would stay buried. Though his limbs had frozen, his eyes shifted frantically, scanning the walls for exits. Was the room getting smaller? Why was it so hot?

As she continued her musings, Carol had trained her gaze on Vee, but Lucinda was staring at him, her brow creased and eyes narrowed. Had she noticed his distress?

Oh God. He really had to get out of the room before he vomited or passed out.

A noise like an angry wasp came from under Vee's leg. She yelped and jumped up to answer her phone, which had been trapped between her thigh and the sofa.

'Sorry,' she said. 'It's the housekeeper.'

'What on earth does she want?' asked Carol.

'What? OK, OK, I'll come now.' Vee hung up. 'Hubert's missing.'

'Don't be absurd.' Carol shook her head. 'He'll be exploring the grounds. He'll come back later when he's hungry.'

'But he's used to being at my house. He doesn't know the estate and he's practically still a pup. What if he chases a rabbit and gets stuck in a warren?'

Alex blinked and silently thanked Hubert. Time in the fresh air, concentrating on nothing more complicated than finding a lost dog, would give him the chance to regain his composure. 'I'll help you look for him,' he said as he sprang to his feet, the decisive action easing the tightness in his chest and clearing his vision.

'I'll help too,' said Lucinda.

Surprised, Alex glanced at Lucinda as she pushed out of her chair and met his widened gaze with her penetrating green stare.

'Thank you!' Vee beamed at her eager volunteers. She gestured to her gossamer-thin tea dress and four-inch stilettos before turning towards the door. 'I'll just run and change.'

Carol, who must also have been musing on sartorial inadequacy, gave Alex and Lucinda a critical head-to-toe scan. 'Your clothes are fine.' She sniffed at her guests' jeans and casual sweaters. 'But you'll need to borrow coats and boots. There should be something suitable in the mud room. Follow me.'

Chapter 14

As she had threaded her way through the crowds at Waterloo station earlier that afternoon, Lucinda's plan had been simple: grit her teeth and apologise to Alex, enjoy some cake with Carol and be on her way home by six at the latest. But now, as the time approached six fifteen, she was being marched through a country mansion by the daughter of a duke in preparation for a beagle hunt.

Lucinda and Alex scurried to keep up with Carol as she strode across the hall, down a hidden staircase and along a stark white corridor peppered with forbidding mahogany-framed doorways. To her left, Lucinda caught a glimpse of a cavernous kitchen with two island units and an array of tantalisingly modern fixtures and fittings. She slowed her step to peer into the room and was tempted to sneak inside. But the idea of Hubert lost or trapped underground, whimpering in the darkness, made her stomach roll and she quickened her pace to catch up with their host.

'The mud room is through here,' Carol said as she came

to a halt in front of a door at the end of the passageway. 'Help yourself to coats and boots. I'll find Veronica and tell her to join you here. You two should check the bottom meadow.'

'The bottom meadow?' Lucinda asked, her tummy performing an elaborate series of somersaults. How many meadows could there be? How ruddy enormous was the estate?

Carol replied with a bewildering set of directions involving a reflecting pool, something called a 'lesser folly' and great abbey ruins. Lucinda lost track after the mention of the walled garden and was glad when their rude, nosy, patronising host stomped away, leaving her and Alex to fend for themselves.

Lucinda's simmering irritation, which had been thoroughly stoked by Carol's unauthorised snooping, was not soothed by her rummage through the mud room's supplies. The best she could turn up were wellington boots four sizes too large and a monstrous oilskin coat which hung down past her knees.

And, amid all the unthinkable weirdness of the afternoon, the most unsettling element was also the most familiar: Alex.

Alex, who stood next to her in an outfit similar to her own. But, of course, on him, the black boots and navy gabardine coat were fabulous and transformed him into some sort of dashing moor-stalking groundsman who was about to do a photoshoot for Burberry. Meanwhile, in her formless olive coat and brown boots, she looked like something vomited up by the tide and left to rot on a barren shingle beach.

This unfortunate contrast wasn't helped by the reappearance of Vee, whose new outfit—a fitted tweed jacket, crisp white shirt, skintight beige jodhpurs and thigh-high leather boots—made her look like an equestrian events catalogue model.

'Goody, you're ready!' Vee said as she shimmied through the door and retrieved a crash helmet from a shelf to her right. 'I'll get the quad bike and ride over to the deer park. You head for the bottom meadow. You'll know it when you reach the wooden fence. You'll have to climb over it, I'm afraid.'

'You're not coming with us?' Lucinda asked, the slight squeak in her voice betraying her dismay. She had been banking on Vee acting as a buffer between her and Alex as they combed the grounds.

'We'll cover more ground if we split up.' Vee grinned as she made the infuriatingly sound point.

Alex, who appeared to be having difficulty keeping his eyes off the contours of Vee's lower half, asked, 'Carol gave us directions, but would you mind running through them again?'

Ha! thought Lucinda. It wasn't just her who was directionally challenged.

Vee opened the outer door and turned back, her hand resting on the frame. 'Go that way'—she pointed to a track of grass sloping away into the distance—'over the north lawn. Past the bigger outdoor pool and tennis courts. You can't go wrong because the lesser folly will be on the mound to your right.' Vee nodded at them. 'Right. If I find Huey, I'll come and get you. If not, I'll see you back here.'

Alex and Lucinda followed Vee out onto a paved area

overlooking the lawns and watched as she scurried around the corner of the building out of sight.

'I guess,' Alex said, 'we head over the grass and hope we recognise some landmarks?'

Lucinda shrugged. Vee's directions had been as muddy as Carol's. A pragmatic trial-and-error approach to navigating their way around the estate would probably be as good as any.

She tilted her head towards the lawns. 'Let's go.'

They trudged across the waterlogged lawn, breaking the silence periodically to shout Hubert's name. The humid air was heavy with the scent of wet earth and a light drizzle began to fall as they neared the tennis courts. Even so, Lucinda was pleased Hubert's escape had provided a reason to flee the drawing room. It had looked beautiful from the threshold with glittering gilding on almost every surface—from the chandelier and the frames of the mirrors to the legs of the side tables—giving the space an opulent shine. But once Carol and Vee had started poking around in her private life, Lucinda had felt as if she were trapped in a shrinking gold box.

She glanced at Alex as they drew level with the tennis courts. He paced forwards with confidence, his left hand in his pocket. Drizzle lay in tiny beads along the sandy waves of his hair, shimmering like sea foam.

His behaviour that afternoon had left her more confused about him than ever. After his icy greeting, he had gone out of his way to give her due credit for saving Carol's life and she suspected he'd stepped in with his own marriage story to draw the heat off her. In fact, she had just started to think she should apologise to him after all when Carol had made some ridiculous comment about the children of single-parent families and the relaxed lines of his body had gone rigid. His skin had paled and eyes turned glassy. It was the same distant, frozen expression he had worn in the lift when Carol had lost consciousness. Lucinda had been on the verge of reaching across the coffee table to touch his hand and ask if he was OK when Vee's announcement had roused him. Perhaps there was a deeper explanation behind his frosty welcome? Perhaps he was quietly dealing with all manner of difficult stuff and she should give him the benefit of the doubt?

Then again, maybe he'd just been bored and zoned out from Carol's droning for a moment. Maybe he had mentioned his marriage because he felt cold out of the spotlight. He was an actor after all. And weren't they all huge show-offs?

Lucinda bit her lip as she followed Alex's sure steps up another slippery incline and considered her latest theory. As well as getting everyone's attention, Alex's romantic yarn had given him an excuse to cosy up to Vee. When he'd smiled at her and delivered that corny line about not having ruled another marriage out—ugh!—Lucinda had struggled not to choke on her cake. And, as if the flirting weren't nauseating enough in itself, he had a girlfriend! He'd kept her quiet, hadn't he?

'Here we are,' said Alex, interrupting Lucinda's churning thoughts. He glanced left and right, taking in the long wooden fence which disappeared into forested areas in the distance, and smiled. 'So I guess we made it to the lower meadow without getting lost. Now we just have to get over this ...'

Alex hopped onto the lower panel of the fence and sailed over the barrier, droplets of water flying from his locks and the tail of his coat sailing out behind him. The landing, with both feet squared next to each other, was worthy of an Olympic gymnast.

Lucinda closed her mouth. Huh. That little display would have sent Vee and other members of the Alex Fraser fan club into raptures. Thankfully she had more sense. She refused to be bowled over by the sight of a stupid man vaulting a ruddy fence! No matter how good—or indeed athletic and graceful—he might have looked doing it.

Harrumphing and glaring at the wood as if daring it to give her a splinter, she grasped the top bar with both hands and planted her left foot on the bottom panel. The soles of her boots were clogged with mud and it took three attempts to get a solid grip. Fighting the restriction of the ridiculous coat around her knees, she swung her right foot onto the top panel. It rested there for a moment as she contemplated her next move and the bigger questions. How had she let Jay persuade her to come here? Where was all the fun, relaxation and pampering? Fun? Ha! And how the heck was she supposed to get over this sodding fence without—

'May I give you a hand over?'

Frozen with her right leg extended along the top of the fence, like a six-year-old in a ballet class having their first attempt at the barre, Lucinda glared at Alex and covered her embarrassment with one of her old friends: haughty scorn.

'No, thank you.' What was it with men? Did they go about their lives assuming women were incapable and needed saving? Grunting, she moved her right leg back to the lower bar. Her feet firmly underneath her, she shot Alex a venomous glance and said, 'I don't need looking after!'

To her surprise, Alex chuckled. 'Lucinda. Anyone who meets you must know, within seconds, that you are the last person on earth who needs to be looked after.'

Oh. Lucinda frowned and channelled her pique into swinging her legs over the barrier until she was sitting on top of it. There! She'd cracked it. And by herself, thank you very much.

Alex nodded at her success and stepped forwards so his waist was a few inches from her knees. With Lucinda perched on the fence, their faces were on a level and, as his gaze collided with hers, she noticed the gold flecks in his dark eyes. He dropped his voice and inclined his head, as if he had a secret he wanted to share with her alone, and said, 'I wasn't trying to look after you. I was trying to look *out* for you.'

The left side of his mouth curled upwards a fraction and Lucinda's traitorous insides fizzed in response. Her lips parted as she scrabbled to cook up a fitting reply, but before she could speak Alex strode away.

Oh drat. Lucinda sprang down from the fence and brushed her hands on her coat, her nerves buzzing from Alex's words and sly smile. Just when she'd worked herself up into a comfortable strop, he had to go and ruin it by saying something disgustingly reasonable, insightful and clever! He really was making it much harder for her to dislike him. Dammit.

On the upside, they were now inside the lower meadow. Clumps of ox-eye daisies, bright blue cornflowers and purple foxgloves shone out among the tall grasses which swished against their coats as they stalked forwards, shouting for Hubert.

Wanting to know the time, and unwilling to ask Alex, Lucinda was rummaging under her coat, trying to fish her phone from her jeans pocket, when it buzzed. She had turned it to silent before sitting down to afternoon tea and, in the urgency to start the hunt for Hubert, hadn't turned the ringer back on.

She had six missed calls. One from Jay, one from Chris and four from her brother, Michael. She'd have to contact Jay when she got back to the house and pray she didn't need her help urgently.

Chris would be calling to tell her to ring her brother. She'd send him a message later.

Michael ... She sighed. Michael could only be calling her to discuss their mother's apparent slide into love-struck madness. A highly disturbing turn of events Lucinda had blissfully forgotten for the past hour.

What was to be done about Mum? If anything? She was certainly old enough to make her own decisions. And mistakes. But, Lucinda realised, her mood souring as the gathering clouds above turned from drizzling grey to stormy black, the other question around her mother's impending nuptials needling her was: what did it all mean? If Mum could reconsider her 'true love is humbug' credo and recant her deepest, most strongly held beliefs, where did that leave those she had raised to share those beliefs?

'There's no sign of Hubert here.' Alex spun round to face her, arms stretched wide above the grass. 'I think we should head back and find Vee. She might have him already.'

Lucinda bit the inside of her cheek. Though the weather was getting worse, she hadn't thought Alex would have given up so fast. In fact, she mused, her eyes narrowing, he now seemed keener on finding Vee than the lost dog. But then, perhaps that was why he had volunteered for the search? Had he hoped to be alone with Vee this whole time but had been lumbered with her instead?

The rain began to fall in earnest. Lucinda yanked up her hood, her blood running hot with annoyance at the baffling man in front of her. But, as strong as her irritation was, it didn't explain the tears which sprang into her eyes. She usually had such fierce control over her emotions. What in the world was wrong with her?

'Are you OK?' Alex stepped closer. His coat didn't have a hood, and his fair hair was slick with rain. He ran a hand across the droplets on his face and gave her a reassuring smile. 'Hubert seemed pretty smart. I'm sure he'll have found his way back to the house by now.'

Mortified he had caught her on the verge of tears, Lucinda stammered an excuse. 'I'm fine. Just not looking forward to returning to the Berkshire inquisition.'

He huffed a short laugh. 'I'm not happy about Carol having us investigated either. You know ...'

Beyond Alex's voice, Lucinda swore she heard a faint barking. She pulled back her hood and began to wander towards the sound. Alex followed her and, pulling up by her side, continued his monologue. Lucinda closed her eyes to better concentrate ... Yes! There was the barking again! But where was it coming from? Drat! It was impossible to make out the direction with Alex droning on. Couldn't he hear it too? Would he never shut up?

She held a hand up and used her sharpest tone to cut over his rambling. 'Could you be quiet for a second? I heard barking and would like to listen for it. Even if you want to, I'm not about to give up on Hubert. Some of us came out here because we genuinely care about finding him.'

Alex's eyes widened. 'What? What exactly are you implying? You honestly think I don't care about finding …' Alex pressed his lips together, bunched his fists and half turned away, before wheeling back to her. 'You know what? Think whatever you want. I've had it! Lord knows I've tried, but you are impossible!'

'Tried? You've tried?'

'Yes! I have. Unlike you!'

The light dimmed as the storm approached and the rain fell in bulging droplets which formed puddles in the soggy earth. In the distance, a rumble of thunder shook the air.

Lucinda glared at Alex, meeting the furious challenge in his eyes square on, relieved and thrilled to be giving vent to her seething tangle of feelings. 'The only person you've tried anything with today is Vee!'

'What are you talking about?'

'Oh please. She's been all over you like a rash and you're just as bad!' She rolled her eyes and raised the pitch of her voice into a sycophantic simper. 'Vee, can I pour you some more tea? Please let me muse on the idea of marriage as I gaze into your big blue eyes. And let me have a good ogle of your backside in those riding trousers!'

'For your information, I was being polite and friendly. You probably don't know what that looks like, but if you pay attention perhaps you'll learn something.'

'What's that supposed to mean?'

'Listen. I don't know what you think I did to you, but you've been a total bitch to me pretty much since the second we met which, I might remind you, was when I did you the favour of stopping you smacking your head against the side of a lift.'

The sound of barking was closer now. Lucinda couldn't be sure, but the happy yapping might even have been coming from somewhere within the meadow.

She brandished a hand in the air between them and said, 'I don't have to listen to this,' before striding off towards the barking.

But Alex clearly had more to say and was eager to continue. He scurried after Lucinda, keeping pace with her brisk stride. Meanwhile, Lucinda refused to slow her furious strut in her determination to keep on Hubert's trail.

'It all makes sense now!' Alex shouted through the rain. 'If, on top of your delightful rudeness and sarcasm, you can't tell the difference between flirting and being friendly, it's no wonder you're single!'

Lucinda glared at him, but refused to slow her enraged stomping. He was close enough that she could see the angry flush in his cheeks and feel the heat of his breath. She raised her voice to compete with the hiss of the rain and to match his as they paced, sniping at and over each other.

'How dare you—'

'—looking down your nose at me ever since we—'

'—arrogant, attention-seeking—'

'—I've noticed the eye-rolling—'

' —who thinks all women should fall at his feet—'

'—behaving like some jealous, sharp-tongued harpy!'

'Harpy!' Lucinda halted abruptly and whirled to face Alex who reared back, eyes wide, as if he feared—with reason—she might breathe fire. 'Well, *Mr Fraser*,' Lucinda spat with as much contempt as she could muster, 'you know what you can do? You can go fu—'

Lucinda's witty, eloquent retort was lost to a squeal as, stepping back onto a particularly treacherous patch of ground, her foot flew out from under her. Mid-expletive, she dropped straight down to earth, leaving the decorous suggestion she'd been in the middle of delivering incomplete and her on her backside in a pool of mud.

Chapter 15

Alex stared in goggle-eyed horror. In a large puddle at his feet, Lucinda sat stunned, her green eyes glistening in her mud-freckled face.

She'd slipped so fast, he hadn't had time to grab her. Luckily the soft earth would have cushioned her fall. The only thing wounded would be her pride, wouldn't it?

He longed to reach down and check she was all right, but their row had left him wary and he feared any offer of assistance would be unwelcome. How had their argument started anyway? He recalled little except for a sudden and overwhelming need to get through to her. To make her see that he wasn't the bad guy. And apparently yelling and calling her names had been the best way to get that across. No wonder she thought he was an idiot!

Taking a tentative step forwards, he heard muted sounds coming from between her parted lips, but they were drowned out by loud barking approaching at speed.

With a triumphant yelp, Hubert burst out of the long

grass and hurtled into Lucinda, almost knocking her further back into the mud. Lucinda gasped and let her head fall forwards to touch the dog's back as she raised a hand to stroke him. Her shoulders started to heave and Alex's heart clenched. Right, that was it. She could scream at him if she liked, but he couldn't bear to leave her sobbing on the wet ground.

He was about to take another step forwards when Lucinda straightened. Her hood slipped back and he realised the noise he'd thought had been crying, was chuckling. As she stared into Hubert's eyes, the low giggle accelerated and swelled until it was a wonderfully filthy cackle. Alex found himself grinning in response and, when she glanced up at him, her genuine mirth had softened the hard set of her features. The transformation was striking: it was as if she had been lit up from the inside.

Although he was loath to bring the mesmerising display of levity to an end, Alex leant towards her, trying to keep one foot out of the worst of the mud. He extended his right hand. 'Hand up?'

Lucinda stopped laughing long enough to say, 'Why, thank you, Mr Fraser!'

As she reached for his fingers, their gazes locked and he was unable to tear his eyes away from the intriguing glint in hers. Too late, he recognised the emerald gleam for what it was: pure devilry.

With a wicked grin, Lucinda clamped her hand around his wrist and heaved. Already off balance, Alex slid to the ground with a yelp and landed with a resounding squelch on his bottom next to her.

His tumble was met with another enthusiastic bout of jumping and barking from Hubert, while Lucinda waited until his gaze met hers to break into another gale of giggles. The collective joy of woman and dog was so contagious that, even as his boots filled with water, Alex found himself closing his eyes, tipping his head back and roaring with laughter at the absurdity of the entire situation.

Tears had left tracks through the freckles of mud on Lucinda's cheeks. Still grinning at Alex, she scooped up a palmful of mud and flung it at him as she said, 'Harpy!' and set off into another fit of hilarity.

Alex winced as the soft projectile struck his cheek. He was tempted to lob a clod back at her: how would she react to that? But he didn't want to do anything that might change her features: the unaffected grin, feline eyes shining with playful amusement and all the ridiculous mud splatter. She was beautiful.

The last thought made Alex's breath hitch and smile slip. Lucinda must have noticed because, grin still in place, she asked, 'What? Never seen a harpy taking a mud bath with a beagle before?' Her laughter subsided to a quieter wheezing, which was swamped by the approaching roar of a diesel engine.

Reluctantly dragging his gaze away from Lucinda, Alex glanced over his shoulder and said, 'I think the cavalry's coming. Here, help me up.'

They rolled onto their knees until they were face to face and planted their hands on each other's shoulders. Slowly, they rose to their feet while Hubert darted between their legs, doing his best to unbalance them again. For a moment they stood holding on to each other and, though their laughter was quieter and a little awkward, the ice between them had finally broken. Perhaps, Alex thought as Lucinda lifted her hands away from his shoulders, they'd get on much better if they spent less time talking.

'There you are!'

A black two-seater vehicle, the sturdy love child of a quad bike and a golf buggy, growled to a halt on the other side of the meadow fence. Vee leapt up from the driver's seat. 'You found Hubert!'

An ecstatic Hubert sprinted for the fence and was under it and in Vee's arms in seconds. Alex and Lucinda took longer to trudge across to the buggy, but their welcome from Vee was no less enthusiastic.

'Thank you so much!' she said, cuddling the beagle without a care for the paw prints he was leaving on her jacket. 'Goodness!' Her eyes widened as she inspected the dog rescuers. 'Whatever happened to you?'

'We had a run-in with gravity,' said Lucinda, gripping Alex's hand to steady herself as she swung over the fence.

'And gravity won,' Alex said. He grinned as Lucinda landed safely and released his hand, leaving his fingers tingling.

'Oh dear,' said Vee. 'Let's get you to the house. We can all squeeze on the bike. Come on!'

Vee suggested Alex ride in the co-pilot seat, but he insisted Lucinda and Hubert take the chair. It had a seat belt. And the dog would be much happier on Lucinda's lap and next to its owner. This left him with the uncomfortable option of perching on the metal shelf at the rear of the vehicle, his legs dangling over the side while he clung to the bars of the roll cage.

Fortunately, Vee made short work of the bumpy drive to the mansion. And not only because it meant Alex's teeth weren't rattled free of his head. The rain, which had eased to drizzle when Vee arrived, began to fall on them in a spiteful torrent as they reached the house. Freshly soaked, humans and dog sprinted away from the buggy and for the stifling warmth of the mud room.

As they peeled off their soggy boots and swampy coats, Carol exploded through the door brandishing a stack of towels.

'All this mess for that stupid animal.'

'I'm just glad Hubert's OK,' said Lucinda.

'Oh course he's fine!' said Carol, giving Hubert a withering stare. 'He's had three people at his beck and call for hours.'

Hubert, who was enveloped in a fluffy towel and being rubbed dry by Vee, had the good sense to stay quiet.

His socks thoroughly drenched, Alex finished drying his feet and pushed them naked into his shoes. He stood. 'I should get going.'

'Me too,' said Lucinda, holding her own socks between thumb and forefinger.

'Would you like a lift to the station?' asked Alex.

'Yes, please,' she said, getting to her feet. 'If you wouldn't—'

'Nonsense!' Carol's tone was the verbal equivalent of a foot being put down. 'The storm won't ease for hours and your clothes are filthy. You'll stay here tonight. I'll have two of the guest rooms prepared.'

Alex and Lucinda exchanged a glance. Her slight pout seemed to reflect his own reluctance to accept Carol's invitation. She turned her gaze back to Carol and said, 'That's very kind, but—'

Her words were cut off by a sound like an avalanche of small rocks falling against the outside door as a violent gust of wind slammed a wall of water against the wood.

Carol's lips twisted into a smug smile as she nodded at the weather's intervention. 'You see? You'll be washed or blown away in that. I insist you stay. Supper will be in an hour. That will give you time to shower and change. There will be no problem finding suitable clothing for you, Alex.' Carol paused, giving Lucinda a look of puzzled dismay. 'And I'm sure something can be found for you too, Lucinda.'

Vee chimed in, 'It'll be dark soon. And you can be off early tomorrow.'

Alex glanced at his phone. It was five minutes past seven. 'It'll be light for at least another couple of hours. I'm sure we can make it through the rain. As Lucinda said, it's very kind of you to offer—'

'Marvellous. That's settled. Vee will show you to your rooms.'

As the door clicked shut behind Carol, Vee looked up from Hubert and said, 'There's no use arguing. Trust me.'

Alex turned to Lucinda who was scrunching the ends of her hair between the white folds of a towel. Rather than appearing annoyed or frustrated by Carol's latest orders, she wore a small, enigmatic smile. And, as he observed her, Alex decided if Lucinda wanted to make a break for it, he'd happily be her getaway driver. But, if she chose to comply with Carol's demands, he would stay and share the heat of whatever grilling awaited them at supper. He wasn't one to leave a man behind.

'What do you think?' he asked her.

'To be honest, I don't fancy making the journey home this late. Or through that.' She nodded towards the outer door where ominous bangs and rattles made it clear the elements were continuing their malevolent attempts to break through. She shrugged. 'I'll stay if you stay.'

As his eyes met Lucinda's calm green stare, Alex knew he should brave the storm and head back to London immediately. He had to pack for his extended stay with Sarah and James. And he had to have a difficult chat with Nicole. If he left that conversation until the next morning it would be more rushed than he would like. Then again, depending on how Nicole took the news, his having to leave the flat and stay away for a few weeks might be for the best.

He nodded at Lucinda. 'All right.'

Vee squealed and clapped her hands, making Hubert jump out of the towel. 'That's terrific! I'll go and check the staff know what's what. I'll meet you in the hall upstairs.'

'OK,' said Alex. 'I have to make a quick call anyway.'

'And I have to send some messages,' said Lucinda, unlocking her phone screen. 'I'll see you both up there.'

Chapter 16

Vee squealed again and danced out of the mud room, leaving Lucinda and Alex alone.

Alex made to follow her, then paused by the door and turned back. 'Are you really OK with staying?' he asked, his brow creased in concern. 'Because I honestly don't mind taking you to the station.'

'It's fine. I don't fancy going home this late and getting half drowned in the process. And when else will I get the chance to stay in a place like this?' She smiled as Alex's frown eased. 'But thank you.'

As they both busied themselves with patting the final drips from their hair, silence descended and a shiver of awkwardness crept across the back of Lucinda's neck. She rolled her shoulders and realised the tension which had been sinking its claws deep into her neck muscles for the past five years had vanished. The fall must have jolted it loose along with her simmering store of irritation and anxiety.

Harbouring resentment, making harsh judgements and picking fights had got her nothing but a sore bum and probably a few more wrinkles. Why continue fighting to keep her balance if the universe was going to continue pelting her with seismic shocks? Perhaps it was time to relax and be philosophical about her setbacks rather than furious?

So when Carol had declared they were to stay overnight, Lucinda had weighed her options calmly. Option one: head home through the rain and dark. Chris would open the door, take one look at her damp and dishevelled appearance and remind her he had told her that she should stay home. Then he'd bug her to call her brother. Ugh. More stress.

Option two: give herself the night off and luxuriate in being a guest in a great country house. Indulge in the rest she had hoped for. The idea made her smile: Jay would be delighted.

Although she wouldn't have stayed if Alex had decided to go. There would be nothing relaxing about going up against Carol's questioning without reinforcements and Becky had been right when she praised the strengths of a good team.

Thoughts of Becky reminded Lucinda of something she had been planning to do earlier in the afternoon. Putting the towel down on the bench next to her, she glanced at Alex. His right hand was resting on the door handle while his left swiped at his phone screen. She cleared her throat to get his attention and said, 'Jay wanted me to thank you.'

Alex looked up and his eyebrows lifted as Lucinda continued, 'For helping out with the creep at the dinner who grabbed her. You know, with the police thing you did. Thank you.'

'My pleasure.' Alex grinned. 'I was happy to be able to help.'

'Right. And, I suppose ... Well, I wanted to say sorry.' Alex's eyebrows twitched, apparently unable to rise any further. She swallowed and pushed on. 'For the thing I said about your roles. It was mean and ... I think I was taking something out on you which I shouldn't have. So I'm sorry.'

There! Lucinda allowed herself a small smile of satisfaction. She might have to accept that there were many things beyond her control, but at least she had finally put one small corner of her world to rights. If they'd been in the room, Jay and Becky would have been impressed. And Chris and Michael would have been amazed: they knew better than anyone how rare her apologies were.

Alex's grin stretched a little wider and his eyes sparkled. 'Apology accepted. And while we're on the subject, I'm sorry for shouting at you out there just now and—'

'No, no. There's no need. I definitely gave as good as I got. I'd had a really weird day and I was annoyed with Carol. But that was no reason for what I said just before I fell over.'

Alex tilted his head to one side and blinked, his features the perfect picture of puzzlement. Oh Lord, he wasn't going to make her say it again, was he?

Lucinda stammered. 'You remember? When I slipped I was in the middle of telling you to go fu—'

'You mean,' said Alex, his eyes wide and innocent, 'when you suggested I leave your presence to go and make love to myself with vigour?'

Lucinda snorted as the laughter bubbling in her chest spilled out. 'With vigour! Ha!'

Alex was quickly infected and, as she squeezed his eyes shut and chuckled along with her, Lucinda recalled their mutual giggling fit while sitting in the boggy meadow. When had she last laughed this much? And with someone else?

As the last of their laughter faded, Lucinda took a step towards Alex. 'How about we just agree to forget about it?' She extended her hand. 'Truce?'

He nodded and, as he shook her hand, a pleasurable buzz shot up Lucinda's arm. A feeling which fanned across her chest as Alex treated her to a dazzling smile and said, 'Truce.'

Chapter 17

Alone in the ground floor entrance hall, Alex sent Nicole a message to warn her he was about to call. He didn't want her to leap to answer, expecting news about her audition, only to be disappointed.

'Hey. What's going on?'

'It's a long story, but Carol's insisting we stay the night. I'll tell you all about it when I get home tomorrow.' Alex lifted his gaze from the marble floor to the chandelier. Where to start an explanation of the afternoon's events? 'I'm sorry—'

'It's absolutely fine, don't worry about it.'

Alex frowned. Nicole had never been jealous or possessive, but even by her breezy standards, she was being unusually relaxed.

'I should be back by lunchtime. If anything changes—'

'That's great, babe. Thanks for letting me know, but I really have to go, someone else is trying to get through. Enjoy your evening!'

The line went dead. Alex tapped the phone off his chin. Could Nicole's dismissiveness be explained by her waiting to hear back about her audition? Or was something else—

'I don't know exactly when. I guess before lunch if the trains are on time.' Lucinda marched into the hall from the back staircase, her voice honed to a sharp point. 'No ... Because I don't want you to come out in such terrible weather to get me, thank you ... OK, I'll let you know ... OK, bye.'

Pushing her phone into her back pocket, Lucinda joined Alex at the foot of the grand staircase. Her eyes were narrowed and she was biting her lower lip. Eager to prevent the phone call causing her to return to cool spikiness, Alex decided to throw caution to the wind and attempt another joke.

'Is some poor fool trying to look after you?'

Lucinda gave him a wry smile and her flinty glare softened: encouraging signs which caused his heart to skip a beat. 'Unfortunately, yes.' She sighed and her gaze mellowed further. 'He means well. But he never learns.'

Intrigued by who this troublesome 'he' might be, and pleased she had answered so easily, Alex was opening his mouth to follow up, when Vee bounded down the stairs.

'Everything's ready! Follow me!'

Halfway to the initial landing, Vee threaded her arm through Alex's. 'Please make yourselves at home. I made sure you're in the recently refurbished rooms. They're the best in this part of the house.' She beamed at Alex and, as she squeezed his arm, Lucinda's sneering comments about brazen flirting came back to him. Could Lucinda be right? Was Vee interested in him?

He waited in the corridor while Vee showed Lucinda her room. Listening to the younger woman's light, bubbly chatter, he leant towards the conclusion Vee was simply a tactile, friendly person. Although this tentative position was quickly undermined as she grabbed his arm to escort him the few metres to his room and clung on limpet-like once they'd crossed the threshold.

Maybe Lucinda had a point.

'You see!' Vee swept a hand to take in the gleaming oak floorboards, heavy velvet drapes and enormous double bed. Alex blinked: partly in astonishment that Russell House could continue to be ever more impressive; and partly against the glare from the many glittering surfaces.

'And through there'—Vee gestured to a door to the right of the bed—'is your bathroom. The shower is wonderful. It's a walk-in with oodles of jets and nozzles.' She gazed up at Alex through her long lashes and lowered her voice as she added, 'You know, it's large enough for two.'

Drat, he thought as he ushered Vee to the door with polite determination. Lucinda definitely had a point.

A fantastically scorching shower *alone* went some way to soothing his concerns about Vee and, for a few blissful minutes, Alex forgot the details of the bizarre situation he'd tumbled into.

Emerging from the bathroom wrapped in an ivory bath sheet and a billowing cloud of steam, he found an invisible presence had vanished his dirty clothes and left alternative garments on the bed. On first approach he thought they were the pieces of a simple black suit, but closer inspection revealed a dinner jacket with notched labels in a contrasting satin. Holding the pristine white shirt up to the light, Alex realised he was looking at a vintage ensemble which was almost identical to the outfits he'd seen on rails during his costume fittings for the film he was making at Compton Hall. And that was a period drama set in the 1920s.

Alex rubbed a hand across his forehead. His sensible side contemplated begging his host for more casual attire. But his inner child, who had always loved dressing up, was bouncing on his toes with excitement. Besides, he didn't want to appear picky or ungrateful, did he?

In a nod to the present century and the warmth of the day, Alex decided to go without the bow tie and left the top two buttons of the shirt open. Giving his reflection a critical appraisal in the mirror by the bathroom door, he had to admit the final result was striking, although maybe he was a little skinny? He'd always been slender, which had been a bonus when going up for roles in his twenties. But over the last decade he'd been forced to invest time in 'bulking up'. Apparently everyone now expected men on screen to have chiselled abs and bulging biceps. He frowned as a gloomy heaviness settled on his chest. Bloody wall-to-wall superhero movies! They were mostly to blame for such unrealistic standards. Them and ruddy Poldark.

He was tying the laces on the impeccably polished Oxford shoes he'd found nestling next to the bed when a quiet knocking made him startle. It seemed to be coming from the door to the left of the bedhead, which he had assumed opened into a cupboard. Although, as he drew nearer, he realised it was unlikely a cupboard would need a brass slide bolt underneath the handle.

The knocking was followed by a faint, 'Hello?' and, despite it being muffled by a heavy oak door, Alex recognised the voice immediately. The weight that had been squeezing his ribs lifted, replaced by a fluttering in his stomach, as he flicked back the bolt and flung open the door to find Lucinda standing in a room the mirror image of his own.

Her jaw dropped. 'Wow,' she muttered as she squared up to him and scanned his body from head to toe. Alex's skin prickled as her bright eyes lingered on his figure. Perhaps the spark between them wasn't one-sided after all? Maybe—

Lucinda laughed. And while it was a warm sound, it was a bucket of icy water over Alex's hopes and the fizzing in his tummy hardened into a cold knot of disappointment. She gestured to his suit. 'Wow!' she said again. 'No favouritism going on here at all. Oh no. Fair's fair!'

It was a somewhat cynical observation but, as he dropped his gaze from her face to glance at her clothing, Alex had to admit she was right again. While his clothes had been temporarily replaced by a dapper suit, Lucinda had been given ... a pale grey sack. The collar was high and frilly. There were more frills at the wrists. But otherwise the plain material dropped in a shapeless tube from neck to mid-calf. There was a proper word for that type of dress. He'd done a job a few years back where some of the supporting cast had to wear something similar. A tunic? A shift?

'Smock,' Lucinda said, pinching the front of the offending item and giving it a contemptuous tweak. 'If you're wondering what the heck this beauty is, it's a bloody smock.'

'It's not that bad.'

'You don't have to be polite. It's hideous.'

The crease between Lucinda's eyes told Alex there was no point trying to sugar-coat something so obviously bitter. 'Yes,' he said. 'You're right. It's hideous.'

Lucinda laughed again and completed a playful twirl, giving Alex the opportunity to shamelessly ogle the parts of her not covered by the washed-out slip: the small shuffle of her bare feet, the taper of her delicate ankles, and the soft waves of her damp hair. The butterflies in his tummy stirred again, threatening to take flight. 'But you look charming nonetheless. Are you ready for a light supper and heavy interrogation?'

'As I'll ever be. Oh, wait a sec.' Lucinda bustled over to the bed and slipped her feet into a pair of kitten-heel slippers. From the baby-blue fluff perched on the toe strap, Alex guessed they were a donation from Vee. 'That suit's an amazing fit,' said Lucinda as she grabbed her handbag from the bed and rummaged inside. 'Your shoes aren't quite as snazzy as mine though. Do they fit too?'

Alex watched as Lucinda extracted a pink tube from the bag and scurried over to the mirror. 'They're a couple of sizes too big. But the rest fits quite ...' He trailed off, distracted by Lucinda's no-nonsense lipstick application. She dabbed a few spots of the raspberry colour on her lips and then used her index finger to spread the tint. The final result was a subtle, smudged flush which made her lips appear a little swollen, as if—the thought came before Alex could swerve it—they had been kissed. Thoroughly kissed. With considerable energy and enthusiasm. By some lucky—

'There!' Lucinda rubbed the residual colour on her finger into her cheeks and turned to face him. 'What do you think?'

'Um…' Tearing his gaze from her lips before he was guilty of leering, Alex was grateful his mouth had gone dry. Snapping his mouth shut and swallowing gave him the seconds he needed to quash the perverse desire to answer her question truthfully. He ran a finger around the sides of his collar which, though unbuttoned, seemed to be straining against his racing pulse. Had it got tighter? And was it warmer in Lucinda's room than his?

Lucinda rolled her eyes at his stammering. 'That good, huh? Oh well, it'll have to do. Come on, comrade.' She beckoned for him to follow as she made for the door. 'Let's go and face the next round of the inquisition.'

Chapter 18

'Alex, darling! You look wonderful!'

'I knew that suit of Father's would fit you. And look how right I was. Like a glove!'

Loitering at the entrance to the dining room as Vee and Carol greeted Alex with thunderous enthusiasm, Lucinda considered the well-dressed trio as they moved to take their seats. Carol wore a floor-length salmon satin gown with a beaded neckline. Meanwhile, Vee was decked out in an open-backed velvet gown in midnight blue which flowed over her slender figure like an haute couture waterfall.

As she shuffled her straight-backed chair closer to the table, Lucinda glanced down at her grey dishrag of a dress. She was definitely the Cinderella at this ball. Although Cinderella would probably have had the skills to sew a few improving darts into the smock. Or persuade some woodland creatures to do it for her.

A member of the household staff drew thick damask drapes to shut out the rain-blackened sky, their movements stirring a faint smell of wood smoke from the fireplace. In the absence of natural light, two chandeliers struggled to chase the gloom from a space dominated by patterned burgundy wallpaper and mahogany furnishings. The imposing dining table, long enough to seat five along each side, dominated the room.

Poor Hubert had been banished from the gathering by Carol. Fidgeting with the white linen napkin in her lap, Lucinda realised she missed the beagle and the levity he would have brought to the stifling, formal atmosphere. Fussing over the little dog would also have been a pleasant distraction from the exhausting spectacle on the opposite side of the table: Vee flirting with Alex.

'I'll never be able to thank you enough for rescuing my Huey!' the young woman said in a breathy voice as she batted her eyelashes at Alex and pressed her fingers to the back of his hand.

Giving her a tight-lipped smile, Alex lifted his hand away from her touch and towards Lucinda. 'Honestly, Lucinda had far more to do with finding him than I did. I didn't really—'

'And you really do look amazing in that suit!' The non sequitur was accompanied by more eyelash fluttering and the back of her fingers trailing along Alex's sleeve.

'Um. Thank you. It's very well made.'

Oblivious to Alex's small twitches of discomfort and the clipped tone of his replies, Vee opened her mouth to no doubt further her advances when—thank the Lord!— Carol cut in. 'Ah! At last!' Their host straightened in her seat as the staff member returned to the room carrying two large plates. 'Here's supper.'

Lucinda's stomach rumbled in anticipation of food but when her plate was laid on the table her tummy flipped and squeezed as if shrinking back in self-defence. She knew overcooked, reheated meat when she saw it. The cut sprawled on her plate had been abandoned in a pool of brown, gelatinous goop, accompanied in its hellish afterlife by a few unrecognisable root vegetables.

As Lucinda poked at the lumpy gloop with her fork—she would rather die than dare serve anything so substandard!—Alex lifted a forkful of generic vegetables to his mouth. Chewing and swallowing followed and Lucinda wrinkled her nose again at the thought of their stringy texture. But her eyes widened as her gaze followed the fork back to the table and observed the vegetables still skewered on the prongs. A smile played at the corners of her mouth as she cut off a scrap of meat. Was 'Pretend Eating 101' an official acting class? And, more importantly, could she pull off the same trick without Alex's training?

'Do you not like the lamb, Alex?' asked Carol from the head of the table.

'Um, yes. Usually I do. But ...' Lucinda's eyes widened further. If he told the truth about the inedible fare she would be shocked by his rudeness. But he would also have her unqualified respect for calling out such offensive catering. It would be a struggle not to applaud.

She held her breath as he continued. 'But I'm on this vegan challenge thing at the moment. So I can't—'

'Oh yes!' Vee—who was opting for a liquid diet of red wine—gave Alex a knowing smile. 'I saw that on Nicole's Instagram. The thirty-day Vegan Challenge. What a wonderful idea!'

'Yes. Wonderful,' said Alex in the dejected tone of a man who Lucinda suspected would kill for a medium-rare peppercorn steak. Although, she reasoned as she jabbed at the so-called lamb on her plate, he must care for his girlfriend a lot to support her by joining in on a challenge he didn't seem overly enthused by.

'Nicole's amazing on Instagram,' Vee said, beaming at the side of Alex's face.

Alex made a non-committal grunt while hacking at another anonymous vegetable.

Undeterred, Vee continued. 'I've noticed you're not on social media much, though.'

'Not really. I try to remember to post about work but I'm not great at that stuff. I always worry I'll press the wrong button and break the internet.'

Lucinda nodded in an expression of fellow feeling. She muddled through on Facebook to keep up with what her mum and brother were up to in Spain. But Misha and Jay had taken over updating the business's Instagram and other accounts when it became clear to them it was a task far from Lucinda's forte.

'How funny!' Vee giggled and knocked back another sizeable gulp of wine. 'Given the recent interest in you online, I mean.'

Having won the fight against a mouthful of gummy lamb, Carol said, 'You didn't finish explaining all that business to me, Veronica. Perhaps Alex can enlighten me.'

Every line of Alex's loose posture snapped into an expectant rigidity. For a moment Lucinda worried he was freezing again, but then she noticed the dash of pink creeping across his cheeks. That was new.

She frowned. Jay had mentioned something about Mumsweb and Alex going viral, hadn't she? Surely that would be a good thing for his career? Why would talking about it make him uncomfortable?

Alex shook his head and trained his attention on his plate. 'Oh, it was a lot of fuss over nothing.'

'Hardly!' Vee drained her glass and grabbed the bottle. The glugging of the Bordeaux formed a liquid accompaniment to her speech as she directed her words to Carol, probably assuming Lucinda was already up to speed. 'Someone started a thread—that's like an online group conversation—asking people about the sexiest children's television presenters.' Carol tutted and rolled her eyes, but Vee carried on. 'Which soon developed into a conversation about weird crushes. And that was when someone mentioned they fancied the guy who did the voiceover on an advert even though they hadn't seen him. And then loads of people were like "Oh my God, you're right, his voice is sooo dreamy"'—she paused to bat her eyelashes at Alex, a pointless move because he was staring determinedly at his cutlery—'and then I guess the thread went viral because of everyone agreeing and also because it was so ... well ... odd.'

An angry flush stole across the alluring *V* of bare skin at Alex's neck and his jaw muscles tensed. Lucinda's frown deepened as she sipped her water. What could possibly be mortally embarrassing about this advert?

'Odd?' Carol paused her sawing at the excuse for meat on her plate. 'How so?'

'I suppose in this case, people thought it was odd for the woman who originally wrote the post to find the voice attractive because of what the advert was for.' Vee shrugged. 'You know, because it was for Salvan.'

Lucinda spluttered, choking on her water. She grabbed for her napkin and covered her mouth as she coughed.

'And I am supposed to have heard of this Salvan?' asked Carol.

Having merrily recounted most of the story, Vee now stammered. 'It's … um … well, it's …'

Alex flicked his gaze up to Carol and then back to the table. 'It's haemorrhoid ointment,' he said, his voice a low blast of air from between gritted teeth.

Lucinda coughed again, her shoulders trembling as she hid her twitching lips behind her napkin. She shouldn't laugh. It was a puerile response to the mention of a thoroughly practical product. A medical one at that. Nope. It wasn't funny. Not at all.

Her sobering thoughts did nothing to quell her childish urge to giggle. However, where mature reasoning had failed, the sight of Alex succeeded. A chill trickled down her spine as she noticed the flush of mortification had reached his hairline and he was fiddling with the handle of his steak knife as if pondering whether to fall on it.

Lucinda took another sip of water to drown any remaining giggles. What could she do to draw the heat off Alex and out of his face? Perhaps she could use his earlier trick and offer up some personal information to interest her hosts? But did she have anything that could tempt them? Thanks to Carol's private dirt-digging, there could be little she didn't already know.

It was Vee who provided Lucinda with inspiration. 'It's surprising how salacious some of the comments were. Given the website is supposed to be for mothers to exchange advice and—'

'My mum's getting married again!' The words shot out of Lucinda, far louder than she had intended, but they had the desired effect. Carol and Vee's attention swung towards her, like the headlamps of a juggernaut changing course.

'Was this a surprise?' The high pitch of Carol's voice suggested it was certainly news to her.

Ha! thought Lucinda, the great Lady Russell didn't know everything after all. 'Yes,' she said. 'A great surprise.'

'Because she's so old?' Vee asked.

Alex swung a look of appalled astonishment at Vee but Lucinda, who had noticed how the younger woman had started to slur her words, was happy to cut her some slack.

'No,' Lucinda said. 'It's surprising because she swore she'd never marry again.'

'Of course!' Carol paused her vigorous chewing, which must have been putting her recently repaired heart to the test. 'After what happened with your father, that is understandable.'

Determined to lead Carol away from further revelations about her past, Lucinda pushed on with details about the present. 'Yes.' She took a deep breath, preparing herself to deliver the details of her mother's manifesto in a single run. 'But mostly because she's always said true love is nothing but a palliative fiction and marriage is an outdated patriarchal institution which only continues to survive thanks to a romantic mythology which furthers the cynical economic interests of various industries.'

She took another gulp of water and glanced at her dumbstruck audience. Their furrowed brows and open mouths were pretty standard responses. As was the pensive silence, into which the ticking of the ornate gold carriage clock on the mantelpiece boomed.

Alex rallied first. 'So ... if, in your mother's view, love doesn't exist ...' He pressed his lips into a thin line as he considering his next words. 'How does she explain people falling in love all the time?'

Lucinda snorted. 'Your evidence for the existence of love is the falling?'

'After our run-in with gravity today, you must believe in falling?'

'I believe in *physics*, sure. But falling in love? As in—'

'A racing heart, sweaty palms ... You can't wait to be with the object of your affection, you dream about them, think about them all the time and you feel ... almost euphoric in their company.'

As if Alex's words had conjured the effect they described, Lucinda's pulse accelerated as she held his dark stare.

'How do you explain all that,' he asked, 'if it's all a lie cooked up by capitalism?'

Lucinda cleared her throat, relieved to be back on solid ground. She had this part of the sermon down pat. 'It all starts with attraction. Hormones, pheromones, whatever. Your body makes dopamine, adrenaline and serotonin.' She extended three fingers one at a time for emphasis. 'They give you a natural, addictive high. Your body basically drugs you. But you get used to it and the effect wears off in time.'

'Hmn.' Alex took a sip of water and Lucinda was unable to tear her gaze from his sparkling eyes. A pleasant wooziness—which she would have attributed to the wine if she had drunk any—rolled along her limbs as he held her stare. 'And you agree with your mother's theories?' he asked, placing his drink back on the table.

'Yes.' Lucinda tipped her head from side to side. 'On the whole.'

'So you don't believe in true love?'

'Not as any magical, mystical force that makes the world go round. No.'

'But as a temporary effect of serotonin, adrenaline and ...'

'Dopamine.'

'Right, dopamine, yes. So, what I think you're saying is: you don't believe in true love, but you don't deny the very real existence and undeniable power of *chemistry*.'

He dropped his pitch as he uttered the final word and raised an eyebrow. His lips curled at one side and Lucinda's face heated as her own lips parted. Once again she was struck by conflicting impulses: part of her ached to drive the point of a feathery slipper into his shin as payback for being such an infuriatingly witty smartarse, while another urged her to throw herself across the table, wrap herself round him and kiss all the smug off his gorgeous face.

The clatter of steel striking china made Lucinda startle. Carol had laid down her cutlery, a sign of surrender in the face of the lamb's enduring opposition. Lucinda blinked as she emerged from her trance and reached for her glass with a shaky hand.

'Well!' said Vee, draping a hand on Alex's shoulder. 'I, for one, believe in the undeniabu ...' She squinted and took another slurred run at the pesky polysyllables, 'Undeniabubull power of chemistry.' A droopy-eyed stare accompanied the sentiment, making Alex stammer and direct his gaze back to the table top.

Enough was enough. Lucinda swept up her napkin and dropped it beside her plate. It was time to take control of another small slice of her destiny before Vee's flirting and the smell of the 'food' made her nauseous. 'If you'll excuse me,' she said, pushing her chair back, 'I suddenly feel exhausted. I think all the excitement from the search for Hubert has caught up with me.'

'Blasted mongrel!' said Carol. 'Are you sure you won't stay for dessert?'

Lucinda's stomach turned over at the thought of what congealed horrors awaited them in the kitchen. 'No, thank you. I think I'll head straight up to bed.'

'I'll come with you. That is ... I mean ... I think I'll do the same,' said Alex, jumping to his feet. 'It's getting late.'

'But it's only nine o'clock!' said Vee with a disappointed whine.

'I suppose I should also retire,' said Carol, making no effort to stand. 'I am still recuperating.'

Lucinda saw her opportunity and leapt for it. 'That's probably a good idea. Thank you for dinner. Goodnight.'

Lucinda loitered at the bottom of the stairs, waiting to make sure Alex also escaped. He appeared in the dining room doorway a moment after she had fled, but his progress was halted by Vee. The young woman placed a hand on Alex's arm and stood on tiptoe to put her lips close to his ear. Whatever she whispered made Alex recoil as if stung, whirl around and stride across the hall.

'Shall we?' he said to Lucinda as he passed her, attacking the stairs two at a time.

Lucinda kicked off her slippers and hurried after him. She didn't catch up until he had sprinted through his bedroom door and slammed it behind him. A second later, he yanked it open and glanced at Lucinda from under his furrowed brow. With a weak half-smile, he said, 'Goodnight, Lucinda.'

'Goodnight, Alex,' she said as he vanished once more into his room.

Lucinda closed her own door carefully and placed the slippers by the bed. She strolled into the centre of the room, enjoying the softness of the colourful floor rug underfoot. After being smothered by the fire-warmed air of the dining room, the pleasant room temperature and the absence of offensive food smells made it much easier to think. She stared at the connecting door to Alex's room and mulled over his flight from the dining room. What had Vee said to him?

Eventually, her gaze settled on the open brass bolt beneath the door handle which, she noticed, was identical to the one on her room's outer door.

An idea taking shape, she paced over to the connecting door and knocked. 'Alex?'

Muffled footsteps approached and the door was flung open. Alex's harassed expression had been replaced by pinched concern. 'Are you OK?'

'Yes, I'm fine. Thanks. I just wanted to check something.' Keeping her feet planted in her own room, she leant over the threshold enough to get a clear view of his outer door. And ... there! She knew it! She swayed back and rested her shoulder against the door frame. 'We should swap rooms.'

'What? Why?'

'Your bedroom door doesn't have a lock.' She tilted her head back towards her own door. 'Mine does.'

Alex frowned and stepped forwards. The height difference between them brought Lucinda's face close to his chest and, as a delicious smell of citrus and—was that mint?—washed over her, she was transported back to the moment she had fallen against him in the lift. It was a struggle not to lift her nose and sniff to better appreciate the scent.

Meanwhile, the crease between Alex's eyes deepened as he peered over Lucinda's head in the direction of her outer bedroom door. 'I see,' he said. 'That is odd.'

'Odd both rooms don't have a lock, or odd Vee just happened to give you the one without one?'

'Huh.' Alex rubbed the furrows on his brow. 'Both, although the latter could be seen as more suspicious—'

'If we switch rooms we could save everyone a lot of embarrassment.'

'Yes, I suppose.'

'Unless, of course, you'd like a midnight visitor—'

Alex's eyes widened in horror. 'No!'

'She's very pretty,' said Lucinda, her blithe tone a sharp contrast to that of the voice inside her head which was asking her what on earth she was doing. Why was she suddenly in the business of encouraging men with girlfriends into flings? 'And she's obviously keen.'

'She's almost twenty years younger than me and obviously drunk.'

'That would be some guys' type.'

Alex's lips drew into a firm line and tone shifted into a hard mixture of hurt and annoyance. 'Well it certainly isn't mine.'

'OK. Sorry.' Lucinda's insides clenched as if she'd made the mistake of eating the lamb. She bit her lip. How could she claw this one back? 'I didn't mean to suggest you were ... Sorry. Really.'

Alex shoved his hands into his pockets and trained his gaze on the floor.

'Please swap with me,' said Lucinda. 'Come on. It'll make me feel better about having accidentally suggested you're a pervy cradle-snatching creep.'

Alex laughed and the shine in his eyes suggested amusement had taken the edge off any offence she'd caused. 'I suppose, if it will make you feel better.'

'Great,' she said, a grin spreading across her face. 'Give me a minute.'

As she gathered her belongings, Lucinda replayed their conversation and realised Alex hadn't listed having a girlfriend among his reasons for wanting to dodge Vee. Filing the thought in her rapidly expanding mental folder for interesting Alex-related observations, she left the bathroom and arrived at the doorway at the same time as Alex.

Giving each other nervous smiles and avoiding direct eye contact, they turned to sidle past each other in an incredibly English dance of muttered apologies, all while clutching the bundles of toiletries, towels and the nightwear which had been left by their beds while they were at dinner. As she came within inches of brushing against Alex, Lucinda made sure to breathe through her mouth. The poor excuse for an evening meal had left her famished and if she caught another hint of Alex's scent she wasn't sure she would be able to resist taking a bite out of him.

Alex turned to close the connecting door. 'Lucinda?'

'Hmn?'

'Thanks for switching rooms. Thanks'—he paused and fixed her with a meaningful stare before continuing—'for *looking out* for me.'

Lucinda's raised her eyebrows as one side of Alex's mouth curved into his cheeky, lopsided smile and a twinkle stole into his eyes. Whatever his flaws, his talent for elegant point-scoring was undeniable. In contrast, her own technique was blunt and childish. But, in her experience, also effective.

Her heartbeat picking up in anticipation of the shot she was about to fire, she said, 'You're welcome. I wouldn't want to make myself a pain in the backside. Even though I guess you already have a cream for that.'

'Oof!' Alex grimaced, then smiled. 'Was that a Salvan joke?'

Fighting to suppress a rising wave of giggles, she shrugged. 'Might have been.'

'And I'm guessing it's not your only one, is it?'

'Oh no. I have *piles* and *piles* of them.'

Alex clutched his guts as if her words had been bullets and threw himself face down onto the bed with a dramatic groan. Without lifting his head from the mattress he said, 'I asked for that. Goodnight, Lucinda.'

'I mean obviously no one likes to be the *butt* of a joke—'

'*Goodnight*, Lucinda.'

'Goodnight, Alex.'

Lucinda clicked the door shut and rested her back against it, enjoying the gentle squeezing sensation which was swelling against her ribs and blooming into a warm tingling in her limbs. It was an unfamiliar but pleasant feeling, not entirely unlike a hug.

Chapter 19

A summer breeze chased clusters of smoky clouds across the sky as the earliest stars burned into view over the gardens. The weather had calmed and, as he swept a curtain across the window with a sigh, Alex wished he could say the same about his turbulent mind.

How was he supposed to sleep with his thoughts and feelings in such a tangle? He was relieved to have dodged Vee, worried about Nicole and work, and charmed by Lucinda's increasingly fascinating company. And even contemplating sleep brought an additional layer of anxiety for, based on his experience over the past week, it was likely to evade him and be peppered with nightmares when it finally showed up.

But, overriding all these competing claims for his attention was his empty belly. He pressed a hand to his stomach as it issued another roar of neglect. Whatever might be going on in his head, he stood absolutely no chance of getting to sleep without silencing the gnawing racket.

There was nothing else for it: a mission to the kitchen was the only solution. There might be a member of the household staff down there and they were unlikely to deny him some toast if asked politely, right?

As he removed his jacket and rolled up his shirtsleeves, he glanced at the connecting door to Lucinda's room and considered inviting her along. From the fleeting wrinkle of her nose as she had prodded her food, he assumed she had found the meal as repulsive as he did.

He wandered over to the connecting door and was raising his hand to knock when he paused. He had taken Lucinda's earlier claims of exhaustion to be a polite excuse for abandoning the dining room—a smart ploy he wished had occurred to him—but perhaps she truly had been tired and was already asleep. Pressing his ear to the wood, he held his breath. But the sole return for his patient listening was a stab of disappointment.

Not wanting to disturb Lucinda or his hosts, Alex crept down to the hall, banked left, ducked under the wall hanging at the back of the room and tiptoed down the gloomy iron staircase to the basement.

His progress was halted by an unlikely sound echoing along the bare walls of the narrow corridor: the strains of late eighties synth-pop. Following the melody along the passageway, Alex found the door to the third room on the left was ajar and he nudged it with his fingertips.

While singing along to 'Just Can't Get Enough', Lucinda was engrossed in systematically plundering the kitchen. Once the contents of one cabinet had been scanned and prodded, she moved on to the next, flicking the marine-blue cupboard fronts closed with a flourish and swaying

174

along in time with the music. Her hair had been clipped casually into a messy pile at the back of her head and as she grabbed a frying pan and clanked it onto the hob in the centre of the largest island unit a strand came loose.

Alex beamed as Lucinda retrieved a wooden spoon from an under-counter drawer and used it to provide a percussion accompaniment to the chorus. For a moment his hunger lost its dominance, edged out by a glow of affection for the relaxed, comfortable Lucinda who continued to drum the granite countertop as she inspected the contents of one half of a standing fridge the size of a double wardrobe.

Alex would have been content to stay hidden until the end of the song, tapping his foot and enjoying Lucinda's impressive interpretation of a pop classic, but Hubert had other ideas.

The beagle, who had been lying on a tartan velour dog bed next to the garden door, snapped his head towards Alex, barked and padded across the slate floor tiles, his tail wagging furiously.

Alex bent to pat his head and glanced up. Lucinda was depositing the packets and tubs she had removed from the fridge next to the hobs while watching him with the sheepish smile of a child caught raiding the cookie jar.

'I went downstairs and found Vee finishing off the wine. She said I could make myself anything I wanted,' Lucinda said, nervously eyeing the food on the counter.

'In that case, it would be rude not to.' Alex drew up to the opposite side of the island and tipped his head towards Lucinda's phone, the source of the music. 'Depeche Mode, huh?'

'Oh!' Lucinda grabbed her phone and silenced the tune. 'I've got lots of different playlists.'

'I wasn't complaining. It's a great song.'

'It is. And I like allsorts. Although'—she frowned as she scrolled—'the ones I have here are mostly a shedload of eighties and nineties random stuff.'

'A fair description of my adolescence.'

She chuckled. 'Mine too.'

Alex would have loved to ask her what else was on one of her random playlists, but his stomach rumbles escalated to pangs. 'So,' he said, glancing at the spoils of her search, 'what were you making?'

'You would not believe the fantastic produce they have in the fridge and cupboards. Look!' She picked up a packet of bacon. 'This is from a farm right here on the estate. Those eggs too. All free range, organic ...' One of her hands landed on a jutting hip and the other slapped down on the counter. 'I could have made us over a hundred different, tasty dishes. I don't understand how anyone could serve that reheated excuse for lamb.'

She winced and, at the memory of the tough lumps of meat in brown slop, Alex mirrored her grimace. But apparently even the thought of their nausea-inducing supper couldn't dampen Alex's appetite and his tummy grumbled and roared.

Lucinda glanced at his midriff and raised an eyebrow. 'I was going to make the fluffiest scrambled eggs in the world, served with some perfectly crisped rashers of this beautiful salty bacon. And maybe some pan-fried cherry tomatoes. It'll take less than ten minutes.' Under the row of spotlights above the island, her green eyes glinted with mischief. 'Would you like some?'

Alex's mouth had filled with saliva. He swallowed. 'I shouldn't.'

'You're actually doing the vegan thing? I thought that was just a brilliant excuse not to have to eat the lamb.'

Alex stared longingly at the bacon and eggs and pressed a hand to his guts which were yelling at him to take what the nice lady was offering.

'It's great you're supporting your girlfriend,' Lucinda said, plucking an egg from the box and cracking it into a ceramic bowl. 'When are the thirty days up?'

'Today's the last day.'

'Hmn.' She cracked a second egg. 'Then you have fewer than three hours left.' The third egg split. 'So if you eat this now, how about you promise not to eat any cheeseburgers between midnight and 3 a.m. to compensate?'

She broke the final egg, picked up a whisk and twirled the handle between her fingers. Her impish smile and stare formed a coy challenge, the irresistible offer of an emerald-eyed temptress.

'Well?' Lucinda poured some milk into the bowl and began to whisk. 'Can I tempt you?'

'Yes,' he said, answering a little too quickly.

'Great. Although I expect you'll have to defend your bacon from Hubert. Could you go through the cupboards and see if there's anything more dog friendly? Biscuits or something?'

As Lucinda drizzled olive oil into a pan, Alex paced over to the right side of the kitchen and began opening cupboards, grateful for a task to distract him from his gnawing insides. He turned up a stack of white plates and carried two over to Lucinda. 'I thought these might be useful.'

'Thanks. Just put them there. Tomatoes sorted.' She put a lid on the pan and moved on to the bacon. Within moments it was sizzling and the smell was so terrific, Alex retreated to the far cupboards to stop himself drooling.

Lucinda drew in a long, slow breath through her nose and sighed as she turned the bacon over. 'I honestly don't know how your girlfriend persuaded you to sign up for that challenge. One sniff of bacon and my resolve would crumble.'

'I didn't have much of a say in it. I came home to find the kitchen had been emptied of all animal products.'

'What?!'

'I know.' The pinch of the memory was softened by the triumph of finding a sack of dog biscuits in a low cupboard. Alex grabbed it and Hubert trailed him back to the island.

'Was it a lot of stuff?

'A bit of milk, butter, a few eggs, cheese and some sausages.'

Lucinda poured the beaten eggs into the third pan and looked up, her gaze serious. 'Please don't tell me she binned it ...' Alex raised his eyebrows and Lucinda made a grunt of disgust. 'That is criminal. You're a better person than me. I'd have been straight down the nearest kebab shop in protest.'

Alex chuckled and, as Lucinda heaped scrambled eggs onto their plates, decided to risk asking her a personal question. 'Speaking of protests, I got the impression you weren't delighted with Carol's snooping either.'

'Not overly impressed, no.' Lucinda rapped the spoon off the pan to dislodge the last of the eggs, probably imagining the metal was Carol's meddling head.

'So, if you don't want to answer, I get it, but ...'

Lucinda snorted as she served up the bacon and tomatoes. 'I will happily answer as long as you let me eat a few mouthfuls of this first.' Nodding in satisfaction at her work, she pushed one of the plates towards Alex and handed him cutlery.

'Deal.' He scooped a forkful of the fluffiest, creamiest scrambled eggs he'd ever tasted into his mouth and closed his eyes, basking in the heavenly flavours caressing his taste buds. 'Mmm. This is so good.'

Lucinda paused her chewing to give him a smug smile. 'Told you.' She took a large bite of bacon before rummaging in the bag Alex had left on the counter and crouching to give a whingeing Hubert a biscuit. 'Anyway ... You have questions?'

Alex leant an elbow against the counter and frowned as he remembered Carol's revelations about Lucinda's ex-fiancé. Fortified and emboldened by divine calories, but keeping one eye on Lucinda's knife just in case, he asked, 'If true love is a ...'

'Palliative fiction.'

'Thank you. Then why were you engaged? If you were going to marry someone, weren't you in love with them?'

'I loved him. Still do, actually. Chris is a great bloke.' She considered her next words while swallowing another mouthful. 'I guess it made sense? We met at work when we were in our twenties, became friends in our early thirties and when we started dating it was really ... comfortable.' She winced, possibly touched by how underwhelming her choice of word made her decision to date Chris sound. 'And then we were spending so much time at each other's places, it seemed sensible to move in together. He was about to start working in his parents' restaurant and suggested we buy a place near them. Which is how we ended up in the Comptons. We'd been in the house a couple of years when he proposed and he's a great guy, we had a joint mortgage and his family had adopted me.' She shrugged. 'Marriage seemed like the logical next step.'

'Makes sense.' Alex nodded and noticed the tension in Lucinda's shoulders release. Had she been worried about his opinion? Lucinda hadn't struck him as someone who was particularly concerned about anyone else judging her. The thought she might care about what he thought about anything made him itch to turn the eighties and nineties tunes back on and dance. It was with effort he kept his feet still as he asked, 'You split up before the wedding?'

'Yes.'

'But you still live together?'

'We live in the same house.'

'OK … Do you mind if I ask what happened?'

'Uf! That's a story.' Lucinda removed two tall glasses from a cupboard behind her. 'Tap water all right?'

'Great, thank you.' As Lucinda filled the glasses, Alex finished his meal and sighed as he appreciated the final bite which had been as delicious as the first. Lucinda must have ended her engagement to Chris because who in their right mind would willingly split up with someone who could cook such fantastic food?

Lucinda took a sip of water. 'We'd been engaged nearly a year, living together for two. He was doing his normal shift at work, looked through the serving hatch and noticed a customer. Their eyes met across the dining room and he said it was like being run over by a high-speed train.'

Alex's lips parted as he recognised the description. It wasn't too different from how he'd felt the first time he'd laid eyes on Kelly. In a stunned whisper, he said, 'The lightning bolt.'

'Yep. A dopamine, serotonin and adrenaline-supercharged lightning bolt.'

'I'm sorry. That must have been rubbish for you.'

She waved a hand in front of her face. 'It was probably for the best.'

'So how come he's still living with you if he found this soulmate elsewhere?'

Lucinda huffed a laugh. 'Unfortunately for Chris, Janine didn't feel the same irresistible pull towards him.'

Alex's jaw dropped. 'What ... but ... it went nowhere?'

'Correct.'

'And he still told you about it?'

'Ha! If you'd met Chris, you'd get it. Chris ... he doesn't have much of a filter. Which can be great, because you know he won't lie to you, but it doesn't do him any favours.'

Alex shook his head, hoping it would settle his incredulity. 'So he tells you—the woman he's going to marry—he's fallen in love with another woman at first sight, without having checked her feelings about this?'

'Crazy, right? But he said he couldn't marry me. He was completely bowled over, love-struck, mad about her. And he'd never felt that way ... about me.'

For Alex, learning to act had mostly been an exercise in understanding how to truly listen. How to hear and understand more than someone's words. And in Lucinda's pause he heard the downwards flicker of one side of her mouth, the brief contraction of her brows and the sheen in her eyes as she finished her sentence. He heard how much Chris's candour had hurt her.

Lucinda shrugged. 'I had to admire his honesty. After all, he sleeps in the same house as me and knows how handy I am with a knife.'

Alex chuckled and hoped she wouldn't notice his smile didn't reach his eyes.

'And his mother tortures him about it, even now.' Lucinda grinned. 'Now she *does* love me.' Her smile fell. 'Seriously, though. It was really sad watching his heart break when Janine turned him down. He's a good person and didn't set out to hurt anyone.'

'A good man brought down by chemistry.'

'Ha! Exactly.'

'But … what about *your* heart?'

'A bit bruised, but intact. I guess if you don't give someone your whole heart it's pretty hard for them to break it.'

Alex nodded, a heaviness settling in his stomach as Lucinda's words hit home. Though he hadn't realised it until a couple of years ago, he'd been shielding his heart since Kelly had left him and their marriage. The epiphany had come while playing a small part in a television drama series. His character was a long-term commitment-phobe and, during a confrontational scene, was told by an angry ex that he only ever went into a relationship if it had a built-in escape hatch. The idea had resonated with him at the time and, after turning it over, the truth became unavoidable: since Kelly, he hadn't started dating a woman if he couldn't already envisage how their affair would end. And end with minimal damage to them both.

Lucinda refilled his glass. As she set it on the counter in front of him, he noted her pinched expression and sensed she was about to say something she found difficult.

'I watched *Napier*,' she said. 'I've still got the last two episodes left, so no spoilers!' She smiled and lowered her gaze to follow her finger along one of the silver veins in the countertop. 'I see what all the fuss is about. It's a great show.'

'Thank you.'

'And I think you're perfectly cast as Dexter Hartford. Your family must be proud of you.'

'Huh.' Alex didn't want to unburden the depths of his mum's and brother's disapproval of his choice of career onto Lucinda, but felt compelled to give her more. 'My family have never been delighted by what I do for a living. They think I should have gone into something more reliable.'

'It must be hard. Not always knowing what your next job is. Especially with having to afford London prices.' Lucinda lifted her gaze to meet his. 'Did you ever think of doing something else?'

'Sure.' Alex knew of no actor who, after seemingly endless rejections, hadn't thought of packing it in. Those who stayed in the business grew a thick skin fast. Although Alex found it wasn't the horrifically personal rejections which did the most damage, but the false hope of the near misses. Friends transitioning to successful alternative careers with regular incomes and private pensions had given him pause. But for all the precariousness, Alex knew he'd never be happy doing anything else. Acting was possibly the only job on the planet where by becoming someone else you got the chance to discover who you were. Ugh! He rubbed a thumb over his brow. How could he say any of that to Lucinda without sounding like a pretentious tit?

'I've thought about getting a nine-to-five job loads of times. Mostly in my late twenties. But … but …'

'You're not a quitter.'

Alex nodded. It wasn't exactly what he'd been trying to say, but it was close enough. Besides, he liked the way Lucinda looked at him as she said it. A warm gleam flashed in her eyes that might have been respect and, as he noticed it, a matching shimmer of warmth coursed throughout Alex's entire body.

'Dessert?' she asked. 'I could whip us up a jam sponge pudding.'

Alex placed a hand on his quiet, content belly. 'I shouldn't.'

'If it's the lack of custard that's putting you off, I can make some in fifteen minutes. It won't be my best, but what is a pudding without custard?'

'Um … It's tempting, but …'

'It's not your favourite.'

'No, but—'

'What is?'

'Uh …' Alex scanned a mental gallery of all the puddings he loved but rarely ate. 'Sticky toffee pudding. With custard.'

'Good choice. I make an excellent sticky toffee pud. But it'd be midnight before it would be finished—'

'Honestly, it's fine. I have to fit into some pretty tight trousers on Monday.'

'Because you always start the week with tight-fitting clothes, or …'

'I start filming at Compton Hall. It's a period drama and the trousers are, let's say … snug around the waist.' And everywhere else. He should probably do a few squats and lunges before going to bed.

'That's this Monday? Wow. How long will you be in the Comptons for?'

'Three to four weeks. Perhaps a bit longer.'

'And you're commuting from north London?'

'I'm staying at my brother's place. He and his wife live in Wolston.'

'You'll be down the road! That's handy,' Lucinda said as she began to fill the sink with water.

'Hey! Leave that. You cooked. I'm washing up.' Alex moved to Lucinda's side and poured dish soap into the sink.

'Are you looking forward to your triumphant return to Compton Hall?' Lucinda stepped back and leant against the counter, watching him clean the dishes. 'Hopefully this time you won't have to deal with any creeps.'

'Hmn,' said Alex, his thoughts flying to Ray.

'Oh dear. Did I speak too soon?'

Alex sighed. He hated badmouthing anyone. And, like most industries, it was unwise in case a moment's indiscretion came back to bite you. But Lucinda had no connection to anyone involved, so perhaps it couldn't hurt. 'Ray Veasey is in the cast.'

'Ray Veasey as in the guy who plays Frank Buchanan in *Napier*?'

Alex paused his scrubbing and glanced at Lucinda, impressed. 'That's the one.'

'Is he stalking you?'

Alex snorted. 'You might think that. He was in my year at drama school. We're the same age, similar heights, builds, colouring … we've been going to the same auditions our whole careers. We've been the last two for jobs a few times.'

'And if you didn't get the job, Ray did.'

'And vice versa.' Alex scrubbed the last of the pans viciously, picturing Ray's smug face as he told him he'd got the part. Again. 'We played brothers once.'

Lucinda must have noticed the energetic scouring. 'But you don't get on?'

'Oh everyone gets on with Ray. He's *a character*. Charming, tells funny stories … but he can be cruel and I've seen him be rude to anyone he considers less important than him.'

Lucinda twisted her lips, considering. 'Hmn. Is he rude to the caterers?'

'Yes.'

'Say no more. He's clearly a total knob.'

Alex laughed, relaxing into a proper chuckle as he pulled the plug out of the sink and dried his hands. 'You said it, not me.'

Giggling and whispering, Lucinda and Alex sneaked back upstairs. Alex was so distracted by the fizz of happiness in his chest, it took him a moment to notice they had accidentally returned to their original rooms. As he was walking towards the connecting door there was a knock from the other side.

The door swung open and, still chuckling, Lucinda said, 'Wrong room.'

Alex smiled and allowed himself a second to take her in. She was still wearing the hideous grey shift but, ever since they went into the puddle, it was as if she was surrounded by a colourful aura not even a washed-out smock could dampen.

They passed each other in the doorway and Alex paused. Perhaps he should risk another question. One that would probably have earned him death from pre-puddle Lucinda.

'I've been thinking about your mum's theories. About true love and whatnot. They're rules, right?'

Lucinda shrugged. 'I suppose.'

'But isn't there an exception to every rule? And your mum, she's found it with ...' He circled his hand, waiting for Lucinda to supply a name.

'Graham.'

'Right.'

Lucinda blinked. 'You're saying *Graham* is ... *exceptional*?'

'Yes. I guess I am.'

'Huh.'

A cute wrinkle appeared between Lucinda's eyebrows as she bit her bottom lip. Alex decided he had pushed his luck far enough. He sketched a deep bow. 'And on that bombshell ...'

Lucinda laughed at his flourish and gave a mock salute in return as she turned towards her bed. 'Goodnight, Alex. Sleep well.'

'See you in the morning.'

Alex lingered by the closed door with his fingers resting on the door handle. The sound of Lucinda giggling reached him from the other side of the wall and he smiled, marvelling at how radically the tense, nervous mood in which he had started the day had changed. An hour ago he had stood on the same spot contemplating a restless night of hunger and worry, and now he was going to bed with a full stomach and heart.

Chapter 20

When the antique clocks throughout Russell House chimed midnight, Lucinda was curled up in bed finishing season three of *Napier*. The house elves had left a phone charger on her nightstand, allowing her to enjoy the series cliffhanger and then—after some qualms about whether it was snooping or reasonable due diligence—spend an hour of the early morning googling Alex Fraser.

The biographical and career details she could find were spare and matter of fact, but the recent explosion of comments following the Mumsweb shenanigans were fascinating and scurrilous. It turned out Vee had been downplaying how filthy some of the comments about Alex and his 'golden voice' were. Lucinda found it alternatingly hilarious and cringe-inducing, particularly once the observations swung from his voice to his physique, with universal admiration being expressed for his gravity-defying rear.

As she closed the browser and set an alarm for half past eight, Lucinda's mind drifted. Had all this attention come from Alex doing any job other than advertising haemorrhoid cream, would it have swelled his ego rather than mortifying him? Surely it would be impossible not to become boundlessly conceited when thousands of strangers were debating what grade of gorgeous you were and jostling for a place in the queue to sleep with you? And—as a final thought before slipping into sleep—how could any one person compete with the love of an army of adoring, if intimidating, fans?

Lucinda woke moments before her alarm. A shaft of sunlight edged around the heavy curtains, warming the amber tones in the floorboards and setting the gold threads in the counterpane sparkling.

Her sleep had been untroubled. Either Vee had thought better of her seduction plans, passed out in a wine-induced stupor or had tried the door handle so stealthily the noise of it moving had failed to disturb her.

Lucinda yawned and skipped over to the bathroom. Here there was no need to clean someone else's toothpaste spatter from the mirror or hang up their damp towels. She grinned as she collected her toothbrush from the porcelain cup by the sink, revelling in the carefree holiday feeling.

Emerging into the bedroom in a buoyant mood, Lucinda sprinted towards the bed and launched herself into its downy embrace. She stretched out her arms as her gaze settled on the other side of the bed, where the counterpane and pillows remained undisturbed, and a pang of loneliness pinched her heart. After spending two years sleeping solo, it would be nice to wake up next to someone. To laze in his strong arms and brush her cheek against his warm skin. To stare into his dark brown eyes while teasing her fingers through his sandy curls—

A polite knock on the outer door shattered the fantasy and drew Lucinda towards the corridor. Her hand resting on the door handle, she glanced down at the white frilly nightie she'd been given to sleep in and decided to open the door only enough to peer round it. No one needed to be treated to the sight of her in floor-length nightwear that would only look good on a doomed maiden in a gothic romance.

Her caution was rewarded immediately. In the corridor stood Alex, dressed in comfortable clothing from the current century. His black jeans and dark blue sweater were worlds away from the structured formality of the previous evening's dinner suit, but he looked no less attractive. In fact, the colour of the top did wonders for his complexion. And it looked really soft. Huggable.

'Hi.' Alex beamed, his face lighting up as if Lucinda had given him an enthusiastic welcome, rather than peeking round the door at him like a suspicious loon.

'Hi.' Lucinda took a moment to treat herself to the pleasure of gazing at Alex's broad grin of greeting before dragging her stare away from the gleam in his warm brown eyes long enough to notice he was clutching a bundle of clothes. 'Are those mine?'

'Oh, yeah. Sorry.' Alex held the pile of folded laundry out to her. 'No one knew we'd swapped rooms so they left them outside mine.'

Lucinda reached a hand around the door to take her clothes. 'Thank you. Are you off down to breakfast?'

'Yes. Hopefully it's better than dinner. If not, I might give it a miss.'

'Oh, OK. And you'll be leaving right after?'

'Yes.' Alex frowned, his eyebrows seeming to sink under heavy thoughts of the important things he had to be getting on with. 'I won't hang about. I should get going.'

'Right. Sure.' Lucinda's stomach lurched. There went her lift to the train station. He had forgotten about it. Which wasn't surprising. He was probably only being polite yesterday when he'd offered. And by now he likely wanted a break from her anyway. 'You must have a lot to do before work tomorrow.'

'Yes. I do.' Alex shrugged as he slid his hands into his back pockets. 'Would you still like a lift to the station?'

'Yes!' Lucinda cleared her throat. That had sounded a little too eager. 'I mean, that would be so helpful. Thank you. Um, I'll get dressed and be down in a minute.'

'Great.' His frown lifted and his smile returned. 'I'll leave you to it.'

The evening storms had swept the atmosphere clean of all clamminess. Flushed from rushed dressing, Lucinda was grateful for the drop in temperature as she descended the staircase while running her right thumb over her phone screen. Should she text Jay again? Her head chef had sent her two messages yesterday to report the weddings they had been catering in Great Compton had been plain sailing. And, as always when hearing a local event had passed off without a hint of drama, Lucinda had wondered if Becky had been lurking in the shadows.

Lucinda sighed: she should call Becky. They hadn't seen each other since the whole fake police officer routine and Lucinda needed to apologise for her bizarre behaviour.

Downstairs, the dining room had also benefited from the change in weather. One of the tall windows was ajar, and the circulating air had banished the lamb slop stench and replaced it with light scents from the roses and freesias on the side tables.

Alex, Vee and Carol were in the same seats as the night before, working their way through cereal and toast. Lucinda raised an eyebrow at the absence of a cooked breakfast but reasoned that perhaps Carol, for the good of her heart, was permanently banned from the delights of bacon and eggs.

If their host was disappointed by her muesli, she didn't show it. As immaculate as ever in a black trouser suit trimmed with white piping and her hair styled in a simple bun, Carol nodded at Lucinda as she took a seat while continuing her monologue listing her posts on various national and regional committees, boards and judging panels.

Carol paused to draw breath and Lucinda jumped in. 'That's amazing, Carol. And what do you do, Vee?'

'Oh, you know!' Vee shrugged and tossed her head. In contrast to Lucinda's rushed twist-and-clip approach to hairstyling, Vee had found time to shape her blonde hair into an enviable glory of ringlet curls, and the movement of her head sent them bouncing. 'I'm studying.'

'Yes,' said Carol, the one word replete with disapproval. 'As Veronica approaches twenty-five I fear she will become a perpetual student.'

'Lots of people do more than one degree.' Carol harrumphed, prompting Vee to continue her defence. 'And, besides, everyone goes to university, don't they?'

Lucinda considered keeping her mouth shut, but a perverse, point-scoring inclination loosened her tongue. 'I didn't.'

'I didn't either,' said Alex, glancing up and meeting Lucinda's gaze. 'I went straight to drama school.'

'I went to catering college,' said Lucinda as she spread a thick layer of jam on a slice of toast. 'Eventually.'

'Ah yes, *eventually*.' Carol shook her spoon in Lucinda's direction. 'That was the most intriguing bit of your file.'

File? The sweetness of the strawberry jam soured on Lucinda tongue. She had known Carol's snooping had been thorough, but the idea she had an actual dossier on her, some thick tan-coloured folder stashed in a tall cabinet, was horrifying.

She swallowed with difficulty and managed to stutter, 'Sorry?'

'Your missing years!' Carol drained her cup and set the dainty porcelain back in its matching saucer. 'You finished high school here in England, your mother moved you and your brother to Spain and then you vanished until reappearing at a catering college in London almost four years later.'

Lucinda's appetite having also disappeared, she put her toast back on her plate. Certain her eyes spoke of murder, she risked a glance up and found Alex watching her. His stare was determined but not unfriendly and, when he flicked his gaze to the door, Lucinda fancied he was offering to take her hand and make a run for it.

'How mysterious!' Vee said. 'What were you up to?'

Without breaking eye contact with Lucinda, Alex tipped his head towards the exit and raised an eyebrow. Bolstered by this further sign of his support, Lucinda found herself possessed by the petulant impishness she often found hard to control.

She frowned, hoping Alex would rate the performance she was about to give, and adopted a flat, serious tone as she said, 'I suppose, as I'm among friends here, I can tell you I spent some time travelling continental Europe. But beyond that'—she darted furtive, timid glances at Vee and Carol—'I'm afraid I can't say anything else.'

Carol gave an incredulous gasp. 'Come now, Lucinda. I'm sure whatever it is you can tell—'

'No, sorry. I really can't.' Lucinda waited until Vee turned her head to exchange a glance with Carol so she could wink at Alex unseen. 'You see, I signed the Official Secrets Act.'

Lucinda bit the inside of her cheek, focusing on the pain to stop herself laughing at Vee and Carol's gobsmacked expressions. Meanwhile, poor Alex was having great difficulty swallowing his tea. From his flared nostrils and trembling shoulders, Lucinda guessed he was trying not to release a guffaw which would have sent hot liquid spraying in all directions.

Before she could think where she would take the lie next, Lucinda's phone trilled. 'Sorry,' she said, springing to her feet. 'Please excuse me a moment.' And, caring not a jot what Vee or Carol might think of her, she waltzed out of the room.

'Jay?' Lucinda answered the call as she crossed the hall to the foot of the stairs. 'What's going on?'

'OK. Don't panic.'

Never a good start. 'But?'

'Tyler called in sick.'

'Right.' Lucinda ran through what she could remember of that day's booking: preparing three courses for a twelve-person lunch to be delivered by noon. Gazpacho, fish parcel and chocolate soufflé. 'Perhaps Peter is free—'

'Peter's not answering his phone!' Jay's voice rose to a squeak. 'Sorry. I normally wouldn't stress like this. I can prep everything on my own, but I'd need an extra hour at least.'

'I could call the customer. Perhaps they'll—'

'That's just it! The customer is Nancy sodding Sheridan.'

'Oh.' Lucinda gripped the bannister and sank onto the stairs. Nancy Sheridan was vice president of the South Compton Art Society and one of the best-connected people in the local area. She had been a loyal customer for the past three years and had made a point of informing Lucinda she had her to thank for several new contracts after recommending Lucinda's Catering to many of her wealthy friends. However, from the brief periods Lucinda had spent with Nancy, and snippets she'd gleaned from Becky, she had the impression messing up Nancy's lunch order would lead to a spree of spiteful bad-mouthing that would cause her to lose most of her business in the Comptons area.

'Lucinda? What do I do?'

Lucinda swallowed the bile rising up her throat. 'Keep going with the prep and keep trying Peter. I'll come up with something and call you back in ten minutes. Hang in there.'

Not for the first time in the past twenty-four hours, Lucinda wished she'd stayed at home. She could have been at the premises in under fifteen minutes and what threatened to be a business-maiming disaster would have been nothing more than a Sunday-morning hiccough. Checking the train timetables confirmed her worst fears: replacement bus services. It would take over three hours to get back to the Comptons by public transport.

As she re-entered the dining room, a final resort option came to her: she could ask Chris to nip down to the industrial park to help Jay. The thought of begging for such a huge favour made her stomach churn. It would give Chris more ammunition for his ongoing campaign to get her to throw in the towel on entrepreneurialism and return to working with him at his parents' restaurant.

Lucinda composed her features and donned a tight smile as Carol, Vee and Alex swung their collective stare towards her. Alex's welcoming grin dropped as he scanned her face and asked, 'What's wrong?'

Lucinda blinked. Clearly she was going to have to practise her poker face if she hoped to fool Alex. 'Um ... It's just ... Work emergency.'

'Can I help?'

'Thanks, but I don't—' Lucinda paused, struck by an idea which would solve her problem and free them both from the Berkshire Inquisition. 'Actually, I don't suppose you could give me a lift back to the Comptons, could you?' She winced, aware it was a significant detour for him. 'Jay needs me there now and the trains are up the creek and—'

'No problem at all,' said Alex, leaping out of his seat. 'Let's go.'

'Do you have to rush off?' Vee jumped after Alex, her ringlets swaying as she laid an arresting hand on his arm. 'You've barely finished your breakfast! And the Comptons is in the opposite direction to your way home.' She squeezed Alex's bicep as she gave Lucinda a pointed stare. 'Surely Lucinda can find another solution?'

Though it pained Lucinda to admit it, Vee was right. 'Um I suppose I could ask Chris to—'

'There! See!' Vee beamed at Alex. 'Now you can stay a while longer. The housekeeper can call a taxi to take Lucinda to the station.'

Lucinda's heart sank as Alex turned to face Vee. The younger woman batted her eyelashes and smiled, showing off her straight pearly white teeth. The docile blue stare and adoring disposition of such an attractive young woman would be more than enough to persuade most men to stay put. Especially when the alternative was a long unnecessary car journey with a harpy.

Though dejected at the thought of how far the odds were stacked against her, Lucinda refused to be easily defeated. While she didn't believe anyone could push their will onto someone else via telepathy, she gave it a try. Balling her fingers into fists and fixing her stare on the back of Alex's neck, she willed him to take her hand and run.

Chapter 21

Vee's last-minute intervention caught Alex off guard. The grip of her slender fingers on his upper arm was surprisingly firm, but the sensation paled in comparison to the electric prickling at the back of his neck. Alex rotated away from Vee and his gaze collided with Lucinda's. Her stare was insistent but—as opposed to Vee's eyelash-wiggling ogle—calm and neutral. A closer inspection revealed a fractional narrowing of her eyes, a tensing of her upper lip and a tiny twitch of her nose. Alex's stomach churned at the thought of Lucinda leaving without him, but he imagined she was also suffering as she entertained the possibility of asking Chris to come to her rescue.

Alex took a deep breath. Chris had had his chance and squandered it. 'No, no,' he said, a little louder than necessary, as he twisted out of Vee's grasp. 'You've been incredibly kind, but we've trespassed on your hospitality for far too long.'

While Vee let out a whine of disappointment, Carol—

who was possibly as delighted by the prospect of their departure as they were to go—chimed in. 'If you're in a hurry to get off the estate, there is a shorter route to the main road. From the stables, take the track to the right and go past the sculpture garden, between the upper and lower lakes.'

Through a sizeable pout, Vee muttered, 'Just keep the old stone bridge and cascades on your left, you'll be fine.'

Gawping in confusion at his hosts, Alex hoped Lucinda had got all that. Honestly, were there no simple directions to get around this place?

They trooped across the hall and exchanged farewells while Lucinda swung her bag onto her shoulder and tapped out a message on her phone, presumably informing Jay the cavalry was en route. As they neared the open front door, with the scent of freshly cut grass on the air and a cool breeze caressing his brow, Alex's spirits soared up after the birds swooping through the flawless azure sky. Almost giddy with relief, he beamed at Lucinda as she slid her sunglasses onto her nose. Hanging back a step to let her exit first, he dashed across the threshold to regain his place at her side.

Lucinda glanced at him as she strode across the gravel and the sunlight glinted off her sunglasses. 'Where's your car?'

'I was ordered to park it past the stables.'

She turned her head left and right, taking in the verdant lawns on all sides. 'And where the heck is that when it's at home?'

Alex pointed towards an incline that would take them up to the shade of a row of beech trees. As they began to climb, he twisted his vowels into a passable impression of Carol's accent. 'Oh come now, Lucinda. The stables! They're just past the labyrinth, over the golf course and next to the roller coaster!'

Her eyebrows flickered and, even shaded by the glasses, Alex swore he saw a mischievous glint in her eye as they reached the top of the hill and began the descent to the stables. 'Now, now, Alex,' she said, in her own decent imitation of Carol's voice. 'I think you'll find you've got that quite wrong. The roller coaster is next to the intergalactic spaceport while the golf course—'

'The eighteen-hole or the dinosaur-themed crazy golf?'

'Ugh! The eighteen-hole, naturally. Do keep up, dear boy! The course is to be found where it has been since time immemorial.'

'Which is?'

'Between the model village and the jazz club.'

Alex had considerable professional practice suppressing giggles but, as the stables came into view, his straight face cracked into chuckles. Lucinda joined in and by the time they reached the front of his car, he was slightly out of breath and fuzzy headed.

Lucinda's laughter subsided into a smile. 'Honestly— and forgive me for saying this—but there were times being stuck in the lift with her was less stress. I'm so glad we're getting out of here.'

As he was in complete agreement with her, Alex forgave Lucinda before she'd finished her sentence. He swallowed the last of his laughter and said, 'Me too.'

They stood smiling at each other, Lucinda twisting the toes of her shoes against the gravel underfoot. 'Your car,

I presume?' she said, gesturing at the front bumper of his aged blue Fiesta.

Alex had only ever viewed his car as a convenient way of getting from A to B. But, as Lucinda swept her eyes over the vehicle, no doubt taking in the scratched paint, cracked licence plate and rust patches, he wished it were a little bigger, newer and, more than anything, that he had bothered to wash it. 'It's not much. But it's roadworthy.'

'My car is a catering van. This is terrific.' Lucinda pushed her sunglasses up into her hair as the charming curve of her lips fell into a serious line. 'Thank you for driving me to work. I'm sure you've got lots of better things to do.'

Alex's mind flew to Nicole and the weight of the most important thing he had to do that morning dragged the edges of his smile down. 'It's fine. What are friends for?'

The words had barely left his lips when they were followed by a painful internal wince. Was he jumping the gun to declare them friends? A couple of intense shared experiences do not a friendship make, right? And he guessed it was probably the sort of overfamiliarity which would encourage giggly dazzling Lucinda to scarper, leaving frosty intimidating Lucinda to take her place. He held his breath. Which woman would come out in response to his question?

Lucinda lifted her gaze to meet his. The smile shining in her green eyes made his heart swell and head light. Her lips twitched, possibly tugged by the mysterious electric force which fixed Alex's gaze on her face and made the flesh on his arms prickle. And as they stood opposite each other, less than a stride apart, Alex's mouth went dry and his heart began to pound. How he would love to trace a knuckle along the soft skin of her jaw, apply the gentlest of pressures to tilt her chin upwards and, staring deep into those mesmerizing eyes, lean down to—

'Thanks,' she said, nudging him out of his reverie by tapping his upper arm, a playful gesture which caused Alex's thudding heart to knock against his ribcage. 'I'll have to return the favour ... I know!' Inspiration spread her smile into a grin. 'I'll cook for you some time.'

'You already did that last night,' Alex said as they moved to opposite sides of the car. Meanwhile a stern voice in his head screamed at him. *Shut up! That was practically an invitation to dinner! Are you trying to put her off?*

Shaking his head to silence his inner critic, Alex said, 'If anything, I owe you a favour for saving me from a sleepless night listening to my stomach rumbling.'

Oh very cool Alex, well done, added the voice. *Trying to recover from your previous gaffe by mentioning the seductive noises made by your bodily functions? Sooo attractive.*

Alex was grateful to be able to focus on the physical processes of opening the car door and getting into the driver's seat. Why did talking always seem to complicate things? And how did Lucinda have the power to turn him back into the gangly, tongue-tied adolescent who girls would laugh at rather than chat to?

Apparently unaware of his unease, Lucinda slid into the passenger seat and fastened her belt. 'That's true,' she said. 'But I didn't get to make you that sticky toffee pudding. Did I?'

Don't mess this up, Alex. Go with it!

'With custard?' he asked.

Lucinda nodded. 'The best in England.'

Accept, goddammit, man!

'In that case, I'm in.'

The engine growled to life and, as the tyres rumbled over the gravel, Alex told himself it was perfectly normal for friends to eat together. Even if, and a wave of excitement swept over him at the thought, their agreement sounded a lot like a date.

A short drive past assorted improbable landmarks brought a small lodge, a boundary wall and open gates into view. Lucinda wound down her window and cheerful birdsong became the soundtrack to their escape. A wordless tune came to Alex's lips, but no amount of jaunty humming could drown out the screeching guilt seething in his belly, stronger than the hunger pangs of the night before.

Alex bit his lip. However well it might be going, whatever this undeniably thrilling new thing with Lucinda was, it would have to wait. His mission was clear: drop Lucinda at work, get home to Nicole and put things right. After all, now they were on their way—far from high-spirited beagles and overly keen heiresses—surely there could be no further delays ahead.

Chapter 22

The boundary wall sparkled like a mirage in the near distance as Lucinda snuck a glance at Alex's profile and admired his strong jawline. It was currently defined by a dusting of stubble which she'd first noticed when they were standing in front of his car and he made a comment about being friends. As he waited for her reply, his features had arranged themselves into an expression she now recognised—his eyebrows drawn together while his eyes sparkled like he was expecting her to provide the punchline to a joke—and a part of her had ached to grab his shoulders, rise to tiptoe and press her lips to his.

Birds sang as they looped through the sky and Alex joined them by humming a melody she didn't recognise. A traitorous smile tugged at the corners of her mouth before Lucinda was able to remind herself she found humming and whistling unforgiveable annoyances.

Sighing in frustration at her increasingly nonsensical behaviour, Lucinda wound down her window, rested her elbow on the frame and covered her apparently uncontrollable lips with her hand. That was the trouble with Alex: he kept saying things that made her smile. She'd always been drawn to guys who could make her laugh. And, in his specific case, everything he said came gift-wrapped in that low voice which was steady and silky but edged with an even deeper rasp, like a shower of soft kisses followed by a light brush of stubble—

The car dipped into a pothole, jolting Lucinda out of her train of thought and giving her sceptical inner voice the chance to observe she was in danger of becoming one of the Mumsweb weirdos. She'd barely spent any time with Alex. How could she be sure the wit he'd displayed so far hadn't been a fluke?

Besides, it was all moot because the man had a girlfriend! She needed to focus on work and refuse to let her hormones distract her from what was truly important.

As if answering an unspoken call for help against the evil forces of dopamine, her phone buzzed in her hand. Lucinda wound up her window as she took the call. 'Jay? How's it going?'

Jay's response was a flurry of words barely separated by breath. 'I couldn't find anyone to help in the kitchen.'

'Ah. Perhaps I should call Nancy—'

'I called her housekeeper. We are to deliver by twelve o'clock. If we are late then Mrs Sheridan will not be ordering from us again and neither will any of her friends.'

'OK. High noon it is then.' Lucinda squeezed the ache building above her eyebrows with the thumb and index finger of her free hand. 'If Lucinda's Catering want to work south of the Watford Gap ever again ...'

'We can't be late.' Jay's voice was accompanied by the rattle of plastic. 'I'm about to turn on the blender. When will you be here?'

'A little over an hour. Keep doing what you can.' Jay started the blender and Lucinda raised her voice to say, 'I'll see you soon.'

Ending the call silenced the grinding whizz of the blender, but the noise seemed to continue in Lucinda's mind. Her brain fizzed painfully with ideas which, bumping against an uncooperative wall of anxiety, failed to provide a solution to the age-old dilemma of having a heap of stuff to do and not enough time to do it in.

Alex cleared his throat. 'Are you OK?'

'Not exactly. But there's not much I can do until I get there. And we're on our way now. That helps. Thanks.'

Alex slowed the car to a crawl as they passed through the gap in the boundary wall and came to a halt just beyond the entry to the estate. On the other side of a single-lane rough track lay an unbroken sea of purple lavender which rippled under shafts of sunlight.

Although the satnav ordered a right turn with total confidence, Lucinda would have been reassured by a road sign, markings or even some tarmac.

'Oh my ...' She glanced at Alex. 'Where's the road?'

Alex turned towards her and, in a perfect American accent, quoted a line from a movie she'd watched more times than was probably healthy. 'Roads? Where we're going—'

'We don't need'—Lucinda flicked her sunglasses down onto her nose—'roads.'

Pulling onto the track, Alex beamed at her. 'Thank goodness you got that.'

Appalled anyone survived without exhaustive knowledge of the greatest movies of the 1980s, Lucinda gaped at Alex and asked, 'Who wouldn't get it?'

'This may shock you, but I have it on good authority there are people out there, living productive lives, who have never seen *Back to the Future*.'

'Great Scott!' They shared another smile while Lucinda wondered if 'people' meant Nicole, and her petty, competitive streak pushed her to say, 'I have an original foyer poster at home.' She turned her head to the window to hide a cringe. Why did she always have to push her luck? That had been too geeky, surely?

'I used to have a copy on my wall in one of the rooms I rented in London.' He shrugged. 'It's a classic.'

Relieved, and deciding to clamp her mouth shut before she revealed she also had *Indiana Jones* and *Star Wars* posters—no need to stress-test their friendship on its first official day—Lucinda sent a brief update to Chris. His response was two emojis: a thumbs up and a four-leaf clover.

She would need the luck from a million four-leaf clovers if she were to deliver Nancy's order by midday. But there was nothing she could do about it for another hour.

To distract herself, she reached for the radio. 'Oh, sorry'—she paused, fingers hovering by the button—'do you mind if we have the radio on?'

'Good idea,' Alex said. 'I think one of the programmed stations plays eighties and nineties "oldies".'

'Oldies for us oldies, you mean?'

Alex smiled. 'My nieces think I'm ancient. They can't imagine being eighteen, let alone forty-three.'

Lucinda flicked through the stations while hoping her

expression hadn't revealed that Alex's age came as no surprise. It was listed in his Wikipedia entry which she had skimmed in the early hours of the morning.

Her skin suddenly itchy, she squirmed in her seat. It wasn't long ago she'd wanted to throttle Carol for researching her life, and what she'd been doing to Alex by poking around the internet wasn't that different. Although at least she'd only read information that was a matter of public record. And wasn't it 'normal' nowadays to google someone when you met them?

The chorus of 'Don't Look Back in Anger' erupted from the radio, triggering simultaneous exclamations of delight from Alex and Lucinda. Her mission accomplished, Lucinda sat back and joined Alex in singing along. Gradually, the tension in her shoulders and neck began to release, until adverts interrupted the track seconds before its proper conclusion.

'I hope I'm not signing my death warrant with this question ...' Alex glanced at Lucinda, one eyebrow raised. 'But I take it you're not really a spy?'

Lucinda huffed a laugh. 'No. To date, all my kills have been completely unlicensed.'

'In that case, may I ask what you were doing in your "missing years"?'

'I'm afraid it's not that exciting. I was learning to cook.' She shrugged. 'Mum moved us to Spain when I finished high school. I needed some money and had to improve my dreadful Spanish, so I got a job washing dishes in a local restaurant. One day they were short-staffed and let me peel some vegetables. When I didn't stuff that up they let me do it again, and then chop some stuff, then stir ...'

'And you discovered you were good at it?'

'I was OK. More importantly, I enjoyed it.'

The initial few months in Spain had been tough. Despite all Lucinda's protests, her mother had dragged her children away from their friends and everything they had ever known to drop them in a foreign country. And while her mother had blossomed in the southern sunshine like the local displays of fuchsia bougainvillea, Lucinda had wilted. By the time she found a job in the tiny restaurant at the touristy end of the esplanade, she was in a state of quiet dejection and had expected to keep her head down at the sink and disappear. But cooking had been a revelation.

Lucinda smiled at the memory. 'And then one of my friends at the restaurant, a waiter, he was nineteen ... He said he and a group of mates were going to France to work their way around the country and see the sights. And I thought, why not?'

The full truth was Lucinda had leapt at the chance to get away from her mother. Back in the UK she had lived with Marion's suffocating sermons and downbeat ranting for almost seven years, but her mother's newly found and loud enthusiasm for all things Spanish was almost harder to bear. The only thing keeping her from leaping into her friend's car and racing to the border was Michael. She was loath to leave her little brother, even though he had adapted to their move remarkably well. In the two months before starting his new school he improved his Spanish to near fluency. And while he'd been awkward and withdrawn in England, in Spain he came out of his shell and quickly gained a large group of friends. When Lucinda told him she was thinking of going travelling, he couldn't have been more excited for her.

Lucinda frowned as she stared out at the green and yellow fields flanking the track. Her brother was still happily living in Spain, running a successful language school a few doors down from the first restaurant she had ever worked in. He met up with Mum at least once a week. Surely he had noticed her growing attachment to Graham? Or had the news of their upcoming nuptials floored him too?

Lost in thoughts of family, Lucinda stewed in silence, until Alex—who was apparently still interested in her travels—prompted her to continue. 'And you spent nearly four years in France?'

'About a year. Then different groups of us went on to Belgium, Germany, down to Italy, over to Greece ... We hopped from one kitchen gig to the next. The best were the tiny local places. That's where I learnt the classics. If you're honestly interested, people are usually happy to share their family recipes.'

'You must be fluent in a few languages.'

'I wish!' Lucinda snorted. 'I can say "hello" and "thank you". And words to do with food stick in here too.' She tapped her temple. 'Everything else slips away. Languages were never my strong suit.'

'Is that one of the reasons you came back to England?'

'Yeah, I suppose. I wanted to study cookery properly and didn't have the language skills to do it in anything other than English.'

'How did you go from there to owning your own business in the Comptons?'

'I guess I have Chris to thank for that. We met in London and were friends for years before dating. After a while we both wanted to get on the property ladder and living together and sharing the costs made sense.'

A wince contracted Lucinda's brows. Inside her head, buying a house and moving in with Chris had always seemed eminently sensible. But now, said out loud, and especially to a man whose own story of starry-eyed elopement had been old-Hollywood levels of romantic, it sounded like such a dry and loveless decision. She had dated a string of flirtatious, lying, narcissistic frogs in her twenties, and her continued failure to find her prince had only borne out her mother's assertions about true love being a lie for the weak and gullible. But when she and Chris had started going out, he'd been a known quantity. An honest friend who she loved and got on well with. And when he seemed to be equally fond of her, she had decided she was lucky to have found him and settled for what she believed was the best she could expect.

'And,' she said, the word coming out like a sigh, 'there was no way we could afford to buy anything in London and Chris's parents had been hassling him for ages about taking over their restaurant in the centre of Compton. So we decided to house-hunt locally and both work for the family business.'

'And that didn't work out?'

Lucinda bit her bottom lip. 'Not exactly. I don't think living *and* working with someone is the best idea.'

It had all been great in the beginning. House-hunting turned out to be fun. And finding the right place— somewhere she could leave her mark and make a real, permanent home—had been exhilarating. Even with everything that had happened between her and Chris since, the memory of grasping the keys and opening the front door for the first time remained bright and untarnished.

Unfortunately, working with her significant other soon became a nightmare. Ninety-nine per cent of the time Chris was a kind, gentle guy. But, like Lucinda herself, when under fire he became prone to explosive outbursts. And while Lucinda had been hollered at in various kitchens by many red-faced chefs, it was an entirely different experience when the chef in question was your boyfriend and the kitchen was owned by his parents.

Alex pulled the car onto the grass verge to give an approaching vehicle space to squeeze past. 'That's understandable. But you could have gone to another kitchen. Why a catering business?'

'A friend of Chris's parents had a catering company in the Comptons. They were retiring and wanted to sell off their equipment. And it gave me the idea of buying up their stuff. That was over five years ago and I think we're finally getting somewhere.'

Unless we muck it up today, she added to herself as she glanced down at the clock on her phone again.

'It must be stressful sometimes,' said Alex. 'The responsibility that comes with being the owner.'

Not sometimes, thought Lucinda. All the ruddy time. 'It is,' she said as she laid a hand over the ache in her belly.

'So why do it?'

Lucinda stared at the side of Alex's face, considering the tone of the question. Chris liked to ask her the same thing, but it wasn't an honest enquiry. His exasperated lilt and stare of desperation as he posed the question conveyed his opinion: she should sell up. She should quit and come back to his kitchen where she belonged.

In contrast, Alex's tone and open expression spoke of genuine interest. So she decided to give him an honest answer.

'I don't like being in the kitchen all the time. You hardly ever get to see anyone enjoy—or even hate—something you've made. And, while I love cooking and I'm pretty good at it—'

'From last night's bacon and eggs, I'd say you're better than pretty good.'

'Thanks.' Lucinda beamed at the compliment, letting it settle like a delicate balm around the raw edges of the pain in her tummy. 'But I'm not like Chris. He's ... This might sound pretentious, but he's an artist. He always wants to create new things and push himself to find better flavours and textures. He'd be experimenting with liquid nitrogen if he didn't think his mum would kill him!' She chuckled. 'Me? I just want to make simple favourites well and serve them in decent portions so everyone goes home full and happy.'

Not many people understood how crucial food was to the success of an event. If it was good, the client would be satisfied, Lucinda might get a couple of positive comments from guests and, if she were lucky, they might recommend her to others. If the food was bad, everyone would be grumpy and an otherwise perfect occasion would be irreparably soured. The power to make or break someone's big day was in your hands.

Aware her last thought risked casting her as a megalomaniac, Lucinda voiced her less power-hungry motives. 'And there's more variety to the job. I get out of the kitchen to meet clients, visit venues. I can work with lots of different people on the staff. It's busy and interesting. And, I suppose the universe sort of decided it for me, in a way ...'

Why was she still talking? A naturally private person, Lucinda couldn't remember the last time she had spoken about herself this much, if ever.

But Alex didn't seem to mind her monologuing and asked, 'How so?'

'I'd heard about the equipment sale and had the idea for the business, but I'd sunk any savings I had into the deposit for the house. I couldn't get a loan without some money of my own and then ... my dad died and my brother and I inherited his house. We sold it and I used my share of the money to set up the company.'

Alex slowed the car into another passing place and, while the oncoming four-by-four roared past them, turned to meet Lucinda's gaze. His features were pinched with sympathy as he said, 'Sorry about your dad.'

'Don't be.' Lucinda appreciated the sentiment, but didn't want Alex to waste his sorrow on someone who didn't deserve it. 'We hadn't seen or heard from him since I was twelve. Apparently family life became too much for him. Or it wasn't what he'd thought it would be. So he took off.'

Alex's expression shifted into one of concern and then his eyebrows lifted as understanding dawned. 'Hence your mum's rules.'

'Yep.' Lucinda put as much caustic bitterness into the pop of the final *p* as she could. 'Dad was the love of Mum's life, her soulmate, her other half ...' She trailed off, unable to voice the whole truth: that Dad had been the love of her life too. He had been her superhero, her idol. He had told her he loved her more than anything. To the moon and back. But clearly that hadn't been enough.

Her eyes began to water and she swallowed hard. Not wanting to shed a single tear more for someone she doubted had cried over her, she summoned her anger. 'He took the dog too.'

'What?'

'The family dog. *My* dog.' She ground her teeth. 'He left his two kids without saying goodbye but apparently leaving the dog was unthinkable. So he took her from us as well.'

'Bloody hell.' Alex shook his head and opened his mouth to say something, then closed it again. His nostrils flared as he exhaled noisily and asked, 'What was your dog called?'

'Bear.' Lucinda smiled as she remembered the golden retriever's shining black eyes. 'She was already two when we got her—she was a rescue—and my brother was three. And to Michael she was a huge, soppy, cuddly bear.'

Lucinda hadn't thought about Bear for a long time. It was difficult to detangle positive memories of the dog from black thoughts about Dad, and so she avoided them both. The blame for their resurgence probably lay with Hubert, and Lucinda hoped the mischievous beagle had been fully forgiven for his antics and was managing to stay out of trouble.

The jingle for the ten o'clock radio news bulletin cut into Lucinda's canine-related reverie. Where were they and what time was it? How had she managed to wander so far from the here and now?

She glanced at Alex, taking in the crinkle between his eyebrows, and wondered if he found her ridiculous and self-absorbed. She had done nothing but talk about herself since they left Russell House!

Wanting to show she wasn't a total egotist, she attempted to give him the floor. 'How about your parents? Are they married?'

'They were. But my dad died when I was nine.'

Lucinda's mouth went dry. 'Oh Alex, I'm so sorry.'

'It was a long time ago. But it's good I can tell you about it because ... I'd like you to understand ...' As he tailed off a second time, Lucinda watched Alex's brows settle over his narrowed eyes to form a look of such intent concentration, he might have been trying to assemble a ten-thousand-piece puzzle depicting an unbroken stretch of blue sky.

'Actually,' he said, 'if we're going to talk about it, would you mind if we stop here for a second?' He pointed to a passing place by a field gate a little way ahead. 'I won't keep us back more than a few minutes, I promise.'

'Of course, that's fine,' said Lucinda, her heart heavy with concern. 'But if you'd rather not talk about it—'

'No, I do want to. Because, you see, it has to do with the way I behaved when we first met.'

'Oh. OK.'

Lucinda bit her bottom lip as Alex brought the car to a halt. She had told him about her own dad's death in such a blasé manner. If, by some good fortune, he didn't regard her as ridiculous and self-absorbed, surely he must think her a right callous cow.

But, she mused as she scanned the taut muscles of his

cheeks and jaw, she might be able to undo some of that impression by offering a willing and sympathetic ear. And by keeping her mouth shut. After the favours he had done her since they met, it was the least she could do.

Chapter 23

Alex approached his story cautiously, hoping that doing so might stave off an attack of dizziness and nausea. Keeping his gaze fixed on the road, he spoke at a steady, deliberate pace. 'Dad used to take my brother and me to the park at the weekends.'

He swallowed and blinked. Tears welled in his eyes and his pulse beat a little quicker than usual, but otherwise he felt clear headed and in control. The previous night he had slept peacefully, waking refreshed and with no memories of any dreams good or bad. He had begun to believe that spending so much time with Carol and finding her stunningly vital and, frankly, rather annoying, had settled the ghost which had come back to haunt him since her collapse. And explaining everything to Lucinda, especially after she had spoken so openly about her own father, seemed like the ideal opportunity to see if he was right to be optimistic. But just in case he had thought it best to stop the car.

He exhaled slowly and continued. 'One weekend, when I was nine, we were playing football down the park and he just dropped to the ground. Turns out he'd had a stroke and went into cardiac arrest. And I ... I froze. I just stood there. I couldn't move.'

Alex shivered and glanced at Lucinda. Meeting his gaze, she gave him a flicker of a smile in encouragement and placed a hand lightly on his forearm. The warmth of her touch chased away the chill that had been creeping along Alex's spine and he was pleased to discover he was able to return her smile. Recalling the events of that day now, it was as if he were a distant observer. One sitting in Lucinda's reassuring presence, witnessing something incredibly sad and nonsensical happening to two young boys he used to know. It was so unlike what had happened in the lift back in April. Then, as Carol's chest had stilled, he had been transported back in time to relive his past. Lucinda and everyone else in the cabin had vanished for a moment, and he had been seized by the terror of a small boy watching helplessly as their dad fell and didn't get back up.

Lucinda squeezed his arm gently and the light pressure spurred him on. 'Luckily my brother—he was seven—was shouting and that brought help, but it was too late for Dad.' Alex took a deep breath. 'I thought I'd got past it. But when Carol collapsed, it was ... I froze again.'

A car roared along the track and Alex and Lucinda turned to watch as it shot past them. As it disappeared around the bend ahead, Lucinda said, 'Alex, I'm ...' A deep crease appeared between her eyes. 'I was so shouty and mean to you in the lift.' She gasped. 'Oh my God! I hit you!' She whipped her hand away from his arm and slapped it over her eyes. 'But I didn't … I'm sorry …'

'Don't worry about it.'

'No, bloody hell. I'm so sorry. I was awful!'

'You weren't. You needed help. Carol needed us. Both of us. And I didn't want to be back there, reliving that day. You did me a favour, snapping me out of it.'

'You don't have to say that just to make me feel better. I—'

'Lucinda.' Alex waited until she uncovered her eyes to continue. 'I mean it. Please, don't feel bad about it.'

She shook her head. 'Seeing Carol this weekend must have been difficult. Did it happen again, the freezing thing, yesterday afternoon when she mentioned your dad?'

Alex's lips parted. So she had noticed!

'A bit. But seeing her fully recovered has helped. I mean, I'm talking about it now and look!' He held up his hands, which were remarkably steady. 'I'm fine.'

'You're sure?' Lucinda gestured to the steering wheel. 'I could drive the rest of the way. If a white van driver taking the wheel of your car wouldn't make things worse.'

Alex smirked, started the engine and pulled onto the track. 'Thank you, but I'm OK. I just wanted you to know what really happened. So you didn't spend the rest of your life thinking I was entirely useless.'

'I didn't—' Lucinda snapped her mouth closed, checking her outrage. 'I *don't* think that!'

Ha! Alex smirked again. So she had thought he was useless! Well, that wasn't great, but at least he seemed to be changing her mind.

'I'm very glad to hear it. And look!' He pointed ahead at a sign for the motorway. 'More good news.'

'Hallelujah!' Lucinda leant forwards to get a better look at the sign. 'If you'd told me yesterday I'd ever be this happy to join the M25, I'd have said you were crazy.'

'I'll be able to put my foot down now. Make up some time.'

'Thanks. I'll send Jay another message.'

Alex rolled his shoulders and found his neck muscles were looser than they had been for weeks. Talking to Lucinda about his dad seemed to have finally dispersed the dark cloud which had been following him since the day of Carol's heart attack. And now, after crawling along the narrow country track, accelerating smoothly along the motorway provided further relief.

He glanced at Lucinda as she finished her message to Jay and his recently buoyed spirits sank. For while he was relaxing as their journey progressed, Lucinda seemed to be winding herself into a tight ball. Her head bowed, she slouched into her seat, her right hand clutching her phone while the other rapped out an agitated SOS against her left knee.

Alex scanned the road as he sought inspiration. Back at the start of their trip she had laughed a few times. But then that was before the conversation drifted into the troubled waters of family. Could he steer it back to those earlier calmer waters? If only he could think of a neutral topic …

Aha! He nodded to himself as he examined the subject for potential stress triggers and, having found none, decided to go for it.

'So,' he said, 'are you going to watch the last two episodes of *Napier*?'

Bingo! Lucinda's frown vanished and she straightened

out of her slump as she turned towards him, her eyes and smile radiating excitement. 'I watched them last night! The cliffhanger is superb. Annoying, but superb.'

Alex laughed. Only Lucinda could add an edge of grouchiness to enthusiastic praise. 'Before you ask, I can't tell you anything. No spoilers.'

'Can't or shouldn't?'

'Can't. I don't think they've written the next series yet and they certainly don't tell me anything ahead of time.'

'Do you think you, sorry, I mean Dexter, could be the mole?'

'I hope not.'

'Why? Surely that would be huge?'

'Yes, but whoever the mole turns out to be, I guess they'll be killed off, sent to prison or have to flee the country. And I'd like to stay in the series.'

'Is *Napier* your favourite thing you've worked on?'

'Definitely. I love my character, the writing and the whole team, the cast and crew, are wonderful. Especially Diana. She plays my ... well, *Dexter's* wife.'

The first season of *Napier* had launched Diana Carter to superstardom. Playing the titular role of DCI Alisia Napier with an intelligent, commanding brilliance, she had caught the eye of Hollywood. Now, when not filming the TV show which had made her name, she was busy tackling lead parts in international blockbusters.

'It's unusual to get to work with the same people over and over,' explained Alex, 'and it's sort of like going back to a family.'

'Even if it includes creepy Uncle Ray?

Alex grinned. 'Even then.'

'So you're going to do more?'

'Probably. We all signed contracts for three series but we haven't renewed yet.'

'But the series finished on a giant cliffhanger. There has to be more, right?'

'I hope so.'

'This might sound daft ... But there was all that stuff at the end of series two with your character and the kidnapping ... And I thought they were setting up a storyline for you in series three, but then there wasn't one. I mean, don't get me wrong, you appeared a lot in series three but mostly in more of a side plot. Maybe. I've probably got that all wrong—'

'No, I thought the same. I'm still worried I managed to piss the writers off.'

'I wouldn't worry. If you'd offended someone they'd have dreamt up some unpleasant way to kill you off.'

Alex snorted. 'Is that your professional opinion, 007?'

'Absolutely. So watch your step: more driving, less sarcasm.'

'Yes ma'am.' Alex shot her his lopsided smile and raised a joking salute.

Lucinda's phone pinged. 'Hmn.' Lucinda rubbed an eyebrow as she glanced up from the screen. 'Jay says, "No pressure but hurry up please".'

Alex checked the speedometer as his heart accelerated. The stress Lucinda was doing her best to contain within herself was beginning to get to him. Blimey. Living with that sort of pressure long term couldn't be good for you. 'I'm already doing the limit, I'm afraid, but we'll be there soon. Are all your jobs like this?'

'Not all of them. But catering for smaller dinner parties can often be more hassle than huge events.'

'How so?'

Alex listened as Lucinda explained—with some impressively expressive hand gestures—the many potential pitfalls of feeding the demanding clientele of the Comptons, and was surprised to learn many people had partly prepared food delivered to their home to finish cooking it there. The problematic Nancy Sheridan being one of them.

'I don't get it. Why not make it from scratch in her kitchen?'

'That's a service we offer,' Lucinda said. 'But Nancy doesn't want a load of strangers in her kitchen all morning clanging pots and pans while she's preparing for twelve guests.'

Alex understood but couldn't imagine having the money to afford such a luxury. He glanced at Lucinda, whose tight jaw and taut lips told him she was worrying again. Hoping that enquiring after small details might soothe her mind, at least for a while, he asked, 'What's Nancy serving for pudding? Please tell me there's pudding.'

'Come on! As if I'd work for a dessert traitor.' Lucinda grinned. 'Chocolate soufflé.'

'Delicious.' Alex drummed his fingers on the steering wheel, considering. 'But aren't soufflés tricky?'

'We have a foolproof recipe. Whoever is going with the delivery will have to put them in the oven when Nancy's guests are halfway through their mains. And then …'

Alex took in Lucinda's furrowed brow. 'What's wrong?'

'I just thought … Tyler, he's a more junior chef, he was

supposed help Jay prep everything and then he was going to go to Nancy's, put things in the oven, plate up ... But he's the one who hasn't turned up.'

'Can Jay do it?'

'She could and I'm sure she would if I ask her to. But it's not her job. She's my head chef.'

'I'm sure she won't mind.'

The radio DJ announced the time was coming up to a quarter to eleven as Alex pulled off the main road leading to Great Compton and into an industrial park. Sunday had rendered it a ghost town, and the smooth rumble of the car's engine seemed unnaturally loud as they drove along treeless streets lined with shuttered warehousing units.

A tapping drew Alex's attention back to Lucinda. She was staring at her phone screen and pursing her lips as she knocked her nail against the phone's plastic frame.

'Still worrying about Jay?'

Lucinda glanced towards him, shaking her head. 'No, you're right. She's always been flexible with changes to plan.'

Her dejected tone belied the nonchalance of her reply. 'But...?'

'But, she's really good. Talented. I worry I'll lose her to some exciting restaurant. I've been giving her more responsibility and not looking over her shoulder too much. Which I find hard, but I'm trying.' She pointed to the side of the road ahead. 'It's the next on the left and straight down to the end.'

In the corner of the estate, surrounded by sycamore trees, squatted four single-storey buildings. Unlike the warehouses they'd passed earlier, they were unintimidating brick constructions which resembled small houses with gable roofs and built-in garages. A Lucinda's Catering van was parked outside the second unit on the right and Alex pulled into the space next to it.

The engine stuttered to a standstill and, as Lucinda removed her seat belt, Alex's heart faltered at the thought of saying goodbye. And, although he knew she was rushing to beat a deadline, he sought to prolong their conversation for a moment more.

'And you think Jay might find today a little too much responsibility?'

Her hand resting on the door handle, Lucinda replied, 'She usually thrives on stress, but …' Her eyebrows shot skywards and Alex could almost see the light bulb above her head. 'Hey! Would you come in and say "hello"? She's a big *Napier* fan and it might cheer her up, or at least make her think about something other than a resignation letter.'

Alex's mouth moved before the part of him which kept insisting on remembering his own deadlines could stop it. 'Sure,' he said, scrambling out of the car and following Lucinda through the white-framed door.

Chapter 24

Lucinda barrelled across the beige box which formed her business's reception area and through the swing door into the kitchen. A gust of humid air hit Alex as he stepped after her, which was closely followed by the pungent smell of fish. Narrowing his eyes against the fluorescent lighting and drone of extractor fans, Alex squinted at the many features of the large rectangular room. Silvery linoleum coated the floor, while stainless-steel counters banked the outside of the space and formed three spotless workbenches in its centre. The walls were lined with square ivory tiles, and strip lights nestled in the blank snowy ceiling.

The steady mundanity of the greyscale décor was disrupted by Jay who stood at the middle of the workbenches in a scarlet chef's jacket and matching headscarf and was using an apparently incredibly sharp knife to separate a fish from its spine. Evidence of her industry could be seen in both the sheen on her brow and the items arranged on almost every surface: a simmering pan of water perched on one of the burner ranges, trays filled with tinfoil parcels, a pile of potatoes with the peeler abandoned beside them ... Alex blinked but failed to take it all in.

He was still struggling when Jay, without looking up from her task, said, 'Gazpacho in three flasks in fridge ready to go. Cucumber and pepper needs dicing. Half of the fish ready and parcelled, six to go. Potatoes to peel, chop and parboil. Roasting trays are ready by the ovens. I've peeled, topped and tailed the carrots—they're in the covered bowls beside you there—still to chop. Soufflé ingredients all in one place on the workstation nearest the sink.'

Her status report was delivered with the swift precision of a paramedic upon arriving at hospital. Alex wasn't sure he'd caught all of it, but Lucinda responded immediately. 'When does the van have to leave here?'

'11.35. Loading at 11.30 at the latest.'

Lucinda glanced at her phone. 'It's 10.50. We have forty minutes till loading.'

'Yep.' Jay set her knife down and glanced up. Her gaze snagged on Alex and she beamed. 'Hi, Alex! Bet you didn't think you'd be back at Lucinda's Catering this soon.' She transferred the fish to a sheet of baking foil as she spoke. 'Did Lucinda pass on my thanks?'

'She did. And you're welcome.'

'Great!' Jay beamed. 'I've been looking forward to talking to you about the final episode of *Napier*. Oh my God, it was completely insane ...'

Jay's voice faded to background chatter as Alex's attention narrowed to the creases in Lucinda's brow and the way she was biting her lower lip. His fingers twitched: there had to be something he could do to help.

Lucinda strode to the side of her head chef and began to offer solutions. 'I can do the soufflés in about thirty minutes.'

Moving on to the next fish, Jay shot back, 'More like thirty-five to forty if you want the ramekins perfectly filled, covered and on the trays for transport.'

'But that still gives me a few minutes to get the potatoes in the water.'

'I'll be done with the bream in about thirty minutes. Then I can move on to dicing the veg for the gazpacho.'

Though he was no culinary expert, Alex's maths skills were advanced enough to know the two of them couldn't get everything done in time. But with three pairs of hands …

With the women absorbed in their calculations, Alex stole over to the hand basin and scrubbed in as if he were preparing to perform surgery. Gliding over to the workbench nearest the door, he uncovered the bowl Jay had mentioned earlier, removed the peeled carrots and placed one on the chopping board. He snatched up the knife waiting next to the bowl and, using rapid, efficient cuts, squared off the carrot before gripping it in his clawed left hand and rocking the knife gently until he had produced a neat block of batons. Pleased with his first attempt, he glanced up and tuned back into the conversation in the middle of the room.

Lucinda planted her hand on her hip, her gaze shifting from Jay's face to the fish under her knife. 'Perhaps you could go ahead and I could deliver the soufflés a bit later—'

Jay shook her head. 'They won't like that. They're picky about—'

Alex raised his voice. 'Excuse me! If you're going to

roast them, I'm guessing the carrots need to be batons, right?'

'What are you doing?' Jay's tone rose to an aghast squeak.

'Chopping carrots.' The women exchanged stunned glances, giving Alex the chance to push on. 'Look, the two of you can't get this done in time. I can help.'

Lucinda crossed her arms. 'It's a kind offer, Alex, but Nancy's such a demanding customer—'

'Honestly, I can help—'

'—that we can't risk serving her anything not up to a professional standard—'

'But that's what I'm trying to tell you—'

'You've already done enough today by bringing me here. Jay and I can—'

Alex struggled to contain a growl of frustration. Clearly the only way to get Lucinda to accept something was to let her see it with her own eyes. Pushing his irritation into his movements, he snatched up the knife, clamped the batons in his left hand and in a blur of smooth strokes diced the sticks into a pile of perfectly regular cubes.

This time when he looked up, Jay and Lucinda were wide eyed and open mouthed.

Jay recovered first. 'What ... the ... actual ... hell?'

Alex shrugged. 'I played a sous chef once. I wanted to look like I knew what I was doing, so I worked in a kitchen for a few weeks.'

Jay jabbed a finger in the direction of the carrot cubes and, in a sceptical tone, asked, 'A few weeks?'

Alex grinned. 'It might have been a month. Or nearly two.'

Jay returned his smile. 'For a part? Do you have to do that?'

No, thought Alex. The simple answer was 'no'. But he never found any way of preparing for a role which made him as comfortable as exhaustive research.

He looked at Jay's raised eyebrow and replied, 'I like to be prepared.'

The women exchanged glances again, but the twitches at the corners of Lucinda's mouth told Alex she was beginning to waver. Focusing his gaze squarely on her green eyes, he made a final attempt to win her over. 'I want to help. And I can't do much harm peeling potatoes, can I?'

Lucinda glanced at the clock on her phone again. Uncrossing her arms, she raised her gaze to Alex and nodded. 'OK. I'll get you a jacket.'

Jay spluttered. 'But you never let anyone unqualified anywhere near your kitchen, how—'

Lucinda silenced her with a glare. 'He's right. We need help if we're going to do this. And he evidently'—she waved at the chopping board in front of Alex—'knows what he's doing. Needs must.'

'All right,' said Jay as Lucinda passed Alex a black jacket. 'How do you want to do this?'

The question seemed to snap Lucinda into battle mode. She lifted her chin and, as she slid into her own jacket, a familiar glint of steely determination crept into her eyes. 'I'll do the soufflés. Alex, those carrots in two-inch batons, please. Then get on with peeling the potatoes. Jay, supervise him. I have to concentrate because if these soufflés don't rise, Nancy will give us the boot anyway.'

The next thirty minutes sped by in a blur of slicing, peeling and boiling. Jay's initial reluctance to accept Alex's assistance vanished the second he replied to her instructions with an enthusiastic 'Yes, chef!' and what he liked to think was a winning smile.

She chuckled and nudged him in the ribs, 'Get you!' She returned to the fish while muttering 'Yes, chef' and shaking her head.

Occasionally, when he glanced up from his task, his gaze met Lucinda's. Her steady stare would sweep across his work and she would give him an almost imperceptible nod. These tiny signs of approval made Alex want to burst into song and, not wanting to be a distraction, he had to channel his surge of happiness into a low hum which was safely disguised by the drone of the extractor fans.

At half past eleven, Ethan and Lukas slouched through the door—one ready to clean up after them and the other to load and drive the van—and leant against the wall in the corner of the room, awaiting their orders while blissfully unaware they were witnessing a triumphant victory snatched from the jaws of defeat.

As Lucinda had expected, Jay volunteered to accompany the food to its destination. And rather than being annoyed at having to complete a task Lucinda believed to be beneath her, Jay's elation at having pulled off a time-defying culinary feat was so great she was even enthusiastic about it.

'I can go if you had something else planned,' said Lucinda.

'Are you kidding? I'm making sure nothing goes wrong at the final hurdle!' Jay grinned as she breezed past Alex and Lucinda holding the last tray of soufflés.

Alex followed Lucinda out of the kitchen and into the office area. He pointed at his jacket, which he was rather pleased to have kept almost spotless. 'What do I do with this?'

'Oh, um … give it to me. I'll take it home and put it in the wash with mine.'

Alex struggled out of the jacket which clung stubbornly to his arms. Eventually he was free of it, but not before it caused his sweater to stretch and ride up, exposing a strip of midriff to the relatively cool air of the office. As he tugged his top down over his belt he glanced up and caught Lucinda swerving her gaze to the floor. His suspicions she had been staring at his bare skin grew as her cheeks began to glow pink.

Alex's pulse thudded and lips quirked at this sign Lucinda found him attractive. A bit. Maybe. And, as he handed her the jacket—his smile stretching when he noticed she took it and draped it over her arm all while refusing to meet his eye—her flushed face gave him the confidence to ask her out for a drink. It was the question he'd first attempted to put to her back in the London lobby of the Richards Group building and, after the events of the past twenty-four hours, they had, once again, more than earned it. Besides, there could be no harm in a friendly drink, could there?

He took a breath, his stern inner voice ordering him to stop overthinking and ask her. 'I was wondering if—'

Lucinda spoke over him, 'I don't suppose—'

They both laughed and gestured for the other to continue. 'No, please, you first,' said Alex.

'OK, thanks. It's a cheeky favour to ask, but would you mind dropping me home? It's a ten-minute drive. I could walk, but there's no path at one point and I'd have to walk next to the main road—'

'Of course. No problem.'

Lucinda grinned in gratitude. 'Thank you. For all your

help.' Her smile thinned into a slightly embarrassed smirk. 'I will honestly stop bothering you soon.'

Please don't, was the response on the tip of Alex's tongue, which he fortunately managed to trap behind his teeth. For as much as he was gladdened by the prospect of more time with Lucinda, he knew he should be prioritising getting home to Nicole.

Jay was closing the rear van doors as they stepped out into the sunshine. The purr of the engine sent her scurrying to open the passenger door. 'It was lovely to see you again, Alex. Thanks so much for the help. Again.' She planted a foot on the step, ready to hoist herself up into the vehicle, then froze. 'Oh! And sorry about *Napier*,' she said, offering Alex a wince of sympathy.

Completely at a loss, Alex asked, 'What about *Napier*?'

Jay's sorrowful stare lifted as her eyes widened and her lashes fluttered in a spasm of nervous blinking. 'Er … um … you should look at Twitter.'

A swirling nausea flooded Alex's stomach. He was silenced by a suffocating sense of foreboding and it was Lucinda who asked for clarification.

'What's going on, Jay?'

'They announced, earlier this morning … They're not renewing it.'

Bile threatened to rise into Alex's throat and he swallowed hard as Lucinda half shouted, 'What?'

'It's been cancelled.' Jay turned her gaze to Alex, the sympathy having returned to her eyes. 'I'm sorry.' She tilted her head towards the van. 'I have to go. It was great seeing you again. Bye!'

Somewhere in the far distance, Lucinda asked Jay to call her later, a door slammed and an engine rumbled as the van left the car park. The sounds were distorted by a dizzying fog of disbelief and an inner monologue which, at its most basic, was an agonised scream of despair.

'Alex, I'm sorry.' Lucinda glanced up from her phone, her expression strained. 'I've looked at Twitter and ... I think it's true.'

Alex squeezed his eyes shut, tipped his head back and let sunlight wash over his face. He refused to believe it. Someone could have got the wrong end of the stick. Rumours about shows getting cancelled spread like wildfire and tended to hang around even when disproved. It was the sort of ludicrous thing Ray would have started just for fun.

It was likely to be a silly misunderstanding. But the writhing anxiety in his guts wouldn't settle until he knew for sure.

He turned to Lucinda. 'Do you mind if we get going? I think I should get home and make a couple of calls.'

Chapter 25

The sapphire sky filling the car windows reflected Lucinda's joy at having completed Nancy's order. Unfortunately, the only sunshine inside the car was being provided by the upbeat tunes from the oldies radio station. Alex's lips were set in a thin line and he didn't bob his head, not even a fraction, in time to the music when a classic a-ha track was followed by 'Wake Me Up Before You Go-Go'. Lucinda chewed her bottom lip. You knew things were bad when Wham! couldn't help.

Unable to think of any words that might comfort him, she spoke only to give Alex directions. Frustrated and restless, she attempted to distract herself by trailing her fingers over the stitching on the black chef's jacket in her lap. Alex had looked marvellous in it but had struggled to take it off. His top had risen to reveal an inch of skin above his jeans. Her fingers had tingled in response to the sight, twitching as she ached to stroke the tanned muscle, hook her thumb over his waistband and pull him hard against her.

The back of her neck prickled with heat as the memory was followed by another: he'd caught her looking. Thankfully he hadn't said anything. Perhaps he was used to being ogled by deranged fans.

As they neared her house, Lucinda exhaled slowly and wrung the jacket fabric in her fists. She needed to wrest control of herself back from her hormones. If Alex were to put on another display of decisive proficiency, inside or outside a kitchen, she wasn't sure she would be able to hold herself back. Why were confidence and competence such an attractive combination? A sexy cocktail too powerful to resist—

Oh no.

A pulse began to thud in Lucinda's temples as Alex drove past her house and pulled into a space on the opposite side of the street. There could be no mistaking the vehicles she had seen. Her dreams of unpacking the events of the previous twenty-four hours in blissful privacy, and perhaps the luxury of a scalding hot bath, were shattered.

Chris had told her he'd be having lunch at his parents', but his black saloon squatted on the drive like a fat shiny bug. And, equally distressing, his parents' silver hatchback was stationed on the road in front of the house next door.

She rummaged in her bag for her keys, finding them, as ever, thanks to her heart key-ring charm. Its size and colour made it a bright beacon among the dim jumble of bits and bobs which she must have deemed essential at some point in the past. The crimson enamel heart filled her palm as she slipped two fingers through the puzzle-shaped hole in its centre and tugged, freeing her keys from the handbag detritus with a triumphant jangle.

Pushing her index finger to the stress headache blooming behind her right eyebrow, she knew she should get inside and make polite small talk. Let Alex get home.

And yet, when she turned to face him, Alex's expression was so drawn that her British crisis instincts kicked in.

'Would you like to come in for a cup of tea?'

Alex blinked, the distance in his eyes shrinking. 'Uh. Actually, could I just use your bathroom?'

'Of course. Follow me.'

Lucinda's house was a mid-terrace in an unremarkable row of brick buildings. Bay windows and arched porches created the mildest hint of character. Some of the properties preserved their low front walls and gardens while others—like Lucinda and Chris's—had a short driveway.

As they approached the house, the patter of their footsteps were the only sounds troubling the Sunday afternoon hush. The suburban silence, together with Alex's glum reticence, made Lucinda twitchy, and she gave her keys a reassuring rattle as she stepped up to the front door. Few visitors had stepped through it and, as Alex waited for her to turn the key in the lock, Lucinda's heart began to knock against her ribs: what would he make of her nest? And could she get him in and out without having to introduce him to Chris and his parents?

Inside, a few strides separated the entrance from the staircase. Two doors to the left of the narrow hallway—one before and one after the foot of the stairs—opened into the lounge and kitchen. As she tiptoed across the threshold Lucinda noted a faint scent of lily and jasmine in the air: Chris's mum was nearby. She eased the door closed behind Alex and winced at the click of the latch as if she were a rebellious adolescent sneaking back into her parents' house after midnight.

Lucinda pointed to a third door beyond the entrance to the kitchen and said, 'Through the door with the stained-glass panel. The loo is to the right.'

Alex nodded and said, 'Thanks,' as he shuffled past her.

The door had barely shut behind him when Lucinda was assaulted by the sound of her name flying out of the lounge. She rolled her shoulders back as if preparing to step into a boxing ring and nudged the door open.

'Lucinda! At last!' Chris's mum sprang off the sofa under the bay window and strode forwards to kiss Lucinda's cheeks. The heels of her black ankle boots clacked against the laminate flooring. Their colour was a perfect match to her cropped hair, which was a uniform and, Lucinda suspected, expensive raven hue. Lucinda envied anyone who could carry off such a short cut, and Chris's mum, who bulldozed her way through life with unassailable confidence, did it terrifically.

Chris's dad stepped forwards as his wife released her grasp on Lucinda's arms. 'Nice to see you,' he said and laid a careful peck on her cheek.

'You too,' said Lucinda as she scanned his friendly face. While Chris's mum was able to use dye to fight the signs of ageing, his dad didn't have that option, having gone bald over ten years previously. Perhaps that was why he refused to shave his dapper white moustache and neat beard.

Chris levered himself off the arm of the sofa and slunk forwards, rubbing his fingers over the stubble lining his jaw. A navy cotton jacket was slung over his left arm and his parents were also carrying their coats. Were they about to go out? Had they been waiting for her to get back?

Perhaps following Lucinda's gaze to his arm, Chris gestured to the chef jackets hanging from hers. 'So did you and Jay get it sorted?'

'Yes, thank you. Crisis averted.'

Mrs Georgiou tutted. 'You should come back to the restaurant.' She tapped Lucinda's forehead. 'Look at these lines. Worry is ageing.'

'Lucinda is beautiful, Helena,' said Chris's dad in a firm tone which presented his opinions as fact. 'And her business is very successful. Remember you were the one who wanted to start our business. You would not stop her doing the same, would you?'

God bless Mr Georgiou, thought Lucinda as her headache began to retreat. The man was a tonic.

Her initial line of attack rebuffed, Mrs Georgiou began another assault. 'Did we hear you talking to someone just now?'

'Oh! Yes. Um ...' Lucinda flailed as she realised there was no chance of smuggling Alex out of house. Or avoiding having to explain what he was to her. 'It's my ... that is, he's my friend.' Lucinda smiled. That had been surprisingly easy. And the idea of Alex as her friend produced a warm glow inside her which resisted the freeze of her audience's enquiring stares.

'Do we know him?'

'You might ... Sort of ...'

'Does he live locally? What's his name?'

'No, he doesn't. He's called'—Lucinda glanced to her left as Alex appeared in the doorway—'Alex!' Her smile widened and, as Alex stepped into the room, she turned her gaze back to the others. 'This is Alex.'

As the Georgious gawped at him, Lucinda realised she had become used to Alex's company. Trying to view him as if it were for the first time, she noticed his height and relaxed stance. Beyond his handsome features and strong, slim build, he had an undeniable *presence*, as if the space around him shimmered with energy.

Apparently unaware of the force field around him, Alex smiled awkwardly and raised his hand in an unnecessary wave. 'Hello everyone.'

Rushing to complete the introductions, Lucinda said, 'Alex, this is Chris and his parents, Mr and Mrs Georgiou.'

'Nice to meet you.'

Chris managed to shut his mouth long enough to swallow before he said, 'You're Alex Fraser.'

'That I am.' Alex laughed nervously and extended a hand.

Chris's gaze shuttled between Alex's face and their joined hands as he loosed a stream of appreciation. 'I'm a huge fan of *Napier*. I just rewatched it all with Lucinda because she hadn't seen it and I didn't mind because I thought it would be good to catch up before the latest series. And it was amazing. That cliffhanger! Incredible!'

Alex laughed again as he rescued his hand from Chris's grip. 'Thank you. I'm pleased you enjoyed it.'

Chris's mum shot a huff of air from her nostrils. 'I'm sorry but I have no idea—'

'Mum!' Chris interrupted with all the horror of a teenager about to be shamed by a parent's lack of cool. 'He's in *Napier*. The detective show I keep telling you to watch.'

'Uf! My love, I have enough with my gardening and cooking programmes.'

'You'd like it. The end of the last series was ace. Although'—Chris frowned and glanced at Alex—'it looks like we might never find out what happens next if the cancellation rumours are true.'

Lucinda's stomach dropped as Alex's smile fell. Desperate to steer the conversation away from the likelihood of Alex having lost his beloved job, she said, 'Did you find it OK, Alex?' before kicking herself for asking such a lame question. As if the man would have got lost in a two-bed terrace!

'Yes, fine thanks.' Alex glanced around at the four sets of eyes fixed on him and pushed his hands deep into his pockets. 'I like the tiles behind the sink.'

Lucinda gave a short laugh of pleased surprise. She'd had the tiles printed with a multicoloured pattern of tessellating stars based on one of the stunning mosaics in the Alhambra. She'd seen the original during a visit to the beautiful hilltop palace complex with her brother and mother. A trip which was probably her happiest memory of her brief time with her family in Spain.

'Oh no,' Chris said with a groan. 'Don't encourage her. She wanted to do the whole area around the shower like that.' He chuckled at the ridiculousness of the idea, and Lucinda's delight at Alex's comment was replaced by an echo of the teeth-grinding frustration she'd experienced during her and Chris's heated discussions about how best to decorate the house.

Ignoring Chris's comments, Alex continued to look at Lucinda as he said, 'It made me think of something I saw in Spain once.'

'It was based on a design in the Alhambra. Have you been to Granada?'

'Not yet. A friend got married in Andalucia a few years ago, but I couldn't make it. I'd love to go.'

'That reminds me!' Chris's mum gave Lucinda's elbow a sharp squeeze, forcing her to drag her attention away from Alex. 'Did Chris tell you his cousin Theo is getting married? You met him at our anniversary party.' She drew a few inches closer to Lucinda and lowered her voice to the loudest of stage whispers. 'You remember Theo? A sweet boy, but not the smartest. When it was raining brains he was carrying an umbrella!'

'Mum!'

'It's true! Anyway, Chris needs a plus one and I said you should go with him.'

This time Chris's pained shout of 'Mum!' also expressed Lucinda's horror.

'What? She's practically family.'

Lucinda's skin itched and burned under Chris's mum's hopeful gaze. The awkwardness she had experienced around Chris's parents since the split had mellowed of late, but occasionally Mrs Georgiou insisted on making ham-fisted attempts to push her and Chris back together. In these tricky moments, as well as unease, Lucinda was troubled by a quiver of sadness. She had enjoyed spending time with Chris's large extended family. They were accepting, noisy and fun; unlike her own in almost every way.

'Um, it's kind of you to invite me,' Lucinda said. 'But I'm sure Chris would rather take someone else.'

'Nonsense! Why would he? You are single. He is single. This is perfect.'

We are single because your son dumped me for a woman he barely knew! Lucinda bit her tongue to keep the reply from slipping out of her mouth. Why did people keep behaving as if the break-up was somehow her fault?

The fire in her cheeks swelled as a dash of angry resentment fanned the flames of embarrassment. Lucinda swallowed and tried to rein in her chagrin. Although, the added complication of Alex's presence—the poor man had stumbled into the role of unwitting bystander to a family drama—didn't help. He must have thought them all dysfunctional at best and, at worst, deranged. Although, thankfully, he seemed to have zoned out of the conversation and was staring past Chris, his eyes scanning her bookshelves.

No one had ever inspected her collection before and, even if they had, she wouldn't have cared. But now, as Alex ran his inquisitive stare over her carefully arranged detective novels and spy fiction, she chewed her lip. What did her favourite volumes by Christie and Le Carré say about her? Whatever it was, it was probably more cryptic than the larger, non-fiction books on the lower shelves which included two tomes about the making of *Back to the Future*, a guide to the best movies of the 1980s, and a *Star Wars* visual dictionary. And, in case the titles didn't make her preferences obvious enough, all doubt was removed by the vinyl figurine of Princess Leia standing in the corner of the bottom shelf.

Chris grinned, swung close enough to Alex to nudge him and said, in a mocking tone, 'Admiring Lucinda's shrine to the past?'

Alex fixed Chris with a penetrating level gaze as if he were trying to stare into Lucinda's ex's soul and weigh his character. His expression neutral, he replied, 'She has an interesting collection of books about film.'

Chris chuckled. 'If you know what's good for you, you won't get her started on all that geeky stuff'—he jabbed a finger towards the Princess Leia figurine, which he'd moaned about being on the shelf since the day Lucinda had unboxed it, and banned Lucinda from putting Han Solo next to her—'or she'll never stop bending your ear about it!'

Alex's brows rose and he blinked rapidly as they settled. A coolness crept into his eyes as he shrugged and said, 'Sounds good to me.'

He shifted his gaze to Lucinda and, as their eyes met they smiled at each other. The heat in Lucinda's face began to calm as she focused on their shared smile: a conspiratorial grin that brought to mind beagle-hunting in a bog, sneakily scoffing bacon and eggs and locating a car somewhere between the adventure golf course and model village.

Mr Georgiou coughed, jolting Lucinda from her reverie. She should let Alex get home. He must be desperate to find out what was happening with *Napier*. And the very last thing he needed was to get caught up in her Chris-related stresses.

She glanced at the clock above the fireplace and, upon seeing it was nearly one o'clock, the caterer in her turned to Alex and asked, 'Did you want some lunch before you go?'

'Thank you, but I'm fine. I should be heading off.'

'So should we,' said Chris's dad, touching his wife's elbow and glaring at Chris.

Lucinda followed the others to the front door. Squinting against the sunshine, she realised she had hoped to speak to Alex in private before he left. To thank him properly for giving her a lift and helping in the kitchen. To wish him luck with the whole *Napier* situation. And then there was the small matter of the sticky toffee pudding. They'd agreed to meet up for dessert and she'd been looking forward to impressing him with her baking.

A chill of disappointment snaked down her spine. Their pudding date seemed unlikely to happen now. Not that it would have been a *date,* of course. Because he had a girlfriend. And they were just friends, after all.

Pausing on the driveway, Alex spun to face the house. As he moved, the sun's beams caught the blonde tones in his hair and added a golden glow to what Lucinda was beginning to regard as his undeniable allure. 'It was nice to meet you all,' he said, raising his hand in a polite half wave and nodding at the reciprocal murmurs from Mr and Mrs Georgiou.

Chris took a step back so he was standing beside Lucinda on the front step. His arm brushed against hers and she fought the urge to shrink away. She was opening her mouth to say goodbye to Alex when Chris cut across her. 'Bye then. Thanks for driving Lucinda home.'

The crease between Lucinda's eyebrows deepened as Chris wrapped an unwanted arm around her shoulders. Her neck muscles clenched as if trying to shrug him off, and if his parents and Alex hadn't been standing in front of them she would have foregone all social niceties and shoved Chris down the step.

'It was my pleasure.' Alex shifted his gaze to Lucinda. 'Any time. Goodbye, Lucinda.'

Staring at Alex's slightly sad smile, Lucinda momentarily

forgot about the heat of Chris's arm and matched Alex's rueful expression. 'Bye, Alex. Fingers crossed for good news about *Napier*.'

As Alex crossed the road, Chris squeezed Lucinda's upper arm and she reluctantly dragged her focus from Alex's retreating figure. 'You should come to lunch with us,' Chris said, his voice loud enough to be heard by the whole street, and certainly by Alex who was opening his car door as the invitation was issued.

'No,' said Lucinda, twisting out from under Chris's arm, 'that's nice of you, but I'm tired after this morning.'

Chris's mum swung her support behind her son's idea. 'You can ride in Chris's car.' She poked Lucinda in the tummy, hitting the exact spot where a knot of discomfort was tightening by the second. 'You could do with a good feed.'

'Thank you, but—'

'If you won't come with us, I'll make you something!' said Chris. 'Mum's right—'

'Come on, you two,' said Mr Georgiou, using the grim tone of someone who had reached their shenanigans limit. He placed a hand on his wife's arm and steered her down the driveway. 'Lucinda is busy. And she's certainly capable of making herself food.' He glanced over his shoulder and his moustache twitched as he threw Lucinda a fleeting smile. 'It was good seeing you, Lucinda.'

'You too!' said Lucinda, hoping he would hear the genuine love in her words.

As Chris's parents drove away, Lucinda brushed her fingers over the perfect paint finish she had applied to the front door. The idea of ever parting from the shine of the silky crimson gloss—a regular reminder of how hard work could have spectacularly pleasing results—pained her, tugging at the knot in her stomach.

'The guys at work won't believe it when I tell them Alex Fraser was in my house!' Chris said as he unlocked his car and opened the driver's door.

Lucinda lurched forwards onto the front step, moved by a sudden need to prevent Alex from being reduced to one of Chris's anecdotes. 'Don't say anything, Chris. Please.'

'Why not?'

'Well, it's just …' Lucinda fumbled about for any reason other than an inexplicably strong instinct to defend the privacy of a man she barely knew. 'There are these rumours *Napier* is going to be cancelled—'

'I know. It's all over Twitter. They left this last series on such a cliffhanger I couldn't believe they'd pull the plug, but now …'

Tiny prickles, like an army of ants, crept over Lucinda's skin. 'But now *what*?'

Chris sighed. 'When I tried to talk to Alex about the show, did you notice how he barely said anything? I mean, he could have shown a bit more enthusiasm!'

Lucinda's jaw fell slack as the feet of the invisible ants began to burn. How had Chris read Alex's modest response to his overexcited fanboying as indifference?

'I mean,' Chris continued, unaware Lucinda was mentally measuring him up for a coffin, 'if you can't show more passion for a job than that, you probably don't deserve it anyway. Right?' He shrugged. 'Makes you think he's been lucky to get the jobs he has up to now.'

Lucinda's lips moved but no sound came out as Chris hopped into his car and reversed down the drive. She was immobilised by the scorching heat thundering through her and had no answer to his comments which wouldn't have been the blood-curdling screech of an offended harpy.

Allowing herself a short growl, she whirled into the hall and thumped the door into its frame, not caring if the resulting tremors brought every tile and brick of her cherished house tumbling down around her.

Chapter 26

As he accelerated away from Lucinda's, Alex's thoughts spiralled. He had probably lost the best job he'd ever had, he was on his way home to break up with his girlfriend, he had a new gig starting tomorrow, and Chris definitely wanted to get back together with Lucinda. But did she want that too?

Round and round his thoughts spun, with Lucinda on the tail of every twisting coil. The image of her and Chris, his arm wrapped casually around her shoulders, standing in the doorway of their house, his parents standing next to them ... It was a neat family picture. One with no place for anyone else. No place for *him*.

When James called an hour into his trip, Alex ignored the phone's insistent chirp while marvelling at his brother's sixth sense for knowing when the worst possible moment was to bother him. But when the phone rang again seconds after the first attempt had cut off, Alex growled and jabbed the handset to accept the call.

'I'm driving!' he said, hoping to keep the conversation brief.

'I can hear,' James said, his tone equally curt. 'I need to know if you'll be here for dinner this evening.'

Alex sighed. It was a reasonable question. And he should be showering his brother and Sarah with gratitude for putting him up for a few weeks. In a gentler voice, he said, 'Sorry. I should be. I'm nearly home. I can try and be with you by six. Is that OK?'

'Sure. Sarah says we can give the girls their dinner at the usual time and then eat together later if you need more time to get here.'

'Tell her, thank you. She's a saint.'

'Too true. Oh, and, um …' James's voice trailed off in a crackle of interference.

'James? Are you still there?'

'Yeah. I … I wanted to …'

Alex frowned and hoped he was losing phone coverage. Otherwise, from James's halting approach, it was likely his kid brother was building up to telling him something difficult, and more difficulties was something he could really do without.

'What's up?'

'I heard about *Napier*.'

'It's just rumours.'

'Actually, I think it's been confirmed.' Alex rolled his eyes. That was James: always happy to drop the blunt hard truth. 'The online news is running the story.'

James's voice was interrupted by a number of message alerts which Alex suspected came from the *Napier* WhatsApp group.

'Al? Are you OK?'

'Yeah,' Alex lied as a tightness gripped his chest. 'I'll see you later.'

Alex completed the rest of the journey in a thickening cloud of gloom only punctuated by regular beeps from his phone which his overactive imagination began to regard as the chimes of doom.

Shortly before two o'clock, Alex scrolled through the disbelieving and increasingly desperate messages flying among the *Napier* cast and crew as he climbed the stairs to his flat. Though he trudged steadily upwards, he felt as though a sharp slope was unfurling behind him and he was in danger of tumbling down it into darkness below.

And arriving home offered little comfort. Opening the front door, he was struck by how cramped and featureless the living space appeared. While this was partly a side effect of having spent a significant part of the previous twenty-four hours rattling around a stately home, even Lucinda's slender terraced house seemed like an airy palace in comparison. And her place had many stylish, thoughtful touches, like the bathroom tiles and her bookshelves. Meanwhile his flat remained a bland, impersonal box, with a tenancy agreement which forbade almost all forms of decoration. And while the tiny window in the kitchenette was open, any air which might have dared to enter the room had nowhere to go, leaving the space clammy and airless.

'He's picking me up in a few minutes ... I know! I can't wait! It's going to be beyond amazing!' Nicole's excited chatter bounced into the room, followed by the woman herself in a cloying haze of vanilla and rose. The handle of an enormous silver suitcase was in her left hand, her phone in her right. She was dressed suitably for the sauna-like conditions in the flat in a sleeveless lavender minidress and sparkly gold sandals. When she saw Alex her eyes widened. 'Babe, Alex is back. I have to go. I'll talk to you later. Love you, bye!' Grinning broadly, she stepped past the sofa towards him. 'You're finally here!'

Alex met her grin with a wary smile and nodded to the suitcase. 'Going somewhere?'

Nicole inhaled noisily through her nose, her chest inflating with the news she could barely contain. 'I got the part!'

'What? That's ... that's fantastic!' Alex's lips stretched into a genuine grin. Nicole worked hard, was a great actor and it was about time she got a break. Besides, only the most miserable of people would have been unaffected by the joy radiating from every inch of her, swelling her petite form to near bursting. 'Did they call you this morning?'

'Yesterday afternoon. Not long after you left.' She let out a squeal and clapped her hands together in a gesture that reminded Alex of his nieces' innocent delight at the smallest things. He frowned. Suddenly he felt very, very old. 'They want me over there right away,' Nicole said. 'Jackson'll be here in a minute to take me to the airport.'

'Airport?' Alex's thoughts were sluggish, not helped by the suffocating warmth in the room. As beads of sweat formed at his hairline, he struggled to get past the revelation Nicole must have known she had the part when he had spoken to her the previous evening. Why hadn't she told him then?

'They're flying me to LA. Production starts in a couple of days.' She tittered and flicked her hair from her shoulder. 'Your memory is getting worse, old man.'

Alex gave a half-hearted laugh, but he was distracted from Nicole's teasing by two stacks of cardboard boxes next to the kitchenette. 'That's great, really exciting.' He pointed towards the boxes. 'What's in those?'

'Oh, right.' Nicole's smile slipped. 'The lettings agency called yesterday to say the landlord wants to sell the flat. They're giving us a month's notice to leave.'

Alex shook his head to clear a wave of wooziness. 'A month?'

'I'm so sorry, babe, I should have told you yesterday, but it's been absolutely crazy since I got the call about going to the States. It's been a blur, honestly. But I did look into the notice period and apparently it's normal and in the contract ...' She waved towards the boxes. 'I don't know when I'll be back, and I didn't want you to have to worry about my stuff so I boxed it up and Jackson will pick it up. You'll be busy with filming from Monday so I'll give Jackson my key and he can let himself in, if that's OK with you.'

She took another step forwards and reached for his hand, her dainty fingers curling around his. 'And uh... as I can't say when or even if'—she broke off and a more timid version of her excited grin returned—'I'll be back ... I think, you and me ... well, you know I love you, but long distance never works, does it? We've had such a great time together, I think it's best to end things now rather than drag it out over video calls. And'—she shrugged and her smile fell as her tone turned quiet and serious—'this is such an amazing opportunity for me, Alex. I think I need to give it my all. I need to be completely focused on me for a while.'

Gobsmacked, Alex stared down into Nicole's blue eyes: after worrying about breaking up with her for weeks, she had beaten him to it. Her unexpected initiative, yet another surprise in what was proving to be an eventful and bewildering weekend, made his lips twitch and he barely managed to contain hysterical laughter at how swiftly his life was descending into farce.

He cleared his throat. 'Of course. I understand.'

Encouraged by his tentative smile, Nicole squeezed his hand. 'I knew you would. You've always been so supportive.' Gazing into his eyes, she ran a hand over her hair, and Alex did his best not to blink. After all, this was the last time she would use him as a convenient mirror.

Stray strands tamed to her satisfaction, Nicole released Alex's hand. 'I know you aren't looking forward to it, but I'm pleased you're staying at your brother's for a while. It'll give you more time to find somewhere new in London.'

The intercom by the front door buzzed. 'That'll be Jackson!' Nicole skipped over to push the entry button with considerable agility for a woman wearing four-inch heels. A few more hops took her back to her suitcase.

The sight of her slender fingers grasping the handle of the case jolted Alex out of his shocked trance. 'Would you like help with that?'

Nicole shooed him away with her free hand as she dragged the case to the front door. 'Jackson will come up and carry it down for me.'

'Will you let me know when you get there?'

She laughed and stepped away from her case just long enough to peck him on the cheek. 'You're such an old worrier.'

Back in the days when he was a young worrier, Alex had made his first trip to LA for pilot season. He'd been brimming with optimism, convinced he was a step away from a big break which stubbornly refused to show up. Looking at Nicole's glowing expression of youthful excitement, he hoped she had better luck.

Now her ex, Alex decided he no longer cared if he sounded like her dad. 'Please send me a quick message. I want to know you've arrived safely.'

'I'll try. But I'll be so busy I'll probably forget!' She loosed another squeal. 'OK. Here I go!'

Wheeling the case onto the landing, Nicole broke into a high-pitched greeting to Jackson and didn't glance back as Alex followed her to say goodbye. The door slammed inches from Alex's nose, leaving him staring at the scratched white paintwork and listening through the wood as Nicole's bubbly chatter and Jackson's low murmurs grew distant.

Alex staggered back and dropped onto the sofa. He exhaled slowly as he imagined Nicole strutting around LA while he was begging his baby brother to let him stay for a couple of extra weeks until he could find another depressing, characterless matchbox to live in.

He let his head thud back onto the seat cushion. Staring at the beige walls, he made some effort to resist wallowing in self-pity by drafting a mental inventory of what he had to pack before leaving for James's. But the list was depressingly short. A sad showing for a man of forty-three.

A dull heaviness settled into his limbs. A part of him suggested shaking it off and getting on with packing. But the leaden sensation slithered up his spine, dragging his eyes shut and encouraging him to slide down into the darkness he had sensed on his arrival at the flat.

His drop into despair was halted by the cheerful chirp of his phone. Groaning, Alex opened his eyes and swiped at the screen. *What the hell now?*

The message was brief. He read it once. Twice. Then he shot upright so fast the phone jumped from his fingers and clattered to the floor.

Cursing, he grabbed the phone and scanned the text again.

14:04

Hi Alex. This is Lucinda. I hope you got home OK and don't mind me texting you. I asked Misha for your number. She had it on file from when you worked with us at Compton Hall.

The creeping numbness lifted as his pulse accelerated. Lucinda had gone to the trouble of tracking down his number. Although she hadn't said why.

He slumped back into the sofa again and massaged his brow with his thumb and forefinger. Sweat began to form at his nape as he urged his sluggish brain to come up with the perfect reply. Something friendly, but not too friendly. Something brilliant, witty and winning.

He typed, erased and retyped, muttering to himself to vent his frustration. Eventually, he glanced at the clock and realised ten whole minutes—practically an eternity if you were waiting for someone to reply—had passed since he read her message. Rolling his eyes at his own indecision, he tapped out his first draft and muttering, 'Sod it,' pressed send.

14:14
Hi. It's good to hear from you. Is everything OK? Did Jay sort the rest of the grand luncheon?

Alex grimaced at the banality of his reply and his poor attempt at humour. She had probably moved on to more important things while he was worrying about his punctuation.

But, as if Lucinda wasn't on board with furthering his natural tendency to wallow in setbacks, she replied almost instantly.

14:16
Everything's fine, thanks. Jay reports the lunch was a triumph. Everyone very impressed. Nancy happy.

Alex surged to his feet. Buoyed by the success of the lunch and his initial message, he paced in front of the sofa, trying to imagine Lucinda was standing in front of him. Talking was always easier than writing. If she were in the room, what would he say to her?

This time it only took four agonising minutes to come up with thirteen words and—absolutely crucially—an emoji.

14:20
All down to the superior chopping of the carrots and potatoes, I'm sure ☺

14:21
Undoubtedly ☺ I'm not keeping you back from packing, am I?

Alex grinned. She'd sent an emoji back! That had to be good, right? Perhaps not overthinking it was the key. Perhaps, he thought, as he began typing, he should reply with whatever came immediately to mind.

Reading her latest message again, her mention of packing gave him pause and dented his elation. He mustn't get to James's later than six. And he hadn't even dug his bag out from under the bed. He should be getting on with it.

But he couldn't leave Lucinda unanswered. That would be rude. Besides, the sight of the small smiley face, and his memory of the alluring smile of the woman behind it, sent a fizz of excitement shooting through his veins. Receiving another emoji might give him the energy he needed to get the packing done in record time. Two might send him into orbit.

14:22
Not at all. It won't take long to throw some things in a suitcase.

14:23
OK, if you're sure ☺
I know it's not any of my business, and you can tell me to get lost if you like, but I wanted to talk to you about Napier.

14:25
Are you about to offer me a job in your kitchen? Because from what I've been reading on the cast and crew WhatsApp group, I might need it.

14:28
We'd be lucky to have you, but I think that'd be a shameful waste of your talents.

And when I called Jay to check how it went with Nancy, she gave me an idea about saving the show.

14.29
Napier???

14.31
The one and only. You're going to your brother's later, right? And he lives in Wolston?

14.31
Yes ...

14:33
Would it be OK if I came round this evening? It'll be easier to explain in person.

14:34
Sure! I should be there by six. 24 Rose Lane, CP2 7RB. If you have trouble finding it, give me a call.

14.35
If I come around 7, I won't be interrupting dinner, will I?

14:35
7 would be perfect.

14:36
OK, see you then ☺☺

14:36
Looking forward to it! ☺☺

Chapter 27

Lucinda retrieved the large plastic tub from the passenger footwell and slammed the van door. As she strolled across the charcoal-block paving towards Alex's brother's house she admired it with a covetous stare. The cladding looked brand new. And expensive. What achingly sensible and well-paid things must the owners do for a living?

Drawing closer to the front door, she balanced the tub on top of the bunch of keys in her left hand and used her right to tuck two stray strands of hair behind her ears. Her fingers trembled as she pushed the doorbell. Get a grip, she told herself. This was Alex's brother's place, not a lions' den.

A tall woman wearing black leggings and an oversized pink pullover opened the door. Her chestnut hair was tied back in a low ponytail and her feet were bare. She was slightly out of breath and a dash of red highlighted her cheekbones in her otherwise pale face. On seeing Lucinda, a wide smile lit up her eyes. 'Hello! You must be Lucinda. I'm Sarah, please come in.'

Lucinda stepped into the relative gloom of the hallway as Sarah closed the door behind her and lowered her voice to say, 'I'm glad you're here. I'm hoping *you* can cheer Alex up.' She threw a glance down the corridor which led to a staircase and a number of open doors. 'You know it's bad when the girls' antics haven't been able to raise a single smile.'

Lucinda's eyebrows shot upwards. Alex had seemed sombre when he'd left her house earlier, but not miserable. And she found it hard to imagine Alex despondent, although the idea came with an unpleasant, queasy pang. 'Is it that bad?'

'I've never seen Alex look so much as unhappy. But today he is miserable. And, I don't mean to be harsh, but I think he's being a bit *dramatic* about it all.' She chuckled. 'For an actor he's usually fairly stoic. But then I suppose he is having a hell of a day. He hasn't gone into details, but I think Nicole dumped him.'

Lucinda's mouth fell open and her heart began to pound. 'Oh. That's ... that's...' Finding the words on the tip of her tongue were 'great' and 'terrific', she clamped her lips together while casting about for a more appropriate response. 'He must be upset.'

'Huh.' Sarah raised a sceptical eyebrow. 'Between you and me, it was going to come to an end sooner rather than later.' Her pulse now racing, Lucinda leant towards Sarah as her host continued, 'They were hardly made for each other and she was far too young. To be honest, I think he's more stressed by their landlord having told them they have a month to get out. Now he has that to think about as well as the new job starting tomorrow. And the *Napier* calamity, of course.'

'Oh. That is ... a lot for one day,' said Lucinda, still captivated by the revelation Alex was single. It was shameful she was experiencing an adrenaline rush in response to the news of Alex's break-up, particularly if it was contributing to his unhappiness. But her body didn't seem to care and her galloping heartbeat was joined by clammy palms.

'You're right. I guess we can forgive him some dramatics. Come on through, they're in the lounge.'

Lucinda followed Sarah down the corridor, hanging back a step to admire the colourful family photos covering the walls. A cool breeze fanned her face, carrying the unmistakeable aroma of fried sausages. 'I didn't interrupt your dinner, did I?'

'No, we eat early because of the girls. They've had their bath and should be going to bed any minute.' Sarah turned to face Lucinda. 'Tomorrow is a school day.'

'I brought some dessert.' Lucinda offered the plastic container to Sarah. 'It's just chocolate brownies, but probably best not to give them to children right before bed.

'Ooo!' Sarah gripped the proffered tub eagerly. 'You're right, that sounds like food for adults.' She opened the edge of the lid and inhaled the rich smell of chocolate. 'That is divine! I love you already.' She gave Lucinda another open smile and Lucinda suspected Sarah was her kind of person, a hunch confirmed when she said, 'I'll put these on a plate. I'm making tea, would you like one?'

'Yes, please.'

'Good woman. Go on into the lounge. I'll bring the tea in a minute.' Sarah nodded to the doorway on the right before striding away.

The vertical blinds hanging on the left-hand wall of the lounge swayed in the air entering through the open bay windows. The wall directly in front of Lucinda was home to an enormous flat-screen television. Beneath it, lying on their bellies on the oatmeal-coloured carpet, were two small girls wearing matching blue pyjamas. Their chins rested on their hands as they listened to the bedtime story on the screen while one swayed her feet and the other wriggled her toes. Also facing the television, forming a barrier between Lucinda and the girls, was a black, two-seater sofa. Alex was sitting on the left—Lucinda recognised his fair hair and broad shoulders. She assumed the marginally shorter man to his right, whose mousey hair was beginning to thin on his crown, was James.

She opened her mouth to say hello, but paused when James turned his head towards Alex and said, 'You can stay here as long as you need.'

Alex kept his gaze forwards as he replied, 'Thanks, but I'll start looking for somewhere tomorrow night. I don't want to be in your way.'

Alex's words were polite and measured, but something about his clipped tone meant all Lucinda could hear was *'Drop it and leave me alone'*. But James was either accustomed, indifferent or oblivious to the stern note in his brother's voice and pushed on. 'It's no problem. You could babysit. Sarah and I could take some nights off.'

A polite rebuff having failed to deter his brother, Alex resorted to shrugging one shoulder and harrumphing.

James continued, 'You should think about getting out of London. City rents are crazy. You're paying over a grand a month for a shoebox in Barnet!'

'Half of that. Nicole was paying the other half.' Alex's tone sharpened another notch. 'And it's in North Finchley, not Barnet.'

'Same difference.'

Alex gave a grunt which Lucinda recognised. It was a sound she produced when her brother or mother said something outrageously inaccurate but she didn't have the energy to argue the point.

'The important thing,' said James, 'is that a bit more than half of that would cover a mortgage on a small place round here.'

Alex grunted again and while Lucinda sympathised with his frustration, James was only speaking the truth. London prices had been one of the main reasons she'd moved down to the Comptons six years ago.

'Who are you?'

The younger of the girls had turned away from the television and was staring at Lucinda, her enquiring gaze as direct as her question.

Three other heads swivelled to follow her gaze. Finding herself in the crosshairs of four dark brown stares, Lucinda raised her right hand in an awkward greeting. 'Hi,' she said quietly, the keys in her left hand rattling as she fidgeted with them. 'I'm Lucinda.' She looked past the men to the girls as she said, 'I'm a friend of your uncle's.'

Her cheeks began to warm but, despite her discomfort at being the centre of attention, Lucinda was pleased when Alex's frown lifted and the suggestion of a smile pulled at the edge of his mouth.

The girls leapt to their feet with enviable agility and bounded round the sofa for a close-up inspection of the new arrival. Their chestnut hair was still damp from their bath and smelt faintly of apples.

The elder said, 'I'm Olivia and that's Emily.'

Not to be beaten by her sister, Emily added, 'I'm six and she's seven.'

The names and ages were delivered deadpan, as if they were vital information, and Lucinda was trying to work how to respond when their dad came to her rescue.

'I'm James.' He reached over the back of the sofa to shake Lucinda's hand. His face was a rounder version of Alex's with thinner lips and thicker brows.

'Daddy is forty-one,' said Olivia with a hint of scandal in her voice.

'But Uncle Alex is *even older*,' added Emily.

'Thanks, kids,' said Alex. He trained his gaze on Lucinda. 'Hi.'

'Hi.' Lucinda held his gaze, the warmth in her cheeks spreading to the rest of her face.

'I like your key ring,' said Olivia, poking at the bunch of keys which Lucinda had absent-mindedly been moving between her fingers.

Sinking down to her knees, Lucinda gripped the large red heart charm between her thumb and forefinger and offered it to Olivia for proper examination.

'Who gave it to you?' The girl poked her index finger through the puzzle-shaped hole in the middle of the heart. 'And where's the missing piece?'

That was quite a story. Lucinda bit her lip and did her best to simplify it for her young audience. 'My dad gave it to me when I was about your age. I gave him the puzzle piece. It was on a keychain too.'

Olivia nodded. 'My best friend River and me, we have necklaces and they're both half of the same heart. It's like that. Does your dad still have the missing piece?'

Alex jabbed James's arm and tilted his head towards the girls. 'What? Oh, right.' James nodded at his brother and said to his oldest daughter, 'Olivia, don't be nosey.'

'It's OK. It's a good question.' Lucinda gave Olivia a rueful smile. 'My dad kept it. But my brother has it now.'

Six years ago, weeks after being notified of their father's death and their inheritance, Lucinda and her brother had gone to empty the house that was now theirs. While Michael began to tackle the contents of the upstairs rooms, Lucinda sat at the kitchen table and sorted through the items which had been in her dad's pockets when he had been cut from the wreckage of his car. The contents of the envelope had thudded onto the table and, shining out from among an assortment of monochrome items, Lucinda had been astounded to see the bright red enamel of the missing puzzle piece. The sign her father hadn't entirely forgotten her made Lucinda cry for the first time since receiving the news of his passing.

She had stared at the puzzle charm until the tear tracks on her cheeks dried themselves and then darted upstairs to give it to her brother. She could remember five-year-old Michael sitting on their dad's lap, playing with his keys, fascinated by the ruby-red key ring. And his stunned expression as she handed it to him and asked him to keep it told her he could remember it too. For a moment, she had considered giving it to Chris, but he would have thought it soppy and never used it. Besides, there was no one in the world she loved more than Michael and no one else she trusted to keep the charm safe.

'Why did you give it to your brother?' Emily asked, her button nose wrinkling to indicate her bafflement.

'Well ...' Lucinda had stalled—should she raise the subject of death in front of children?—when Sarah bustled into the room carrying two steaming mugs of tea.

'Up to bed, girls. No, go on!' She raised her voice over howls of protest. 'I'll be up in few minutes to check on you.' Her stern expression melted away as the girls ran past her and thudded up the stairs. 'Lucinda, you can take this chair,' she said, depositing one of the cups on a side table next to the armchair to the left of the television. 'Alex says you have an idea about saving *Napier*. Just so you know'—she paused as she sank into the armchair opposite Lucinda's—'whatever it is, we're in. They can't leave it on that cliffhanger!'

Lucinda took the seat as directed and reached for her cup. 'The credit should go to my colleague, Jay. She's a huge fan of the show and is very upset about it being cancelled. She told me lots of people on Twitter and Instagram are using the hashtag "save *Napier*" and that made me think.' To escape the weight of the expectant stares on her, Lucinda took a scalding sip of tea before continuing. 'Other shows have been cancelled but then picked up by another channel after fans protested. Right?'

James, who had been relaxing against the backrest of the sofa, sat forwards. 'Yeah, it's happened a few times.' He poked Alex's knee. 'There was that sci-fi series last year, remember?'

Alex sank back against the sofa cushions, letting out a loud huff of resignation. Staring up at the ceiling, he said, 'I doubt it would work. We'd need everyone to get behind it, and from the messages I've been reading from the cast and crew, I'm not sure they're up for a fight.'

As he closed his eyes and released a long sigh which ended in a weary moan, Lucinda understood what Sarah had meant when she suggested Alex might be indulging his dramatic side. But pandering to his performative wallowing wouldn't solve his problem. Far better to press on with practicalities. 'Jay said you had quite a few followers on social media. I looked at the number of followers of the cast as a whole. If you put them all together, even with overlap, you're nearly at two million.'

James nodded. 'Particularly Diana Carter. She's had over a million followers on Instagram since she's been in that superhero movie. That first post of her in her costume got a few million likes.'

'Spent a while appreciating Ms Carter in her outfit, did you, my love?' asked Sarah in a barbed, though playful, tone. 'Revealing, was it?'

'No, not really,' James said, responding so quickly Lucinda was certain he'd ogled the picture more than once. 'Um … I mean, I heard about it. Indirectly. Probably from someone at work.'

Lucinda jumped in before James could incriminate himself further. 'I'm not sure how you'd go about getting your followers to join a "save *Napier*" campaign.' She paused, waiting for Alex to open his eyes and look her way. 'But I thought perhaps if you put out a short video message on social media then the Mumsweb lot might be persuaded to get behind it?'

Sarah snorted. 'Oh they'd love to get *behind* him, all right.'

Lucinda blinked, completely lost, while Alex groaned and bent to drop his head into his hands.

Sarah chuckled. 'It started with the voice thing, but now they've created a "Sexy Dexy" fan forum. You know, because his character in the series is called Dexter. Anyway, they've already launched their own campaign. After that bit in episode two of the latest series where you see him coming out of the shower naked—'

'It was important to the story! And it was less than a second!' Alex snapped his head up to protest before returning his forehead to his hands and muttering something which Lucinda thought sounded like, 'Sodding Poldark.'

'Yes, well, a second or not,' said Sarah, 'they're now trying to get Alex nominated for the Rear of the Year Award.'

James tipped his head back and guffawed, his laughter calming as he slapped his brother on the back. 'Ah, mate, come on. It's poetic. Your backside up for an award after your adverts for Salvan set off this mania in the first place.'

Lucinda bit the inside of her cheek and hid the lower half of her face behind her mug. Alex's face was concealed by his hands but, as James continued to chuckle, his neck turned a deep red. Not wanting to add to his discomfort, she strained to contain her own giggles while trying to think of how to steer the conversation back to ground absent of all adolescent humour.

'What does sexy mean?'

Emily's innocent, bell-like voice rang through the room and the adults turned as one to where the girl was standing in the doorway, clutching a teddy bear and looking not at all like someone ready to go to sleep.

Sarah, who was still sniggering, said, 'Ask your father.'

With a solemn expression, Emily padded around the sofa and climbed onto James's knees. 'Daddy, what does sexy mean?'

'Yes, James,' said Alex, a vengeful smile playing on his lips as he watched his brother splutter and fidget. 'Emily wants you to explain it.'

'Um ... er ... well ...'

Sarah allowed Alex to enjoy his brother's distress for a moment before coming to her husband's aid. 'It means good-looking.'

Emily's brows contracted in a crease of confusion. 'People think Uncle Alex is good-looking?'

'Yes,' said Sarah. 'Quite a lot of people.'

'But he's not good-looking!'

'Well said.' James patted his daughter's shoulder as he nodded in agreement.

Spurred by her father's encouragement, Emily added, 'He pulls funny faces and pretends to be a dinosaur.'

Alex groaned again and returned his face to his hands while Lucinda took a sip of tea to hide another smile. The movement must have drawn Emily's attention as the girl turned to stare Lucinda in the eye and ask, 'Do *you* think Uncle Alex is good-looking?'

Lucinda risked a glance at Alex, whose fingers had parted slightly to reveal his eyes, and pushed as much nonchalance as she could into her reply. 'Yes, I do. I think most people do.'

Emily's shook her head. 'I don't.'

James patted his daughter again. 'Me neither, kiddo. Time for bed.'

'But the sun is out.' The summer solstice was only a week away and it would be light for another couple of hours at least. James stuttered, foolishly leaving a gap for his youngest to deliver a killer follow-up question. 'What's the Rear of the Year Award?'

Sarah, apparently more experienced at answering difficult queries than her husband, said, 'It's a prize for having a nice bottom.'

Emily grimaced. 'Eww. That's super stupid.'

Alex lifted his face from his hands and laughed. 'You are one smart kid.'

'Yes. I am.' She turned her stare to Lucinda. 'Do you think Uncle Alex's bottom should win a prize?'

'I ... um ... wow, that's quite the question.' Lucinda chuckled nervously and glanced at the other adults for help. But Emily's parents gazed at her with neutral expressions, as if politely awaiting her answer. Alex pressed his lips into a thin line and blinked at her, the picture of wide-eyed innocence. But a single twitch at the side of his mouth gave him away. He was laughing at her predicament! The cheek!

Lucinda's inner warrior bristled and her blood began pumping as if she'd been challenged to single combat. It would serve Alex right if she went ahead and announced her innermost musings on his rear right in front of everyone. But they definitely weren't child appropriate. And no matter how bad a day he might be having, no one needed their ego stroking that badly.

Her face starting to burn, Lucinda turned back to Emily and lied. 'I haven't really thought about it.'

Emily nodded sagely. 'Because it's silly.'

'Exactly!' said Alex. 'Come on. Bed!'

Emily jumped off her father's lap, skipped over the carpet and leant on the armrest of Lucinda's chair. 'I like you,' she said, her hazel gaze fixed on Lucinda's. 'Are you going to be Uncle Alex's girlfriend now?'

Lucinda managed to stammer a few incoherent sounds before Emily continued, 'Because he doesn't have one any more. She's gone to America. Mum says it's probably for the—'

'Emily!' Sarah and James shouted and jumped up together. 'Bed! Now.'

Emily gave Lucinda an apologetic shrug, spun round with a swish of auburn hair and was chased out of the room by her parents, leaving Lucinda and Alex alone.

Chapter 28

'Sorry about Nicole.' Lucinda moved from the armchair to the space on the sofa next to Alex. She scrunched her nose in an adorable half-smile. 'And Sarah told me about you having to leave your flat.'

Alex allowed himself a second to stare at Lucinda's sympathetic green stare and pretty pink lips. How did she look even more gorgeous than she had earlier that afternoon? He, on the other hand, must look dreadful. A compressing weight continued to squat on his chest, a sensation not alleviated by his family doing everything in their power to crush him with embarrassment.

He returned Lucinda's smile. He appreciated her concern but, now the shock was wearing off, he had to admit Nicole's cut-all-ties departure had been the relationship equivalent of a get-out-of-jail-free card. And he was incredibly lucky his imminent eviction, while a hassle, wasn't the end of the world. 'Thanks,' he said. 'But I'm pleased for Nicole. The job in LA could be something big for her.' He glanced towards the hallway to check for eavesdroppers. 'I'm not delighted I'll probably end up living with my little brother, but it could be worse.'

Lucinda's smile widened and it occurred to Alex a benefit of a longer stay with James would be his proximity to the Comptons and Lucinda. Should he say that out loud? His luck that afternoon hadn't been the greatest. Perhaps he shouldn't tempt fate. But then again, could things get any worse?

Throwing caution to the wind, he took a breath and said, 'Actually, one of the nice things about being here in Wolston is that I'll be—'

'So, Alex, have you figured out what you're going to say to whip your loyal devotees into a *Napier*-saving frenzy?' said Sarah as she bustled back into the room carrying a plate piled high with brownies. 'Or do we need to have a brainstorm using these spectacular brownies as rocket fuel?'

Sarah offered the plate out to Alex, defusing his irritation at her interruption with the tempting sight and irresistible aroma of chocolate. Only one person could have baked something that delectable. He turned to Lucinda. 'I'm guessing you made those.'

Lucinda nodded.

'Then I vote for brainstorming,' Alex said, taking a huge slice of brownie.

Lucinda frowned, but Alex recognised the devilish twinkle in her eyes as she said, 'Careful now, remember the extra-tight trousers you have to fit into tomorrow.'

Alex raised an eyebrow at her and took a large bite, which was immediately followed by a deep groan of pleasure as rich gooey deliciousness enveloped his taste buds.

Lucinda's lips twitched and Alex guessed she was holding in the smile of a chef witnessing the best possible reaction to one of their creations. 'Now, now,' she said in a playful tone as she leant towards him, 'you don't want to be in trouble with the costume people. Maybe you should stop there.' She reached for the brownie and Alex grunted with indignation and twisted away, lifting the precious snack just beyond her reach.

'I'll go for a run later,' he said. 'And if that doesn't help, I'll skip breakfast.' He fired a mischievous smile at her and shoved the rest of the brownie into the safety of his mouth. Enthusiastic chewing, accompanied by equally enthusiastic 'mmm' sounds, meant the treat was sadly gone too soon and, as he swallowed the last crumb, Alex wondered if he could sneak another. 'I don't care if wardrobe kill me. It will have been worth it. That was best brownie ever.'

'Really?' said Lucinda, widening her eyes in mock surprise. 'I never would have guessed from all the yummy noises, but thanks for clearing that up.' She grinned at him before taking a genteel bite of her own slice.

Mirroring her grin, Alex admired the wicked glint lingering in her bright emerald eyes and said, 'Seriously amazing.'

A phony bout of coughing to his left dragged his attention from Lucinda and reminded him Sarah was in the room. She had returned to her armchair and was observing him and Lucinda over the top of her mug.

Worried he had been ignoring his gracious host, Alex tried to make amends. 'Sarah, you have to try a brownie.'

277

'Ha! While you've been gabbing, I've already finished one.' Sarah nodded at the slice in her hand. 'This is my second.'

'Hey! Leave some for me!' James strode into the room and over to his wife's seat. He grabbed a brownie from the plate and took a seat in the armchair Lucinda had vacated. A bite of brownie later and he too was making appreciative noises. 'Mmm, that is good.' He turned to Lucinda. 'Would you like to move in too?'

'You beat me to it.' Sarah raised her mug in her husband's direction as if toasting his great idea. 'I gladly second that invitation.'

The room fell quiet apart from companiable chewing as Lucinda, Sarah and James finished their brownies and, as he glanced around at the others, Alex realised the tightness in his chest had eased.

James finished his brownie first. 'Do we need to script this video thing or are you going to wing it?'

Alex's mouth dried and the lingering sweetness of the brownie soured. Was he really going to do this? The idea of actually being able to *do* something which could save the show made his nerves jangle with excitement. But while he knew how to go about being someone else on camera, being himself on film wasn't something he'd practised. What would he say? He could make something up, but then he'd likely end up tripping over his tongue.

'It only has to be a minute long,' said Lucinda, using the calm tone of a woman who was excellent in a crisis. 'We could come up with some main points you want to cover and I could hold them up next to the camera if you need a reminder.'

'I'll operate the camera,' said James, leaping in to stake a confident claim on the director's chair. 'I'm always taking videos of the kids. I know what I'm doing.'

'Get a load of Kubrick over there, would you?' Sarah scoffed. 'Shoving your phone in Alex's face and pressing one button to start and stop filming isn't exactly complicated.'

A queasy combination of elation and dread made Alex's stomach roll. 'But what will I say?'

Lucinda shuffled a little closer towards him. 'Whatever you think best. But I guess you say how sad you are the show is being struck down in its prime and how much you've loved working on it. How it's like having a family.'

Alex smiled, pleased Lucinda had remembered and understood his feelings.

'Say you make it for the audience,' she continued. 'That it wouldn't be the success it is without them and you've seen some of them would like to save it and you think with their help that might be possible.'

James jumped back into the conversation with a typically practical contribution. 'And then some stuff about what they can do to help.'

Alex nodded, but the sickness sloshing about his tummy persisted. His misgivings must have shown on his face because Lucinda laid a gentle hand on his forearm and asked, 'What's wrong?'

'I'd do almost anything to save *Napier*. But if this is going to work, everyone on the show has to get behind it. What if they don't and it's just me left looking like some sort of pathetic attention-seeker?'

'Huh.' Lucinda took her hand away from his arm and tapped her index finger against her lips. 'Could you talk to Diana before we put the video up? She's the star, right? So if she's on board, I don't think anyone could say you're trying to make it about you.'

'She's filming in Australia at the moment. She probably wouldn't reply to any message I sent her.'

James cleared his throat. 'I don't think you've much to lose by giving it a go, mate.' He shrugged and when he spoke again his voice was quiet and soft. 'It's like Dad used to say: if you don't try, you'll never know.'

Alex's lips parted, but no words could pass the lump in his throat. James had only been seven when their dad died and Alex hadn't thought his little brother would have remembered one of Dad's favourite sayings. The motto of a man unwilling to quit at anything.

And Dad had loved making home movies. Whatever primary school production Alex was in, no matter how insignificant his part, Dad would be in the audience with a cine film camera pressed to his face, the machine unable to fully cover his enormous grin of pride. To this day, if he was on stage and noticed an empty seat in the theatre, Alex took comfort in imagining his dad standing there, radiating silent support.

Alex risked another glance at his brother. James looked up and, in the eagerness of his expression, Alex caught a glimpse of the fun-filled boy who had constantly begged his big brother to play with him. When was the last time they had done anything even remotely enjoyable together?

Perhaps letting James unleash his inner director wouldn't be such a bad idea. On family trips, after some pestering, Dad used to let them hold the camera and look through the viewfinder. Who knew? Had Dad lived, perhaps film-making projects would have been something they did together regularly. And he had always hoped his brother would one day be more positive about his career. Surely it would be daft not to let him make a constructive contribution now?

Alex's resistance was crumbling when Sarah said, 'And if you won't do it for your army of mummy fans, do it for me. I have to know who the mole is, Alex. They cannot leave the story on a cliffhanger that enormous. It's cruel. And possibly illegal.'

Alex chuckled, but the gloomy thought of never getting the chance to wrap up such a terrific storyline cut his mirth short.

Glancing at the expectant faces around him, Alex realised he was too emotionally involved in the outcome of any attempt to save *Napier* to make a level-headed decision. At this point he could probably be convinced to run naked down the street if he thought it would save the show. What he needed was the opinion of a sensible person. Someone so rational they even regarded true love as a cosy fiction.

He turned his gaze to meet Lucinda's. 'You think this is a good idea?'

'Yes.' She answered without hesitation. 'I think it's definitely worth a try.'

'OK then'. He clapped his hands together and gave her a genuine grin as the churning in his stomach transformed into flutters of excitement. 'Let's do it.'

Chapter 29

Monday 15 June

It was evening when Alex parked on James's driveway. His mind was foggy after his first day on set at Compton Hall and, as he switched on his phone, he was looking forward to a quick meal and perhaps a good movie to help him relax and disconnect from the reality of an Edwardian butler. But as he dragged his feet towards the house his simple plan was assaulted by a cacophony of chimes and beeps. With a creased brow, Alex stared at his phone screen and a seemingly endless string of notifications. He was still scrolling through them when James opened the door and launched into a breathless summary of all that Alex was now catching up on.

Alex was certain many of the messages and missed calls were important. Indeed, some of them were perhaps crucial to the success of his future career. But only four of them made his heart race.

10:32 Lucinda
Hi Alex. Hope your first day of filming at the Hall is going well.

Please say thanks again to Sarah and James for last night. I thought I was competitive, but your brother is a Pictionary fiend! I hope he's recovered from the trauma of us winning and I didn't outstay my welcome.

11:45 Lucinda
Oh my God, Jay tells me the video has gone viral. Diana Carter shared it.

14:36 Lucinda
OK. Diana's done her own video and it's awesome. Though obviously not as good as yours. I mean, hers wasn't directed by James and doesn't feature a cameo by Emily.

15:55 Lucinda
#SaveNapier is trending on Twitter! Are you EVER going to turn your phone on?!

Alex grinned, imagining Lucinda's small frown and huff of exasperation as she had punched out the last message. Not wanting to keep her waiting any longer, he swiftly passed on Lucinda's thanks to James and Sarah and tapped out a reply.

20:14 Alex
Sorry, sorry. I was on set and my phone was off. This is madness!

20:15 Alex
Back at James's now. Sarah says you're very welcome and James eventually stopped moaning at her about losing last night.

Alex stared at the screen and chewed his lip. He shouldn't expect Lucinda to answer any time soon. Almost ten hours had passed since she had first tried to contact him and she was probably busy with work. Perhaps he should set about looking for a movie to watch rather than gawking dumbly at his phone or—

His musings were interrupted by another beep.

20:17 Lucinda
Glad you're home safe and I'm not banned from the premises.

If the Napier stuff is too exciting and you need a distraction, Indiana Jones and the Last Crusade (the best Indy film, don't fight me on this) is on TV later.

Alex's grin returned. The woman was truly brilliant.

20:20 Alex
No fight from me on that one. If the demon Pictionary Master lets me have the remote control, I'll be watching.

Tuesday 16 June

After a pleasurable evening exchanging eighties movie trivia with Alex, Lucinda struggled to squash the urge to contact him again. She eventually surrendered to it on Tuesday afternoon after Jay had given plenty of unwitting assistance. Her head chef's frequent #SaveNapier updates provided Lucinda with an invaluable pretext for contacting Alex and hopefully prevented her from sounding too eager.

15:48 Lucinda

Hello! Jay told me Nicole shared your video and it gave it a big Instagram boost. That was nice of her. How is she doing in LA?

#SaveNapier still trending on Twitter which is great. Hope work is going well. We have two midweek weddings this week so all busy in the kitchen. Jay says 'hi'.

Alex's silence stretched on into the evening and Lucinda was in the kitchens at the Old Grange Hotel, where her team were catering a modest engagement party, when a message from him finally arrived.

19:44 Alex

Hi! Another good day at work. Hope wedding prep is going well. 'Hi' back at Jay ☺ Nicole arrived safely, but that's the last I heard from her. I'm sure she's busy with her new job.

Beaming as she formulated possible replies, Lucinda hurried through the door to the staff corridor and collided with Misha, who was returning an empty canapé tray.

'Lucinda!' Misha hugged the tray to her chest to halt its slide. 'Mrs Barry would like to talk to you. She's in the library.'

Lucinda frowned. When the organiser of an event requested a private audience it was rarely good news. Alex would have to wait.

Thankfully Mrs Barry had summoned Lucinda to shower her with praise. And, as gratifying as it was to listen—for ten minutes of jaw-aching smiling and nodding—to how delighted a customer was with her company's services,

Lucinda was relieved when she was left alone. In the privacy of the library, she rushed to fumble her phone from her pocket, almost letting it slip from her trembling, impatient grasp.

She was unlocking the screen when another message arrived.

20:01 Alex
My agent just called. Apparently, The Breakfast Show want to interview me tomorrow morning about Napier. Not sure how I feel about it ...

Lucinda gasped and answered his message without a moment's hesitation. If she didn't hurry, Alex's aversion to self-promotion would swamp common sense and he'd talk himself out of what was a terrific opportunity. Enthusiasm, encouragement, and perhaps a little tough love, were in order.

20:02 Lucinda
You have to do it!

20:03 Alex
Really?

20:04 Lucinda
Of course! It'll be amazing! Do you have to go into London?

20:05 Alex
No, we can use video call. And it would be before work ... But I don't know ...

20:06 Lucinda
Alex Fraser, so help me - don't make me come round there.

20:08 Alex

Has anyone ever told you that your inner harpy comes across surprisingly loud and shrill through messenger?

20:09 Lucinda

Good. Now call your agent and choose what you'll be wearing tomorrow morning. And not that you need my opinion, but dark blue suits you.

Wednesday 17 June

8:05 Lucinda

Just seen the interview. You were terrific.

8:06 Alex

It was mortifying.

8:08 Lucinda

What, you mean when they threw the Mumsweb Salvan hysteria, 'Sexy Dexy' and the Rear of the Year nomination (congratulations!) at you in a single 'What's it like to be a sex symbol' question, and you stammered and went a charming shade of puce?

8:09 Alex

Ha ruddy ha.

8:10 Lucinda

Oh cheer up. You'll have double the number of admirers by the end of the day. Trust me.

20:06 Alex
checks follower numbers
Lucinda. Tell me the truth. Are you actually a witch?

20:08 Lucinda
See! I'm not one to say I told you so, but …

♥♥♥

Friday 19 June

7:33 Alex
Sarah wanted to know if you'd like to come over for dinner tomorrow night. I think she may be after more brownies. And James has a Pictionary score to settle.

7:48 Lucinda
That would be lovely, but Jay goes on a two-week holiday starting today so I'm flat out at work for the next couple of weeks. No free evenings

Although we would win Pictionary again. And you can tell him that 😊

7:53 Alex
I would tell him, but I can't risk eviction. Don't worry though, Sarah's said she'll tell him. I think she's looking forward to it.

♥♥♥

Monday 22 June

19:12 Alex

Hello! How was your weekend? Did you have to push anyone off a balcony?

We're not shooting on Sundays so James and I went to London to pack up the flat.

19:25 Lucinda

Very busy, but lots of happy customers and thankfully no guests who needed fake/real police intervention.

Any word on Napier? I saw Ray had been doing some interviews. Isn't he working with you at the Hall at the moment?

19:29 Alex

He starts this week. He's playing one of the 'upstairs' lot. The son and heir of the lord of the Hall. A bit of a rogue and a bounder. A nasty piece of work.

19:31 Lucinda

I'm sure he'll find that a stretch.

19:32 Alex

You said it. I couldn't possibly comment.
Speaking of the nobility, Vee called me yesterday.

19:33 Lucinda

How is Carol? Is Hubert OK?

19:34 Alex

Carol's very well. From the yapping in the background I'm guessing Hubert is fine.

Vee said there were a couple of calls to the house from reporters interested in Lady Russell's health, what had happened to her in a certain lift and who'd been involved. But I don't think she told them much.

19:37 Lucinda
I suppose there's nothing really to report. Carol was unwell. Some bystanders helped her. The fantastic paramedics showed up. Some fantastic doctors operated. She's OK now.

19:39 Alex
And they all lived happily ever after.

19:40 Lucinda
I do so admire your optimism.

Wednesday 25 June

12:23 Lucinda
How many interviews have you done now?

12:28 Alex
Honestly? I've lost count.

12:32 Lucinda
The one you did for Mumsweb … The questions got a bit personal, didn't they?

12:34 Alex
Everything short of my inside leg measurement.

12:35 Lucinda

I thought you deflected brilliantly—steering the conversation back to your character and Napier. I couldn't do it. I'd walk out.

12:36 Alex

Because you signed the Official Secrets Act and would have to kill them if you told them too much?

12:37 Lucinda

That, yes. And I've sworn to protect the secrecy of the coven

And I do actually like to keep my private life private.

12:38 Alex

So do I.

I suppose you have to decide where the line is. And, at the moment, if it'll save Napier, I'm happy to let the line get a little blurry.

♥♥♥

Saturday 27 June

22:48 Alex

I have repeat requests from everyone here that you return as soon as possible with more of those brownies. And, of course, they'd like to see you as well.

22:52 Lucinda

It's always nice to be valued for yourself.

22:53 Alex

James is attempting to fill the brownie-shaped void by bringing home biscuits and pastries left over from work meetings (it's good to see where your council tax is going).

22:56 Lucinda

Aren't you worried about getting into trouble with the costume people? How are the trousers?

22:57 Alex

Fine at the moment. Thank you for your concern.

22:58 Lucinda

They haven't put extra padding in them then?

22:58 Alex

????

22:59 Lucinda

Well now your rear is award-nominated, surely the terms of the insurance must demand they protect it at all costs?

23:00 Alex

Oh, piss off.

23:01 Lucinda

☺☺

Monday 29 June

11:22 Lucinda

ALEX!!!! You did it! #NapierSaved— Congratulations!

12:41 Alex

Thank you 🙂 The Napier WhatsApp group is on fire. Everyone's ecstatic. I may have whooped and hugged Ray.

Apparently it's taken a while to confirm because they had TWO platforms after it. Ha!

12:44 Lucinda

This is incredible! Jay has been sending me excited messages all morning.

12:46 Alex

When is she back from her break?

12:46 Lucinda

Friday morning.

12:47 Alex

Are you free on Sunday evening?

12:47 Lucinda

Yes ...

12:48 Alex

Good. And Saturday afternoon?

12:48 Lucinda

Why? What did you have in mind?

Chapter 30

Lucinda left the van in the car park and, picnic basket swinging from her arm, strode towards Compton Hall along one of the main footpaths. As the basket jostled her thigh, she was pleased she had decided to wear her knee-length pedal pushers. The blue denim shorts, twinned with a magenta off-the-shoulder top, were a more practical choice than the floaty floral dress which had also been in the running as she had spent far too long choosing what to wear for her lunch date with Alex. Which probably wasn't a *date* date. Or, at least, not *officially* a date.

She slowed her pace. The borders of elm trees along both sides of the path reached up and over to meet each other, forming a corridor of cool green shade. Even so, beads of sweat formed on the back of Lucinda's neck and, while she was pleased she had taken the precaution of wearing comfortable ballet pumps and clipping her hair up, she did not want to meet Alex red faced and out of breath.

After two weeks of capricious weather, July had arrived bringing uninterrupted sunshine. The part of the Hall's grounds open to the public buzzed with visitors. In the park area to the west of the house, families relaxing on blankets occupied the shade under the dense canopies of the beech trees spotted across the otherwise open space. Children ran in and out of the shadows, squealing as they dodged around adults basking in the rays and those using their Saturday lunchtime to get some exercise.

The cheerful yapping of dogs brought a nostalgic smile to Lucinda's face as she remembered the last time she had traversed the grounds of a stately home. She hitched the wicker hamper up her arm and balanced it on her hip, taking a moment to push her sunglasses further up her nose, catch her breath and admire the view.

Although not as quite as impressive as its front aspect, Compton Hall's profile—with its three storeys of russet brick, tall white-framed windows and ornate chimney stacks—was still an imposing sight. However, the historic grandeur of the ground floor of the seventeenth-century structure was presently marred by a row of grey metal portable cabins forming an ugly temporary barrier between the park and the house.

As Lucinda drew nearer, a far more pleasant twenty-first-century feature came into view. Alex was leaning against the side of one of the cabins, scanning the horizon to the south, his hand lifted to shield his eyes against the glare. The naturally sandy waves of his hair were inky black and had been straightened and flattened either side of an off-centre parting. He was wearing dark blue jeans and a tight-fitting black T-shirt which showcased his lean muscular figure but left Lucinda a little disappointed. Having heard so much about his costume, she had been hoping to see him wearing it before the movie made it to the big screen.

Alex dropped his hand away from his face as he caught sight of her. He raised an arm in an exuberant wave and began to trot down the incline towards her, Lucinda's heartbeat accelerating with his every step.

'You made it!' he said, a wide grin spreading across his face. His eyes sparkled as he stared at her and, not wanting to appear overkeen, Lucinda was pleased her sunglasses were concealing what she was sure would be the obvious delight in her own.

'Yep,' she said, unsure what the acceptable greeting for a non-date date was. Should she hug him? Peck him on the cheek?

Floundering for something to say to cover her indecision, she asked, 'Did you miss me?' and immediately wished for the ground to open up and swallow her whole.

'Of course.' Alex replied without hesitation. His grin remained shining and steady as he answered, and Lucinda found it impossible to tell if he was being sarcastic, polite or honest. Or maybe all three at once.

Once again wrong-footed, she managed a nervous smile and fidgeted with the basket. The motion drew Alex's attention to the hamper and his smile slipped. 'Wow! That looks impressive. And heavy. Should I ... I mean I'm sure you have it under control. But you've already carried it a long way. It must be my turn. Right?'

Lucinda smile broadened in response to Alex's valiant attempts to offer help in a way which wouldn't needle her fiercely independent inner harpy. He held out a hand for the basket and Lucinda muttered, 'Thanks,' as she passed it over, grateful to be unburdened but with the new problem of what to do with her hands.

She stuffed her left hand into her pocket and used the right to point at Alex's artificially dark hair. 'Love your new do.'

Alex lifted his free hand to his head. 'Oh, yeah. I forget. The make-up and costume I can take off, but this ...' He glanced behind him. 'I've just ... I was in a rush and I forgot something. I need to go back to set for a second to get it. Do you mind coming with me?'

'Not at all.'

'Great, thanks.'

As they set off towards the cabins, Lucinda asked. 'How do they get your hair so straight?'

'They tracked down some sort of traditional miracle pomade.'

'Huh. Well, I'm sure it's very Edwardian. And'—Lucinda paused and used a supposed inspection of Alex's hair as a good excuse to stare openly at his handsome face—'I think you carry it off. You'll be the smartest butler ever on film.'

'Thank you. I'll settle for convincing.' They reached the base of the incline and he glanced at her as they strolled up the slope. 'You're looking lovely, as ever.'

'Thanks,' Lucinda said, smoothing the base hem of her top with lightly trembling fingers. She had been beginning to relax into Alex's company but, never good at taking compliments, his open admiration left her flustered. 'You too. Although I was hoping to catch a glimpse of the infamous costume.'

They rounded the corner of the nearest cabin and Alex exchanged nods with a broad, stony-faced man who Lucinda assumed was a member of set security.

'I'm sorry you won't get to see it.' Alex chuckled. 'But they'd never let me take it off set. If I lost it the wardrobe supervisor would kill me. We still have another couple of weeks of filming.'

'Here?'

'Here until the middle of next week here. Then most of us are moving to Shepperton to shoot some interior scenes on a sound stage.'

They paused on the lawn bordering the brick wall which enclosed the Hall's rose gardens to let two women carrying cream parasols cross their path. Lucinda gaped at their beautiful clothes: the rows of dainty pearl buttons and the elegant lace details on their collars and cuffs. The purple and blue folds of their floor-length skirts swung out in front of their feet while the rear drapes seemed to catch up after a slight delay, creating a bobbing motion like that of two peacocks strutting in the sunshine.

She turned back to Alex who, apparently completely acclimatized to life in the early twentieth century, hadn't even glanced in the direction of the women. 'Shepperton isn't too far from here, is it?'

'No, I've been lucky. The commute from James's is a little longer, but still not far.'

'How's everything with Sarah and James?'

'Fine. Although he has started dropping hints about me looking for somewhere else to live.'

'We should've let him win Pictionary.'

Alex chuckled as he ushered her underneath a pop-up gazebo and set the hamper down next to a scattered collection of folding chairs. 'Do you mind waiting here? I'll only be a few minutes.'

'Sure. No problem.'

'Sorry. I would introduce you to everyone, but they're really busy and time will be against them—'

'Alex, it's fine. I get it. I don't exactly welcome interruptions when we're in the middle of dishing up for two hundred. Go on. I promise I won't wander off.'

Alex threw a glance back at her before disappearing through the gap in the garden wall and Lucinda gave him a reassuring smile. But the second he was out of sight she sighed and ran her damp hands along the back of her shorts. The shade under the gazebo was welcome, but it failed to counteract the heat and jitters inside her. Perhaps she should sit down. But then the metal seats looked hard and uninviting, and Alex had said he'd only be a couple of minutes.

She sighed again, this time in despair at her skittishness. She needed to calm down. She was here for a nice lunch with a nice guy. The way she was carrying on, anyone would think she was about to encounter an ogre or—

'Hello.'

Lucinda squawked as she wheeled round to face the stealthy man who had entered the gazebo. Unlike Alex, he was in costume: trousers with a subtle grey stripe, a black morning coat over a grey waistcoat, high-collared white shirt and russet-coloured silk tie. He was staring at her open mouth and wide eyes while sporting a sly grin which made Lucinda believe he had been trying to scare her. Her annoyance at such mean behaviour hardened as she

recognised him: Ray Veasey, better known to her as *Napier*'s
DI Frank Buchanan. A man she knew was routinely rude to
catering staff and therefore a complete dickhead.

'Hello,' she said, hoping she'd injected enough venom
into the two syllables he would hear them as, *'Get lost.'*

But Ray wasn't easily deterred. 'I'm Ray,' he said,
extending his hand and another slick smile.

Lucinda eyed his hand for a moment, hoping her
reticence to touch it was clear. 'Lucinda,' she replied as
she put her hand in his, planning to make it the briefest
handshake of her life.

But Ray gripped her hand and pulled it towards him.
If she hadn't been in flat shoes, she would have stumbled.
Instead she pulled back with equal force and gave Ray the
stare she reserved for customers she would like to push off
balconies.

Taking the hint, he released her, chuckling as if her
annoyance had amused him. 'I haven't seen you around
before. What is it that you do?'

He tilted his head and, as he raised an eyebrow, Lucinda
saw it: the faintest resemblance to Alex. No wonder they'd
been competing for parts over two decades. They were
a similar height and build, but Ray's features lacked the
definition and expression of Alex's. It was as if Ray was
a blurrier, greasier version of Alex: the man you would
get if you dipped Alex in a vat of hot oil and gave him a
thorough shake.

Lucinda was deciding whether to give him a vague, civil
answer or tell him to mind his own business, when Alex
marched back into the gazebo carrying a rolled tartan rug
under his left arm.

'Ray!' Alex gave his colleague a pat on the back which landed between his shoulder blades with a hollow thud and enough force to make Ray sway. 'I think you're needed back in the house.

Alex smiled at Ray, but his eyes were cold and Lucinda would have sworn they contained a glint of menace. He stooped to recover the picnic hamper and turned his back to Ray as he asked Lucinda, 'Ready to go?'

'Picnicking in the park, are we?' said Ray.

Alex rolled his eyes but when he turned to face Ray his features were composed in a convincing display of nonchalance. 'That was the plan. See you on Monday.'

Lucinda strode after Alex and they had just stepped back into the sunshine when Ray called after them, 'If you want a quiet spot, you might want to try the oak trees in the north-west corner near the path to the car park. We've had a few more reporters and fans digging around today and you wouldn't want anyone interrupting your lunch. Plus, it'll make it easier for Lucinda to get back to her car, assuming she drove here.'

'Thanks,' said Alex. 'We'll keep that in mind.'

'Ciao!' Ray said to their backs. 'It was wonderful to meet you, Lucinda.'

The slimy way he extended the first syllable of her name made Lucinda want to shudder, but she restrained the impulse until the security guy and cabins came into view. 'Ugh!' She slid her sunglasses into place and gave the bridge of them an irritated prod. 'I'm glad I met him before I ate. Definitely a total knob.'

Alex gave a short laugh but the crease between his eyes lingered as they made their way down the slope.

'Is it just me,' said Lucinda, 'or has Ray done something to annoy you in addition to being his charming self?'

'Is it that obvious?' He shook his head. 'Sally, one of *Napier*'s executive producers, called me earlier this week to thank me for kicking off the campaign to save the show and for doing interviews and social media stuff. She said how surprised everyone was because they were all under the impression I wasn't that dedicated to the show.'

'What?' Lucinda blinked and brought her voice down to ask, 'Who the heck is everyone and how could they think that?'

'All the people high up enough to make decisions. Apparently they had been planning to give my character more to do in series three—'

'I knew it!'

'But then several of them were told by a reliable source that I was only marking time on *Napier* and planning to scarper the second a bigger and better job came along. So the writers shelved the idea they'd had to give Dexter his own storyline in series three.'

'Let me guess. The "reliable source" behind all this rubbish was Ray.'

'Yep. And it turns out it isn't only me he's been making trouble for. I got the impression from what Sally said they're not very happy with him.'

'Well I hope he gets his comeuppance next series. Or sooner. There are a couple of high balconies back at the Hall. I'll happily shove him off one if you want.'

They laughed as they crossed the park and Alex's frown finally lifted. He pointed to a cluster of oak trees in the far right corner of the open area. 'I hate to say it, but I think Ray may have been right about the quiet spot over there.'

Alex's arm muscles bulged and flexed as he dropped his arm and swung the hamper from one hand to the other. Her eyes hidden behind her sunglasses, Lucinda ran the tip of her tongue over her bottom lip as she allowed her gaze to linger on his strong forearms and impressive biceps and imagined running her fingers over his—

A squeal knocked her out of her reverie as a group of children chased each other through the gap between her and Alex, forcing them further apart. Lucinda shot a glare after the pesky interlopers then swung her head in the direction of the promised quiet spot. Right now she didn't much care who had recommended it if it would give her the chance to get Alex alone. All to herself. Without interruptions.

She dropped her chin to wink at Alex over the top of her sunglasses. 'Well I won't tell him if you don't.'

Chapter 31

Alex spread the picnic rug under the largest tree in the wooded area and the red, green and white stripes of the blanket were immediately dappled with sunshine filtering through the canopy above. Lucinda kicked off her shoes and enjoyed the brush of the fleecy fabric on her bare feet as she knelt and opened the hamper. The chatter, shouting and barking which hung in the air in the main park had retreated to muffled background noise, as if they had snuck off to a private room during a garden party.

Alex sat opposite her, the hamper between them, and watched as Lucinda unpacked its contents.

'I brought my own non-alcoholic fruit punch or—just in case you want to insult me and my mixing skills—shop-bought iced tea.' She held up two steel flasks. 'I would have brought something more exciting, like Pimm's or G & T, but we're both driving.'

'No, that's very sensible. And I would like to try your no doubt life-changing punch, please,' said Alex, taking two plastic tumblers out of the hamper and holding one towards Lucinda.

Having poured the drinks, Lucinda moved on to the sandwiches. 'OK, I wasn't sure what you'd like, so we have turkey club or honey-roast ham with Cheddar.'

'I like both, but please could I start with ham and cheese. And by the way, this punch is delicious.' Lucinda beamed as she passed Alex a plate, her chest swelling in response to his praise. And a few minutes later, when he had devoured the sandwich and asked for another—her favourite sign a customer was happy with her food—a blush of pleasure began to creep into her cheeks.

She had spent more time weighing up filling options than when dealing with even her pickiest customers. Anything containing garlic had been ruled out instantly because you didn't have to be a vampire to shrink from garlic breath. The heat in her face intensified as she peered over the top of her tumbler to watch Alex raise his own cup to his lips and pondered, as she had more than once while deciding on their lunch menu, what it would be like to kiss him.

'How's the wedding planning going?'

'Hmn? Sorry?' Lost in her own imaginings, Lucinda took a moment to refocus on Alex's eyes and what he had said. 'Whose wedding?'

'You mum's. She is still marrying the exceptional … Graham, wasn't it?'

'She certainly is.'

'Have they set a date yet?'

'Ugh. No. Apparently it's complicated. But probably spring next year.'

'And what about Chris's cousin's wedding? Are you going to that?'

Lucinda took a moment to finish her sandwich and consider Alex's tone. His last questions had sounded a little too nonchalant. Was he was jealous of Chris? Or was that wishful thinking on her part? 'No. I'm not. It would be nice. Chris's family are lovely and know how to throw a party. But it wouldn't be fair to give anyone the impression Chris and I are ever getting back together.'

'Hmn.' Alex nodded, accepting her answer with a neutral expression that made Lucinda's heart sink to her shoes. Why did she have to fancy an actor? Why couldn't she have developed some sort of weird magnetic connection with a man who, helpfully enough, was unable to conceal his feelings?

Alex stretched his long legs out along the rug and reclined so his weight was resting on his forearms. And, as he tilted his head back, his face was touched by the muted gold of the rays piercing the leaves above them.

Lucinda stared, her pulse accelerating. Did he try to look like he had fallen out of a movie?

Worried she would soon begin drooling, Lucinda snatched a plastic tub from the hamper and shuffled towards him on her knees. 'Dessert?'

'Yes, please,' he said, inspecting the contents of the box. 'What are they?'

'Mini lemon tartlets. Designed to be eaten in two bites, or one if you're in a hurry or no one's watching.' She glanced down at the delicate shortcrust pastry shells, filled with rich lemon curd infused with a hint of basil. 'Topped with either toasted French meringue or you can go for the ones dusted with icing sugar.'

'I think I'll start with a meringue one. Thanks.'

As she passed Alex the box, Lucinda dipped her head over his and caught a new scent. A mysterious sweet note, mingling harmoniously with his usual hints of citrus and spice. It was so intriguing, Lucinda was reluctant to pull away.

'Lucinda?' Alex glanced up at her, his forehead creased. 'Are you OK?'

Drat. She must have drifted off. 'Fine. Um ... It's ... Is there honey in whatever they put on your hair?'

Alex swallowed the second bite of his pastry and grinned. 'Yes, chef. Sort of. I think they said it contains beeswax and almond oil.'

'Right. Makes sense.' Lucinda avoided his gaze as she sat down and tucked her legs to her right side, leaving her left hip inches from Alex's waist. She shuffled her feet against the rug and when she looked at Alex again he was still smiling and staring at her, his eyes shining with a glimmer of amusement and—she hoped, although she couldn't be certain—a hint of something more urgent and hungry.

The heat in Lucinda's face stole down to her neck and chest. She dragged her eyes away from Alex's and stirred herself to ask a question before all the skin above the magenta neckline of her top turned a matching pink. 'Have you figured out where you'll be living next?'

Alex polished off a second tartlet with an appreciative hum and rubbed his fingers together to remove traces of icing sugar. 'I think James might be right about searching for somewhere around Wolston. As long as I can get the train to London, it should work out. And I'll be renting, so I can always move. It'll be a lot cheaper. And'—he dropped his gaze to the blanket, where he drew circles on the fleece with his left index finger—'there is another reason I'd like to hang around.'

'Oh?'

'There's this rather interesting person I've met who also lives locally. And it'd be nice to spend more time with her.'

'Oh. Really?' Though she had been aiming for a casual tone, Lucinda's question emerged with a squeak.

'Yes. She has great taste in music and films. She's smart and funny. And I suspect she might be the best cook in the world.'

Alex looked Lucinda in the eye and, at this solid evidence he was interested in her—although if it turned out he was calling someone else the best cook in the world she would cheerfully wallop him with the picnic hamper—she came over light headed. And he thought she was funny! Had she mistakenly put alcohol in the punch?

She swallowed and said, in a joking tone, 'She sounds awesome.'

'She is. Although, she did promise me sticky toffee pudding, and yet—' He sat up and made a show of searching in the empty hamper.

'Hey! Come on!' Lucinda reached across Alex and flicked the hamper shut. She slapped her left hand on the lid and rested it there as she defended her corner. 'It's best served warm and I can carry a lot, but not an oven.' She lifted her nose in the air. 'Besides, I refuse to serve custard from a thermos flask. I have standards.'

Alex reached over to the hamper and laid his right hand on top of Lucinda's left. 'And I would never ask you to compromise them. Another time?'

'OK.' Lucinda was sure her skin must be flaming scarlet, but her woozy head and certainty about Alex's feelings made her brave. She was tired of having to use her imagination when reality was sitting right next to her, his lips dusted with sugar. 'OK,' she said again. 'And'—she leant towards him, pausing when her face was close enough to his that she could appreciate the shards of amber in his eyes—'in the meantime ...'

Lucinda pressed her lips gently to Alex's and ran her fingertips across the soft hair and warm skin at the back of his neck. Her pulse drummed in her ears, downing out the birdsong in the canopy above, as a fuzzy, floating sensation filled her. And when Alex brushed a knuckle along her jaw, the enduring spark between them flared and flashed along Lucinda's nerves until she was convinced her skin must be rippling and sparkling all at once, like sunlight on flowing water.

Alex pulled back to lay his forehead against hers and muttered her name in a low whisper. Deep inside Lucinda, the sparks blazed into raging flames and when she opened her eyes to meet Alex's, she saw her own smouldering need reflected there.

Lucinda opened her lips to respond, then paused. She didn't want to talk. She wanted to lie in the sunshine, enjoy the electricity thrumming under the surface of her skin and kiss Alex until she was drunk on him and the sweet taste of powdered sugar.

She wrapped her hand around his neck and sank down onto the blanket. Alex slid with her, deftly removing her hair clip as they descended, until they were lying side by side, Lucinda on her back, Alex above her, propped up on his left forearm which Lucinda was more than happy to use as a makeshift pillow. Especially as this pillow insisted on running his clever fingers through her hair and tenderly brushing her neck in slow tantalising strokes.

When Alex deepened their kiss and skimmed his right hand along the denim covering her thigh, she prayed the gentle pressure would evaporate the fabric. With a moan of frustration, she slipped her hand under his top and ran her hand over the firm muscles above his waistband. Burning from head to toe, she grabbed a handful of his T-shirt, threw her leg over his and rolled towards him, but she couldn't get close enough and, as her fingers roamed across his chest and biceps, she realised she didn't have enough hands.

Alex broke away and gently squeezed the leg which was hooked over his. He bit his bottom lip. 'We have a problem.'

Lucinda took the opportunity to loop her left hand around his belt and tug him towards her. Breathlessly, but with absolute confidence, she replied, 'We do. Too many clothes.'

Alex laughed and the deep rolling chuckle made Lucinda's insides flutter. 'I was going to say that we're in a public place.' He sighed as he ran a fingertip along the neckline of her top, his eyes following its progress from one shoulder to the other, and Lucinda could have sworn her heart stopped. When he lifted his gaze to meet hers, the dark intensity she had seen earlier had crept back into his eyes. Dropping his voice to its lowest register, somewhere between a purr and a growl, he said, 'But I don't disagree with you about the clothes.'

His lips curled and a familiar sparkle returned to his eyes. He released a long sigh which spoke of great reluctance and restraint and bent to place a light kiss on her forehead.

It was Lucinda's turn to sigh. As tempting as it was to get completely carried away in some sort of mad midsummer al fresco frenzy, this was only their first date. And not even an official one. Alex was right. Again. Damn him! That was such an annoying habit.

'OK,' she said, gripping his biceps and using them as an anchor to drag herself up to sitting. 'You have a point.' She cast a longing glance at his impressive muscles as she gave his arms a final squeeze and then busied her hands with the far chaster task of reclipping her hair. 'To be continued?'

Alex grinned as he stood and offered her his hand. 'To be continued.'

Chapter 32

Keen to extend his time with Lucinda by every possible second, Alex set a deliberately glacial pace as they strolled back to the car park. His gaze lingered on her beautiful smile and dazzling eyes but he suspected if he were to glance up he would find a revolving circle of stars or bluebirds above his head.

'Do you know what you're working on next?' Lucinda asked as she repositioned the empty picnic hamper into the crook of her arm. Alex had considered offering to carry it, but thought better of it when he noticed the determination with which she grabbed the basket and told him to retrieve the blanket.

'I may be in Stratford for a few weeks. There's an outdoor production of *A Midsummer Night's Dream*. One of the actors has just pulled out and the director thought of me.'

'Stratford-upon-Avon?'

'That's the one.'

A crinkle appeared between Lucinda's eyebrows. 'For how long?'

'All of August. It's not really that far away.' He glanced at her, hoping the crease in her forehead would vanish, but it persisted. 'And I can start looking for a place to rent around Wolston in September.' Lucinda nodded and Alex was relieved when her brow relaxed. 'You'll have to come to the show. I should be able to get you a good seat.'

'Yeah. Sounds great,' said Lucinda, with all the enthusiasm of someone talking about invasive dentistry.

'What have you got against Shakespeare?'

Lucinda sighed. 'I don't know. I guess, at school our English teacher made it out to be such a trial. I think he hated teaching us. And it always seemed like a lot of gobbledygook, flouncing about, misery and then everyone dies.'

Alex laughed at Lucinda's flippancy, but would gladly have wrung her teacher's neck. He had been lucky to have a terrific English teacher who had made Shakespeare relevant and lively. He found it hard to imagine not enjoying it. 'I'm guessing you studied the tragedies. But I promise there's no misery or death in *A Midsummer Night's Dream*. It's actually funny in places. Even the flouncing is pretty comical.'

'Hmn. Maybe.'

'Sarah and James and the girls will be coming up. You could come with them.'

Lucinda lifted her gaze to the trees overhead and a hint of a smile twitched the corner of her mouth as she asked, 'Will there be ice cream available in the interval?'

'I should think so.'

'The posh handmade stuff that comes in those little tubs with wooden spoons?'

'If there isn't, I'll ask Sarah to bring some.'

'Then count me in.' She grinned. 'And it would be great to see your family again.'

'They'll be delighted. Ecstatic if you bring some brownies to go with that ice cream.'

Up ahead, the end of the path and the car park beyond it came into view. And while the sun continued to shine and Alex had a tremendous amount to be happy about, a shadow crept across his buoyant mood at the idea of parting from Lucinda. He couldn't let her leave without having arranged to see her again soon. Since their first meeting he had tried and failed twice to ask her out for a drink. But today would be different. The management of Compton Hall were in the middle of a big push to promote the stately home as a filming location. As part of their efforts to woo the current shoot's production team, they had organised a dinner for the cast and crew on Sunday night in the Grand Saloon. From the moment he had heard about it, Alex had been looking forward to inviting Lucinda and introducing her to everyone.

He shuffled to a stop, a few paces from the nearest line of cars, and reached for Lucinda's hand, bringing her to a halt next to him.

'Hey!' She smiled, glanced down at their intertwined fingers and gave his hand a light shake. 'What's up?'

'Nothing. I just wanted ... I've been trying to ask you—'

'There he is!'

'Alex! Alex!'

'He's over there!'

A frothing gaggle brandishing cameras and microphones bore down on them, and they were soon surrounded by a cloud of booming questions and dazzling flashes.

'Alex! How do you feel about being called a hero?'

'What will you do now you saved *Napier*?'

'How did you know how to save Lady Russell's life?'

'Do you have a message for your fans?'

'There're saying you are single-handedly responsible for saving Lady Russell—'

'How do you feel about the calls for you to be knighted?'

Alex's lips parted but he only managed to stammer incoherently. For while the reporters were loud and unrelenting, most of his attention was fixed on wondering why his hand was suddenly cold and the space at his side dismally empty. Where was Lucinda? Was she all right?

Rising to his tiptoes and craning forwards to peer over the bank of cameras, he was rewarded with a glimpse of lustrous wavy hair and a fetching figure in a dark pink top retreating towards a white van on the right side of the car park.

His heart hammering in his chest, he threw out a hand to part the crowd. 'Excuse me—' he began, but had only advanced a step when his breath was knocked out of him by a body slamming into his.

'My love!' Nicole wrapped her arms around his neck and planted a loud kiss on his cheek as camera flashes exploded around them. 'Isn't this amazing!'

Alex gawped at his ex-girlfriend. Her pearly teeth, shining blonde mane and bronzed skin seemed too bright in the banal setting of a car park. Nicole was supposed to be in America, not at Compton Hall digging her manicure into the back of his neck. How was she here at the exact moment of a media ambush? And, most importantly, where the heck was Lucinda?

'Now, now, everyone.' Nicole lifted a hand to brush her hair from her shoulder. 'Please. If you would back up a little, I'm sure my gorgeous boyfriend will be delighted to speak to you.'

Alex tore his gaze from where he had last seen Lucinda to gawk at Nicole in open-mouthed disbelief. While he stuttered, she continued to smile serenely and swayed to turn her best side towards the photographers. Alex swallowed and managed to blurt, 'Nicole—'

'I know, babe,' she said. 'I've missed you too!'

Nicole threw her arms around him again, burying her head in his neck as another fireworks display of flashes made him blink and squint. The crowd began to fire questions but, beyond the roar, Alex heard an engine splutter into life. His stomach rolling, he peeled Nicole from him and, muttering curses, hustled his way through the scrum, emerging on the other side in time to see Lucinda's van accelerating away.

Chapter 33

'Oh my God, Alex! You should see the amazing pics I got of the photographers! I can't wait to put these on Insta!' Nicole swiped at her phone, her broad grin a sharp contrast to the grim set of Alex's lips.

He glanced in the rear-view mirror. For a while he had thought a couple of cars were following them, but his meanderings through Greater Compton's dense warren of residential streets seemed to have shaken off any possible tail. Not that Nicole cared. She would probably be thrilled by the idea of paparazzi covering her every move. If he hadn't taken her arm and ushered her to her car, fending off all questions with nods and smiles as he prised the key from her fingers, she would no doubt still be posing in the centre ring of the media circus.

As he pulled over at the end of a deserted cul-de-sac, Nicole continued, 'Do you think they'll use the pictures of us together?' She almost bounced off her seat in excitement. 'Do you think they'll make the nationals?'

Alex ground his teeth, attempting to squash his anger before speaking. However tempting, shouting at Nicole right now would be like batting an overexcited puppy on the nose with a newspaper.

'Nicole.' He reached out to place a hand over her phone screen, forcing her to look up and meet his gaze. 'Why are you here? I thought you were in the States.'

Her smile dimmed and her eyes turned glassy. Her bottom lip would start wobbling soon if he wasn't careful. 'What's going on, Nicole? Are you OK?'

Nicole sniffed and shrugged. 'It was great at first. The filming went really well and everyone was so positive. But my part wasn't as big as I'd thought and then it didn't even matter because the pilot didn't get picked up.'

'Sorry,' said Alex, his compassion genuine. Even though he could shake Nicole for her cameo role in the press ambush which had ruined what had been shaping up to be the best day of his life, he took no joy in her disappointment. He and many of his friends had been through the same thing. Many times.

But her depression didn't last long. Straightening, Nicole flicked her hair off her shoulders as her smile returned. 'And then I started following the *Napier* thing, which is great, Alex, I'm so pleased it's been picked up. And you were being interviewed everywhere! It was just so exciting I felt like I had to come home and be a part of it!'

'That's ... nice.' Nicole's enthusiastic support was welcome, even though Alex suspected it was largely motivated by a desire to piggyback on his reluctant fifteen minutes of fame.

'I got back to London yesterday and I wanted to talk to you and then I got a message from Ray saying—'

'You got a message from *Ray*?'

'Yeah, it was a bit odd. I haven't heard from him in ages and then he sent me a message—'

'Wait. How does Ray even have your number?'

'He doesn't. He messaged me on Insta, duh!' She rolled her eyes. 'That was only a couple of hours ago. He'd seen from my latest posts I was back in London and he said you were free this afternoon and I should come to set. I'd just parked and I saw all the camera flashes and there you were, in the middle of it all! It was such a fantastic surprise. What brilliant timing!'

Alex's relief that Nicole had nothing to do with tipping off the press was balanced by rage at Ray's meddling. Chances were the oily snake arranged the photographer tsunami before inviting Nicole down to the Hall.

A throbbing started in his temples and the overpowering sweetness of Nicole's perfume made the back of his throat itch. Closing his eyes, he wound down the window and directed his face towards the cool breeze outside.

Apparently unaffected by the prickling discomfort which was needling Alex all over, Nicole continued, 'I've been thinking, this could be a sign, Alex. This is a chance for you and me to try again as a couple. Think of my time away as a break. We'd still have to find somewhere new to live, but—'

'Nicole!' He grimaced, that had come out as more of a bark than he had intended. He was still annoyed with her—and sodding Ray—but most of his anger was reserved for himself. This was his fault. If he hadn't dithered pathetically for weeks about telling Nicole he wanted to break up with her they wouldn't be in this situation.

He softened his tone. 'You were right to end things between us. We're too different. And, honestly, I think you'll be happier with someone closer to your own age. You're so bright and energetic and in the long term I worry I'd become more of a grumpy, forgetful dad to you than your boyfriend.'

Nicole winced, her features contracting as if she'd been stung, and Alex knew the truth of his words had hit home. 'You're sure? You wouldn't even consider some sort of—'

'No, Nicole.'

She dropped her gaze to her lap and seemed to shrink in on herself. Her sparkle faded and when she glanced up at him again she appeared younger and more fragile. 'I'm not going to be able to change your mind about this, am I?'

'No. Sorry.' He sighed and, as he ran the tip of his tongue over his bottom lip, he fancied he could still taste powdered sugar. His mind flooding with memories of his and Lucinda's kiss—which he had hoped would be the first of many, and that had been before it turned out to be more incredible than anything he'd been able to imagine— he said, 'The perfect person for everyone is out there, Nicole. And in your case, I bet they listen to music from this century.'

'Yeah, I guess,' she said in a small voice. 'Can I get a hug though? You're really good at them.'

Alex shuffled to the edge of his seat. 'Come here,' he said as he wrapped an arm around her shoulders and rested his chin on top of her head. 'Please don't let what happened in America get you down. Don't give up. You're talented, beautiful and determined. You're going to go far.'

Nicole lifted her head from his shoulder to look him in the eye. 'You really think so?'

Her question was accompanied by an impressive set of glistening Bambi eyes. How could someone who could produce that expression at will not get everything they wanted in life?

He squeezed the top of her arm. 'Really.'

'Thank you.' She swayed back into her seat and sniffed as she wiped the corners of her eyes gently with her fingers.

Alex hated upsetting anyone, but any desire to comfort Nicole was trounced by his need to know if Lucinda was all right. 'I need to go back to Compton Hall. My car is there,' he said. 'Do you mind if I drive yours a bit longer?'

Nicole shrugged. 'Sure.' She swept up her phone and set about using the front-facing camera to check her appearance. 'Do you think any of the photographers might still be hanging around?'

'I don't know. Maybe.'

Nicole let out a squeal of excitement and returned to perfecting her appearance. 'Alex, babe?'

Alex stifled a sigh as he swung the car back onto the road. 'Yes?'

'If this whole *Napier* saviour thing leads you to international mega stardom, you will mention me to all the important people, right?'

As Nicole deployed her weapons-grade puppy eyes again, Alex's lingering concerns about having wounded her vanished. She was going to be fine. He, on the other hand, wouldn't be able to rest until he had spoken to Lucinda.

In the cupholder in the centre console, his phone buzzed and chirped. Oh please, he prayed, let it be Lucinda. Maybe she was as worried about him as he was about her? Could he be that lucky? Perhaps finally speaking to Nicole had reversed his bad karma and he was one short conversation away from getting his love life back on track?

Muttering apologies to Nicole, he brought the car to a halt once more and reached for the handset.

Chapter 34

By eight o'clock on Saturday evening, Alex was close to taking a sledgehammer to his phone. Anything to stop the incessant buzzing and ringing.

His nieces had kept him busy for most of the afternoon, merrily involving him in ever more convoluted outdoor games, and he had been grateful for the distraction. But now they had gone to bed the kitchen was too quiet and his phone impossible to ignore. Even the delicious smell of roast chicken—the only remnant of a favourite family dinner—failed to lift his spirits. He hadn't been able to bring himself to eat anything since lunchtime. A rolling ache worried the pit of his stomach every time his phone made a sound.

His overactive imagination was torturing him with various disastrous scenarios. In the worst case, Lucinda drove off believing *he* had spread a story taking sole credit for saving Carol and had lied about breaking up with Nicole. She arrived home furious and disappointed to find Chris—the annoyingly handsome devil she knew—waiting to comfort her with some of his genius artistic cookery magic. Ever pragmatic, Lucinda would decide she was better off with her former fiancé in their ready-made home, rather than taking a gamble on an unreliable, untrustworthy flirt she suspected was a charlatan and a fame whore. She'd attend Chris's cousin's wedding and, while there, Chris would propose again and she'd think, 'Why not?' given that true love is a load of illusory nonsen—

'Hey!' Sarah came into the kitchen from the garden, interrupting Alex's slide down his latest doom spiral. 'Cheer up, it might never happen.' Glancing out the window, she planted her hands on her hips. 'James can tidy up the rest of the stuff out there. I'm done in.' She surveyed Alex's slumped posture. 'Hmn. Wine o'clock, I think.' She opened a cupboard and removed three large glasses with slender stems. Placing them on the island in front of Alex, she nodded towards his phone and said, 'You can silence those things.'

'I know. But then I wouldn't hear if Lucinda replied to my messages.'

'Fair point.' Sarah retrieved a bottle of Chablis from the fridge and poked through the drawer in search of a corkscrew. 'Have you considered *talking* to one of these reporters who keep hounding you? Perhaps then they'd all leave you alone?'

'You sound like my agent.'

'It's not a stupid idea,' said James. Having completed the Herculean task of getting the girls to bed, he crossed the kitchen with a jubilant strut, hopped onto the bar stool to the left of Alex's and held a wine glass out towards his wife. 'That way you could get your side of the story across.'

Alex ran his hands through his hair, tugging at the roots. 'You mean how the "heroic saviour of *Napier*"'—he raised his fingers to sketch sarcastic air quotes—'absolutely *didn't* single-handedly save Lady Russell from the jaws of death?'

'Exactly,' said Sarah, pouring a generous measure into the glasses, leaving her husband's until last. She swung herself up onto the stool to Alex's right and nudged him with her elbow. 'You can put the story straight.'

'I don't know.' Alex swirled his glass and raised it to his lips. He had never been a big drinker, but as he took a sip he was tempted to finish the wine in a few glugs and pour himself another. 'It'd probably just backfire.'

Sarah exchanged a significant glance with James who cleared his throat and asked, 'So what's happening with Lucinda?'

Alex downed his wine in one. He'd hoped it would act as a form of immediate anaesthesia, but the ache in his stomach persisted. 'She hasn't replied to my messages. But she's read them.'

'And you explained about Nicole and—'

'Of course I did!' Alex reached for the bottle and poured himself another glass. 'Sorry. I didn't mean to snap.' He drummed his fingers on the counter. 'I told her everything and apologised. But she's a really private person and all those people and cameras … It probably scared her off.'

James took a swig of his wine. 'How did they know where to find you anyway?'

'I'd put good money on Ray, given it was him who sent

Nicole in our direction.' Alex gripped the stem of his glass, wishing it was Ray's scrawny neck.

'But things are OK with you and Nicole now?'

'Yeah. We had a chat.'

James topped up his glass. 'So it was Nicole who told the press about Carol's heart attack?'

'No. Weirdly enough, it was the other guy in the lift.'

'Wait, what?' James frowned. 'There was someone else in the lift?'

'I told you at the time. Hipster guy, remember? Turns out he's a *Napier* superfan and was keen to further the whole "Alex saves *Napier*" story with his version of my "heroics". A version in which I feature as the sole messianic saviour and Lucinda doesn't get a mention.'

Sarah drained her glass. 'I'm so confused. Maybe I should switch to water now before it gets worse.'

James strode over to the sink and set about filling three glasses from the tap. Alex's gaze swung after his brother and snagged on the view of the garden through the windows. A white-and-blue paddling pool sat in the middle of the lawn. The kids' toys were strewn around it: sparkly hula hoops, fluorescent orange tennis rackets and discarded water pistols. These colourful reminders of their laughter would usually have made Alex smile. But now, staring at the remnants of their energy, the evidence of a busy family life, only added another leaden layer to the heavy cloak of loneliness he'd been wearing since he watched Lucinda's van race away.

James returned to the island with the water and, as if reading his thoughts, said, 'Getting back to Lucinda. I know she's not speaking to you right now, but you're not going to let it go, are you?'

Alex ignored the water and reached for his wine glass. 'Let what go?'

'The amazing thing!' James thumped the countertop. 'The *thing* between you two.'

'What *thing*?'

'Oh come on, Alex!' Sarah smacked his arm with the back of her hand. 'It was like there was an invisible force field shimmering around you two whenever you got within a few feet of each other.'

James added, in the steady tone of one imparting ancient wisdom, 'It was sex.'

Sarah rolled her eyes. 'It wasn't just sex,' she said to James before turning her attention back to Alex. 'It was like you were having a conversation without speaking.'

'Oh. Right.' Alex gazed down into the bottom of his glass, but instead of answers he found greater confusion when he noticed it was somehow empty again.

Sarah prodded his arm, this time with a touch of menace. 'If you let that go without a fight, you're—and I say this with love—an enormous stinking idiot.'

They sipped their drinks and their gazes became unfocused as their thoughts turned inwards. The contemplative silence grew thick and when Alex's phone rang they all startled. Alex glanced eagerly at the screen but the heaviness in his stomach redoubled when, yet again, the caller was not Lucinda.

When he looked up, Sarah and James were watching him. Their identical frowns spoke of their concern and Alex decided he should let them know the full magnitude of what he was up against. 'It's not that simple with Lucinda. You see … She doesn't believe in love.'

Sarah's and James's frowns vanished as their eyebrows flew upwards and they chorused, 'What?'

'Her dad abandoned the family. After that her mum adopted these rules and some ... I guess you'd call them "beliefs". And apparently true love is a load of rubbish. Nothing more than a ...' Alex paused. The alcohol was taking effect and he feared he would trip over the upcoming syllables. He frowned and took another run at the sentence. 'Nothing more than a palliative fiction.'

James huffed a laugh. 'What a load of—'

'Now, now,' said Sarah. 'Don't make me remind you of your annual Valentine's Day rant.'

'That's different.'

'Saying it's all a cynical capitalist campaign to exploit silly dreams of romance for commercial gain?' Sarah gave James a barbed stare and he dropped his gaze to his glass. 'It may just be your excuse for forgetting to get me anything, but it doesn't sound too different to what Alex is talking about.'

'It is a bit like that,' said Alex. 'But applied more widely. And stubbornly.'

'Huh.' Sarah shrugged. 'Well, that's as maybe, but Lucinda seems like a sensible person to me. It's hard for someone like that to reject the evidence of their eyes and ears. I think she could be persuaded. And you've always been a romantic, so I guess you'll have to believe enough for the both of you.'

Alex huffed a laugh. 'I'm not sure that's how it works.' He polished off the dregs of his wine and closed his eyes for a moment to savour the wooziness which was making his head swim. 'Besides, perhaps sometimes you need to know when to quit.'

'Maybe.' James nodded and tapped the back of Alex's hand to make him look up. 'But if you don't try, you'll never know.'

Alex's heart thudded, as if the full force of his dad's motto had landed on his chest. He was opening his mouth to reply, when James continued, 'And I wouldn't hit you with the emotional blackmail of Dad's greatest advice if I didn't think it was important, mate.'

Alex nodded. James was right. It was important. The alcohol had risen to his brain and his thoughts were increasingly blurry, but he knew the feelings Lucinda stirred in him were powerful. And he was pretty sure they were the opposite of the icy emptiness which had made a home in his guts as the afternoon had worn on without word from her.

He stared at the sheen of the late sunlight on the glossy cupboard fronts and, fighting the rising fog of intoxication, tried to pin down what was so wonderful about Lucinda's company. There was—of course—the rush of undeniable attraction, the way he could relax knowing she would understand his references and jokes, and, most importantly, a sort of inexplicable deep contentment.

The last thought brought an unexpected vivid image to mind. When Sarah and James began dating, she owned a cat. An enormous fluffy ginger lion of a creature who loved to lie on the windowsill on sunny days. With its belly stretched towards the warm rays and its eyes squeezed shut, it would stretch and purr with gusto until it sounded like a feline motorbike. It was like the creature was in love with the sunshine itself—

That was it!

He slammed his fist against the countertop. 'She makes me the cat!'

'Okey-dokey,' said Sarah, sliding the glass and bottle away from him. 'Enough wine for you, mister.'

Alex grinned, his head swimming with the epiphany—and possibly, he had to admit, more wine than he could tolerate on an empty stomach—that Lucinda was quite possibly to key to his future happiness.

He grabbed James by his shoulders. If he'd had one more glass of wine, he would have hugged him. 'James! You're absolutely right!'

'I'm going to need that in writing.' James laughed. 'And, if possible, I'd like it as my ringtone.'

'I'm going to go for it!' Alex jumped off the stool and began to pace across the tiles beside the sink.

'Hallelujah, the leading man is back!' said Sarah. 'Whatever it takes, we're going to help you speak to Lucinda. I need that woman back here with more of those brownies, Alex.'

'Amen,' said James, raising his water glass in a toast.

'And,' said Sarah, tilting her head from side to side, 'I also happen to like her a lot. So tell us, how can we help?'

Alex groaned and lifted his hands to his head. He should have stopped drinking after one glass of wine. This was a situation that required sharp, critical thinking. The sort of thing Lucinda was good at.

'I don't know.' He dragged a hand down his face. 'She's not replying to my messages or taking my calls. What do I try next?'

'I do have one idea,' said Sarah, her eyes glittering with inspiration.

'Anything. I'll try anything.'

'That's the attitude.' Her gaze flickered to the countertop, where Alex's phone was buzzing again. 'I think you should give whichever of your persistent callers has the greatest audience the interview they're so desperate for.'

Chapter 35

Lucinda had never thought of herself as someone who ran away from the unexpected or difficult. But, as the swarm of photographers bore down on them, a powerful flight response overwhelmed her. Her breathing grew shallow and her hands trembled as the air vibrated with raised voices and blinding lights and she didn't truly realise she had abandoned Alex until she was next to the van.

Lucinda drew in deep calming breaths, her heartbeat slowing as her face reddened: she had deserted him. She had turned tail and left him there alone.

As she whirled round to try to glimpse Alex behind the huddle of photographers, she chastised herself further: she was usually so good in a crisis. But the sort of problems she was used to dealing with occurred in the privacy of kitchens, behind marquees and, lately, in lifts. Life hadn't prepared her for having a bank of cameras shoved in her face. The mere idea of being the centre of attention made her skin crawl.

But all that was no excuse for having left Alex to face them alone.

Lucinda was scanning the group over by the path, planning the safest way to approach and extract Alex, when a late arrival barged through the scrum and threw herself at him. The polished, glamorous woman swung from Alex's neck and, as Lucinda watched open mouthed, embraced him in a passionate kiss.

The crimson waves of Lucinda's guilt were washed away by a torrent of jealous green. Jay had shown her enough posts from Nicole's Instagram feed for her to recognise the blonde hair and glittering youth of Alex's ex-girlfriend. Or *supposed* ex-girlfriend.

Lucinda yanked the van door open, threw the hamper onto the passenger seat, slammed the door and sped away without looking back. Alex had an enthusiastic volunteer to help him sort out whatever the heck was going on. He had his hands full of Nicole's golden mane and perky figure and probably wouldn't even miss gullible old Lucinda.

While the sky at Compton Hall had been an uninterrupted sheet of pale blue, heavy grey clouds hovered over Great Compton and the darkest of them seemed to have taken the spiteful decision to gather above Lucinda's street. Not that Lucinda was able to give the weather much thought. Her mind was swamped in a fog of confusion, jealousy and residual panic, which began to lift as she pulled the van into her driveway and shut off the engine.

Groaning at her own irrational behaviour, Lucinda slumped forwards and let her forehead strike the steering wheel. Could Alex have known about the waiting press? Had he lied about splitting up with Nicole?

Lucinda considered the possibilities for a few seconds before harrumphing and shaking her head. What melodramatic nonsense! Alex was a terrific actor, but she'd bet her house his shock at the presence of the photographers had been genuine. And why would he have told Sarah and James that Nicole had left him if she hadn't?

As she leapt out of the van and raised her keys to open the front door, her hand wobbled and her calm inner voice—which was normally right about most things—suggested retreating to her bedroom with a cup of tea might be for the best.

Her drink had cooled enough to risk sipping it when the first message arrived from Alex. It confirmed her suspicions: Alex had no idea what had happened and he and Nicole were not an item.

Pausing occasionally to take a sip of scalding tea, Lucinda made several attempts at composing replies but deleted them all. She needed to think.

She set her phone down next to her on the bed and exhaled slowly. Her fingers were still quivering as she pressed them to her ribcage which shuddered as her heart boomed against it. The calm inner voice returned: *There are no photographers here now, Lucinda. What are you really afraid of?*

She rolled her eyes. Ruddy smartarse inner voice.

Things had been going very well with Alex until you were interrupted. What would have happened next? What would 'to be continued' have looked like? Where would that happen? Would you ever be comfortable inviting Alex back here, into this room and this bed, knowing Chris's bedroom is the other side of that wall?

Lucinda shuddered and covered her eyes with her hands. From his message she knew Alex was upset and worried. He would have been frowning as he typed, that cute crinkle appearing between his sad brown eyes. Her heart ached at the thought and she longed to jump back in the van and race round to James's to see him. But at the same time, the competing image of Nicole showering him with kisses filled her with a fierce desire to kick something.

Raindrops knocked at the window as the sun cast a weak beam of light across the foot of her bed. Lucinda gazed out at the shifting colours of the clouds and asked herself the question which had been troubling her for the past couple of months: what the blazes was wrong with her? Every time she tried to think her way towards Alex and the idea of a future which included him, she reached a dead end of anxiety-laden uncertainty. It was if she were standing on a high ledge overlooking a murky chasm and, before she could leap, she needed a better idea of what was below. Because, right now, the brightly lit safety of the uneventful life a few steps back from the ledge was beginning to look like her best option. Even if it was Alex-free territory. At least there she had never felt in danger of losing her mind.

She collapsed back onto the bed and curled into a ball, hugging her knees. Her limbs were heavy and her temples throbbed. Perhaps she should rest for a few minutes. Close her eyes, have a short nap, give her mind a break from Alex and wake up with all the answers ...

Lucinda smiled as she snuggled further into Alex's embrace. A cosy tartan blanket held them tightly as he stroked her back and whispered into her hair, and Lucinda was close to purring with pleasure when the hornet appeared. It dived towards them as she swatted at the angry buzzing ball. Swinging her arm wildly, she tottered and plummeted into the gaping hole which opened at her feet—

Lucinda startled awake and squinted at the vibrating black block juddering on the pillow next to her head. The words 'phone' and 'ringing' crawled to the front of her sluggish brain and she grabbed for it, successfully clutching it on the third clumsy attempt.

'Hello?'

'Lucinda? What's wrong with you? Were you asleep?'

The bubble of hope that it might be Alex on the other end of the line burst. Lucinda rubbed her sore eyes. How long had she been asleep? 'Hi, Mum. What time is it?'

'A little after six here.'

She'd slept for more than three hours! Maybe exhaustion was part of her problem. It would probably be easier to think clearly about Alex after nine hours of uninterrupted sleep. Particularly if the sleep included pleasant dreams of rolling about on cosy picnic blankets with him. Without being interrupted by giant stinging insects or phone calls from her—

'Lucinda? Were you sleeping?'

Lucinda shook her head and sat up. 'Only for a minute.'

'You work far too hard. You've barely had a minute off while Jay's been on holiday. I bet you're working tomorrow too.'

336

Lucinda was working the next day and her Mum was right about her recent schedule. Despite her longer than intended nap, her head was groggy. An early night would be a good idea.

Not wanting to admit her mum was doubly correct, she made a non-committal humming sound and waited.

It didn't take her mum long to jump into the silence. 'I was calling to let you know we've narrowed down wedding dates. It'll either be April or May next year.'

'That's great. I'll book it out as soon as you have a final date.'

'You won't be coming alone will you, darling?' Her mum's tone turned sugary and Lucinda braced herself. 'I'm sure Chris would love a holiday over here. You had such a nice time when you came together. What was that, three years ago? It was lovely to see him and Michael getting on too. They'll both look handsome in morning suits—'

'Mum! Chris and I are over. He fell in love with someone else. At first sight. Remember? And anyway, even if he hadn't, I don't think I was ever in love with him.'

'Oh.' Her mum fell silent and Lucinda dared to dream she might actually be lost for words. But it didn't take her long to rally. 'But you're such a good couple. You get on so well and have lots in common.'

'No, Mum!' Lucinda was not going to let it go this time. 'I don't think we do, not really. He never made me feel ...' *What?* she asked herself. What had been missing?

The air in the room had become stuffy and stale while she slept. Lucinda rolled off the bed, opened the window and inhaled as a rain-cooled breeze drifted over her face.

'Mum?'

'Yes, darling?'

'You love Graham, don't you?'

'Of course!' Her mum laughed. 'Why else would I be marrying him?'

'Right. Yes. Right.' Lucinda perched on the edge of the dressing table and rubbed her brow ridge. 'But how did you know you were in love with him?'

'I ... well ... I suppose because he makes me very happy.'

Lucinda thought about her mum's renaissance in Spain. 'You have friends who make you happy. And Michael.'

'Yes, that's true. But it's not the same.'

'How?' Lucinda pressed the phone closer to her ear. If she could have reached down the line, grabbed her mum by the shoulders and shaken the precious information out of her, she would. 'How is it different?'

'Gosh, Lucinda. You are asking the oddest questions today.' Her mum clicked her tongue off her teeth. 'I suppose it's a sort of bubbly, fizzy happiness. When he calls and I see his name on my phone, for example. It's exciting.'

Lucinda's thoughts returned to the jolly, independent life her mum had been leading for nearly three decades. She seemed fine and she'd always said she had no desire for romance. Which was all deceptive, dangerous rubbish anyway. 'But weren't you happy before you met him?'

'I was. But I'm happier now.'

'But you'd have been OK ...' Lucinda paused. She sensed she was getting closer to what she wanted to know. 'You would be OK without him?'

Her mother tutted. 'Lucinda. It's not about needing Graham. I don't *need* him in my life. I *want* him in my life.'

Lucinda's fingers ached from how tightly she was

gripping the phone. She bit her lip as she transferred it to the other hand and pondered her mum's response.

'What's this all about, Lucinda? Are you all right?'

Oh, don't worry, Mum. I just suspect you and your years of 'true love is harmful crap' rants may have ruined my chances of finding what you, the original sceptic, have now found with Graham! No big deal.

Swallowing the bitterness rising up her throat, Lucinda fought the tremor creeping into her voice and replied, 'You said true love wasn't real. That it's hormones making us crazy. That it doesn't last forever because it wears off. You ... You had rules, Mum!'

The silence on the other end of the line was so complete, Lucinda thought she must have been cut off and glanced at the screen. 'Mum?'

A slow sigh prefaced her mum's halting reply. 'Yes. You're right. I did say that. Because, all that time, after your father ... I was hurt. And angry. And that's what I believed. Honestly believed. But, with Graham ... I guess it turns out that all rules do have exceptions.'

Lucinda squeezed her eyes shut, remembering the moment in their adjoining bedrooms at Russell House when Alex had said almost exactly the same thing. His being right was becoming a habit. 'And Graham is yours? Your exception?'

'Yes.'

'What if you're wrong now?'

'Sorry?'

'What if it wears off? The bubbly, fizzy feeling? What if it turns out you were right before? That there are no exceptions.'

Her mum sucked in a sharp breath. Her answer, when it eventually came, was firm. 'I did ask myself that. And, in the end, I thought, "To hell with it." Life flies past, always faster and faster. And I want to be happy. Whatever happens, I'll be glad to have met him.'

Lucinda nodded and blinked back tears. And, for the first time in years, she wished she was sitting next to her mum, holding her hand.

She held the phone away from her face while she sniffed and ran a finger under her eye. Trusting her voice would be steady, she returned to the reasons for her mum's call. 'So it's an April or May wedding then. The weather should be perfect.'

'Exactly! Not too hot yet. Apparently Bella, that's Graham's eldest, is terribly sensitive to the heat.'

Lucinda rolled her eyes. The desire to run to her mum vanished with the mention of her soon-to-be stepsister. Although it was nice to know Graham's perfect daughter had one chink in her flawless armour. 'I suppose lots of people are.'

'Hmn. I don't like to think of you coming alone. Is there no one else you could bring?'

Lucinda's mind strayed to an image of Alex resplendent in a morning suit. For a fraction of a second her mood soared, but then her nagging doubts wound themselves into a heavy lump and started to roll around her guts. Pressing her hand to her belly, Lucinda gazed out of the window at the grey-blue clouds in the distance. 'I'm not sure yet, Mum. I'll let you know.'

Chapter 36

Sunday morning was humid and overcast. As she drove to work, Lucinda prayed the painkillers she had swallowed instead of breakfast would soon take effect. A determined ache was pulsing above her eyebrows and, despite not having eaten the previous evening, she felt queasy rather than hungry.

The headache eventually dulled, but she struggled to concentrate nonetheless. Even the simplest of tasks—chopping vegetables—brought distracting thoughts of Alex, buttoned up to his strong jawline in a smart chef's jacket, wielding a knife with surprising, alluring competence. She hoped Jay, who was merrily chattering about the highlights of her recent holiday, wouldn't notice her unusual sloppiness. Although in the end it was her stomach that drew notice, not her inept dicing.

'Oh my life!' Jay stared at Lucinda's tummy. 'You should go outside for a break and eat something before your guts start to digest your vital organs.' The head chef's complexion was radiant and her eyes shining with the energetic glow of the well-rested. But though she was poking fun, there was something a little sly about her tone as she added, 'And while you're there, I strongly recommend checking out the video I sent you a minute ago.' She flicked a cloth at Lucinda, shooing her towards the door. 'Go on!'

A mixture of intrigue and dread hurried Lucinda to the far corner of the car park where she sank onto the bench underneath the elm tree and opened the link in Jay's message.

A video from the latest episode of *The Sunday Breakfast Show* popped up and there, in the palm of her hand, was Alex. He was sitting in James's spare bedroom—his preferred remote studio—and accessorising a black, tight-fitting jersey top with white EarPods and a nervous smile.

Lucinda growled as the video refused to load. Glaring at the rotating circle of doom in the centre of the screen, she pulled her keys from her pocket and fidgeted with her heart key-ring charm, running her fingertips over the smooth red enamel and the scratches around the golden metal rim. Seconds of infuriating waiting later, she was about to bite it to stop herself screaming, when it began to play.

'This morning we're delighted to be joined by Alex Fraser, who is best known for playing Dexter Hartford alongside Diana Carter in hit police drama *Napier*. Although lately he's been starring in real-life drama.'

The gurning presenter proceeded to give an overview of what had happened to Carol in the lift and Alex's image on the large flat screen next to her vanished for a moment, replaced with a recent picture of Carol, Lady Russell, decked out in diamonds and a sleek black gown.

Alex managed to keep a strained smile in place while the presenter spoke, looking only marginally like a man who would have preferred thumbscrews to sitting through the interview.

'So, Alex. Loving the black hair, by the way.' The presenter batted her eyelashes and shuffled further towards the television. If she could have climbed through the screen and onto Alex's lap, Lucinda bet she would. 'Many of your fans are calling for your "Saviour of *Napier*" label to be extended to—'

'Well, that's the thing, you see,' said Alex, using his smoothest tone to interrupt as graciously as possible. 'I don't deserve the credit for saving Lady Russell. There was another passenger in the lift who knew what to do. If it hadn't been for her staying calm and getting on with first aid … I dread to think what would have happened.'

'But, according to Lady Russell's own account, you helped?'

'Yes. But, as I said, I would have been useless without the other passenger telling me what to do.' He chuckled and Lucinda's chest swelled as tears pricked her eyes. 'I'm an actor. I guess I need direction.'

The presenter responded with a shrill giggle which dried Lucinda's eyes and made her cringe with second-hand shame. 'And, I know we don't have you for long, but I have to ask you about the statement Nicole Allen posted on her Instagram earlier this morning. After pictures were circulating yesterday afternoon of you two together, she wanted to make it clear you are no longer an item. Is that right?'

'Yes. Nicole and I are good friends. She's a wonderful person and actor and I wish her well in LA.'

'So you're single?'

Lucinda cringed again, but also brought her phone closer to her face and turned the volume up a few notches.

'Yes.' Alex nodded and gave another nervous smile as two dashes of pink spread along his cheekbones.

'I'm sure lots of our viewers will be very happy to hear that.'

Well they can get in line, Lucinda thought as Alex laughed the comment off with adorable modesty. She loved all his laughs, although the embarrassed chuckle with a side order of bashful blinking was one of her favourites.

As the presenter thanked Alex for coming on the show and he raised a hand in an unnecessary goodbye wave, Lucinda found she was squeezing her key ring so hard the metal rim had left an angry groove in her palm.

She pursed her lips and stared at her keys. The keys to her and Chris's house. She tapped a nail off the red enamel of the charm and frowned. The heart had been invisible to her for such a long time. But since Olivia had admired it, every glance at it had made her remember how she hadn't wanted to give the missing puzzle piece to Chris. The day they completed their house purchase had been one of their happiest together. Lucinda remembered standing side by side in their new kitchen. And as they both gazed in awe at their sets of keys—keys to their own house!—it would have been the perfect moment to give him the key ring which completed hers. But she hadn't.

Lucinda shifted her gaze to her phone. She should reply to Alex's messages. Imagining him worrying because he thought she was upset or angry brought the thudding in her temples surging back. She rattled her house keys and sighed. She would talk to Alex, but there was something she had to do first. Something she should have done some time ago.

Acting quickly, before she could change her mind, she sprang up, stuffed her keys into her pocket and dashed off a message to Chris.

11:07 Lucinda

Hi. I need to talk to you. Will you be home at around 4 today? x

Chapter 37

'Hello?'

A rustling in the front room was followed by Chris's voice. 'I'm in here.'

Heart racing, Lucinda was tempted to spin round, throw open the door and bolt. But her stubborn side refused to make the mistake of running away from someone she cared about twice in one weekend. Besides, she reasoned as she squeezed her key ring, this had to be done. If she wanted to start a new chapter in her life, she had to turn the page.

And, as she sidled into the front room and Chris rose from the sofa to greet her, she realised she should have asked for this conversation sooner. Chris was sporting his best powder-blue shirt and favourite navy tie. Lucinda suspected his brown hair, always short and neat, had been freshly trimmed. The same barber might have also taken a razor to the blunt angles of his jaw which were unusually stubble-free.

He was also wearing a tight, nervous smile and, as

Lucinda's pounding heart sank, he bent to snatch up a bouquet of red roses from the coffee table. 'These are for you,' he said, extending the flowers towards her.

Lucinda returned his timid smile and took them. 'Thank you. They're lovely. Chris—'

'I was so pleased to get your message.' Chris's words rushed out on one breath. 'I've been wanting to talk to you properly for a while. We seem to keep missing each other.'

Lucinda thought about how many times she had avoided Chris over the past couple of years and a trickle of guilt wormed its way down her spine. She set the flowers down on the table slowly, as if they might shatter, and perched on the edge of the sofa. 'Chris, I'm sorry if I've given you the wrong impression—'

'No, I'm sorry.' Chris sank down next to her. He took her left hand in his right and ran his thumb gently over the back of it. 'Lu, I know I was an idiot and stuffed up things between us. But I think we can—'

'Chris.' Lucinda twisted her hand in his and squeezed his fingers. 'There's no easy way to say this.' She took a deep breath and the thick perfume of Chris's well-intentioned but misguided roses spurred her on. 'I want to sell the house.'

Her words landed like a hard slap. Chris's jaw dropped and his eyes filled with disbelief. For a moment, his expression was so sad and lost she longed to take it back. She did love the house and the little things she had done to make it cosy, to create a permanent space which was hers. But there were no finishing touches which could counteract the awkwardness of sharing it with Chris. And that wasn't going to change.

Home was a place you were safe and at ease. Somewhere you belonged. And the only place Lucinda had felt like that in recent memory was in Alex's arms.

Shaking his head, Chris asked, 'But, why? Why do you want to sell now? We've been happy here, haven't we?'

'Yes. We have. And no, not so much. It's been awkward since we split up. We've been tiptoeing round each other. Neither of us should have to do that.'

'But we wouldn't have to if we gave it another go.' He shifted to face her, a hopeful shine chasing some of the sorrow from his eyes. 'I love you. My family love you.' His voice dropped to a near whisper, a tender plea. 'We're perfect together. We could make it work.'

Tears rushed into Lucinda's eyes and her heart ached for the kind, caring man she had once planned to grow old with. If she hadn't met Alex, if her mum hadn't decided to get married and believe in exceptions to unshakeable rules, perhaps she and Chris would have fallen back into their former patterns and been content to muddle through. But now that wasn't enough. Lucinda had decided she didn't want to settle for anything less than the exceptional. And Chris shouldn't have to either.

'I care about you very much and I love your family too. They're amazing and have been incredibly kind to me. But … You deserve more. What you felt for Janine.' Chris winced at the name as if he'd been struck again and Lucinda hurried on. 'You deserve someone who makes your heart race and your palms clammy. Someone who, every time you're going to see them or speak to them … it's exciting and dizzying but also slightly terrifying in a weirdly good way that makes you feel … that makes you feel …'

'Alive.'

Lucinda nodded, pleased Chris understood the electrifying power of the lightning bolt. She had been sleepwalking through life. But the spark that had jumped between her and Alex at their first meeting had set something smouldering within her which every subsequent meeting and conversation had fanned into a bright flame. Hers had been an increasingly cold and lonely existence. And she didn't want to go back to merely existing now she had a chance to live.

Chris mirrored her nod and let his head hang forwards. He sniffed and the sight of his dejection sent the tears welling in Lucinda's eyes rolling down her cheeks.

'Come here,' she said, pulling him into a hug. 'Look at it this way: you'll be escaping my unpalatable taste in bathroom tiles and film posters.' They both chuckled and, reassured by the amused rumble shaking Chris's chest, she eased out of the embrace.

As they dried their eyes, the curl at the edge of Chris's lips dropped. 'Mum's going to kill me.'

'Ah, she'll get over it. If it'll help, I'll tell her it's my fault.'

'No. Nope. Absolutely not.' Chris shook his head and thumped his palms against his knees. 'You're not to blame for anything.'

Finally! Someone else had said it! Lucinda gave him a nod of gratitude and they fell into a companiable silence, gazing out through the window as a car rolled down the quiet street which had been home for almost seven years. A breeze stirred the edge of the curtains, a sign of the approaching change in the weather which was also visible in the distant billowing towers of cloud whose light charcoal and midnight-blue shades spoke of imminent thunderstorms and clearer skies to come. As the fresh air brushed over her skin Lucinda inhaled slowly and the heady scent of the roses stirred thoughts of romance, weddings and anniversaries. Of what could have been and what still could be.

Soon she had wandered so far into the forest of missed opportunities and captivating possibilities she startled when Chris spoke.

'So. What happens now?'

Lucinda's phone chimed shortly after Chris had removed his tie and set off for work. Keen to keep herself busy, Lucinda had plucked a vase from the back of a kitchen cupboard and was trimming the rose stems when another message from Alex arrived.

16:34 Alex
Hi Lucinda.

Me again, sorry.
I don't know if you've seen the interview I did this morning for The Sunday Breakfast Show. I hope you have. I wanted to set the story straight about Carol. And Nicole.

I'd really like to speak to you. The managers of Compton Hall are putting on a dinner party thing for the cast and crew tonight from 7 p.m. I'd love you to come. If know it's a bit last minute but I really hope you can make it.

Anyway, I just wanted to check you're OK after yesterday. Hope to see you tonight xx

Lucinda stared at the two x's at the end of the message and smiled. They were a new development, despite Alex having sent her dozens of texts. The pair of little crosses transported her back to the warmth of the sun-dappled picnic blanket and Alex's embrace.

Lucinda had experienced quite a few first kisses. Some had been good, some disappointing, and some head-buttingly, teeth-collidingly terrible. But none compared to her kiss with Alex. Just the thought of it made her knees weak and lips tingle. She doubted another could ever compete and concluded she wouldn't care if she didn't have another first kiss ever again. And, when you found yourself having thoughts that radical, you had to do something about it.

Scanning the message again, she tapped her thumb against the side of the phone as an idea brewed. It was a good one but she would need help and possibly a little magic to pull it off. And whenever she had found herself in a work-related jam which required sorcery to solve, there was only one person to call. Which was why she had her number on speed dial.

Please pick up, please pick up, Lucinda prayed as she listened to the dial tone. After a nerve-jangling eternity, the call connected and a steady, pleasant voice said, 'Hi Lucinda, how are you?'

'Becky! I need a favour,' Lucinda blurted, then winced.

She probably should have gone with a bit of polite small talk before asking for help.

Thankfully Becky didn't seem bothered by Lucinda having skipped questions about family and the weather. 'Always happy to help my favourite caterer,' said Becky. 'What's up?' The tension in Lucinda's shoulders eased. She hadn't been sure, given how stupidly she'd acted last time she'd seen Becky—after the police-impersonation escapade—whether the Comptons' only behind-the-scenes miracle worker would want to help her ever again.

Lucinda sent up another prayer: this time of thanks. 'There's a dinner party thing up at the Hall tonight and I want to go, but not actually attend the party.' She rolled her eyes at her own incoherence. 'There's someone I need to talk to, but want to do it privately. So I want to get into the Hall, without being seen or thrown out by security, and then be able to talk to this person without interruptions.'

In the silence at the other end of the line, Lucinda swore she could hear the millions of tiny interlocking cogs in Becky's Machiavellian mind whirring. Eventually, Becky asked, 'Has this got something to do with Alex?'

Lucinda's jaw dropped. Maybe the woman was a witch after all. 'What makes you think that?'

'More hope than think, to be honest.'

'If it did have something to do with him, would you be more likely to help me?'

Becky laughed. 'I'd help you anyway. But if Alex is involved, I'll be extra motivated. Anyone who can make you act like a jealous ...'

'Harpy?'

Becky's chuckle escalated to a cackle. 'A bit harsh, but that's a fantastic word, so let's go with it.' She huffed another laugh. 'Yes. If the man can make you act that crazy after you'd met him twice … I'd say that's worth exploring. Come on. Let's make it happen.'

Chapter 38

As Sunday afternoon wore on, a gentle westerly breeze cleared the grey clouds to reveal unbroken blue skies. The evening was unarguably glorious and completely at odds with Alex's internal weather, which was a raging hurricane peppered with ragged splinters of hail.

One shaft of light broke through Alex's inner gloom as he mingled with members of the cast and crew in Compton Hall's entrance hall: the revelation that he was unlikely to see Ray in the near future. His co-star had turned down the party invitation because he had somewhere better to be, thus saving Alex the trouble of punching him square on the nose. The devious, craven snake.

The Hall was as resplendent as ever and a luxurious setting for a modest dinner soirée. The sum of the wood panelling, elaborately painted ceilings, gilded portrait frames and extravagant floral bouquets was dazzling. But Alex found no pleasure in his surroundings and the party might as well have been held at the local dump. While everyone around him swapped amusing anecdotes his mind turned through a carousel of Lucinda-related scenarios. She hated him. She had got back together with Chris. She had been in some sort of accident and had woken in hospital with amnesia. Although, he reasoned, the latter idea was probably the product of having watched too many dubious 1990s romcoms.

A gong sounded, momentarily disrupting Alex's gloomy imaginings. The other guests waltzed merrily towards the Grand Saloon while Alex sighed and ran a hand over his hair, his fingers taut with frustration. There were so many things he hadn't told her. How he longed to see her dance and sing again. How he was crazy about her hair and the way it fell when she unclipped it. How her lipstick application methods were incredibly sexy, if not indecent. How he wanted to kiss every inch of her gorgeous body then enjoy the privilege of having her sleep in his arms.

He would stop short at mentioning the sunbathing cat thing, though. Probably best to keep that to himself.

Alex was so preoccupied with thoughts of Lucinda that, as he dragged his feet to join the last of the party's stragglers, the sound of a low voice saying his name made him startle. Spinning towards the sound, he found Becky Watson, fellow Shakespeare fan, standing against the wall in the shadow of one of the room's ornate columns. Dressed as she had been the last time they'd met—in unassuming black and white—she was doing a good impression of a living statue. How long had she been standing there? And how hadn't he noticed her before?

Keeping the rest of her body immobile, Becky lifted a single finger to beckon him to her side. Alex glanced at the entrance to the Saloon and, confident that none of the other diners had noticed his absence, scurried into the gloom.

Becky's commanding blue gaze flicked left and right before settling on Alex. She inclined towards him a fraction and said, 'I've been asked to tell you that, if you don't mind missing out on dinner, there's sticky toffee pudding and custard waiting for you on the rose garden balcony.'

Alex's lips parted and his heart hammered against his ribs as he struggled to take in what Becky was saying. One overwhelming, joyous thought beat against the front of his mind, keeping time with his pulse: Lucinda was here. Here to see *him*.

Becky's lips curled as her quick eyes scanned his slack jaw and stunned blinking. 'I've also been told that this particular pudding is best enjoyed in private and have been asked to escort you through the back corridors so you won't be seen.' She leant back against the wall behind her and, with a smooth, silent motion Alex had only seen in movies, a concealed door swung inwards to reveal a mahogany-panelled corridor.

Becky glided across the threshold and was a few steps down the passageway when she turned back. 'Are you coming? It's best not to keep a lady waiting.'

Alex stammered and scrambled after her, slipping through the door as it began to slide to a noiseless close.

He rushed after Becky, quickly becoming disorientated as she coasted over the thick teal carpet. They flew past several mahogany doors as the corridor turned a sharp right, left and right again, and Alex had begun to wonder what lay behind them when Becky came to a sharp halt.

She pointed to the crimson curtains covering the end of the passageway. 'I'll leave you to take it from here.'

'Thank you.' Alex nodded and made to pass her, but Becky held up a hand to halt his sprint.

'I've been told you'll soon be appearing in *A Midsummer Night's Dream*. And I was wondering, if it's not too much trouble, whether you could arrange a few tickets for me?'

Alex grinned. That was a favour he'd be delighted to grant. 'Any time. My treat. And thank you again.'

'My pleasure.' Becky inclined her head in the subtlest of bows. 'Now, you'd best hurry along." She patted his arm and winked. 'Break a leg!'

The curve of his smile fading into a determined line, Alex whirled away from Becky and dashed to the end of the corridor, almost tripping over his feet in his eagerness. But when he reached the heavy drapes, he paused. Cool evening air drifted through the gap in the curtains. It soothed his flushed skin as he attempted to calm his jitters with a swift pep talk which mostly consisted in one simple message: *Do not mess this up, Alex.*

Beyond the balcony, a fiery blend of reds and oranges shimmered along the horizon as the upper heavens faded to a delicate baby blue and the first stars appeared. A few paces from him, Lucinda was leaning on the stone balustrade, her forearms resting on the top rail, gazing out over the sunken rose garden and the lawns in the distance. Her raven hair, black jeans and navy top made her a shade against the dying light of the day. An image so peaceful, so striking, that Alex was—for a moment—reluctant to disturb her.

'Hello.'

Lucinda turned her face towards him and her lips twitched into a nervous smile. 'Hello.' Alex approached with careful steps as she continued, 'Becky found you then?'

'Yes, thank you.' He positioned himself to her right at the balustrade and leant forwards slowly to rest his elbows on the top rail. The scent of pink and red roses floated up to them as he interlaced his fingers, seeking the right words. His irritation with himself rising again, he rubbed his thumbs against each other. He'd had tonnes to say to her a few minutes ago. Why was his head now empty of everything except the booming of his pulse?

'Sorry there's no actual sticky toffee pudding,' said Lucinda.

'That's OK.' The words rushed out, impelled by his relief that she had broken the silence with a safe subject. 'An expert told me it's best served warm and I imagine that's difficult to do on a balcony.'

Lucinda smirked, and returned her gaze to the balustrade. 'Indeed.'

Reluctant to let silence settle in again, Alex risked another glance at the side of her face and asked, 'Did you see the interview?'

'I did.' She nodded, her gaze fixed dead ahead. 'It was good. And good work on keeping my identity a secret. I, and Her Majesty's Government, thank you. You may be in line for a knighthood.'

'I'm happy to be of service.'

'But ...' Lucinda frowned and her lips tensed into a grave line. 'I did think the presenter made an unforgiveable omission which let you and the viewers down.'

Alex mirrored her frown and asked, a quaver in his voice, 'Oh? Really?'

'Yes.' She turned her head towards him and raised an eyebrow. 'She made no mention whatsoever of your Rear of the Year nomination. Not even a picture. And they claim to be doing public interest reporting!'

Alex laughed, the tension in his chest easing. Lucinda grinned and said, 'I'm sorry I didn't reply to any of your messages.'

Since stepping onto the balcony, Alex had forgotten about the messages. The pleasant wooziness brought on by Lucinda's smile was such that he was finding it hard to remember or care about anything outside of the moment. 'That's OK—'

'No, it isn't.' Her frown returned. 'It was rude. I suppose ... I guess I freaked out with the photographers and then ... I had a few things I had to sort out. Things I should have sorted out a while ago.' She turned her face back to the gardens, directing her words to the flowers below. 'Chris and I are selling the house.'

Leaping up onto the balustrade, punching the air and yelling *'Yes!'* was Alex's immediate instinct. To stifle it, he gripped the edge of the top rail and focused on the hint of regret in Lucinda's voice. He cleared his throat, taking time to ensure his own voice would be steady when he replied, 'Wow. That's a big decision.'

Lucinda shrugged. 'It was time. I love the house, but I can't stay there with him any more. It isn't fair on him or me.'

Alex's neck grew itchy and hot. He ran his fingers over the prickling skin. What did Lucinda's decision about the house mean, if anything, for him? For *them*?

He put his hand back on the balustrade and purposely trained his gaze on the distant lawns. It was important not to jump to conclusions. Lucinda's living arrangements were complicated and a sensitive situation. And making any kind of comment about Chris would probably only lead him to put him foot in it.

The silence between them stretched. Alex snuck a couple of glances at Lucinda, but she appeared to be making an in-depth horticultural study of the rose beds. But, the third time he peeked in her direction, a flash of green and the smallest movement of her head convinced him he had almost caught her looking at him and a warm thrill shot down his spine.

Remembering Becky, he decided to take the plunge with a neutral topic. 'Becky's asked me for tickets to *A Midsummer Night's Dream.*'

Lucinda huffed a laugh. 'I should have seen that coming. Perhaps she could come to the same performance as me and your brother's family?'

Alex smiled and nodded. 'Sounds great.' She was still planning to come to the play with James and Sarah. That had to be another good sign, didn't it?

Butterflies performing acrobatics in his stomach, Alex pushed off the rail and turned to Lucinda. It was time to finally, *finally* ask her out properly. 'You may have noticed that—actually since the day we first met—I've been trying, and failing, to ask you something.'

Lucinda straightened and turned so they were standing face to face. 'I *have* noticed.' She took a step towards him and laid a hand on his chest, over his pounding heart. 'What did you want to ask me, *Mr Fraser?*'

She eyed him expectantly, and her sly smile, combined with the mischievous drawl she used to say his name, wiped Alex's mind clear of all thoughts but one. Smiling, he gently placed a hand at her waist and lowered his lips to hers.

The kiss was soft and sweet, both tender question and affectionate answer. As his rapidly heating blood raced around his body, it took great restraint to pull away. Not to gather her up in his arms and hold her close. But he feared if he did, he wouldn't be able to let her go.

Blinking at her as her eyes drifted open, he asked, 'So, what do you think?'

'Hmn.' Lucinda narrowed her eyes and shook her head. 'I'm sorry but I'm not sure I got all of it. Could you repeat the last bit?'

He grinned. 'For you, Ms Green, I'd be happy to.' He grasped her waist and, as she rose to her tiptoes, he drew her to him and kissed her again until he hoped they were both seeing the same stars. 'Well?' he asked. 'Any better?'

'Hmn.' Lucinda lifted her gaze to the sky and pouted as if giving his question profound consideration. 'I may need a little more clarification of your question before I can answer it properly.' She gave his right bicep a squeeze as she locked her gaze on to his. 'If you could just repeat the first bit, and this time, maybe let your hands do some of the explaining too.'

Alex laughed, a euphoria of fireworks exploding in his chest. 'I would be happy to explain further and more thoroughly. But perhaps'—he tilted his head towards the increasingly noisy party inside the Grand Saloon—'we should do that at your place?'

Lucinda's brow crinkled in a frown of utter seriousness while her lips twitched as if desperate to smile. 'You know, I think that's probably best. I can be slow to catch on and may have to insist on a lengthy explanation. Plus, we'll have the place to ourselves till midnight.' She grabbed his hand and gave him a grin so deliciously wicked it sparked another jolt of electricity in his chest. And, as she encouraged him towards the concealed corridor, a promising flash of devilry entered her emerald eyes as she said, 'To be continued, Mr Fraser. To be continued!'

Ten months later

Lucinda rose from her chair at the front of the congregation and took a deep breath of balmy sea air. As a caterer she had viewed the settings for dozens of wedding ceremonies, but this one—the pristine golden sands of a private beach caressed by the calm waters of the Mediterranean—was the best so far. And when the strains of a string quartet danced into the air and her mum—elegant in a knee-length ivory dress and lace cape—linked her arm through Graham's to sail down the aisle to general applause, Lucinda realised she was finally at peace with the most unexpected of unions.

Of course, it helped enormously that she hadn't had to come to the event alone. And it helped even more than Alex was nothing short of a living masterpiece in his light blue suit. He might have been relieved not to have won Rear of the Year, but she remained of the opinion—one she guessed was shared by several other guests—that he had been robbed.

Lucinda was also impressed with the catering. The food was so good and the wait staff so proficient that as the afternoon wore on into evening Lucinda was able to relax and devote her attention to Bella, Graham's notoriously fabulous daughter, who turned out to be yet another pleasant surprise.

Unable to escape her high-powered accountancy job until late the previous night, Bella had arrived on the Costa del Sol that morning and had scrambled into a frilly dress that flattered her attractive curves and fair, freckled complexion.

'You're kidding!' Bella snorted and upended her wine glass as Lucinda marvelled at her ability to put it away. 'I can't believe they've been going on about me! While all I've heard is Lucinda this, Lucinda that. "Marion's daughter owns one of the most successful catering businesses in the Home Counties, don't you know? She's just bought a house *and* is dating a famous actor."'

'From what Mum said about you, she made you out to be Wonder Woman and apparently you're going to marry Superman.'

'I wish!' Bella laughed, tipping her head back to lose a thunderous cackle. 'You have bought a house though, haven't you?'

'Back in January. Although it's a lowly end of terrace. Not a superhero lair.'

'We haven't bought yet. London prices.' Bella took another glug of wine. 'And there are serious downsides to house-hunting with an architect. He's so darn picky.'

Lucinda smiled politely. She had only had herself to please when looking for a house. Alex had been renting an apartment five minutes from his brother's house since October. That meant he was a short drive from her new home and, since she had picked up the keys at the start of the year, Alex had been using his spare time to help her decorate. As of the previous weekend—which was mostly taken up with preparing for their first holiday together and a beach wedding—Alex had painted all the rooms except two. He would have already finished, but Lucinda found the sight of him working in a tight paint-flecked T-shirt and scruffy jeans strangely irresistible. As he ran a brush along the wall with long, firm strokes, the muscles in his arms, back and chest would bulge and flex, causing Lucinda's temperature to soar. Eventually, her concentration shattered and skin flushed with desire, she would abandon her own tasks to persuade him to drop the brush and pick her up instead.

Lucinda took a sip of her water. Watching Bella drink was making her mouth parched. 'Hopefully you'll find something you both like,' Lucinda said. 'How's your new job?'

Bella sagged forwards, thudding her elbows onto the tabletop. 'Exhausting. How's your business going?'

'OK, thank you.'

'Better than OK,' said a deep voice behind them. 'Lucinda's Catering is booked solid for the foreseeable.'

Lucinda twisted in her seat to grin at Alex—who had ducked out of the reception to run an errand for the newlyweds—and give him a playful shove. She glanced at Bella. 'He exaggerates. I have a great team. And we've been lucky.'

'It isn't luck,' said Alex. 'It's the inevitable result of Lucinda's hard work and brilliance.'

Lucinda scoffed but was quietly thrilled. Even if Alex was biased. And a romantic.

'And how about you, Alex?' Bella directed a woozy smile at him. 'The latest series of *Napier*'s a huge hit. You were fantastic and the big reveal with the mole! I actually gasped and screamed at the TV.'

'Thank you.' Alex gave Bella a modest smile. 'I'm glad you enjoyed it.'

All six episodes of series four of *Napier* had been available to stream since the beginning of May and viewers had been watching in record numbers. Ray's character—DI Frank Buchanan—was revealed to be the dastardly mole, a secret uncovered thanks to the bravery and ingenuity of Alex's character, former DI Dexter Hartford. After a thrilling chase, Dexter cornered Frank on a high rooftop and Frank decided to jump and risk death rather than face prosecution and prison. When he read the script, Lucinda liked to think Ray had hoped his character would have a soft landing and be left with the possibility of a comeback. Unfortunately for Ray, a last-minute change meant Frank dropped from the roof into a fortuitously placed, fully operational wood chipper. Lucinda had cheered and winced at the gruesome moment when human rodent met whirring steel, while making a mental note never to upset any crime writers.

'I'm guessing there'll be more *Napier*.' Bella finished the last of her wine. 'But what are you up to in the meantime?'

Alex nodded. 'Series five and six are confirmed but we won't be filming till winter. I'll be back in Stratford this summer.'

'For *Macbeth*,' said Lucinda, her voice rising with eagerness. 'Alex is playing Macbeth.'

Attending the production of *A Midsummer Night's Dream* the previous summer had gone some way to making Lucinda a late-life Shakespeare convert. So when Alex had finally landed a lead role in a significant Shakespearean production, the desire she expressed to take up permanent residence in the front row during the run had been entirely genuine. And, if his starring role in the Scottish play weren't exciting enough, Alex was jetting off to LA at the end of May for mysterious 'talks' with some Hollywood bigwigs about top secret projects.

Alex offered to top up Bella's glass.

'No, thank you,' she said. 'I should find Dad. And perhaps'—she squinted into the bottom of her empty glass—'I should find some water too. Or coffee.' She pressed her fists to the table and wobbled to standing. 'See you later.'

As Bella meandered across the dance floor, Lucinda scooped up her silver clutch bag and turned to Alex. 'May I steal you away for a walk?'

'Thought you'd never ask.' Alex grinned and held out a hand to help her to her feet. 'Lead the way.'

The wedding band struck up as they stepped out onto the hotel terrace and the melody of 'It Had to Be You' became the soundtrack for their stroll. Cascades of fuchsia bougainvillea covered the walls of the white stone stairway which led to the beach and, as they reached the foot of the stairs and clasped each other's hand, they were welcomed to the sands by the delicate scent of night-blooming jasmine and the shimmering light of the moon on the water.

Alex glanced at Lucinda as they approached the edge of the waves. 'Have I told you that you are beyond stunning today?'

'You have, thank you.' Lucinda smiled and joined Alex in slipping off her shoes. Never that impressed by her own appearance, she had been quietly pleased with her reflection when the hairdresser had styled her hair into loose ringlets. And the V-neck burgundy chiffon gown her mum had selected for her was flattering. The flat silver sandals, which she placed neatly on the sand next to Alex's black shoes and socks, were a practical choice for a beach wedding and comfortable enough for an evening of dancing.

Lucinda stooped to balance her clutch bag on top of the shoes and stepped forwards to join Alex on the damp sand. 'In fact, you've told me a few times. But please don't let that stop you saying it again. Or showing your appreciation in other ways.' Her smile broadened as she circled his neck with her hands, rose to her tiptoes and pressed her lips to his.

The rhythmic hiss of the waves which gently stroked their feet seemed to fade as Alex wrapped his arms around her. He pressed her to his chest and, as Lucinda's legs began to turn to jelly and her head grew light, she was glad to be held so tightly and have the confidence he would catch her should she fall.

Alex pulled back and, studying her face, ran one of her stray ringlets through his fingers, his eyes dark pools in the dim light. His intent stare and the brush of his hand against her cheek flooded Lucinda's brain with a stream of chemicals, an effect which had proved persistent and showed no signs of diminishing in the near future.

'It's beautiful here,' said Alex, turning to studying the stars twinkling above the water.

Woozy from her latest hit of love hormones, Lucinda replied, in a dreamy drawl, 'Yes, it's lovely. A great place for a holiday.' She frowned. The mention of holidays had sparked a thought, a memory of a promise she had made to two angel-faced but ruthless extortionists before leaving England. 'Did you send the girls any pictures?'

'Don't worry, I remembered.' Alex grinned. 'I'd never have heard the end of it if I'd forgotten. I'll have to get them presents too. They're very jealous as it is. I think their poor parents will have to take them for a day trip to the seaside soon.'

Lucinda imagined Sarah and James cursing them for putting such an idea in their daughters' heads. Compensatory brownies might be in order. Or ... 'Maybe we could take them.'

'To the seaside?'

'Why not? We've taken them to the cinema twice without major incident. I think we can manage a jaunt down to Brighton or Eastbourne.'

'That'd be nice.' Alex beamed. 'Buckets and spades, rock pooling, ice creams on the pier.'

'Fish and chips on the promenade.'

'You punching any seagulls who dare steal our chips.'

Lucinda gasped in mock outrage and batted his arm. 'Mr Fraser! How dare you know me so well!'

Alex chucked as he trailed his fingers up and down Lucinda's back. The deep rumble of his laughter together with the languorous stroking sent ripples of heat along her spine.

She swallowed and shook her hair off her shoulders. *Keep it together*, she told herself. *You have something important to ask him, after all.* 'I was thinking ...'

'Yes?'

'Some of the photos from today could look good in the hallway. If I get them mounted and framed. What do you think?'

'I think they'd look great. But my opinion isn't important. It's your hallway.'

'True. But you painted it. And actually ... wait there a sec!' She skipped over to their shoes and swooped on her bag. Keeping her back to Alex, she retrieved something from inside and tucked it into her palm. 'Speaking of decorating. I was thinking ...' Lucinda dropped the bag onto the sand and scurried back to Alex. Looking into his eyes, she took a deep breath to calm the nerves squirming in her belly. 'I was thinking it'd be a lot easier for you to help me finish the last bits and pieces if you were living on site.'

She opened her palm and a set of house keys jangled free, glittering in the moonlight. Pinched between Lucinda's thumb and forefinger was the key-ring charm: a red enamel puzzle piece, the missing piece of her matching heart.

Alex's mouth dropped open as Lucinda pressed the keys into his hand. He blinked and stammered. 'You're not ... you're...'

'Asking you to move in with me. Keep up!' Her tone was jokey, but her heart thundered as she watched his face. She'd thought explaining to her brother why she needed him to give the keychain back had been nerve-wracking, but this was torture. Was she asking too much of Alex? Was it a step too far, too quickly?

Alex stared at the keys in his palm. 'You're serious?'

'You can give a month's notice on your flat and I know you're off to America and then Stratford but this way you'd be at home when you're home and you've been spending loads of nights at mine anyway, I mean you've a toothbrush in the bathroom ...'

As she rambled on into incoherence, Lucinda thought about how she loved having Alex in the house. How his presence made the building a warmer, more comforting place. That knowing he would be there made her eager to get home. And how supportive he'd been while she had gone through the hellish experience which was buying and selling properties, and lately with moving and decorating. He had helped her to frame and hang her favourite film posters in the living room, struggled valiantly against poor instructions to assemble display units for her collector's edition DVDs and growing collection of *Star Wars* vinyl figures, and had been watching dozens of online DIY videos for an upcoming project to install a wall of Alhambra-inspired tiling over the bath.

Alex' expression remained inscrutable and Lucinda's pulse kicked up a notch as she continued to babble. 'And you've helped me make a start on all the little homey touches and been so involved, really they're as much down to you as to me and I was hoping you might like to add a few finishing touches of your own. And I just thought—'

'Yes.'

'Because it makes sense—'

'Yes, please.'

'And I thought you might—'

'Lucinda.' Alex grabbed her shoulders, bringing her

verbal incontinence to an abrupt halt. His eyes sparkled as he stared into hers. 'I would love to move in with you. Thank you.'

Lucinda gawped as her heart stuttered. She blinked as Alex's reply settled and when it sank in she squealed and threw herself at him, flinging her arms around his neck with enough force to make him stagger. Alex laughed as he regained his footing and swung her off her feet in a wide arc, kissing her before setting her toes back into the whisper of the waves.

'This calls for champagne!' Lucinda grinned. 'Shall we head back to the party?'

They meandered over the powdery sand until their feet were dry enough to reclaim their shoes. As Alex slipped on the second of his loafers, Lucinda shivered. The sea breeze stirred her curls and raised gooseflesh on her arms. The night air had cooled, but Lucinda suspected her sudden chill was also a result of the adrenaline of the previous few minutes ebbing away.

Alex's eyebrows drew together in concern. 'Would you like my jacket?'

'No, no. We'll be inside in a minute. Let's go.'

They drifted up the beach and Alex wrapped his left arm around Lucinda's waist. She snuggled into him, snaking her right arm around his middle and pulling him closer. Above them the opening notes of 'All You Need Is Love' rang out, and when the band reached the chorus, their efforts were joined by boozy audience participation.

The keys in Alex's right hand jangled as he held the puzzle piece up in front of them. 'Are you sure you want me to have this?'

'Absolutely.'

'You know, you should be more careful, Ms Green.'

'How so?'

'You're in danger of giving me the impression you think I'm special.'

Lucinda's lips curled into a half-smile. 'I don't think you're special.'

'Oh?'

'No. In fact'—she paused at the foot of the staircase to twist to look at his face—'after a period of initial research, I suspect that you, Alex Fraser, are *exceptional*.'

The tension in Alex's expression vanished, replaced by a beaming smile which lit his eyes and would warm Lucinda's heart for the rest of the evening.

'Interesting.' Alex kissed the top of her head and released his grip on her waist so she could climb the narrow stairs before him. 'And how do you propose to confirm these suspicions of yours?'

Lucinda shrugged as she reached the top step and waited for him to join her. 'Well, with your support, I was hoping to continue my research ... indefinitely.'

Alex laced her outstretched fingers through his and they crossed the terrace to the lights of the dining room, their clasped hands swaying gently back and forth.

'Sounds like an interesting project.' Alex inclined his head in a small bow. 'And I would be honoured to be your research partner.'

Alex slipped the keys into his pocket and Lucinda's lips curled into a smug smile of complete contentment which was the perfect mirror of his. The certainty that the puzzle piece was safely in the right hands made her heart sing and her feet begin moving in time with the band.

Alex opened the door to the reception, allowing a stream of music and laughter to ripple out into the night air. He stood back to let Lucinda cross the threshold, his glaze flicking down to her shuffling feet and back up to her face. 'And I would be delighted to be your dance partner too, if you'll have me?'

'Why, Mr Fraser!' Lucinda grinned and looped her arm through Alex's. 'I thought you'd never ask.'

Also by Claire Huston

If you enjoyed Lucinda's story, return to the Comptons and find out more about Becky, the area's resident miracle worker ...

Art and Soul

(Love in the Comptons Book 1)

Struggling single mother Becky Watson longs to revive her career as a life-fixer, working miracles to solve her clients' problems, no matter how big or small. Since the birth of her two-year-old son she has been stuck preventing wedding fiascos for the richest and rudest residents of the Comptons, a charming, leafy area of southern England known for its artistic heritage.

So when semi-reclusive local artist Charlie Handren reluctantly hires Becky to fix his six-year creative slump, she's delighted to set him up with a come-back exhibition and Rachel Stone, the woman of his dreams.

Though they get off to a rocky start, Becky and Charlie soon become close. But as the beautiful Rachel becomes Charlie's muse, Becky is forced to wonder: will giving Charlie everything he wants mean giving up her own happily ever after?

Also by Claire Huston

Or maybe you fancy an escape to an idyllic country village?

Elle's A to Z of Love

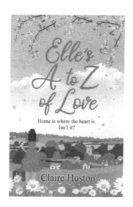

Haileybrook, a beautiful village in the peaceful Cotswolds countryside, is most people's idea of heaven on earth.

Born and raised in this small slice of paradise, Elle Bea can't wait to leave.

It should be easy, but every time she packs her bags for exotic adventures, old loves and loyalties pull her back.

Will Elle be forced to forget her dreams of far-flung places and epic romance, or can she grab one last chance to have it all?

An uplifting, romantic story about friends, family and the relationships that make a place a home.

Acknowledgements

Thank you to everyone who has read *The Only Exception*. An extra big thank you to anyone who has reviewed it or told someone else about it. Thank you to my friends and family for continuing to be interested in my books or at least doing a brilliant job of pretending to be interested. I appreciate all your support.

A few specific thank yous:

My husband and my mum for listening to me going on about my books and for asking everyone they know and meet to buy them. Liz for being my first reader and patient sounding board.

My brilliant editor, Alison May. My fantastic proofreader, Imogen Howson. Gail Bradley for the lovely cover design. Sarah Houldcroft at Goldcrest Books for all her publishing magic.

Rachel Gilbey at Rachel's Random Resources for organising a cover reveal and another great blog tour and to all the wonderful bloggers who took part. And thank you to all the other generous book bloggers who have been so kind as to feature and review the book.

The Romantic Novelists' Association and specifically the members of the Birmingham Chapter who I'm delighted to be able to see again in person.

About the author

Claire Huston lives in Warwickshire, UK, with her husband and two children. She writes uplifting modern love stories about characters who are meant for each other but sometimes need a little help to realise it.

A keen amateur baker, she enjoys making cakes, biscuits and brownies almost as much as eating them. You can find recipes for all the cakes mentioned in her first novel, *Art and Soul*, at www.clairehuston.co.uk along with over 150 other recipes. This is also where she talks about and reviews books.

You can also find her on:

Instagram: @clairehuston_author

Twitter: @ClaraVal

Facebook: clairehustonauthor

Pinterest: claire_huston